With a Voice that is Often Still Confused

But is Becoming Ever LOUDER

and C l e a r e r

The follow-up to his critically acclaimed collection, <u>You Shall Never Know Security</u>, J.R. Hamantaschen returns with another collection of his inimitable brand of weird, dark fiction. At turns despairing, resonant, macabre and insightful, these nine stories intend to stay with you.

Uncharacteristically Kind Words for

J.R. Hamantaschen

As you are already reading (or at least considering) this collection, why not bludgeon you with praise for my first collection, *You Shall Never Know Security?*

"The collection is aptly named - each story inspires a sickening feeling of danger ... a twisted, uneasy, satisfying book."
    –Kirkus Reviews

"A cross between Lovecraft and Chuck Palahniuk, this book of short stories is as memorable as it is terrifying. The Palahniuk comparison doesn't end with a name that's impossible to spell – we haven't been this horrified by a collection of short stories since Chuck's own *Haunted*... You Shall Never Know Security is a wonderful collection of short stories from a dark and original genre voice. That title – it's a promise."
    –Starbust Magazine

"You Shall Never Know Security is aptly titled. Containing 13 tales, all are beautifully written, most are engrossing and there's a vein of loss running throughout. Overall, the book is depressing but still compelling as hell because of Hamantaschen's skill with words. As supernatural as the stories can get, there's still a semblance of 'real life' found in each as sometimes there are just no happy endings. Sometimes the real world just sucks."
    –HorrorTalk

"J.R. Hamantaschen won't be underground for long"
    –HorrorWorld (Note from J.R.: I certainly proved them wrong!)

"The term dark fiction has become a tad diluted by the onslaught of vampire, zombie and pseudo-horror novels that currently dot the literary landscape. However, in J.R. Hamantaschen's You Shall Never Know Security, a collection of 13 short stories, dark fiction is back to what it was meant to be: a bloodcurdling jump into the gloomiest and most sinister corners of the human psyche.

With an elegant and eloquent prose that brings to mind the work of Lovecraft, Hamantaschen repeatedly pulls away the thin cover or normalcy that's usually thrown over our daily lives and unabashedly shows readers what lies beneath. Regret, despair, fear, envy and guilt are all here, and the stories in which they appear are the kind that tend to stick with readers after the reading is over."
  –HP Lovecraft E-Zine

"Here is some boastful praise about this fellow author. My real goal is for you to check out my book. Why else do you think I listed the books I've written?"
  –Sycophantic other Author, Author of Some Other Fiction in the Same Genre

"The language, in places, is evocative, almost elegiac … The stories are so varied in type and emphasis that it is difficult to describe them in a single line or two . . . in all of the above, the author delivers powerful, ugly images, using a battery of verbal pyrotechnics that make the stories demand to be read carefully. Buried in the razzle-dazzle language are clues to the intended meaning. If horror is your poison of choice, these will definitely fill the bill."
  –Innsmouth Free Press

"If you like your fiction unique and on the darker side, if you wonder what Robert Aickman would sound like had he written in the Now instead of the Then...your answer is here."
  –ShockTotem

"The thirteen stories in You Shall Never Know Security are...strange. A character in one story uses the word surrealistic to describe a situation; it is equally appropriate as a description of the entire collection. Another character in another story borrows the oft-overused (although here appropriate) Lovecraftian word eldritch; and again, it resonates through every story—unearthly, weird, eerie."

    –HellNotes

"He has a remarkable grasp of exactly how instinctively predatory the human beast is and the lengths some are apt to go to conceal this fact beneath layers of comforting veneers. He is also a natural story teller, willing to dally at the realizations, the internal struggles to come to grips with the unthinkable, and the often less than satisfying fare that is ultimately one's lot in life rather than the visceral. He also has a macabre sense of humor that creeps into the telling now and again leaving the reader wondering if he has just heard a joke, or if the joke is inevitably on us and from time to time we need to appreciate that fact."

    –Paul Bates, RedRoom

"J.R. Hamantaschen's anthology, 'You Shall Never Know Security,' kicks open the doors of the traditional horror fiction genre and takes the reader to a far darker place. Never relying on gimmicks or gore, Hamantaschen handles some deep topics in these stories, while keeping you thoroughly horrified from beginning to end. This is fiction for readers that like to think, that like to be challenged, that like to squirm."

    –Drabblecast

"J.R. Hamantaschen's stories tap into the cosmic hopelessness of life. His stories are horrific and terrifying, but really shake one's idea of self and your place in the universe."

    –HP Lovecraft Literary Podcast

"Odd, alarming, and almost poetic in nature, J.R Hamantaschen's 'You Shall Never Know Security' is an anthology that will stay with you long after you've turned the last page."

    –OneTitle Magazine

"This anthology of horror and weirdness goes off the charts in the first story. I mean that in a good way."
    –Revolution ScienceFiction

"I recently finished this collection and found it quite good. He is extremely strong with creating character, and his fiction is authentically weird. The prose seemed very modern to me, which is something I sometimes don't enjoy, being an old soul, but I was captivated by these tales. There are places when the descriptions are beautifully poetic. An excellent book."
    –Wilum Pugmire, an author whom I respect and whose opinion I value.

"Bark Bark Bark!" [licks own balls] [falls asleep]
    –Will the Pug

"J.R.'s fiction is raw, startling, and dark. The best examples of his work — stories such as "Jordan, When Are You Going to Settle Down, Get Married and Have Us Some Children?" and "Endemic" — make readers squirm with discomfort, wondering how far the boundaries can be pushed before they break. J.R.'s work isn't comfortable fiction, but it's as often as not thought-provoking fiction wrapped around a grimly philosophical edge."
    –The Harrow

"J.R. Hamantaschen's 'You Shall Never Know Security' is one of the best dark fiction collections ever published. It contains fascinating, disturbing and beautifully written stories that range all the way from dark fantasy to horror."
    –Rising Shadow Magazine

"If you have three pages or so of critical praise, it validates as you as a human being."
    –I wish

Introduction (Of Sorts)

So after four years and just as many suicide attempts (I can't do anything right!), I've returned with another collection of my dark fiction stories. For the potential reader who may not be familiar with me, this is my second collection. *You Shall Never Know Security*, my first collection, was a (minor) critical and (relative) commercial success, so here we are. If you enjoy this one, hope you check out that one as well.

In my first collection, I included a publication history of all the stories contained therein, thinking that was the thing to do. Nowadays, I'm not so sure if anyone cares about that sort of stuff. I'll instead just provide a hat tip to some venues where my work has been published or produced, such as the Drabblecast, Pseudopod, Nossa Morte, 19 Nocturne Boulevard, The Harrow, and Revolution Science Fiction. I appreciate them (and the other magazines that have published my work, some now long-departed) for their support.

This being the sophomore effort, I felt the pressure from some quarters to have another author-friend write some hagiographic piece on my behalf, but who wants that? I've always found it disappointing when a collection exclaims "With an Introduction by [Somewhat More Well Known Author]" and then it's just a tossed-off page or two of nonsense. (Introductions to "graphic novels," I'm looking at you!)

So I'll make this brief (he says after writing several superfluous paragraphs). Far be it from me to suggest how these stories are read, but I'd suggest you read them in order, as some of the stories are related.

If you enjoy these stories in anyway, feel free to email me at jrtaschen@ gmail.com. If you happen to visit the New York City metropolitan area and want to grab coffee, feel free to shoot me an email. Assuming you are not an asshole, of course.

A substantially different version of "The Gulf of Responsibility" was previously published with a preposterously long (but fitting) alternative title. A slightly different version of "Big With The Past, Pregnant with the Future" was published alongside it.

A substantially different version of "Oh Abel, Oh Absalom" was previously published in the 2013 anthology <u>For When the Veil Drops</u>. I mention that anthology specifically because it was a good one, put out by the good folks at West Pigeon Press, and has some other good stories in it.

Other stories herein have been published in various magazines or produced as podcasts or performance pieces. All copyrights are retained by me.

I sometimes stroll through online forums and find it amusing that people request information on where to find bootleg digital copies of <u>You Shall Never Know Security</u> to avoid the onerous burden of purchasing a collection that's priced well below that of a Frappuccino, but I hold no hard feelings. In fact, I understand and am sympathetic. If you happen to be one of these people, and you legitimately cannot afford to purchase any of my work but wish to read them, I'd be more than happy to send you a complimentary copy.

Writing is not how I support myself financially, which explains the general delay in my output. I'm sometimes asked if I ever consider writing full-time, to which I've amassed considerable pithy responses. (One such response: "I have, but I've gotten used to eating daily.") Until the market improves dramatically for depressing, despairing weird fiction that appears exclusively in small press magazines or podcasts and is published by an author with a cookie-inspired nom de plume (google "hamantaschen"), then part-time my writing shall remain.

Sorry for the wait.

Best,
J.R. Hamantaschen
jrtaschen@gmail.com

With a Voice that is Often Still Confused
But is Becoming Ever LOUDER
and C l e a r e r

By J.R. Hamantaschen

This is a work of fiction, and each of the characters, entities, locations, and events portrayed in this work are either products of the author's imagination or are used fictitiously. Any resemblance to actual persons, living or dead, business establishments, events, or locales is entirely coincidental and not intended by the author.

WITH A VOICE THAT IS OFTEN STILL CONFUSED BUT IS BECOMING EVER LOUDER AND CLEARER

Contents

Dedications

None.

Vernichtungsschmerz

JULIA NEVER REMEMBERED her dreams. At most, she'd come back with discrete images that couldn't be cobbled together into a narrative whole, images that would rebound within her memory banks for, at most, several hours, then dissipate to wherever faded memories went. Then, at some point, her attempt to recall them would give way to speculation and conjecture.

She was in a dream now, she knew. She was gently making her way down an azure blue river. Her aunt and her friend Venice were both with her, which was weird. Why not her mother? She found herself questioning the premise of this dream. Why Venice? Was Venice her best friend?

Already the fabric of the dream was tenuous, as she saw herself from the third-person perspective, alongside her aunt and Venice, noting to herself the incongruent angles of the river and the unrealistic color of the raft that carried them. When you became aware of a dream, that's when it ends.

She felt the bobbing of gently-moving water beneath her and looked down at the orangish wood. She was impressed with the granular level of detail in the wood, in the construction of the raft. She knew nothing about handiwork, but she could tell this raft was professionally constructed. She was impressed with herself, that she even had a frame of reference within her to recognize a well-crafted raft.

She let her fingers drift in the water. She distinctly felt them submerge, and instinctively tightened her bladder. Dreams of water meant you were going to pee the bed. She rubbed her fingers in the stream, convinced any minute she'd wake up with a warm, damp bed.

Her aunt and Venice mouthed words, but what they said was a mystery. *What?* she thought, and wasn't sure if that thought made its way into the dream.

Her aunt rocked back and forth. She wore black, which was typical of her.

She didn't see Venice below the waist. It was definitely Venice, tall gangly Venice, large equine mouth and facial features, curly black hair. The rendering was impressive — she made out the impressions of Venice's pronounced teeth, and wondered if she had internalized Venice's insecure impression of herself.

Venice spoke softly and indistinctly.

Julia turned her head to see a large, humanoid creature stand up beside her. It was pale green, long, lean and well-proportioned. It was gilled and scaled. Five hook-shaped claws on each hand, blubbery webbing connecting each claw to one another. Its face was indistinct, like everything else, except its mouth seemed too far back, sprung back almost, but claws forward, as if its claws were the antennae it used to navigate the world.

"Julia. I'm here to help you. Come with me, I'm here to help you."

The impression of shaking her head.

"Come with me Julia, come with me." The webbing of its claws split and new, scythe-like claws emerged continuously, a conveyer belt of sharp angles and scaly blubber.

She shook her head, whether in the dream or in real-life, she didn't know.

Venice and her aunt were gone.

"I do not know what your mind is making me look like to you. I apologize if I appear frightening to you."

Its breath — or perhaps just its presence — was sulfurous, redolent of damp disease.

Her dream jumped-cut to a memory of when she opened what she thought was an empty drawer at her aunt's house and found the corpse of a mouse in a sticky trap, its bottom still plump but covered in its own musty droppings, its upper half feeble and emaciated, a hint of pink color for guts. That smell when she first opened the drawer and realized what she was looking at — that's what this reminded her of.

She was back to her dream-reality. Still on a moving raft, but with just isolated details, nothing that provided a larger impression of her environment, as if her brain didn't have the processing power to create a coherent background.

When she took her focus off something, it disappeared.

"I don't look like anything, I don't smell like anything, I don't sound like anything."

That's odd; she thought mildly, she liked the sound of its voice. Masculine, but in a non-threatening way.

"Everything you perceive, that's just your brain creating a projection that it wants you to believe is true. But it's not true. I don't look like what you are seeing."

The creature reached its arms out, palms up, claws up, long as rakes. So long that they didn't make anatomical sense, how a creature that lives in the water could possibly have claws the size of rakes...

"I am here to help you. I will not make you do anything. I will give you a choice, as much as a choice is possible in your reality. You did not choose any of your urges, preferences or limitations. You did not even choose to be in this sleep state. I am here to tell you that I offer you a painless exit out of existence."

The fetid smell had become overpowering; there was the heavy heat of unwashed body, bacterial build-up. The reeking scene jaundiced all the creature's words, smothered all else, the tinge of genuine sympathy she detected now gone, curdled beneath her base revulsion.

"Of course, your brain wants you to survive and reproduce. That is why you feel pain when you get hurt, to let you know that there is trouble, to get you to avoid those situations so you can survive and reproduce.

"Your brain, your nerves, your senses, they don't want you to listen, for I do bring Death. I bring you the escape from pain, from fear. Your brain will let you feel the pain of disease, of cancer, of decay.

"But I am here to tell you something else. Something your own body, your own mind, will never reveal to you. In your reality, there is no such thing as a painless death. When you die, your brain reacts to get you out of whatever situation is causing your death. To your brain, it is like your finger is in boiling water — it sends the signal to tell you to remove it. But now imagine your entire body is in boiling water, and there is no hope of escape. That's what death is. It's the feeling of your own system in pain, cannibalizing itself. All that pain, you feel it. Time is subjective. The pain lasts forever. It swallows everything you ever did and every memory you ever had. All life ends in a tide of pain. And as your mind controls your perception of time, it's a never-ending tide."

The soaring, uplifting chug of *Bear v. Shark's* "Ma Jolie" flooded her brain space. The dream snapped and she was awake.

It was the dead of night. All was still. "Ma Jolie" was her favorite song, and she'd adopted the opening chord progression as her morning alarm. She checked her phone: it hadn't gone off. She checked the time. 4:27 a.m. The night was long and still.

Try as she might, she was unable to fall back asleep.

>< >< ><

"Man," Julia said, when her three best friends were all seated at the lunch room table the following day, "I used to be jealous of people who could remember their dreams. Not anymore. I had the most fucked-up dream last night."

Clare, Venice, and Lynn didn't jump immediately at the bait like Julia hoped. They were still adjusting themselves, putting their bookbags under the seat, and readying their trays around the table in the outside courtyard. It was chilly outside, but they had warm down jackets and had braved the cold to at least sit outside and get peace and quiet from the loud, obnoxious cafeteria and the table-spanning, shouted conversations.

They were all sixteen and halfway through their junior years at Lakewood High school in Shrub Oak, New York, a middle-class, undistinguished suburb about an hour north of Manhattan. All of them came from families who had uprooted themselves from New York City with hopes of securing themselves a piece of the suburban American dream, decisions made by New Yorkers who lived their formative years in the 1970s and 1980s, when New York City was a metonym for urban disorder. Now, of course, New York City was a locus point of gentrification and the suburbs were steadily and rapidly absorbing the fallout of the recession. Each year, it seemed there were less and less places to go, the odd inverse relationship of more people yet more shuttered businesses. The local Jefferson Valley Mall had just, for example, been placed on the Dying Malls website. All four of them resented losing their New York City birthright, and for what? The drabness of the suburbs with none of the supposed benefits. Suburbs weren't even safer, if you thought about it. More teenagers die from car accidents than gun fire.

Venice took the bait first. Venice was the tallest of group, six foot-one, with long, curly raven hair, a stud tongue ring and belly-button ring, a toothy smile and a subtly elongated facial bone structure that made her resemble a horse. Not really in a bad way; she was pretty and fit and equine in the same way as Julia Roberts. Out of the group, the boys were perhaps most interested in her, some combination of her fit body, her big mouth, her erotic name, and the halo effects of her belly button and tongue rings, which created associations about body image and sexual proclivities that were entirely incidental.

"So, what was it about?" Venice asked.

"A long conversation with a monster about dying."

"Sounds pretty cool to me."

"Yeah," Lynn joined in. "Your plea for sympathy is hereby rejected. I am officially jealous. My dreams are always boring." That last point wasn't true, not recently, but she let the comment stand.

Lynn was bundled especially warmly in a green, cozy-looking knit sweater, which was appropriate for her. She had big clunky brown glasses and the fact that they made her look geek-chic-sexy was purely adventitious. She was short, pert and peppy, about 5'5" and a natural blue-eyed blonde, with a mane which she kept long and well-mannered. Under alternative circumstances — meaning, if you knew nothing about her personality — one could easily imagine her as a cheerleader. Yet no one acted like that was true — years later, classmates would reminisce about her and talk about how cute she was and ponder how odd it was that it seemed like no one ever dated her. Instead of social climbing or dating, she applied that natural pep and go-getterism to doing well in school, fastidiously finishing tasks, getting OCD about her favorite musical genres (emocore and upbeat pop-punk) and making sure her much younger sister got the proper exposure to books and culture.

"Yeah, sounds like a humble-brag to me. What did the monster look like? Was it cool looking?" That was Clare, in between bites of overcooked, droopy school pizza.

"I guess so. It smelled really badly. I was impressed, actually, that my mind could render something like that. I didn't get a good look at the background, though."

Clare was the only one of them who had a boyfriend, which wasn't what you'd expect. She was pleasant and innocuous, an affable wallflower given to bouts of social anxiety. As if form met function, she had a mousy look, with matted-looking brown hair, average height and average weight and a curiously sedimentary, layered countenance, kind of rough and porous, with an atypical bone structure. She had a tendency to sniff her food before eating it, although she only did that in front of her close friends these days. She spoke with a slight lisp, which felt right, given the intangible curiosity of her face.

To boys, she was a nice, pleasant presence, as she had that air of non-judgmental obtainability about her. That's perhaps what lead to her being the only one with a boyfriend, although truth be told, the other girls weren't too concerned about having boyfriends. Clare's boyfriend, Isaac, fit in nicely to their group-centrism, as he was two years older and busy with Westchester Community College and his side job doing light carpentry work for his father. Isaac, when he was around, was an unobtrusive presence, a nod of the head, a filled seat on the couch.

"I had a crazy dream too. I just can't even remember it. I just remember thinking it was crazy. It's weird because I've been reading a lot — " Clare pulled out a used paperback, *Storm Front*, by Jim Butcher — "it's cool, it's got a lot of monsters and supernatural stuff and wizards in it, so I'm disappointed I didn't have a great, vivid dream that I remembered. Usually when I read, my memory gets sharper. I'm jealous, you must be gifted."

"You sounded so cute. If you were a hamster I'd just want to take you home," said Lynn. "Wh-is-zzards": she did her best approximation of how Clare lisped the word.

""Thwwww-wizzards," Venice exaggerated it, using deposited saliva and her tongue ring to great effect. "I love it. How you can be reading that" — Venice looked at the paperback — "oh, I've been meaning to read that actually, heard it's good, but how you are reading that before *Hitchhiker's Guide* is a crime against the universe and a personal insult to me. Do you even still have it?"

"I'll get into it, I promise."

"You have to make good on your promises. Your cute lisp can't save you forever."

"She's done pretty well with it for sixteen years," Lynn deadpanned.

"She perfected it before she could even speak," Julia dead-panned back. They all took pleasure in teasing each other for lapses in logic, malapropisms, and the like. One time Julia pronounced "automaton" as "auto-mate-on" and Lynn had a field day.

"I know, that's what makes it so effective. When you can master something before you even do it, that's the only way you can really be called a Master. You can only be a Master if you can perfect something before you can even do it."

"An illogical but airtight quandary."

"Airtight. Viciously airtight in its ill-logic. Which makes it all the more effective."

They went on for a bit with this inspired nonsense. They could riff off each other all day. They had enough rapport, in-jokes, and meta-references for a Wikipedia entry.

They talked and ate — with a couple call-backs to the lisp-y noises and the foolish Mastery Paradox. Julia ate the peanut-butter sandwich and apple she brought from home and enjoyed the company.

>< >< ><

Julia found herself at the same lunch table under almost identical circumstances. She unwrapped her lunch and again, it was a homemade sandwich, same coarse brown wheat bread, same shiny Red Delicious apple. She unwrapped the sandwich out of the tinfoil and bit into it. It was chewier, smushier than usual, with an overpowering texture on one side and abrasive crunchy pieces on the other. The fractious mismatch of textures made chewing difficult. She opened up her sandwich. It was, literally, peanuts-and-butter. Half of the bread was slicked heavy with dairy butter. The other half was a deposit of whole peanuts.

How could this be possible? Under no circumstances does someone say "Hey, I made a mistake. Instead of peanut butter, I used peanuts-and-butter." Under what sort of haze would someone have to be in to literally take out ill-fitting, cumbersome solid peanuts, and tuck them into one side of the bread, and then slop on a gag-inducing amount of butter onto another side of bread and smush the two pieces together?

She opened up the sandwich to show her friends, as prima facie evidence that something was wrong. The thing spoke for itself.

None of her friends seemed to notice or comment on it.

"My dreams have been weird, too," said Lynn. Lynn was probably the sharpest of the four friends, so Julia was interested in what she had to say. "They are interesting though. I'm interested in them, and what they have to show me."

Julia hmm'ed. *That's an even-keeled attitude to have*, she thought She was speaking to Lynn without seeing her, she realized. She did her best to look at her, but couldn't conjure up a vision of what Lynn looked like. As if in consolation, a show of defeat, she associated her with a green, warm-looking sweater and tight black pants. Was Lynn wearing the same green shirt as yesterday? No, she didn't really wear tight black pants, but they'd suit her in her subtle way.

That wasn't fair, she thought. They were sitting around the table but no one else was eating. When she wasn't looking at Lynn, she seemed to disappear. No one was talking. Maybe James and his group of friends who shared the courtyard with them were doing something interesting and distracting. James' group and their group were cool with each other and sometimes met up, went to local music shows to see the same shitty local bands. She turned and there was nothing behind her. Literally nothing — it's as if she turned her head to espy a niveous stain with the intensity of a supernova.

Her subconscious stirred slightly at the thought of a brief, frustrating fight with her mother. She'd said something mean and impatient toward her mother, more out of hunger pangs and frustration than anything else. But how did that make sense? The timing was all wrong, this was lunch time, she was at school.

Venice spoke while two hands emerged from her mouth, each hand pushing her jaws in opposite directions. Her longish face became even longer, her chin descended at least an inch and her mouth jutted forward, giving her a hook-like shovel face. She didn't scream or react hysterically, but her voice abruptly cut out. The upper part of her face bulged out narrowly, like the beak of a bird.

The top of a figure emerged from her mouth as her body crumpled and broke off around her. *That's not right*, Julia thought. Venice's body should be gore and viscera, blood everywhere, a horror show. Instead, the top-half of a figure just stood upright through Venice's baleen mouth, unfolding and ascending upward in a standing position. Like a seed rapidly germinating into a flower, rising from the flower pot that was Venice's impossibly solid and overstretched jaws.

The figure fully emerged and Venice bloodlessly broke off and tumbled away, like detritus thrown overboard on a moving ship.

"This is another dream," the figure told her. It was silver and featureless, just the outline of a human shape. The dimensions didn't make sense but it was bigger and vaster than she.

"You are dreaming. I'm not here to hurt you. I apologize for however I look to you, if I frighten you. Your brain perceives me as a threat and will do whatever it can to make me seem threatening. Just as it comes so naturally to you to assign negative attributes to spiders or snakes, your brain does the same with me. Just remember that the spider or snake is not evil. It just is, and your brain communicates what it needs to communicate to you to keep you living and procreating.

"Your brain — including the parasites that control it and the forces of natural evolution — does everything within its power to convince you to procreate and extend your genetic legacy. It does what it does. It's a program.

"I am here to offer you a reprieve from living and procreating. No living thing can ever know whether life has been worth living without first experiencing the sensation of dying. No one who has ever died can testify to the experience of dying. Left to your own devices, your brain and existence as you know it will not permit you a quick, painless death. There is no such thing as an instant death. Pain is subjective, controlled by your brain. When you injure yourself, your brain transmits pain to provide you a reason to stop or avoid the injury. The sensation of dying is every nerve, every fiber of your being, being twisted and scorched under the incorrect assumption that transmitting the sensation of pain can cause you to avoid harm. And since the mind controls how you perceive time, death is every nerve and molecule of your being, flayed, in perpetuity.

"Your brain is just a system. If there's a fire, your fire alarm, when triggered, will go off. It responds to stimuli. It will go off even if there is no conceivable possibility that the fire alarm will stop the fire. It just reacts.

"Your brain will react when you die. Every human being who has ever lived and who has ever died has regretted their life, for the sheer pain of dying blots out everything that came before it.

"Do not fear me. I am here to help you."

"You speak well," she heard herself saying in the dream.

It stopped speaking. "Thank you."

"How much of this is real?"

"Nothing of what you are seeing or feeling based on your perceptions is currently real. But everything I am communicating to you is real."

Hmm. She was no longer in the courtyard but instead in some blank, undistinguished mass of space. The figure was no longer visible, just a charged presence.

"Are you a robot or a spirit? Do you have a personality?"

"It is interesting that you are more interested in me than in what I am communicating to you. My history or story is, cosmically speaking, of no significance. I'm here to help you."

"Why should I trust you? And why have you selected me, by the way?"

"You are perceptive, intelligent, and acutely sensitive enough to allow me entry and listen to what I have to say. There are hundreds of millions of others who share this quality who, at the right mental or emotional sensitivity, we reach out to save. I can do nothing to prove to you that what I say is true. I cannot interact with you physically. I can only detach your mind and free you."

"Well, ok, that's all well and good, but maybe you can come back when I'm older and sick or something? When I'm dying. Despite what you may think, I'm actually relatively happy. I like my friends, I like that I'm still young. Things aren't so bad, even if I act like they are."

"I understand. I do not dispute anything you are saying, except there are only limited mental or emotional time periods when you can receive our call, and, as much pleasure and fulfillment you extract from your life experience, on net, the transaction will always be a terrible one. If you could do an accounting after your death, my position would be vindicated.

Of course, that is not within your power. I just bring to you information.

"There would be no pain or fear of suicide. It would just be a transition into exactly what you were before you were."

"That's interesting. I hope I'm able to receive these messages, say, when I'm old and dying and a burden on my family. I don't have any objection to assisted-suicide, given certain circumstances. I think it's a person's right to decide when and how they die."

There was no response. She feared what she said sounded small-minded and childish. She always felt that when expressing political opinions, even though she was fairly confident and adamant about this position. It just seemed ... misguided, miniscule almost. He was talking about something grander, cosmic.

He? Was it a he? More like an It.

Finally It spoke: "And if I am wrong, there is nothing for you to fear. You will be in the same oblivion, absent the pain and ordeal."

"I couldn't do that to my family, at the very least. They'd be so sad and upset. It would devastate them."

There was a pause. "Everything you are saying is true, given your perspective, and it is the great difficulty in this that you are not privy to the knowledge I possess. That is not your fault, though. It is not within your sphere of understanding.

"Unfortunately, it is only a truth that can be learned upon death, and upon death, it is a moot point. All I can communicate is this: In death, there is no shared experience. Your family and friends will not endure the experience nor the pain for you. These concepts of family and the values you associate with them are nothing in the face of death. They are useful concepts during the course of existence but disappear as if they never were upon the commencement of your death."

Hmm. Privy. Priv-vee. That's how that word was pronounced. She was hazily familiar with that word. She'd never pronounced it before and never, she believed, used it in context, but she was confident it had been used correctly. Maybe she had that information tucked away in her subcon-

scious, and the dream had dredged it up. She loved believing that dreams
acted as mental sifters, rooting up trivia or a factoid and allowing them to
waft, gently, into the working canals of her conscious brain.

"Tell me a word I don't know. Or allow me to speak another language.
If I could wake up tomorrow speaking Italian, I'd believe that this was
something beyond a normal dream."

"Sagacious."

"I know that word, I think. I can't define it, but I associate it with like, a
deer. I don't know why, but I have an association with that word."

She realized her dream was no longer visually interesting. It was just
a dark void filled with voices. As if on cue, the figure before her was now
an austere, noble looking white elk, adorned with gleaming antlers that
looked like smooth Amazonian vines that had calcified and hardened into
sheer bone.

"Nostomania. An intense homesickness."

"Hmm, Nos-tuh-mania. Interesting. I like that word. I don't think I
know that one. I don't think I've ever heard it. I'm impressed. Just so you
know, yes, I am looking that word up immediately when I wake up.

"So do you have, like, all the information in the universe? Are you a
God? Are you God?"

"Frigorific. Producing cold."

"That's a cool one. Frig. Frig-o-riffic. It sounds like a fake word, like a
fake curse. Cold, hmm. Homesickness. Cold. Is there a pattern I'm detect-
ing here?" Her palms were sweating. She didn't like that it was complying
with her request; whether because it was going to prove itself correct or
because she felt she now owed it something, she wasn't sure.

"You know, just because you tell me SAT words doesn't mean I'm going
to believe you, you know that, right? If you are so wise, you should know
that. I do appreciate them though. I must have read them somewhere and
be remembering them now, though, thanks for telling me about them."

Her sweat accumulated, pooled in her armpits. She was marinating
in it; it passed through her insides and poured out forcefully between her

legs. She felt its unwelcome presence by her ankles, even in her dream feeling inconvenienced, knowing somewhere she was going to wake up to something unpleasant.

An inkling of a passing suggestion that the elk was transforming into something else that only reinforced the wetness beneath her.

She woke up with a start. Right on time, her bladder was close to bursting.

She made her way, bow-legged, to the bathroom, making sure to close the door so as not to wake up anyone with the light. It was sad, she thought through fatigued reverie, that the dream was over. There was a hidden world inside her, words and experiences and an imagination that she always coveted but never felt she possessed. But it was there, down below, waiting to be unleashed.

A world inside.

Assuming, for the sake of argument that her guest had been real and not just a dream, then its plan had backfired. She was more excited about all the potential that life had to offer than she'd ever been. She liked the interesting presence she'd conjured up and looked forward to meeting it again.

Still, she wasn't particularly eager to fall asleep again. She blamed it on the heat in the room, but made no attempt to toggle the temperature. And of course, she looked up those two words — "nostomania" and "frigorific." They were real and had been defined correctly.

She was impressed. That was one feeling she could identify.

She'd rather not investigate the other feelings.

>< >< ><

Julia breezed through school the next day. Her classwork was simultaneously more interesting and less interesting; more interesting, in the context of how this was part of the wider world beyond her experience, and what lay beyond was so interesting; and less so, in that this classwork was,

well, classwork, busywork, inconsequential, removed in its way from reality. Questions about, say, trigonometry were symbols of the deeper world,
fascinating in helping her to contemplate an entire universe of theories
and connectedness she knew almost nothing about.

But this school wasn't the wider world. School was just a holding pen,
teenage daycare.

She made no mention of her dreams to her friends at lunch time, except
by allusion.

Lynn and Julia were both in Ms. Shaw's Composition Class, and Lynn
was complaining about the essay Ms. Shaw sprung on the class, which she
required the class to complete over the upcoming weekend.

"Frigorific!" Julia replied.

"Frig!" Lynn parroted. She liked the hard consonant sound and thought
it was a cute word Julia had made up on the spot. It felt appropriate.

"Frigorific, I say. It's frigorific, I say," Julia continued.

"Hmm, okay there. No more coffee for you. You've had enough," said
Lynn, in her understated way. "Or your crack. No more crack for you.
Sleeping pills, maybe. Cough drops, sure, why not? What harm could they
do?" She shrugged off her irreverent goofing.

Later, when the whole group was together: "So, anyone have any interesting dreams last night?"

Venice, Claire, Lynn: they all drew a blank in their own patented way;
shrugs, noncommittal faces. "We failed, the whole lot of us," said Lynn.

"Thanks for thinking I could even have interesting dreams, though. I
have something to aspire to," added Clare. The downbeat way she said it
either made her joke more effective, or more harrowing.

"Ven, save us?" pleaded Lynn.

Venice shrugged. "We used Venn diagrams today in class, and one time
I dreamed people were calling out my name, and then I was somehow
stuck in a Venn diagram, like I'd become one, because you know, Venice —"

"Got it," Lynn assured her. "Failure all around."

"So yeah, who knows, maybe I'll have an interesting dream tonight?

But other than that, nah, got nothing," Venice concluded.

Julia didn't know what to expect, or if she'd tell her friends anything about her dreams, unless one of them had shared something eerily analogous or equally hyper-specific. The underlying subject of the dreams would be of casual interest, perhaps most so to Lynn, but she didn't feel like entertaining arguments or even discussions about it.

This was her thing.

>< >< ><

She sat on the floor of the dream cave, Indian-style, looking up in rapt attention. She knew it was a dream cave because, why else would she be in a cave, and why else would the floor appear as nothing more than an inorganic shade of monochromatic light blue, and why else would she be in a cave that had none of the trappings of a cave? No dust, no grime, no darkness, even; she could see fine, everything bathed in soft lambent light. There was no indication, even, that anything would be descending from the ceiling, yet here she sat, prone and waiting.

A brobdingnagian arachnoid shape descended from the unseen ceiling and appeared before her like an ever-stretching monument in a gilded city. *Marked by tremendous size*, she thought somewhere. It descended patiently but inevitably, like the New Year's Ball.

She was naturally afraid of spiders but felt no fear.

In dream-sleep, she'd learned, the perception of size meant nothing, but even with that knowledge in mind, this was perception-altering. Its carapace and abdomen alone were both leagues taller and wider than her.

Each of its eight legs was longer than she, even though there was no reliable form of comparison, for each leg was not actually a leg, but an ethereal projection of a loved friend or family member. Her mother; Venice; Lynn; Clare; a boy named Max she had affection for; her aunt, who she didn't like that much but who was inexplicably present, yet again; her first-grade teacher Mrs. Sullivan, forever her favorite teacher; and her dead grandmother Bernice, all extending outward from the spider's body and wafting like rooted underwater plants.

She didn't have the mental bandwidth to recognize and appreciate all eight projections at once, and she suspected they disappeared, reappeared and changed their order as she exerted herself in making sense of them. Her grandmother in particular was unusual, in that Julia had no working memory of what she looked like when she was alive; she'd died when Julia was only five.

While the other legs were fluid and dynamic — like ghostly projections — her grandmother's was rigid and flat, a brown wall projected behind it. She recognized the image: it was a picture of her grandmother that her mother kept on her night stand. As she looked at the projection, she felt herself inhabit that old space, the musty smell of mothballs and unsavory hard candies, the brown wall cut with three shelves of knick-knacks. She could tell the shelves were occupied, but had no idea with what.

The spider lowered to her level. Its carapace was beautiful and sleek, metallic, appropriate for the antiseptic crystal space. She didn't fear it. She gasped as it flexed its legs, saw the projections of her loved ones adjust, as if they were images changing their aspect ratio.

"I've been dreaming about you," she said, a line that was funny and ridiculous even to herself.

"I'm afraid of spiders. But your appearance is different. If this is my mind trying to make me afraid of you, it backfired." The spider lacked the mandibles, the grubby, crawly sense of alien otherness that made people itch and slap at themselves in disgust. This was more like a crystalline spider ornament, an aesthetic monument to their ability to captivate.

It had not yet spoken to her.

"I'm glad you returned," she offered.

"Yes. I am glad you do not fear me. Your subconscious mind recognizes what I represent, on some level, so it will always inspire you to fear me."

"I want you to show me. I don't....I don't know how to say it. If there is a proper way to say it. I want to follow you wherever you are willing to lead me. I want you to show me."

The enormous crystal spider shape hung motionless. Its eight projected legs continued shimmering. She noted in a micro-second passing that
the legs lost focus and blurred whenever she focused to express herself.

"I am happy to hear that. But I must tell you. I must make you understand. I am not here to show you anything. You will not be seeing anything.
This is not an adventure I am taking you on. Your brain repels me and
makes you fear me, because it wants to survive to reproduce itself and its
genetics, despite the personal cost to you.

"But part of the nature of your brain — your very being — is influenced
by what you've experienced. Your culture prioritizes adventures, journeys
of discovery. You think this is what is expected of you, on some level. This
is not a journey of discovery or self-knowledge. This is not a journey where
you will learn about yourself. This is the end of your existence.

"I am offering you only the escape from the inevitable experience that
awaits you, the most excruciating agony that awaits you. That is all."

"I understand," she said.

"I don't believe that to be true, but I can only work with what is. In this
dream, this image you have created, you are staring up at me, in awe. The
size differential is influencing your decision-making, making you genuflect
before me.

"I do not want you to be unduly influenced. Your type submits and
becomes obedient to differences in height and perceived dominion, and I
do not want that coloring your decision. But perhaps it is inevitable."

"I understand. Thank you. I have made up my mind. I want to follow
you. I want to go with you. I trust you. I'm excited, and I'm curious."

There was no way to calculate time in dream-sleep, she knew. A narrative sequence spanning years in dream-sleep can occur in the objective
length of a second. Yet still, even knowing that, she felt time passing and
passing without a response from the great figure before her.

Finally, after what felt like hours, it spoke.

"I am certain that you are making the correct decision, although perhaps not for the right reason. I am certain that, if you could live out your entire uninterrupted life, experience the agony of natural death, and then situate yourself in this position again, you would understand why this choice was the correct one.

"My hesitation, which you may suspect, is because I want to make sure you are making an informed decision. Even if it is a correct decision, it is my obligation to ensure you are making an informed decision.

"If you agree to this, this is the end of your existence.

"I want you to understand that this is the end of your existence, if you allow me."

She nodded slowly. There was a rumbling excitement within her, an eruption of elation, of grand virgin vistas. Her nerves flared up in panic, but she suppressed it, pushed through it, and smothered it.

There was again a long delay.

"I am confident you are making the right decision."

She closed her eyes — inside the dream, she thought, as her eyes were already closed in 'the real world' — and allowed her guardian to lead her, into the dark of her mind and into the dark of the void. If this were real, it would be amazing. If it were just a dream, she'd wake up and have more fantastic dreams to dream.

>< >< ><

Clare sat in English class. This was a senior class, late in the period and late in the school year. In essence, this class would have no bearing whatsoever on her or her colleagues' academic futures, and they acted accordingly. The class, separated into five distinct groups of about four or five students each, spent a couple of conspicuous seconds of conversation on the assignment at hand and then shifted to talk about practically anything else.

"I just —" Clare trailed off and forgot what she was talking about. Henry, a casual friend and classmate, kept his head arched, ready to nod and be understanding. Henry was a nice, calm Chinese-American student who planned on attending the University of Binghamton, as did she (and as did a fair portion of her graduating class). Since they would both soon be attending the same college, she figured it'd be helpful to get to know him better, since she may be seeing him around on campus next year.

"I just ... I totally blanked on what I was saying."

"You were —" he paused, hoping that maybe she'd remember on her own accord, "you were, talking about Julia's —"

"Funeral, right. Julia's funeral. Oh my god, I can't believe I forgot that. That's so weird." Clare had tracked every day since Julia's passing and since her funeral service, and did not want to contemplate a time when she didn't keep up those efforts.

There was a high-pitched female laughter beside them — the "oh my gawwd" kind— that jolted her like a next-door gun shot. "Anyway, umm, any big plans this summer? Are you going to Corey's party by the lake this weekend?" The end of senior year was a democratizing season, with a built-in reference point for different cliques and groups to hang out.

She wrote *Wuthering Heights* — Reasons on her note book, in big bold letters, in case Ms. Harrison walked around checking on them. She crossed out Reasons and didn't know why she wrote it down to begin with.

She breathed heavily and looked back up at Henry. He was gone. His chair was moved back a space, as if he'd made room to get up and leave. She looked around to see where he went and didn't see him, or see the tail end of the classroom door closing or see anything to suggest he'd left the room or had even ever been in the room.

She looked over in Venice's direction to make sympathetic eye-contact — a general get-me-out-of-here face — and wondered, why not just walk over there, it's already pandemonium in here, no one is paying attention.

She never got Venice's attention.

"*Beyond lies the Wub* puts the Wub in *Wuthering Heights*, it's about a pig," said Susanne, a classmate in her study group. "Did anyone else find it so creepy when the pig's head is on, like, a platter and is still talking to the main character? That freaked me out. That picture freaked me out."

That didn't make any sense, but okay.

Clare was nodding slowly and empathizing. "I remember I read this story once when I was in like, in junior high, in a collection, called *Beyond Lies the Wub*. I thought it had something to do with *Wuthering Heights* for some reason, or maybe was the same thing, I didn't know. All the stories were illustrated, and all I remember about that story was that there was, like, a detailed picture of a hog's, like, decapitated head. It scared the shit out of me. It's so funny you mention that."

She turned to Susanne, who was wearing Henry's face stitched atop her own. It didn't fit over her face properly. Had anyone told her that? The incongruity of Susanne's lush blonde waves over Henry's inscrutable, dried-out, graham-cracker-textured face was too much for her. She almost laughed but contained herself. How did Susanne speak so clearly while wearing Henry's face like that? Crinkly holes were carved for her eyes, but not the mouth, which retained Henry's usual blasé expression.

Susanne raised her hand, didn't receive any response, and walked up and left the class, bringing what remained of Henry along with her.

She imagined Susanne in the bathroom, employing lotions in vain to get that crinkly skin-mask looking smoothed out.

Julia was sitting in front of her, in Susanne's seat ... Julia! Was here! Adrenaline surged inside her; sending everything around her into a whirling paroxysm, like a violently-tossed fish bowl.

Julia was still there when her vision stabilized.

Julia! This couldn't be. This was a dream. The surge of emotion made her perspire, and the whole class room heated up uncomfortably. She felt herself with her hand and felt a down black puff jacket. That's why it was so hot. She thought to take it off but didn't.

"Julia, what are you doing here?"

Julia looked like she always had, she sensed. A dim outline of her mottled brown hair, rounded, moonish pale face, the brown dots of freckles and the red clusters of stubborn zits. Clare identified that pimple — it was a nasty one she'd noticed on Julia the last day she'd ever seen her alive. "A lot of juice is coming out it," Julia had complained. "But at least it's apple juice," she'd joked. The memory of that quip reverberated on the school's loud speaker so everyone could hear it and smile and laugh.

The pimple expanded into its own world, lifting Clare out into the galaxy when it ruptured, and she slid down the expulsion of pus like a toddler on a toboggan.

"I miss you, Julia," she said despite herself. She didn't have a lisp when she spoke, she noted, again despite herself. She didn't care about that.

She knew what this was. This was a dream.

Where is Isaac, why isn't he waking me up?

She pushed herself to flail her arms to force herself awake, but she remained in the dream.

"I know you aren't real, Julia. I know this is a dream."

"I'm not trying to make you believe this is anything but a dream," the voice spoke to her. She knew that voice. It had been the voice that visited her innumerable times, even in her daydreams, whenever her conscious mind wavered.

The voice had always remained patient, understanding, and reassuring. It had explained all about the nature of pain, and how Julia — wisely, after deep consideration — chose to unmake herself rather than await the indescribable agony that awaits us all. It spoke about how Julia one day just no longer was, and how this was a decision of her own making. Don't feel bad for her. Envy her.

Julia had passed in her sleep without medical explanation. No furtive drug habit. No shocking heart attack or brain aneurysm. No unknown allergy. Nothing glorious, poetic or valiant. Not even something gory or tragic but at least understandable, something for which an emotion could be attached and understanding processed, other than whatever emotion or understanding lurked in the aghast, torn space Clare felt in the pit of her stomach. Confusion. Dread. Bewilderment. The space was the cousin of anxiety, churned the way anxiety does, sent its tendrils throughout her system the way anxiety does.

But it was not anxiety, just the absence of something.

"I hate you," she said to the voice, even though she didn't really mean that and was just speaking stupidly. "I hate you. You took her from us. If what you are saying is true, you took her from us. She was my best friend. She had a family who loved her. Did you know that? And now she's gone."

She'd had this conversation so many times and already been through the range of emotions.

She reached her hands out to hug Julia's neck. Julia's head tipped forward and fell hard to the floor like heavy luggage, though it made no sound. Roaches and black bugs crawled from the impossibly-proportioned spigot that was Julia's neck.

Clare screamed without sound, averted her eyes and closed her palms. There were no bugs. Julia was sitting there again, head-and-all, undisturbed.

"You know that does not make sense. That is your brain, trying to scare you off, trying to upset you. It is reaching for the horrific, what it thinks will scare you, disgust you. Julia was cremated. You know that. There would be no roaches. There is no longer even a body. You know this."

She looked back at Julia, which she knew was where the voice emanated from. Clare had been through denial, been upset, furious, depressed, overwhelmed, and even at times felt contented and felt something like acceptant. If what the voice told her was true, then Julia was in a better place: non-existence. She'd avoided the pain of natural death, the voice assured her. No one who loves anyone would permit them to experience a natural death. Having her alive for her company while subjecting her to the possibility of a natural death was, in a sense, selfish.

Clare didn't really believe any of that, not really, but it was a nice thought, to think her friend had made her own choice, made what could be the "correct" choice. That her choice created meaning and understanding to fill — or at least create the semblance of something that could fill — that pit in her stomach.

"If it's good enough for her, well, it's good enough for me," Clare said to the voice, in a half-space of resignation. She said it just to say it, almost as if on a dare. The paroxysms, the violent distortion, of adrenaline-soaked anxiety tore at the fabric of her dream for a moment.

Julia had been lucky, the voice explained. The vast majority of people were on a different mental wave length and could not receive these overtures. In a sense then, she was lucky, too, since here she was....

"I mean it." She doubled-down her provocation.

"I do not believe you mean that. As much as I think it would be in your best interest to believe that, I am not sure you do."

"No, I do. I've had enough of this. I've had enough of this wondering." Her voice sounded faintly contemptuous, even to herself. If she was awake, she'd be sitting cross-armed, curled into herself, steaming in a little tantrum, thinking *fuck everybody else.*

"I want to experience what she experienced. I want to know."

"You do not understand. There is nothing to experience. I offer you the absence of experience. What you will eventually experience otherwise is the unendurable, never-ending pain of your own natural death."

"I don't want to talk anymore." There was an edge in Clare's voice, even though this was nothing but a dream. "I believe you. I've met and spoken with you so many times. I believe. I accept. You would not be so persistent unless you were real. You couldn't know what you know unless this was real. Otherwise, this is just all fake, my crazy imagination, in which case I will just wake up.

"So, here I am. If what you are saying is true, then I believe, take me with you."

She extended her hand and struck a pose of concentration and acceptance.

"I grant you permission, every permission you need. I believe you. I believe. My brain, my impulses, are hard-wired, in the interests of the species' survival but not my personal interest. See? I understand. I believe. I accept, okay?! I accept!"

She extended her hand more forcefully, her look now of determination.

Julia took her hand and held her close. There was no classroom, just them, outside, in space. *This space is the pit in your soul, the emptiness you feel,* Clare felt, and panicked. She had buyer's remorse before the thought was even expressed.

Wake up. Where is Isaac? Piss yourself, shit yourself, wake yourself up. Isaac where are you?! I told you to protect me!

She had been impulsive and didn't want this anymore. She pulled back and before even running was an option she was already making her way toward the door of the classroom.

Clare turned around and saw a Julia of distended limbs and joints launching toward her. Clare was trapped between her limbs now, encaged underneath them, and Julia's goopy neck cascaded down in front of her. Her head flipped back, upside down, revealing her face of ridged teeth.

"No. Embrace this."

"I want to be awake. Isaac, where are you?!"

"You granted me permission. You made the right decision. Shut off what your brain is telling you. There is nothing to fear."

A distended limb ending in the shape of a sharpened asterisk shot out and held her arm. She was trapped between stalk-like growths. The only exit was occupied by Julia's distorted death-face.

A force gripped her throat and soft pads closed over her larynx.

"There is nothing to fear. There is nothing to fear."

Her mind was not assuaged. Every cell in her body revolted, flush with hot terror.

"Isaac where are you?!"

"There is nothing to fear," said the fearsome face, a cacophony of sharp threatening sights, repugnant smells and unsettling booming explosions.

"There is nothing to fear. Your mind has not realized it has lost. You are free from it. There is nothing to fear. This is just your conscious mind's last spasms. This is nothing compared to what you'd experience upon your natural death."

All was nothing.

>< >< ><

Venice pulled into the parking lot of the small shopping courtyard that contained JV Hot Bagels. It was 8:30 a.m. on a Saturday in December. Other
than the post office, JV Hot Bagels was the only business she recognized.
She'd only been upstate in college at Albany for a year and a half — and
truth be told, she'd never been super-observant — but only recognizing
two stores was ... something. A sign. A good sign, bad sign? Maybe a sign
that this place was behind her. She didn't know. It just felt like something,
like moving on.

It was winter. Lakewood High School was not in session, so it wasn't
surprising JV Hot Bagels was empty. The only other customer — a mus-
tached, overweight middle-aged man in a *NY Giants* beanie — gathered his
brown bag and gave her the look-over, as most men did. She was inured to
it, didn't bother her except when she knew the middle-aged man in question, like if it was a friend's father. She didn't know this guy, so what, kinda
icky, but whatever. She was taller than him, and liked being taller than
most men. The door opened, she heard the little bell, and he left without
incident.

She ordered what she had always ordered when she just another high
school regular — pumpernickel bagel, toasted, vegetable cream cheese —
and a coffee, light on the milk and sugar. She was serviced by the owner,
who recognized her, and she made small talk with him. He was a nice guy,
late thirties, gelled hair and muscular, attractive in a typical way. Rumor
was he slept with a couple of the girls who worked here, but for all she
knew those were just rumors, and, whatever, it's a free country. She told
him about what she was majoring in — "Undecided," she said with a smile,
but leaning toward double-majoring in business and sociology — and he
said something about that being impressive and ambitious, as if college
wasn't just a bullshit way station between childhood and adulthood. She
made small talk about how she liked Albany and got along with her room-
mates — yeah, she'd gotten lucky on that end — and how the school lived

up to its reputation as a party school ("I bet," he said, which he'd certainly said a hundred times before).

She took her brown paper bag and said her good-byes. She decided to eat outside, despite the dry cold. Nostalgia required a cold environment, she thought; it wouldn't feel right in a place like Florida, where the warm weather is beckoning and life-affirming. Nostalgia warms you up, in a certain way. It requires gray cold and hot coffee and local restaurants and blue *Giants* beanies.

She could see the edge of the high school from here. She looked at the high school and reminisced without active thoughts. Just about her time there, her friends. There were no real feelings to unearth; it's not like anything was buried here. No dramatic emotions. Just the sad reminders of loss.

Lynn would be back in town next week from R.I.T., which Venice was deeply looking forward to. As college went on, they'd seen each other less, but for valid, expected reasons. Their respective schools were a solid 3.5 hours away from each other, they'd made their own separate friends, and Lynn was an engineering major, so she actually had to study during the school year, especially come finals time. Venice hadn't seen Lynn in about six weeks, actually. There's that obligatory sense of gravitas about being back in town, but hopefully, they could enjoy their free time together without too much painful reminiscing, and hopefully each year onward would get easier and easier.

She put the too-hot coffee in the drink-holder, started the car with her right hand and snacked on the still-hot bagel. She pulled out of the parking lot and thought about pulling up to Lakewood, but didn't. That would be too sentimental, and she really wasn't that type of person. Just thinking about pulling up to her old high school was enough.

She drove down the main road and past the turn-off for Mohegan Lake. She stayed in the right lane, even though everyone rushed into the left-turn-only lane just to cut everyone else off at the light. It didn't bother her. Everyone in town knew about this annoying light and this annoying behavior; it was kind of unifying.

She was multitasking; driving, texting, eating, furtively finger-checking on her coffee cup to see if it was drinkable yet. She should have grabbed a coffee sleeve. She was about ten minutes away from her parents' home off Curry Street. She had a figurative stack full of DVDs and television shows to catch up on, a ton of extra coffee to drink at home, and absolutely jackshit else to do. Ahh, to be home.

She got a hearty scallion chunk in the last bite. Mmm, that was good.

Her phone vibrated. It was jammed right against her coffee. She clamped down on the coffee lid to prevent any from spilling over. She checked the message: Brenda, a friend from college who lived in her dorm. Usual gripes about being back at home. Emoticons and empathy. Continued buzzing vibrations, the red-flashing light of her phone out of the corner of her eye.

Crumpled bag, smeared on its edges with cream cheese. The phone between her legs at a traffic light; a long, hopefully final text until she got home. The coffee was good, she was glad he put in too much sugar.

Starting on the second half of the bagel. Car engine kicked a little bit, some pull-back, whatever. Rushing to make the right on the yellow light. Another insectile buzz from her phone. She checked to see who it was from, turning to make the light, ignoring the uncomfortable sting of the coffee that now dotted her hand.

Turning, that oncoming SUV was retarded, fucker, should stop. It didn't. Nausea overtook her. No, that wasn't right. A moment of dreadful anticipation, a pivot point that lasted a millennium.

The SUV crossed the yellow line while making its left and plowed head-on into her Kia. The metal mousetrap of her surroundings ruptured and exploded, roaring, folded into itself, a ship collapse in perpetuity.

Coroner's report: She died instantly.

>< >< ><

Rowland, six years old, didn't want to go to see Grandma Lynnie. He didn't like the way she looked and the way she smelled. He hadn't seen her for almost two months, ever since she had gotten sick and been in the hospital. He visited her in the hospital once and didn't like it. He didn't say anything about it, just kept to himself and didn't talk. Grandma was nice and usually gave him toys or gifts, and if she did something he didn't understand, his mom and dad would always let him know she did something nice by saying, "oh isn't that nice," and he'd feel comfortable about it.

He was going to visit Lynnie in the hospital. He was dressed in a dark suit and tie that everyone said was so cute and charming but was a little itchy and he didn't like everyone watching over him.

He went with Mom, Dad, and his older brother, Kale, who was ten. Kale was acting like the big boy and telling Rowland to be on his best behavior. Rowland already planned on being good, and even letting Grandma pat him on the head and kiss him.

It took them a long time to get to the hospital. Rowland liked looking out the windows. He liked cars, was fascinated by them. Grandma Lynnie grew up near New York City, a place he'd never been, but he knew there were brightly colored taxis there. The most famous were the bright yellow taxis, Grandma told him. Then were also bright lime-green taxis, she told him, that went to the less crowded areas. And now there were bright purple and bright red taxis, too. And there were trains that went underground where all different kinds of people rode together. He wanted to visit New York and see the taxis and the trains and see the big famous toy stores and candy shops and eat ice cream. He lived in Delaware, and he didn't know why that was funny but he heard people saying Delaware was funny and "no New York."

When he got older, he'd go to New York City. His aunt and uncle and relatives lived somewhere in New York, on an island, but not a fun island, an island that looked a lot like his town except maybe more crowded. They were going to meet them at the hospital, too.

They all crowded into the hospital room. Rowland played by counting them all — One, himself; Two, his brother Kale. Three and Four, Mom and Dad. Five, Grandma who was Mom's Mom, but maybe she didn't count. Ok, then Five: Aunt Josie, Mom's Sister; and Six, her husband William. Seven, Eight, Nine — Josie's children, Auden, Alden, and August.

All in this one room. He was the youngest and everyone paid attention to him but he liked to stay quiet.

His Grandma Lynnie seemed very tired. She always seemed sort of tired and one time he said she should get more sleep, and she said something and everyone laughed. But now she looked really bad, really thin and her eyes were dark-colored. She just didn't look good, and he did not want to tell anyone but he was scared she would get him sick. He was brought over to hug and kiss Grandma Lynnie and he felt bad that he was scared to hug her and he felt bad that she must have realized that.

"Kiss your Grandma Lynnie," his mother said. "Lynnie loves you and you love Lynnie, don't you." He did love Lynnie and he didn't mean to be scared. He knew she wasn't well, she was old, she was in her eighties which was an impossible idea: he was not even in his 'tens' yet. She had been alive eight times as long as his brother, which was amazing. He'd said it was amazing once and everyone laughed.

That laugh he'd liked.

He knew that Grandma Lynnie was special. She had been a successful engineer; he wasn't sure what that was but it was hard to do and you had to be smart for it and read a lot. Plus, engineers worked on trains and helped build cars, although she was not that kind of engineer. Plus-plus, Grandma Lynnie made Mom, and Mom made him.

He hugged Grandma Lynnie and ignored the musky smell that reminded him of his dog when she was wet and sick. Lynnie was covered in a smooth, plastic sheet, kind of like the way his toys came wrapped. This sheet helped to keep her well. She had fallen recently and hurt herself and gotten really weak. He didn't know much about it but she was sick inside. He knew that things disappeared when they died, and that Lynnie would probably disappear soon.

"I love you Row-Row. You're going to go on a boat someday and you promise me to say 'row-row' for me?" He nodded into her shoulder. He'd already been on a boat and people had asked him to do that and he'd done it but he'd do it again. He had never gone on a boat by himself so he could make that promise to do it by himself one day.

She kissed him on his head, but it didn't feel like lips on his head. It felt like a pencil eraser, it was so rough. He didn't say anything.

He thought they would spend a short time there and leave, but they stayed for a long time.

At some point later in the day, his Dad and Uncle came over together with some of the other kids and asked him if he wanted to go to Toys "R" Us for a little bit. Mom and Aunt were going to stay behind. He wanted to be a good, big boy and stay with Grandma Lynnie. He felt it would be a good thing to do, but they insisted and he said ok. They tried to excite him by saying he could get anything he wanted, and that was exciting, but he didn't know how to feel about it and stayed subdued.

It would be the last time he saw Grandma Lynnie.

>< >< ><

Few could be this lucky. Her husband had not been so lucky, her dear beloved Anthony, passed six years ago now, a heart attack. He passed with no one around.

I'll be joining you soon my dear, Lynn told herself. She was surrounded by her daughters, her beautiful daughters, the lights of her life; her large, loving family, her gifts and testament to this world.

She held hands and kissed and embraced. At her age, death was a constant. Even as a child, she remembered, death took her three dearest friends; two of them, bizarre freak occurrences. How else to explain two young girls dying in their sleep, within months of each other, no less? Julia and Clare, she remembered them. Clare: quiet, clever Clare. So clever, so quiet, so reserved. Smarter than she'd let on, didn't talk much because of her lisp, she remembered, but still the first of the group to have a real boyfriend.

And Julia, sweet Julia. It pained her that she couldn't remember much about Julia other than that she had passed first.

Venice, her other young friend, in a terrible car accident a couple years later. While she was home from college, how tragic. Venice, such a beauty, such a beautiful name, such a beautiful girl. So tragic, so terrible.

She remembered a period of consoling dreams she had, where she told herself that Julia and Clare had died peacefully, painlessly. She'd been asked, crazily, to join them, but no, no, she wanted none of that. She'd been scared of death then, as was to be expected, as a teenager. She wasn't so afraid anymore. She'd lived her time. She'd lived a good life.

Well girls, I'll be joining you, and joining all her other dear friends who had taken the next step in the adventure. She hoped she'd join them as teenagers, or else they could greet her as adults of advanced age, as if they hadn't been taken so abruptly.

Voices now sounded like she was underwater. Her daughters were sobbing, clutching each other, trying to be strong but failing. They consoled each other. They spoke as if she'd already passed. *I'm still here, you silly dearies!* she thought, but perhaps not. Perhaps this was passing gracefully. She thanked god for painkillers and all the sweet doctors and nurses helping her, such nice people, all the nice people throughout her life, all the fullness she'd enjoyed when others had been taken so tragically.

She drifted off. She lived eighty-two years on Earth.

Between the synapses of her dying brain, she'd live a millennia in agony.

Beneath the sedatives, she felt a disruption. Placid warm comforting water, boiling in an instant. *A bouleversement*, she thought insanely, a word she didn't remember ever hearing, no, hearing in a dream, one of those crazy dreams from her youth, that now came back to her with its full wretched meaning intact. That's how she'd described death to herself in a dream, after her friends' own deaths, but that was stupid crazy talk from so long ago.

HELP ME! HELP ME! DEAR GOD HELP ME! She reached out, pinioned herself, clamoring against the wall of oblivion encasing her. GOD I FEEL EVERYTHING, HELP ME! HELP ME! HELP ME!

She screamed for her family. FUCK YOU, YOU UNGRATEFUL PIECES OF SHIT, YOU WORTHLESS BITCHES, HELP ME HELP ME!

She reached out in vain but nothing was moving. Every fiber of her being, pin-pricked, aflame, virulent, eyes gouged out, everything organic and important gouged out. KILL THE CHILDREN, KILL THE CHILDREN, she screamed against the perpetual all-consuming pain that all men and women experience upon the precipice of death, the pain that causes them to forsake their loved ones and their lives' work for even just the barest chance of reprieve.

TAKE KALE, TAKE ROWLAND, TAKE AUDEN, and as if this knowledge had always been there, as if she always had known who she'd sacrifice first to make the galaxy of pain crest. She wanted to feel the sensation, tear Rowland asunder, wretch him with her hands, to transfer the bilious suffering from her to the form of another.

She'd tear Rowland in two with her bare hands to make this stop, she'd squeeze him until he exploded, rive him into stumps and pieces, anyone, please god, oh god please anyone else. OHHHHHH GOD PLEASE PLEASE PLEASE PLEASE PLEASE this can't be right, this can't be it, a flooding of experience and pain commanding her to escape, to flee death but it's impossible, she's an animal being cooked over a flame with every fiber of her being broadcasting the pain as an incentive to remove the spit, a lobster in boiling water with the pot jammed closed, OH GOD OH GOD OH GOD and even that's what she intended to think but it was nonsense, gibberish.

The drugs did nothing. There was agony under the fog, gibbering, incessant, liquids of acid and organs of twisting thorn. GOD! GOD!, a scream that renders throats a pulping mess, all her years spent on earth resulting in a perpetuity in a boiling fish bowl.

HELP ME HELP ME ACWKKKK HELP ME! FUCK YOU FOR DOING THIS TO ME! FUCK YOU! FUCK YOU! PLEASE GOD HELP ME! FUCK YOU! FUCK

YOU DO SOMETHING!   HELP ME PLEASE GOD ANYONE!   PLEASE GOD
ANYONE!

>< >< ><

With great sympathy, the doctor consoled the grieving kin.

"It's the best anyone could hope for. She was well-loved, well-cared
for, heavily sedated. She went peacefully," and yes, yes, thank God for that.

A Related Corollary

"SO," CATHY BEGAN, sitting down at the round table at Argo Tea, her with a TeaLuxe Matte Latte, Megan with a Honey Breeze Cooler. The drinks were on Cathy tonight.

Megan sat, slouched, eyes red, facing the wall in the kind of crestfallen way that reeked of unknowing parody. *Dammit, why did it have to be like this?* Even though she had no conscious control over her slouch, even though thinking about it gave way too much import to the random machinations of her musculature, the way she sat, slouched, positioned herself, everything seemed inauthentic, too showy. *Aww, look at me. Look at me sniffle, look at my bright red eyes, all the while I sip my $4 tea drink in a gentrified neighborhood in a city people would kill to live in, in the richest country in the world. Isn't life so tough?* Megan put her hand to her head as if she had a roaring headache, a hot tear skidding down her right cheek.

"So," Megan started, without looking up at Cathy, in a way that wasn't supposed to sound snobby, but did. "I do appreciate you meeting up with me like this, I'm sorry I keep calling you like this, it's just —"

"No, no, it's fine. It's nice to see you again. I just wish you felt better. I wish I could see you being happy." Cathy lowered her head and looked up exaggeratedly to meet Megan's gaze, lifting her eyebrows a bit to signal that she was looking for a response. Her full white face widened, a little bit of a goofy grin across her face when Megan acknowledged her. Several years ago back in college, they'd been driving cross country and passed a billboard featuring a white, round-faced clown with a red afro. Now and again, at just the right, frozen angle, Cathy's white, full face and springy auburn hair brought to mind that lame clown.

Megan smiled.

"Ehh, see, things are looking up already." Cathy took Megan off Constant Attention Watch and took a deep sip of her TeaLuxe Matte Latte. "Mmm, this is delish. You need to try this."

Megan took a sip of Cathy's thick, iced drink, so laden with thickeners and agents that it was questionable to still classify it as tea.

"Mine's good, too," Megan said, took a sparrow-like sip of her honey-tinged tea drink, and passed it over to her friend.

Cathy took a slight sip. "Mmm, that is good. Sweet, but not too sweet. Just sweet enough. And it's black tea, too? That's good for you. Black tea is good for depression," she parroted the science she'd heard before, knowing it was unhelpful and inconsequential.

There were good drinks and good tastes and good experiences in this world, and rather than talk about her Grand Problems, Megan appreciated the implicit premise of enjoying good things in the world, with the expectation of other good things to come.

Arbitrarily, hazy ennui rolled through her emotional landscape like a slow-moving dark cloud. Now she was just sad, just "blah." That she had been briefly in good spirits ... that was something she could acknowledge but not fathom. If there had been a multiple choice test with the question, "Briefly, Megan had enjoyed something and known happiness," she could mark it as True and know she was technically correct, but could do nothing more, come to no further understanding. To try to understand why she had felt happy but no longer did was like trying to fill an empty belly with the memories of a great meal.

This was resignation. There was no sharpness here, no momentous upheaval, no drastic feeling of falling. That feeling was for happy people with expectations of continued happiness, coming to terms with a difficult situation. No, this feeling was the reassertion of the primary. This was the gradual but inevitable overtaking of that which had always lain dormant, that which had always been, that which was. Happiness was a brief signal flare against a sky of coal-shadow.

Cathy, intuitively, saw her friend emotionally overtaken.

"Hey, girl, how are you doing?"

Megan looked around the Argo Tea shop. Aesthetically, she appreciated the bright, vibrant decor, the fashionable, youthful crowd that frequented, their sleek electronic and elegant eye glasses and sophisticated reading material that promised engaging conversations and interesting minds.

She appreciated these things, had a mind for ideas and an eye, even, for fashion. That these things conceivably made her life better was undeniably true but of no mind. How could it be that these things which she enjoyed existed, but her spirit cared not one iota? She was a friendly, well-meaning person, with legitimate interests and a legitimate engagement in the world. Exasperated, frustrated, incredulous, over and over she could think of the friends and images that (theoretically) made her happy, yet the sadness that stood in her way was impermeable, inarticulate.

Cathy eyed Megan with a look best described as triumphant empathy. "Megan, life is worth living. Things get better," she spoke as if she cared or what she said was anything but speculative and clichéd.

Cathy made life sound so good, so intuitive, so full of promise, and for a second Megan could buy into it, but since life as lived is a solitary pursuit, soon she would soon be back in her apartment, tackling the sorrow of the human condition, alone. That bottle of pills promising painless, permanent escape ever-beckoning.

"Megan," Cathy weaved her face into Megan's field of vision, making her acknowledge her. "I'm glad you called me today. You promised me, so many times, that you wouldn't do anything stupid? You promise, right?"

Megan bobbed her head, her mouth a straight horizontal line, just like those showy "smiley" faces she used as an accoutrement when signing her signature, two dots and a horizontal line inside a circle.

"You promise, right? I want to hear that you will never do anything like that."

"Yes, I promise you. Of course, I promise you."

"Good. I'm here to talk to you. I'm here now, and I want you to talk to me."

Megan smiled autonomously.

Just as some cocktail of chemicals and hormones, introduced at certain stages and at certain proportions, led a fetus in utero to become heterosexual or homosexual, this or that, here or there, so too was it with this type of depression. That no name or cause or identifying factor could be pinpointed, no logical assaying could diffuse the mist of sadness that hovered over all which Megan undertook, that by the nature of her make-up such an inquiry was fruitless; well, the science behind that would not be accepted for years to come, and it was of no interest for anyone here. So those pills that offered painless relief stayed stored on the shelf, out of the strength of her reach, high atop the altar of platitudes.

"Things get better," Cathy offered, up-ending precisely everything humankind knows to be intuitively true about the actual flow of life, as if life wasn't a narrative that curdled into decay and death, as if, perhaps for the eight billionth person, perhaps the story this time would have a different ending.

"You have so much to live for. Never forget that," Cathy also offered, which was true in the sense that several others had an interest in Megan's continued, base survival, and society compelled Megan not to disturb that equilibrium.

Cathy smiled warmly, and why wouldn't she? Here was her pathetic, interminable wreck of a friend, whose continued pained existence cast her own doubts and tribulations in a more positive light.

"Of course, I'd never do that," Megan proposed, and Cathy smiled and took it as a victory that Megan would never do anything as stupid as make her own determinations, because the continuation of life, no matter how bleak, that's a victory.

For a second Cathy thought she saw her friend Kyle through the window. He did live in the area. Cathy had a crush on Kyle, and she didn't want to introduce Kyle to Megan. Something about Megan's moody, delicate nature was catnip for the quiet, introverted boys like Kyle.

Cathy noticed Megan's attention had faded and, despite herself, yearned to regain her focus.

"Promise me," she pleaded to Megan.

"I promise you." Megan cemented her promise by extending her hand and putting it atop Cathy's.

While regaining Megan's attention, Cathy was mentally preparing herself on how to handle the Kyle situation and was relieved that she needn't bother. It wasn't Kyle. Her relief came out as an exaggerated smile.

"Great!"

So Megan pledged herself, pushed herself back into life, and life did she have, back through the same dark, encumbering smog that inhabited her to her very core.

So the promise of painless escape went unexplored, so abominable, so abhorrent was that option, as if death would never come unless it was a choice proactively taken;

so noble was the passive retreat into endless, inescapable depression and her living for the benefit of others, as if life was a joint venture experienced concurrently with others rather than a solitary activity, as if promises and overtures meant anything against that fog of dispiriting ennui;

and how so dignified and graceful was her eventual succumbing to death via whatever terrible misfortune befell her, and if only it served, at worst, as the abrupt punctuation mark on the drawn-out sentence of her life rather than another tortuous experience in-and-of itself, part-and-parcel of the whole.

Surely the invisible God(s) and creators we pretended watched our every move were beside themselves with ecstatic cheers of congratulations for a valiant effort, for the noble will to keep on living.

But at least she had pledged herself, to her friend Cathy and others, and they could pat themselves on the back for that. Eventually, of course, their friendship would become wan and brittle, an echo of whatever it had once been; and after Megan moved out of town, Cathy would find other sad-sack friends to feel better than and other activities to reinforce her feelings of superiority.

Megan smiled at Cathy as if she had any belief that the dark weight would ever lift.

The Gulf of Responsibility

"GLORIA, MS. HERNANDEZ ... I can't help but, I've noticed that this is your ... your third *pr-eg-nan-cy* within an 18 month period."

Alex was surprised how his mouth explored every crevice of the word "pregnancy" — the purr of the "pr," the bluntness of the hard "g," the sharpness of the ending "SEE" — surprised at how the word stretched out of his mouth, as if taking twice as long to get the word out meant she'd be doubly attentive to his intent. But the condemnation inherent in his articulated "pr-eg-nan-cy" felt mandatory. Not natural coming from him, that's for sure. Expressing moral outrage seemed so out-of-fashion. Even the term, *moral outrage*, was hyperbolic. Who is really, legitimately *outraged* in America anymore? Not Internet-outraged: actually outraged. It's not cool to pass moral judgment, and that lesson was deeply ingrained in him. But before his subconscious recalled that fact and moved on, it felt good, satisfying, to care about something.

Still, he suppressed his moral outrage and let it transmute into something more palliative and comforting: a sense of superiority. She was in the wrong, he was in the right, and that was enough for him.

"What you mean, 'you notice?' You only visiting me because you knew I'm pregnant. But yeah, so? I took care of those, I'll take care of this, too."

"Okay."

"And why not? It's none of your business. And I am being responsible. What, do you want me to raise a child by myself, without ... without any real income? It's responsible to get an abortion. If I have the baby, then you'd turn around and say, 'how irresponsible, you on welfare and making more babies.' You know, if I wanted to game you and your system and get more money, I'd just have the kids. I know you get more money if you have kids. But I'm not gonna do that, I'm not doing that. I'm being responsible."

Alex nodded, moving his pen on his note pad but not actually writing anything down. She was right, after all. If Gloria Hernandez wanted to secure more money from 'the system,' all she needed to do was pop out some more children. Alex had heard all the horror stories, as did everyone else, apparently. Stories of fat welfare queens passed out drunk mid-day on a ratty couch, their tiny box apartments filled with neglected children squirming in closets, wallowing in filth, covered in freakish amounts of piss and shit ('freakish amounts' in the sense that you were surprised their guardians had fed them enough to even generate any shit and piss, let alone the volume that made headlines in the *New York Post*).

Whenever he described his job as a social worker to strangers, that's the first thing they asked about: the horror stories. But he had yet to personally come across anything so black-and-white, so objectively *evil*. Instead, he encountered slighter moral deviations — a fair amount of substance abuse, sub-optimal work ethics, sexual promiscuity — in the context of three-dimensional people bounded by personal weaknesses, exacerbating the hardships of already shitty circumstances.

"When are you going to get the abortion?"

"Soon. Next week."

"Where?"

Her eyebrows creased hard and she made a disgusted face. The mark of an uncultured person, Alex had learned throughout the course of his job, was the inability to suppress sudden displays of emotion. To be cultured, he'd learned, was to perfect the facade of equanimity. It had been a vestigial remnant of his middle-class upbringing that kept him from looking taken aback after finding out about her upcoming family-planning hat trick. He still had those middle-class values, even if his social worker salary now appended the dreaded 'lower' to 'lower-middle-class.'

"Washington Heights Clinic. Why? It's none of your business."

"I'm just curious. Just interested." He almost forgot that, typically, welfare cases were sycophantically nice to social workers during their monthly status updates. Gloria had integrity for telling him off, that's for sure.

"Do you have anyone to go with you?"

"That's not any of your business."

"Sorry. I was just wondering if you needed anyone to accompany you."

"That in your job description?" she asked, more taken aback than angry.

"I'm sorry ... I don't know why I asked. I was just wondering." It said something about the disenchantment he was feeling that he didn't even know whether that was part of his job description or whether he'd just violated some ethical rules.

"Is social services paying for the abortion?" He adjusted himself in his chair to make himself appear more authoritative, to give the illusion of an interrogative question rather than the embarrassing reality: he didn't even know the answer. He was asking himself the question in his mind and his mouth unwittingly articulated it. Did social services pay for abortions? He was pretty sure it didn't, but he should know stuff like this.

"No."

"No? Who is paying for it? Is the father paying for it?" For a split-second he imagined himself a take-no-prisoners journalist, speaking truth-to-power, busting someone bilking the government. *Dateline*-type shit.

"No."

The circumstances surrounding this ostensibly free abortion were still hanging in the air, but Alex's drive to root out this inconsistency dampened when he remembered he was haranguing a fucking welfare recipient about how she was going to pay for her third abortion. On some days, he could convince himself that his agency was actually designed just to keep tabs on the morals and goings-on of brown-and-black poor families.

Javier, Gloria's six-year old son, tottered into the living room, a big red *Yankees* cap matching his big red shorts and big red-and-white shoes. The kid's fitted *Yankees* cap, Alex noted, was the type he was always too cheap to buy. A cynical person would recognize this child as the anchor baby. Despite what people may think, welfare doesn't really exist for the childless. But a child is the gateway into The System, and once you get into The System — as long as you play along and make your meetings and feign patience with the inevitable administrative fuck-ups — you're in The System to stay. And there were many administrators who had a vested interested in making sure The System was good at keeping people within its confines.

"Come here, Papi." She lifted Javier up into her lap, bouncing him on her knees, and maybe even off her little baby bump. Alex was always a little surprised that his Hispanic clientele actually did say "Papi": he always thought that'd been lazy stereotyping, like whites loving mayonnaise and tuna fish.

"And how is everything else going?"

Alex attempted more natural conversation — talk of family, holidays, usual shit — until these subjects just petered out and the conversation came to its natural end. Gloria provided him an updated resume and some library records to show that she'd applied for home aide and retail jobs. A couple months ago, she'd worked at a *Payless* shoe store down in Harlem (her rent had gone up, accordingly, per New York City Housing Authority rules), but she didn't like the job and quit (her rent then dropping back down, accordingly). Despite her inability to handle the job at *Payless*, and despite submitting several dozen applications to apparently effective silence, she claimed to be optimistic about her chances of securing and retaining some entry-level employment, somewhere.

Alex remembered reading *Gawker* horror stories of despair about college grads sending 400 applications into the Great Unemployment Black Hole. It always surprised him — if surprised was the right word — to find that most of his indigent clients had admirable levels of self-esteem. They were depressed, certainly, but their depression was always blamed on their external circumstances, and rarely based on perceived personal or inherent defects. Maybe this was how it was supposed to be. But he knew his friends and kinda-sorta friends across various social networks griped endlessly about their failures and hardships (real or imagined), intoned daily about their Worst Days Ever, and turned one ambiguous look from a company superior into a prophecy of doom and failure, yet the struggling lower-rung of humanity he dealt with day-in, day-out managed a respectable level of stoicism and perspective.

He felt ashamed of himself for arbitrarily harassing Gloria for unnecessary details. After he'd left her apartment, he even considered going back upstairs and apologizing to her, but he knew that would just be a fumbling, awkward mess. He made the argument to himself that he'd only acted out of genuine concern for Gloria — he wasn't sure if he was convinced, but it was enough to picture Caroline's ruddy smile of approval. Caroline was his girlfriend, but in his mental life she was practically his spirit animal: he thought of her beaming, winning face looking upon him proudly whenever he did something right, and providing him encouragement whenever he felt down on himself.

He thought of her shiny face and took the "A" train back downtown to the Family Services Call Center.

>< >< ><

He should really listen to that jazz standard "Take the 'A' Train." It was indefensible that he had both a growing curiosity about jazz and actually took the "A" train often to commute to work and to his clients' houses, yet couldn't find the time to listen to the track on YouTube or something.

He invented a fake beat and a fake tune and hummed it to himself — "Take-in' the A train, T-T-T-Take-in' the 'A' train —" all the way back to the Family Services Call Center at 132 West 125th Street. Back in the office, he found his coworker Kevin Tharani ensnaring a soon-to-be intern by the stairs.

Ethn-aring? No, he concluded firmly, that play on Kevin's last name was too lame to be vocalized.

"So, guess," Kevin began to his fresh prey. "What do you think I am?"

"Umm, hmmm," she looked at Kevin, smiling toothsomely. She went through the options in her head. She was smart enough not to articulate her process of sorting out what ethnic group Kevin may belong to, in case anyone around her got offended. She was such an overachiever that, despite her smile, she'd kick herself if she got this guess wrong.

"I'd go with … Pers …" — she drew out the 'z' sound, to see if he'd bite and confirm her guess — "Persian?"

"Man," Kevin exalted, slapping his hands together. "That's awesome, everyone says Persian. That's everyone's number one guess. I don't think I've ever met a Persian person, but everyone thinks I'm Persian. I must have been adopted. The best guess I ever got was Puerto Rican. Someone once said half Puerto Rican, half Jewish."

"Well, then, what are you?" she asked with a zeal fueled largely by her status as a lowly prospective intern, and Kevin's status as her potential superior.

"Let me guess," Alex interjected. "If I had to guess, I'd say … let's see, I'd say you are a light-skinned North Indian from Gutenberg, New Jersey who has practically no understanding of his background."

"Dude, you ruined it, man!"

"That was going to be her next guess, I'm sure."

"I know enough about being Indian. Meaning, I know what holidays I can take off."

Alex turned to the future intern. She'd gotten the gig but wouldn't intern until her next semester, and Kevin was just showing her around the place while she picked up her offer letter. "Hey, I'm Alex. I'm the 'other Kevin.' We were the same year in college, have the same job title. We used to be roommayyy – officemates."

She smiled. "I'm Erin."

"Nice to meet you."

They all made small-talk, Alex pleased with himself that he was able to fit in his usual joke whenever the Kevin "Ethnicity Game" came up: "I'd just have guessed he's whatever Ray Romano was, just the darker-skinned version," and she laughed and everyone would agree he looked just like

Ray Romano, except darker.

After some more small talk, she made her exit, spry and happy and bubbly, back to the comforting cocoon of college classes.

Kevin turned to Alex right after she left. "Dude, I'm impressed. She's cute as shit."

"Yeah, she seems cool. Cute as shit, high praise, indeed. I don't know man, you should see my shit, when I put lipstick on it and crimp its eyelashes. It's pretty cute."

Kevin was undeterred. "She's cute enough that even talking about your shit, she's still cute. Even if I realize I compared her to shit, she's still cute."

Kevin refused to take a shit at work, so that was high praise indeed.

"So, how was Gloria? Glorious?"

"Always. She's on abortion number three."

"Damn dude. Well, at least whenever she's pregnant you get to leave the office." When a client was pregnant or otherwise immobile, they got to travel to them and pick up whatever documents they needed.

"Kevin, Medicaid doesn't pay for abortions, right? That's the Hyde Amendment? I wonder how she's paying for it."

Kevin shrugged. "Yeah, sure, I think. Maybe the community volunteered money to keep her from having another child."

"Make-A-Wish Foundation. The community's wish: not dealing with any of her children."

"Word."

Gloria stayed on his mind for the rest of the day. He thought about how he acted differently around Caroline and wondered how she'd interpret his harmless joking with Kevin. He wondered what it must feel like to be pregnant, and how envious he was that Gloria seemed to be completely secure in herself, despite being abjectly poor with one dependent and another abortion-in-tow.

>< >< ><

Alex liked his job, for the most part. It was rewarding (or as rewarding as routine could be), he had minimal supervision, and the pay, while nothing great ...well, that was the sticking point. Being the only child of an industrious father, the inevitable low pay had been the issue hovering over his head throughout college and grad school. The joke throughout college was that a Sociology major concentrating on Poverty Studies was redundant, as a Sociology degree was a lifetime guarantee of a, shall we say, hands-on experience with the subject.

As such, the field attracted a few archetypical practitioners. There were the extremely wealthy children of privilege who didn't have to worry about money, who had an abstract, almost alien relationship to the normal need to earn an income. Then, the most common group, were those, usually women, who were unusually passionate about social justice and practically fierce in their display of empathy and compassion and understanding, and saw this field as their natural calling. Finally, there were the others: the bitter ones, the ones who held an interest in social work but harbored doubts about whether they should commit to this modest field, but lacked the nerve to stray off course and now resented their more successful friends. It says a lot about the nature of his profession that, while so much ink was spilled about the supposed plight of teachers in New York, spend a private minute with a social worker and the resentment toward teachers comes gushing out. (One unarticulated secret kept from the public about social workers was their quiet, dignified struggle with teachers: they presented a united front in their common cause as city workers in constant threat of budget cuts, but a social worker would have to be deaf, dumb and blind not to realize that, when it came to benefits, pay, and job security, they had gotten the short end of the stick.)

Alex had been a social worker long enough to know how to play the politics game with both the true believers and the burn-outs, and adopted some vacillating middle position that tilted a bit toward the latter.

At the advice of Caroline, whom he lived with, he tried to take stock during the day and think about what he should be happy about. To a ten-years-younger Alex, that sounded like something he'd agree to and then never bring up again, but he tried in good faith to stick with it. In that spirit, he told himself (*taking stock*, as Caroline would put it), that he was thankful for his exchange today with Gloria, and was proud of the way he handled himself. So much of this job was passive and reactive; there, he'd been probing and proactive.

All day, he felt he was reacting, putting up appearances with clients that strained the limits of his tenderness and sympathies while his girlfriend, his love, was doing *business* work: deal-making, conquering, doing. Caroline loved him for his sweetness, his understanding, but she spent all day hustling, riding the wave, hunting down commissions. She'd come home and be invigorated — made a commission, got a new deal — and throw her jacket down and announce that they were going out to dinner — her treat — and again he'd be reactive and smile and be appreciative, but made no secret of how he wished he could be the one sweeping her off her feet after some kind of actual success. That he'd spent the afternoon participating in the process, having at it with Gloria, was something ... something good, he supposed. It was a lot more than he could say about how a lot of his co-workers handled matters. At least he'd *reacted*.

Later that night, when he went home back to Bayside, Queens, he was the one who felt invigorated. *Be positive*, he repeated to himself while riding the Long Island Rail Road. *Be positive. You did good, and things are looking up.*

"Hey baby," he said when he came through the door. Not 'baby' in the coquettish way he usually did — spreading the word out like a warm blanket for her to be swaddled up in — no, more like a come-on.

"Hey," she responded, a dulcet tone in her voice, maybe in recognition of his good mood. "How are ya!"

"Good, baby," and he walked over to the couch and kissed her forcefully, and she returned the kiss.

"Why, hello there!"

"Hi!" And he mock-waved in the cutesy way he sometimes did.

They didn't talk much about their day — when you live with someone you've been with for over five years, there wasn't much of a need to provide daily status reports, and, to be honest, unless work was acting as a cause for joy or grief, they were both mutually inclined to avoid talking about the subject.

And sure, despite his moxie, the night transpired in PG-fashion, which he was fine with tonight. He clutched her while they surfed Netflix and ate leftovers on the couch — quite literally clutching her, he held her in a cute bear grip and kissed her left cheek while she stuffed her right cheek with leftover Tikka Masala. She responded appreciatively, both to the kissing and the grub.

He spent the rest of the night with her in such fashion, again putting off calling his friend Brian in San Diego.

"Aww baby you so good to me," she told him after he cleaned up the dishes.

"Nope, just good enough."

"Oh, pshaw."

When going to bed, she kissed him on the lips, sweetly. He'd kiss her back, but he didn't know where to kiss her, as she had retinol on her face and always forewarned him not to kiss her when she was wearing retinol, and he always (or usually) obliged.

"Good night, Gobstopper," she said.

"Good night, Lollipop."

"Ooh, you should be the lollipop." She tugged him teasingly on his hip.

"Ooh la la."

They fell asleep holding each other, her first (because she always fell asleep first), him a couple hours later, as always.

>< >< ><

His natural inclination was to call Gloria the next day and apologize. All that bluster the day before about being proactive somehow frittered away, some gentle alteration of perspective, and now he just felt queasily guilty. But the gears of his mind were already whirring with the rote details of his day: client intake and SCRIE and DRIE forms, oh boy, and the weight of responsibility served its purpose in smothering any rash decision. Better to just let it rest.

Kevin walking toward Alex's office stopped him from doing anything stupid. Kevin stopped by almost every day, usually around lunch. If Alex was in the mood to list things he was thankful for, working with one of his best friends was certainly something to put near the top of the list. Uncouth as Kevin could sometimes be — and seemingly indifferent and callous to issues he didn't care about — he was a good friend to Alex and the only person at the office Alex spoke to on any serious level. Plus, Kevin was something of a cineaste with pretty impressive and wide-ranging tastes, which people didn't expect because of his aforementioned uncouthness, his obsession with sports trivia, and his, shall we say, populist diet (case in point: Kevin had counted down the days until Taco Bell delivered to their office). With those attributes, you wouldn't exactly expect him to be able to sing the praises of *My Neighbor Totoro* and *Bicycle Thieves* in between bites of his Gordita Supreme, but people had a way of surprising you. And even better, Kevin managed to maintain the eating habits of a college freshman and the workout regimen of a lame horse while still keeping a trim waistline, so he was doing something right.

It made no sense, Alex knew, but somehow his interaction with Kevin, and maybe a text he got from Caroline — *Love you Snugglehorse!* — played a role in him declining to call Gloria to apologize. When he did follow up with her a couple weeks later, he simply reminded her to keep in touch, report any changes in income or family composition — which came off as ghastly, in light of her third abortion — and to check in again in another couple of weeks.

So that was how the rest of the month went. Nothing too important, except Caroline retained a bunch of contract attorneys for a law firm to handle a long-term document review project, thereby scoring her a nice monthly bonus. Thinking of all those debt-swamped junior attorneys pulled into working on a brain-deadening part-time contract review project without benefits — he pictured a huge net canvassing Craigslist and capturing poor junior attorneys, snapping and gnawing for escape like crabs — well, it was one of those things that made him glad he went into social work and not law school. So other than that good news — and the extra nights out she insistently paid for — not much else was new for the rest of the month. He continued to love her, and she continued to love him, and their relationship wasn't sex-less but subsisted on less sex than they'd both prefer, which they chalked up to as an unfortunate casualty of living as two working professionals with long commutes.

Work was largely the same, too, except there'd been too many group meetings and conferences for his liking. He didn't dislike his other coworkers, per se; they were a nice enough lot, but hanging out with them for too long made his blood boil. Inevitably, at any office lunch or function, someone would say something so blinkered or so nested on politically correct assumptions that — well, he didn't necessarily disagree with them — in fact, more often than not, he did agree with them -— but he at least recognized what they stated were opinions, not facts, and shouldn't be stated as such.

True to form, his boss, Kaye, made a couple of comments throughout the month about the recent spate of news articles on prominent priests and anti-abortion protestors who recently died of sudden heart attacks, she always said something like "well this will make our job easier" or "won't have to worry about him anymore!" and the other social workers all laughed and agreed, no love lost there. Alex had a pretty cavalier attitude toward issues of life and death and didn't consider himself unusually sensitive — hard to consider yourself sensitive when you've told a dead baby joke or two — but he just hated how everyone there just took for granted how no one would have any problem with what she was saying, even though, in reality, it seemed no one *did* have a problem with what she was saying. At another lunch conference, another coworker commented on how great it was how large, sugary drinks were inevitably going to be been banned in New York and how this would do a great job of reducing obesity and diabetes amongst the working poor, and she made these declarations as if there was no counterargument whatsoever to the paternalism inherent in such a proposal. Not that she necessarily had to agree with the counterarguments, but she and his nodding coworkers gave no impression that they could even comprehend that any counterarguments or differences of opinion even existed regarding the topic.

Be positive, he thought throughout the month. If anything, dealing with his coworkers' self-assured paternalism helped his critical thinking skills and helped him bond with Kevin, who shared his general distaste for their coworkers' strong positions and intolerance of dissent. They were nice people, and he just had to pick his battles. That was all.

So, all-in-all, the month went well.

>< >< ><

The next month he was back to the projects in Washington Heights. Actually, to call Washington Heights, as a whole, "projects" was reductive and silly, as there was actually a complicated ecosystem of industrious Dominicans, retired elderly Jews, and young professionals and grad students priced out of the Upper West Side and Morningside Heights. In reality, the average new rent here in Washington Heights was probably equal to or greater than his more remote Bayside, but old buildings in Washington Heights didn't do it many favors. Someone could — and many a New Yorker did — dismiss Washington Heights out of hand just by seeing the gray, drab and ancient project-style housing,

Rather than allow himself to feel bad about the fact that Gloria lived in a dirt-cheap, spacious apartment in Manhattan whereas he lived in a distant, suburban-style hinterland in Queens without subway access, he contented himself with pretending the whole area consisted of "the projects."

Projects with parking spaces.

The pretty blue and orange NYCHA signs welcomed him to the Audubon Houses.

There were some unsavory young dudes loitering about, but for the
most part there were just elderly Dominicans with endearing smiles and
tottering rolling carts, often times with equally elderly and tottering small
dogs, loved but unkempt, schmutz around their eyes and hair uncombed.
Project puppies, was how he planned on describing them to Caroline (he
anticipated that she would "aww" at that).

"Hello, sir," Alex heard from behind. Alex was on the third floor, Gloria's floor, ready to find her apartment, butterflies fluttering around in his
stomach. He turned around to see a thin, wiry man of average height who
was strangely ageless. He was half-black, maybe half Dominican — a safe
guess, this being Washington Heights — wearing a black *Yankees* fitted cap,
a black Champs sports sweater, navy blue jeans, and black and white Nikes.
He had creases around his mouth.

"Hello."

"You that social worker, right?" he said with a knowing charm. Funny,
that this guy lived in a project, wasn't at work — obviously — was dressed
like a kid, and yet was able to access some vast reservoir of charm and
self-confidence that someone like Alex could never tap into.

"Yes, I am."

"You going to see Ms. Hernandez?"

"Yes."

"Word, no doubt, don't get it twisted, I ain't meant to take up none of
your time or nothing. I heard about FEPS. She on that? I'm only asking
because I heard about that and I want to get on that FEPS."

FEPS? Oh, Family Eviction Protection Supplement, Alex remembered.
"Well, I can give you my card, and you can come into the office and if you
qualify for it, we can help you get on that."

"Hmm." Despite his cocksureness, disappointment was evident. "Is
she on FEPS? Is that what she gets?"

"Well, I'm sorry, I can't divulge —"

"Right, can't divulge, can't divulge. No disrespect, just, how about this. I'll talk to her myself then, and whatever she is on, that's what I want. If she tells me what she's on, can you help me out? I want to get on her plan."

"Ok." Alex handed over his card.

"Good looks, son. I mean sir," he chuckled. "I'm Keith Ortega, nice to meet you." He looked down at the card. "Alex, this your number?"

"Indeed."

"Indeed, I like that, I like that. Good looks. I hope you don't forget about me because I'm going to hit you up soon."

"Okay, nice to meet you, Mr. Ortega. Look forward to hearing from you." Back in high school, if any of his more knuckleheaded friends said "good looks," he'd respond with ironic earnestness: "well, why thank you, I just bought this shirt," or "how kind of you, I just got this haircut." He wouldn't pull that stance with this guy, and wondered, with some concern, why he was so desirous of the affections of cooler, more confident males.

>< >< ><

Gloria's apartment. The boxy rooms; the ugly off-blue couch with the incongruous doilies; even her son playing with trains in the living room felt faintly familiar. The apartment was cleaned up a bit, though, and without the clutter he could confirm his suspicion: yup, this project apartment was bigger than his own apartment out in Bayside. Everything was cleaned, scrubbed, put away, closed and sealed. Even the doilies seemed to be in the right spot (assuming there was ever an appropriate spot for doilies).

Post-abortion Gloria moved with newfound vigor, her load lightened, literally and metaphorically, attending to her son, maintaining eye contact, nodding that was actually connected and related to what Alex was saying, a respectable show of pantomimed interest and concern for whatever Alex was going to say. He didn't know what to say or how to deal with the abortion issue, or whether to avoid it outright and say nothing at all, which should have been fine by him. He had no moral objection to her having an abortion, or anyone having an abortion, but he wasn't sure if *she* was supposed to feel some sort of guilt about it, and whether *he* was supposed to console her about anything. That she gave no indication of overcoming any inner turmoil — or even any indication that she had been suffering any inner turmoil to begin with — left him feeling somewhat ... expectant and perhaps underwhelmed, like something was unfinished, like he should be waiting for something.

But everything was fine, which made the one discrepancy about her apartment all the more glaring. Shit, it wasn't really even a discrepancy, unless she was being judged against some unattainable containment-bunker level of cleanliness. But to Alex, it was jarring in its conspicuity.

Two jacket sleeves — belonging to two separate jackets — were sticking out of the otherwise closed closet door. From his angle, one of the jackets appeared to be hung on the door knob inside the closet; the sleeve was wedged, constricted tight in the door frame. From the look of the other sleeve, the other jacket had been unceremoniously thrown into the closet at a moment's notice. And the oddest thing of all? Unless those coats had accumulated obscene mutant mothballs or something, they were most definitely fur coats. His whole time in her apartment, while he was sipping his tea — she offered him tea, since when did she drink tea? — he kept eyeing those jacket sleeves as if they were waving at him. He only stopped when sex came to mind — he still had that high school talent of transmogrifying anything and everything into a porn metaphor — the too-small closet trying to contain everything hidden underneath, the sleeve like a nipple slip ... Jesus, he was slightly hard, when's the last time he ...

He snapped awake.

"And I do truly appreciate your concern, especially you coming up to visit me —"

"You're going to ruin those jackets," he said while pointing and not thinking.

There was something in her response — her eyes widened by a degree that could only be intuited, an irregularity in her breath, the momentary retreat of her put-upon smile back to its usual mask of low wattage impatience — there was something there, but somewhere between turning her head and meeting Alex's gaze, everything seemed normal and he felt, for a moment, like a fool for thinking otherwise.

"Hah, oh those, no, it's nothing but just old coats."

"None of my business."

He dropped it. But still, fur coats.

Inexplicably, she brought up the abortion later in the conversation. "It was a tough thing to do, but the right thing to do."

"I understand," he consoled.

"Things have been so tough, you know? Raising Javier, alone. It's been hard. Money has been tight. It's always been tight, you know?"

"I know."

"It's tight for everyone, you know, but for me, for me it's been real bad, you know? My mom has been around to help me, a little bit, here and there, you understand, right, but she doesn't have anything either, she lives on disability.

"I ended up paying for it — you know, the procedure — by myself. You understand, right?"

"Yes. You don't need to explain anything to me. It's your affair, it's your business. I am just here to help you, provide you social services. As you know, part of that requires checking your eligibility for time to time, discussing your ... prospects, as it were, your finances, but, you know, that is a personal affair. You don't need to explain yourself to me, or to anyone."

He imagined a desperate woman trying to pay for an abortion on a maxed-out credit card and shook his head. Then, for some reason, he imagined a ghetto Chinese restaurant taking out a lien on the fetus for use as a cheap protein supplement and made a face like he smelled something foul. Gloria looked at him cockeyed.

"Thank you for understanding," she said, speaking a little slower, wondering why he was making that face.

He came back to the reality before him.

"No problem. None at all. No reason to thank me. I hope the recovery is going well, and I will keep in touch."

He hadn't asked her about how she'd paid for it, and the cynical side of him suspected there was some strategic gamesmanship going on there.

>< >< ><

Later that week and several home-cooked meals later, he found himself being seated at *Sushi Samba* with Caroline. She'd made another big commission recently — booked about 70 contract attorneys to work on a huge, six-month document review — so this was a special treat. *Sushi Samba* was her favorite restaurant in the city. To make the whole experience sweeter, they'd booked the reservation using her *OpenTable* account: she loved clocking up redeemable points.

At the table, she put on her airs of excitement. She did love this place, true, but Alex suspected she played up her enthusiasm for his benefit. She cooed at the fare on the menu, the crab and lobster dishes particularly. She took a drink from her glass of water, put the stylish cup up to her face, and struck a playful pose halfway between *Strike a Pose* and *Blue Steel*.

As a condition of going out to dinner, Alex had insisted that he be allowed to pay for it.

The pleasant, ethnically ambiguous waiter came over and took their order. After placing her order, Caroline playfully clapped with the tinny speed of a flapping hummingbird.

"Yay! I'm going to wash my hands," she said, practically on cue. She always brought up hand washing soon after they ordered food at a nice restaurant: she never left to wash her hands until they ordered ("efficient!" as she said, her upright finger the proxy for the implied exclamation mark).

"Cool. I'll wash my hands when you get back." He knew the drill.

"Ooh," she cooed. She loved it when he washed his hands.

"Anything for you, Lil' Panda." He gave her a cheeky finger-point.

"For you, Big Lion!"

First course, naturally, was going to be the yellowtail taquitos, her favorite. *Sushi Samba* was a Japanese-Peruvian-Brazilian fusion restaurant that took the fusion angle straight to its decor, a mélange of bright colors, glass and sharp edges and reflections, lots of reflections. The restaurant was crowded — it was around 8 p.m. on a Tuesday in the West Village, after all — the clientele typical weekday Manhattanites, young urbane professionals without the baby baggage; disparate snatches of conversation, inside baseball-type bitching about young professional life.

He bided his time by skimming through the menu and gazing around at the other patrons. They looked more put-together than him, more deserving and more fit for this environment. He didn't think that pejoratively, just noted it as an observation.

The ambient din of the restaurant mixed well with the unobtrusive Latin American music that registered somewhere in the background, to the extent they sounded like part and parcel of one another. He saw plenty of brightly colored, fruity looking cocktails on several tables and thought, "suckers." That's where these restaurants make money, $12 bucks for some vodka and grenadine and blue curacao.

Caroline came back from the bathroom.

"My turn!" Alex said. He gave her an air high-five. "Tag team! My turn!"

"Yay!" she responded. "Get in there!" She knew he couldn't care less about washing his hands — he had the prevailing 'ignorance is bliss' mindset about invisible vector-spread bacteria — but he knew she appreciated the gesture. He stuck to just washing his hands before meals out with her, just one thing he knew he could do to make her happy, just like how he always pointed out cool-looking thrift stores, and just like how she'd sometimes point out comely models in her fashion magazines with a knowing wink, or push her shoes away from their bedroom door so as not to block the entrance, or stock up on coconut waters because she knew he liked them. In short, they had a loving relationship, something that sounded almost quaint nowadays.

Both children of divorce, both having grown up witnessing the silent power struggles, passive aggressiveness, and quiet resentments of their parents' doomed relationships, they'd somehow managed to create something genuinely heartfelt between them. Alex's parents' relationship had been a leaking relationship — any empathetic love from his father toward his mother had leaked out well before Alex was cognizant of the power dynamics of coupledom — and at some point Alex's father treated his mother less like an active partner and more like a passive responsibility, an additional obligation to be endured until she was out of the house or out to lunch and he could decompress by himself. To his father's credit, that his mother was completely oblivious to any of this — or indifferent to any of this, as long as she was provided for — gave his father some understandable grounding for his feelings. Alex, having always felt like an unloved son of a harried, depressed father and self-absorbed mother, had pledged himself early on to love earnestly and affectionately. As a child, he had love for his friends, and still did — he was quite adroit at keeping in touch with people — but he learned early on that such platonic love had to be held in check, lest it be misinterpreted. So his capacity and desire to love was withheld, stored inside him, bestowed in the interim on appreciative dogs and small animals, just waiting to be lavished on the right person.

And he found that person, Caroline, in college, at a stupid house party in their senior year. She was cute and gawky — her glasses made her look like a cute owl — and he approached her in a perplexing mixture of confidence and hesitation: he'd been confident that he wanted to introduce himself and talk to her, but hesitant because of his fear of weirding her out or coming on too strong, or being unable to suppress his just-below-the-surface desire to be feted over and loved. But fortunately, she recognized his essential goodness and sweetness and was receptive to him. That he wore glasses and was well-spoken and just the right height for her — about six foot — was a social lubricant, too. Living next door to each other didn't hurt, either.

So, as part of his mutual love and respect, he played the kabuki theater role of going to wash his hands ("remember to wrap your hand in your shirt when you open the door!" was another bit of her hygienic advice he followed from time to time, i.e., when she was around to witness it). He made his way through the restaurant, keen to avoid colliding with the donned-in-black waiters and waitresses running to and fro, drinks sloshing perilously on their trays.

Holy shit.

What's that noise used on television shows where there's that overdramatic rewind? That shriek-y record scratching from the 1980s, that abrupt cartoon piercing rewind (skuuuuurrrrrrrrEECH). Alex practically walked backward, as if retracing his steps to move time backward to make sure that he indeed saw what he thought he saw.

Gloria.

Not just Gloria, but a resplendent Gloria — well, her version of resplendence — a fur coat wrapped around her chair, a put-together outfit with a bright, dignified necklace against her heart. She sat across from a middle-aged brown-skinned man in a fitted cap. The only other detail Alex could make out was the man's smile. Suffice to say, the man smiled like a man not used to — or not comfortable with — smiling; maybe because he had a major front tooth missing.

Fuckin' Gloria.

He could spy on them from the bathroom entrance. If only his timing had been sublime and he'd been able to spy on them at the end of their meal ... he was dying to know whether she'd be paying the bill. If her clothing was any indication — and wasn't clothing so wrapped up with identity precisely because it *indicated*? — then she certainly wouldn't be counting on her companion to pony up dough for the yellowtail taquitos and ginger margaritas. He didn't know much about fashion but he knew enough to know her get-up looked pretty expensive, and the fuzzy jacket was definitely the same sleeve stump that reminded him of a Pomeranian back at her apartment.

He kept them in vision, hawk-like, as he circled en route to his table. Fortunately, as "that guy" — white guy, early 30s, undistinguished brown

hair, somewhat average if slightly overweight build, nondescript glasses —
his superpower was going unnoticed.

Caroline waved at him animatedly. Two yellowtail taquitos were waiting for him. She directed him to them like a neon blinking arrow. "Oh yeah
here we go!" He waited a respectful beat — she fucking loved this place
— before going in with the more important news:

"Get this, I just saw one of my clients in here."

Keeping with the jubilant mood, she oohed: "Cool! Did you say hello?"

Eating at *Sushi Samba* was apparently such a joyous occasion that the
thrust of his cynicism was bound to be misperceived. Being a casework-
er was such a charitable profession that everyone just assumed his role
was to be an empathetic partner to his clients and serve no disciplinary
function whatsoever. It was hard to pivot away from the cheery front he
maintained when he was with her. Well, it wasn't a front, per se, as he did
enjoy being with her and she did make him happy. But there was a bit of
theater involved with his enforced cheeriness, and maintaining it all the
time chafed a bit.

"She has no income, supposedly, yet here she is, paying for her and her
friend," he proffered, filling in facts not in evidence to obviate her likely
objections and make his case stronger.

"Well," she offered, no doubt hoping to end the matter, "maybe it's her
birthday! Or maybe she just got a great job!"

He doubted she was so guileless — her job involved a lot of "brass
tacks" business tactics and salesmanship — but something about their
pairing brought out her cutesy side, perhaps because she loved his nur-
turing nature and did what she could to bring it out. He decided to let it
rest — *Sushi Samba, after all* — and the cutesy way she exclaimed "her
birthday!" tipped him off that it was at best futile and at worst selfish and
destructive to push this any further. Maybe it was for the best, because
avoiding the conversation let him stay convinced that something shady
was going on here.

To Alex, Gloria's complete nonchalance regarding her abortion was

evidence of ... something? Perhaps he was naive, but wasn't abortion supposed to be ... difficult? Weren't there supposed to be some kind of emotional consequences? Not that there should be ... just, wasn't it just part
of the package? Asking the very question felt patriarchal and provincial.
But surely, drained of its political implications, there had to be something
unseemly or at least discomforting about a joyous, expensive celebratory
meal less than a couple weeks after your third abortion? *Right? Right?*

Alex and Caroline — two liberal-minded, empathetic, sensitive people
— both had deep reservations about casting aspersions on others' moral
decisions, especially if those others were disenfranchised or disadvantaged
in some obvious way. But surely, she'd have to agree that something didn't
sit well with this, right? But he could think of no sensitive way to bring that
point up, which effectively disqualified exploring the issue with her.

>< >< ><

After their meal, they held hands on the way to the subway, got seats
together, held hands on the way to the Long Island Rail Road, got seats
together, again, and held hands on the ride home. Caroline snuggled
against him, reading a dollar paperback of collected Edgar Allen Poe stories. Alex stared thoughtlessly and dreamily out of the train window, up
at the deep inky purple blackness, sundry lights of cars, houses and street
lights casting their illuminations, and then, gone.

Caroline went into the apartment and he stayed outside to call his friend
Brian. Fucking AT&T, he had to call while he was outside if he wanted to
get a signal; you'd think he was in Alaska instead of a borough of almost 2.5
million people, in the largest urban conglomeration in the United States of
America. He half-wondered whether it was bad form to disrupt the mer-
riment with Caroline to call Brian, but before he could think about it too
much, Brian had picked up:

"Hey Brian, it's Alex. How's it going out in San Diego?"

"Nothing, really. Same shit."

"Oh, ok. How's the job?"

"Sucks."

Alex knew he'd say that. Still, he asked. It was an unexamined but glaring condition of his life that practically all the friends he still kept in regular contact with were more disgruntled or lower on the social totem pole than he. It certainly hadn't been planned that way; maybe he just felt a kinship to Beautiful Losers, a group to which he sometimes felt he belonged. It seemed that people his age were all burgeoning yuppie professionals, struggling hipsters, or the insufferable blend of the two, the trust fund hipsters. In New York, it seemed you were either ballin' or bust (or a student, whereby student loans allowed the illusion of ballin' until graduation, and then, bust).

And out in Bayside, Queens? Forget it, young people didn't live out there.

All this was to say he wasn't making friends too easily, which only exacerbated his natural tendency to stay in touch with anyone he could consider a true friend, including Brian. He and Brian had gone to Hunter College together, but Brian had dropped out sometime in their junior year for some combination of psychological, personal and financial reasons that he'd never fully articulated. After struggling for a couple months in retail hell in New York, he decamped to his mother's apartment in San Diego, where she'd long since relocated from Brian's childhood home of Pelham, New York.

Alex's friendship with Brian had been stuck in a rut for quite a while; hell, Brian hadn't even been back to the East Coast since junior year, hadn't ever met Caroline, even. The fact that Alex had an identifiable career precluded him from bitching to Brian, so he had to act out of character and dole out optimistic aphorisms, ostensibly for Brian's sake.

"How's school?"

"Stupid. Same bullshit classes, same indifferent students. The kids are stupid, the teachers don't care." Ever since Brian moved out west, he'd been a perma-student at San Diego Community College, taking film classes

for some quixotic reason which may have seemed cool three or four years
ago but was now properly understood as fucking pointless and depressing.
Worse, because Brian left New York owing money to Hunter College — in
an amount he wouldn't reveal — Hunter academically cock-blocked him by
preventing the release of his transcripts and transfer credits.

"See any movies or anything recently?"

"No, not really."

There was no way that could be true, given the nature of Brian's course-
work, but whatever.

As depressing and predictable as it was to talk to Brian, Alex kept calling
out of some potent mixture of genuine concern and friendship, civic duty,
and perhaps an acknowledged iota of, well, not exactly schadenfreude, but
perhaps a reminder to be grateful for what he had. After talking to Brian,
he'd be a little more affectionate with Caroline, make sure he got a good
night's sleep, and try to put in a little more effort the next day at work.

>< >< ><

He pored over Gloria's file the next day at work. Nothing jumped out at
him, just the usual smattering of dated forms and NYCHA and HRA appoint-
ments. Her rent was subsidized at $362 a month. She made $288 a month
in EBT and $200, biweekly, in HRA cash allowances. She might have had
some money saved up from her retail job and almost certainly got some
off-the-books help from family and friends. That's all fine and dandy, and
to be expected.

Investigating the finances of an impoverished woman was not inspiring. He felt he was doing a good job, yes, but he wished he could be doing
something more ennobling. He wished Keith Ortega would call him and
set up an appointment, they could go through his situation together, and
Alex could put him on the right path to get all the benefits that were legally
allowable. Maybe Keith would mention an elderly mother or something,
and Alex could suggest SCRIE — Senior Citizen Rent Increase Exemption

— and Keith would light up and pledge to look into it.

Then, months later, Keith's mother would get approved, Keith would call up Alex and thank him profusely.

Then, months later still, maybe they'd run into each other at the Cloisters ... eh, that wasn't realistic ... maybe just the area around Fort Tryon, and Keith would recognize him and wave him over. Keith would tell all his friends how great Alex had been, how Alex had hooked him up, and Keith's friends would look impressed and see him not as a typical bland white boy but a cool, worthwhile guy.

The story expanded with a life of its own as he killed time on Google. It took him a second to realize he'd Googled the Washington Heights clinic where Gloria had her abortion, imaginatively called the Washington Heights Clinic.

He picked up the phone to call Gloria. The fervor of excitement created by his everyday superhero fantasy turned into butterflies of excitement while the phone rang, and then popped into nervous regret when she picked up.

He wasn't being a superhero to her, not at all.

"Hello, Gloria? It's Alex, your case worker."

"Oh hi Alex, I know who you are. I got your number recognized, silly."

"How are you doing?"

"Good. I'm doing good. Thanks for checking up on me."

If he didn't say something soon, there'd go the conversation. "Look, Gloria, I'm sorry, but I'm calling just because there's, there's a discrepancy here. I had to look over your files — my boss, Kaye, remember her? She is making us all prepare and present her an audit of all of our case files, and when I went over yours, I just remembered, I'm going to need a ... I remember you said that you had received money from your friends and family. Was that money put in your bank account? You can't have a certain amount above your bank account to remain eligible for services ...."

She saved him from rambling further.

"I don't got any money. I told you already. I didn't pay for the abortion."

He needed to check his notes, he thought she'd said at one point that family members had helped her pay for it.

"I used all the money I made to pay off my credit cards. I don't got money, I can print you out my bank information. I got like, less than $500 in there until I get my next payment from you guys."

"Wait, what money? You said you used 'the money you made' to pay off your credit cards? What money are we talking about again? Did you get a new job? You need to report that income immediately, if you did."

"Nah, what? I meant the money I got, like, I mean, I made it by getting it, getting it from my mother."

'Making' money and 'getting' money were two vastly different things, and not interchangeable or easily confused, at all.

"Are you sure you didn't make any money, like, earned income, over the last couple of months?"

"Nah. Hold on a second." He held on the phone and heard rustling, emphatic Spanish directed toward her son, heard "Go" and "living room" in English, and then she was back:

"Sorry, just my son acting up. Look, I think actually, yeah I got something like only 50, 100, dollars, something like that, for a clinical test I had done, at that clinic I told you about. While I was going there being seen I signed up for this trial, they just asked me a bunch of questions, it took less than an hour. They gave me a form and I got like 100 dollars, I think. I threw the form out though."

"Okay, well. Thanks for telling me. A hundred dollars is below the reportable amount."

Now he was the one rushing her off. Shit, he had to leave for his own intake clinic in about ten minutes.

Now his head was buzzing.

>< >< ><

His intake clinic ended up being run of the mill. An old Italian women who lived in East Harlem her whole life was in court with her landlord because her dogs were supposedly too noisy (Alex referred her to Legal Aid); a young Puerto Rican male wanted his landlord to assign him his mother's apartment, which he'd lived in all his life (Alex printed out a form explaining the right to succession in rent-controlled apartments and told the guy to find his mother's lease and fax him a copy); a young family wanted help applying for EBT (Alex led them through the process); a skinny, honey-voiced Somali was upset that his landlord refused to renew his lease, even though he'd been a good tenant and paid all his rent (Alex introduced him to the Division of Housing and Community Renewal and went through the forms the man would have to fill out). Alex made sure to give everyone more-than-enough time and apologized to the secretary afterward for making her stay late.

His emotional state, when he thought about it, was warmly perturbed. Something felt awry, there was something unresolved with how things had transpired with Gloria, more questions than answers. He had made a commendable effort to help all the people who came in today, no one left less than satisfied — well, except the Italian woman: who wasn't annoyed when they were referred elsewhere? — but still, he felt bothered, disquieted. Neither his effort at the intake clinic, nor Caroline's company, nor the movie they watched together that night — a giddy French action movie called *District 13* — nor the home-cooked meal Caroline made, nor the soothing bourgeoisie book he read before bedtime titled the *Power of Habit* ... none of these did anything to take his mind off those uncertainties that nagged at him throughout the night.

>< >< ><

His expectations were filtered through a gray, drained Great Depression he never experienced. He was not sure where it came from, really; maybe a corollary of studying Sociology is an inculcated expectation that, wherever there are poor people interfacing with bureaucracy, the situation will be bleak, the atmosphere Hobbesian. Visiting a pawn shop or a payday loan center (not to say Atlantic City, New Jersey, or a Yonkers casino) certainly wouldn't disabuse you of those expectations.

But Washington Heights Clinic didn't seem so bad.

He expected a cattle herd of pregnant women, huddled, pleading. Instead, he found a respectable but not overwhelming number of pregnant young women — almost all minorities, true — most alone, but none looking abject or miserable. Rather than the expected single harried receptionist chewing gum and offering all greeters with a "whaddya want?" he found a sizable staff of nurses and receptionists greeting patients and fetching them water, or bringing Spanish-language magazines to the reclining clientele.

Alex didn't speak Spanish fluently, but the medical professional's pronunciation of the next patient's name sounded passable to his ears; if the client objected, her warm smile and gracious nods didn't convey it. The doctor coaxed his arm snugly around his patient's back and assisted the obviously-pregnant woman into the back of the facility and out of view.

Alex approached the receptionist.

"Hi, I'm Alex, I'm here to see Dr. Rampole about Ms. Hernandez. Gloria Hernandez."

"Yes, please go through the doors and make your second right."

He'd done something responsible and called ahead. A bureaucracy is the closest thing to immortality to be found on Earth, and, in his experience, bureaucracies responded to formal requests with all the rapidity that could be expected from an institution that had no understanding or concern for time. When he'd called, he'd been referred to someone in the records office — what he expected to be the first in an endless loop of referrals — but was mildly impressed when, a couple of minutes later, he was greeted with "Records, how may I help you?" The pleasant-sounding lady on the phone told him what he'd expected: that he needed a HIPAA release to review Gloria's medical records.

He'd had a rebuttal planned. This wasn't a medical record, he had argued, but a financial record to establish her income eligibility for medical and social welfare services. As a recipient of social services, she'd inherently consented to providing all information relating to her finances. Rather than debate with him, the receptionist told him to come in and speak with a Mr. Rampole.

So, a day later, here he was.

He found Mr. Rampole without difficulty, but not without surprise. He'd imagined Mr. Rampole to be a middle-aged man whose owl-like face screamed *HR pain in the ass*. Before Alex even spoke to the man before him, he assembled a case against him. Owl-faced, thinning hair, sharp features conveying *handle with care*. As further corroborating proof that the man before him just had to be the personality type befitting an HR tight-ass, Alex spied the brown, bulbous abnormality tucked under the man's right ear. From that one visible defect, Alex concocted a pop narrative that led inexorably to this man's current life as a HR dickhead: childhood teasing leading to an adult hypersensitivity, his only catharsis found by frustrating the hopes of all that requested his services.

But no, that wasn't Mr. Rampole at all. Whomever that man with the ear abnormality was, well, apparently of no mind. He nodded politely to Alex and walked off somewhere. Alex felt anxious guilt over his prejudices — whatever prejudice it was he was exhibiting, he wasn't sure, prejudice against the owl-faced? — and just hoped that guy hadn't made any snap judgments about the schlubby dude who'd been staring way too intently at his ear.

"Hello," said a perfectly average, six-foot white man in his late-thirties with a sharp outer-borough accent. "I'm Mr. Rampole. I heard you were requesting some information on someone who may have been a patient here."

"Yes, financial information." No harm in framing the issue favorably from the outset. "I'm Gloria Hernandez's case worker. She confirmed to us that she had medical services performed here. The nature of the services are of no concern to us. We are only concerned that, unfortunately,

Ms. Hernandez may not have been entirely forthcoming to us about her income. We are just curious and hoping to cross-check the financial information she provided you with what she has provided us to ensure there are no discrepancies. Are you in charge of her records?"

"I'm in charge of all records of anyone who may be a client." Mr. Rampole exhibited a smile that was both somehow warm and cynical; warm in his empathy, cynical in his underlying world weariness.

"Unfortunately, as explained to you on the phone before, we cannot give out any information without a HIPAA release."

"Yes, but — "

And here Mr. Rampole put up a hand and, again with that smile, cut Alex off at the proverbial knee. "Yes, I'm sorry, as you must know as a social worker, we can't give out that information. If you want, you must get a HIPAA release, or subpoena us."

What had Alex even come here for? Surely, he hadn't expected differently.

Maybe he just needed some hobbies.

Maybe some part of him still expected people to genuflect, out of pity, to the kind requests of an underpaid, underappreciated steward of the poor? In his experience, he found social workers were only appreciated when they were craven and subservient; whenever they challenged the motives of their clientele, people seemed remarkably less sympathetic to them, as if their role was simply to rubberstamp any and all requests without question. He half expected that he got none of the social worker sympathy because, instead of being a cute, fresh-faced true-believer girl out of college, he was that dreaded creature: "That Guy."

Alex's anxieties registered in his tone. "Look, sir, I understand, I really do. But we know that I'm not seeking medical information. Look, I'm a social worker, I know all about client confidences," he exaggerated, giving himself the benefit of the doubt, "but financial documents ... I am sure there are improprieties going on here, between what our client tells us and what is really going on with her finances. I know medical information is sensitive, but we are not interested at all in whatever medical procedures she may or may not have had performed here. It would be to everyone's benefit for us to be able to review her financial documents."

He wished he recorded that. It would be wildly ineffectual, of course, but listen to that tone ... the words ... that left some hair on his chest.

Mr. Rampole just shook his head emphatically.

"I'm sorry, but again, no. And, I must ask, what makes you believe we have any such documents?"

"Well, I assumed ... "

"Ahh," Mr. Rampole stuck up a finger, "that's the problem. Assumed." He may have well had said it with a fucking wink. Asshole.

"I understand how difficult things have been here recently, what with, all that stuff in the news. I read about protests and all that — I don't know if that's happened up here at all at this clinic, but —"

Mr. Rampole nodded graciously, although they continued their conversation as two ships passing each other in the night. Two actors reciting their own lines. There was no point to this.

Mr. Rampole again extended his sympathy regarding Alex's role in all of this, instructed him to return with the necessary documentation, and wished him the best.

The owl-faced man returned and wished him adieu. Literally. Adieu. He then escorted him back to the waiting room.

Funny, Alex noticed. Every single woman being served here was heavily and visibly pregnant. Maybe to be expected — this was an abortion clinic, after all — but where were the frightened teeny boppers here for pregnancy tests or free birth control, or even the early trimester women not visibly carrying a wide load?

Alex remembered how he and his high school girlfriend used to get free birth control pills at their local *Planned Parenthood* clinic. Then, it seemed that everyone was there just for free condoms or birth control pills. Maybe that was the amateur league, and this was the pros. One thing about that *Planned Parenthood* clinic he'd never forget — and which made him think that clinic was amateur league — was its phone number: (914) 666-0295. 666? Seriously? When their political opponents already viewed the world in biblical terms, having your number begin with 666 just seemed like trolling.

>< >< ><

"So," Kevin began, as Kevin was prone to begin, "let me get this straight, and stop me if I'm missing something." Kevin had done mock trial in high school and college, and for all intents and purposes he was now back in the courtroom. The little smirk evident on Kevin's face tipped his hand: he felt he had a good case here against Alex. Kevin loved nothing more than disagreeing with Alex (unless Alex was complaining about a coworker: then they'd become in sync).

"So, this is her third time getting an abortion. Wait, let me back that up. This is her third time being pregnant, not including when she had her son, and, to our knowledge, this is her third abortion. She had an abortion at this Washington Heights Clinic. When you met with her after her last abortion, you felt like she was acting differently somehow."

"Wait dude — "

Kevin put his hand up, his signal for "let me finish." He was making his opening statement. "You felt like she was acting differently, mainly because she is usually uncouth but, at that moment, was acting civil and accommodating. Also, she may have been hiding fancy fur coats. A week or so later, you saw her getting a fancy meal. Also, some guy in her apartment made it sound like he thinks she is getting some kind of good benefits deal. Did I miss anything?"

"Eh." Kevin had fucked up the order of events a bit. Alex also suspected whenever Kevin began a sentence with "also," he'd been downplaying and burying suspicious facts. There was some nice gradual layering of mounting suspicion, he felt, that got lost in Kevin's rendering of events.

"Dude, also, she implied that someone had paid her or helped her get the abortion, I don't know, it was weird. She said 'the money I made,' not the money she borrowed or was given or was gifted, or something like that. 'The money I made.' And this was in reference to her talking about her abortion, definitely. She tried to spin out of it after, but that's how it came out."

"Eh, ok. Then, you go to the clinic, all Sherlock Holmesian, doing no research whatsoever, and, not surprisingly, they don't give a shit about your bullshit and tell you to go fuck off, basically."

"Like you'd have done any research first. Like it would have mattered."

"Word, I wouldn't have done any research, either. You caring at all is more than I'd have done. I am sort of jealous actually, it sounds interesting, more interesting than our usual shit, anyway. I mean, if it were me — well, if it was me, I wouldn't have given a shit to begin with — but, anyway, I'd be shocked if over half our clients weren't just bullshitting us in some way or another. But still I think you should pursue it, just because honestly this job is boring and I want to hear about something exciting."

"Nice logic. I'm consulting fucking Yoda here."

Kevin presaged his attempt at a terrible impression, inhaled too much and looked too excited, which made the impression even that more terrible, "Err pursue the liar you will."

"Ugh, dude."

"Yeah, that was bad. I got to piss, if you want to continue the conversation, follow me, or wait here and I'll be back." That was Kevin, alright. He wasn't joking, he was refreshingly matter-of-fact.

Eh whatever, he shrugged and followed Kevin to the bathroom and they both used adjacent urinals.

Alex scratched his head, keeping his eyes straight. "I'm old enough now to realize that a good life is a necessarily boring life. That's why that Chinese curse is like, 'may you live in interesting times.'" Throughout the day, almost at random, Alex wondered what Caroline would think if she overheard whatever he'd last said. At this stage in their relationship, she'd probably charmingly agree to lead a stable, intertwined, boring life together. "Boring together," he imagined them chanting together, high-fiving and smooching. He smiled inwardly.

Kevin, not noticing or perhaps not caring about Alex's daydreaming: "Word. Anything 'interesting' is usually disruptive."

"Word," (when Alex talked with Kevin, his vocabulary retrogressed to the monosyllabic; not that he was complaining). "Losing your job is an 'interesting' change. I've heard cancer brings interesting changes too. Becoming an orphan probably leads to some interesting changes in perception, also.

"So anyway, Kevin, listen to this, you'll appreciate this" –

Kevin farted as he wrapped up. "Listen to that," he laughed before he could even finish the sentence.

"Dude, what the fuck, man?"

"What? It's a bathroom?"

"Yeah, but I'm right next you. And I was a captive audience, I was stuck peeing right next to you."

"I know, that's what made it funny. It's a bathroom man, anything goes, you can fart without fear in a bathroom."

"False. There are bathroom rules. One is you don't fart when someone is at an adjacent urinal. Another is that you wouldn't fart in the bathroom on a job interview, right? If you were on a job interview, would you have farted in the bathroom?"

"Hmm." Kevin kept his mouth shut and pondered that. "Interesting."

"I win. So anyway," he segued the conversation back to the important stuff after they washed their hands and headed back to their corner of the office. Kevin didn't really care about much — work investigations and farting semantics occupied the same general level of importance to him — so Alex had to make a special effort to keep the conversation on course. "At the clinic, I was like, trying to play the sympathy card."

"Nice. Except no one has sympathy for social workers when we are trying to actually, you know, do our job."

"Word. Anyway, I was like, 'I know things have been difficult, what with some prominent anti-abortion protests, and deaths, and hub-bub and controversy going on — ‘"

"Did you actually say 'hub-bub?'"

"Hah, no."

"Ahh, too bad. I'm sure you'd get sympathy then." Kevin took a bite of an apple he'd kept next to his computer, and didn't let his chewing stop him from talking. "You should have heard Kaye cackling about those protests and like, some prominent protestor activist person dying of a heart attack recently. They found like, plaque build-up in his heart or something weird. Probably some fat fuck. You should read the article in the Post. Pretty weird shit. I thought plaque was for teeth, you know?

"It's pretty funny, actually: whenever, like, a hurricane strikes America or something, these religious people will look at the hurricane info-graphic on the Weather Channel and be like, 'look, it looks like an unborn child! It's a sign from God. Repent!' and all that bullshit. Yet, by their logic, you'd think they would look into the fact that God seems to be killing them off, like, out of the blue, giving all of them random-ass heart attacks."

"Word. It's not God, it's like, Richard Dawkins with voodoo dolls."

"Word. It's Christopher Hitchens, back from the dead. Back for revenge!"

"A revenant."

"Word."

Kevin lined up as if he was taking a free throw shot and lobbed his apple core at the trash. It landed in the trash can with a hard thunk. Kevin raised his arm in victory, his voice now excitable:

"Dude, remember that woman with her 'retarded kids'?" Whenever shady client practices were at issue, the 'retarded kids' story came up. This was a woman who kept coming in with her two kids over the years — the first time, they were aged 2 and 4, then 3 and 5, then 4 and 6 — arguing that they were both functionally retarded, thereby entitling her to Social Security benefits on their behalf. All that stood in her way was the voluminous evidence to the contrary. Blessed, apparently, with the extraordinary power of discerning that her two children were mentally retarded despite any evidence, she'd been dubbed 'the retard whistler' and became a shorthand between them for the lengths some people would go for free money.

"Yeah, I remember her. I actually got a voicemail from her, not too long ago, saying she was going to come in. That was a month ago."

Kevin laughed heartily. "Are you serious? Oh, man."

"Yeah. Makes Gloria look like Mother Theresa. Anyway, I should go."

Alex got up to leave Kevin's office.

"Wait, Kevin, since when the fuck do you eat apples?"

Kevin shrugged.

>< >< ><

A good life, Alex had realized, was an eddy of bemused contentment. To be able to contemplate, ponder and reflect, while being in a generally stable, positive environment. That's it. That's all you can ask for. A high, by its nature, is unsustainable, and can only be recognized as a high in contrast to the metronomic pace of a normal life. You went to work, it paid enough and was manageable and maybe you got some satisfaction out of it. You met someone and stayed with them and encouraged the relationship to become something reliable and sturdy, and in oft-moments you fleetingly remembered the fantasies you'd concocted for yourself or the sexual peaks and frontiers of your tender ages, and your heart beats a bit faster, and that's your high now. The closest true high you'll get is going to the gym, and your heart will pump and you'll feel the world is at your fingertips, you can do anything, you can improve your life in a myriad of ways; but you're old and mature enough to know that soon your heart and hormones will achieve their normal equilibrium, and you'll want an equilibrium too: you'll want stability and security and comfort. Sure, your job is repetitive and your friends and family and loved ones are the same, but imagine having to learn and master new people and experiences and skills every day.

The best life is an ouroboros of contentment.

And, as mopey and beleaguered as he knew he could be, he had to admit that's what he'd achieved, and no transient social media-inspired jealousy changed that crucial truth. That's what life was, and it was oddly glorious. He had his job, his loving girlfriend, his television shows and his books, indeterminate plans to go to Spain with Caroline, the same songs on his iTunes he listened to in college, the eucalyptus plant on his desk to water.

A fucking eucalyptus plant! He had it made.

That's how life was and how it went for the next couple of weeks.

An example: a life where, on one weekday night, Caroline cooked a veggie concoction and he cleaned the dishes, and he showcased a really clean bowl that just minutes ago contained pungent kale and bean soup, and she cooed in melodramatic appreciation.

But whenever he picked up the phone to call Gloria, he felt that this was a moment. Here was, however minutely — and God, it was minutely, it was imperceptible — but there was something, not a high, exactly, but a split-second where the curve of his normal life took a jagged little turn. The phone call — to be honest, this little quest — in this there was a chance of a sharp left turn. However slim. However imperceptible. He didn't think it, he intuited it. Somehow, he could only compare it to that crepuscular nostalgia of bygone youthful days: he'd think of those days and his heart would beat in a different way, he'd view the world in a different way. That was the feeling when he rung Gloria, and he didn't know why it was, but it was what it was.

He was picking up the phone and calling without even thinking. It was like he woke up in the middle of the conversation, as if he could simply not deal with the fact that time was experienced linearly, and he just had to know where this would lead.

He was talking to Gloria — she was being cagey — and there were mixed feelings inside him. Suddenly, he wondered if he was just pinioning this poor woman. Was this malicious? No, he didn't think so, but, as a hedge, all the cards would come out, so if he was enjoying putting the squeeze on her he'd force his hand to make it all be over.

"Gloria, you know I like you. I just want to tell you, that I know. I know. You have to be hiding something from me. I know you have come into a source of money you aren't telling me about. I know. I know you've gone for expensive meals. I know this. So I'm calling you, to ask you, because I like you. Do you have another source of money?"

He said nothing more, was wondering, what the fuck am I doing? He was correct, he knew it, but he had nothing to prove it other than the accumulation of witnessed and intuited knowledge. He didn't even care, really; he didn't give a shit if she was bilking the system: so was practically their entire clientele.

"Do what you gotta do, Alex. Do what you got to do."

Silence.

"Well, what I —"

"No, Alex, you do what you gotta do. That's all I'm going to say. You'd have done the same, if you were me."

"Wait, what? Done what? Do you have another source of money? This clinic you told me about, is that where you've been getting your money from?"

"I didn't know nothing wrong, I got no idea, I did what I did, so you do what you gotta do. I ain't saying no names, I'm saying nothing, I didn't do nothing I didn't think I couldn't do. If they offered it to you, you'd have done the same."

"Done what?"

"Look, Alex, you looking into my money situation, I don't know what you know, but all I sayin', is I did what I did and I stand by it. Do what you do."

He made an inchoate noise — an aborted sentence, he thought — as his brain dealt with that gushing cryptic tumble. "What did ... what? ... Gloria, I am asking you about the clinic, specifically. You said they gave you a hundred dollars to run tests, or for you to fill out some survey? Was it more than a hundred dollars? If I'm wrong, and I'm off-base, just tell me. I know there's some amount of money you are keeping from me."

"You do what you need to do."

"Gloria, ok, fine. I'm sorry, but from what we have learned and heard we're auditing your account, is all, just so you know. So please be forthcoming. I'll be in contact."

He was rolling around the conversation in his head, surprisingly seething. Naturally, he retired for the day to Kevin's office, though, so far, Alex had kept this new business to himself.

>< >< ><

"So, let's see ..." Those three words served as Alex's totemic invocation of their ritual, where they'd test each other to see what they'd each hypothetically be willing to do to keep their salary without working for it. The sacrifices they'd make or depravities they'd undertake varied with the current stressors they were facing. Testing Kevin's moral limits did wonders for Alex's free-floating anxieties; asking Kevin what he'd be willing to do after he'd, say, been chewed out by a succession of ungrateful clients or scheduled against his will for double intake duty was a fantastic way of gaining perspective.

So far, they'd agreed to undertake the following two sacrifices: first, they'd both be willing to have their left hands removed for a lifetime of salary and benefits. (The agreed-upon reason: you could always get an artificial hand, and they were both right handed. Alex had needed more convincing, initially, as he masturbated with his left hand. Kevin had made a good point that masturbating with a prosthetic hand might foster the illusion of an "other.") Second, they'd both agreed that they'd be willing to be stabbed once in the stomach for a year's salary and benefits, assuming no organs were injured and there were no subsequent infections or long-lasting complications.

At Alex's key three words — "so, let's see"— Kevin ceased typing and reclined in his chair, languidly. He sensed what was coming.

"How about this. You manufacture a fake medical report that convinces a pregnant woman she needs to get an abortion to save her life —"

Kevin cackled. "Dude, seriously?"

"Yeah man. Ok, same deal as before, except you authorize or create a fake medical report or diagnostic or some shit that absolutely convinces an otherwise healthy mother to get an abortion, because it somehow convinces her she needs to do it for her health. Like, it's some airtight conspiracy."

"Hmm, very interesting. Could she have another kid after if she wanted to?"

"Honestly, does it matter to you?"

"No." Kevin laughed. Alex knew him well. "Well, yeah, it would, you know. Yeah, for full salary, I'd do that, for sure."

"Eh, I don't believe you. I don't think you'd be able to do that. How about this, if you were a woman —"

"Dear God, here we go."

"— if you were a woman, would you intentionally get pregnant just to have an abortion, for a full year's salary. And you'd have to be watched by some weirdo sex cult who got off on it."

"Do you play this game with Caroline?"

"Of course not, Kevin. Isn't it nice to know that she could never replace you?"

"Word, it is. So, is this hypothetical really just Gloria you're talking about, L-O-L." He actually said each letter aloud.

"Hah, maybe."

"Well, how would I know that the sex cult was safe and wouldn't kill me, or would actually pay me? I'd need tons of references. I'm pro-choice, so I don't think there's anything wrong with having an abortion. Intentionally getting pregnant to have an abortion, well, man, I don't know, I can't say its 'bad' but it's certainly not good. But for a full year's salary, shit, maybe.

"I'll get back to you on that one. I have calls to make and I can't spend all day playing this bullshit game."

"You like this game."

"Word, I do. But you know what I mean."

Alex prepared a little on-the-fly cock-and-bull story to keep Kevin's interest. "I heard about this story — I don't know if it's true — about this woman who like, was paid to have abortions."

"What? Like, a medical study?"

"No, like, some kinky weird group that just wanted to perform abortions, so they'd pay women to get pregnant and then perform abortions on them."

"Sounds risky. Dude, if that shit existed, fucking all of our clients would be doing that shit."

"Word."

"No, really, a ton of them have kids for like, EBT and whatnot. If they could get paid without having a kid, you know they'd totally do it. If that program did exist, we would be encouraged to promote it. L-O-L. Dude, could you imagine if we got a cut, as like, a referral fee?"

"But really, I gotta make phone calls. I'll talk to you later."

Contemplating commissions for abortion referrals: Kevin for you, ladies and gentlemen.

Alex got up from Kevin's guest chair, said his good-byes, checked the hallway to make sure there were no visible supervisors, and headed back to his office.

>< >< ><

She cooked, he cleaned; he pushed the cart, she filled it. He liked walking around the grocery store, ever since he was a little kid. He liked the colors, the clatter, the whole sensory experience. Every product loaded in the cart would be a new experience, like shopping at a bazaar. A new tomato sauce, cool. Caroline was the designated item fetcher, since she did most of the cooking and he didn't really care about what they got, as long as he got his requisite lazy person staples: cereal, some Greek yogurts, some fruits,

some microwavable Thai or Indian meals, some of those sugar-ridden coffee drinks. Caroline was the good one, getting exotic olives or fancy, adjec-
tive-laden sauces and condiments. Being in Bayside, their local grocery
store had a pretty high quality East and South Asian specialty food section
to raid.

It was a nice day, and Caroline looked nice in her outfit: tight black
jeans and a white, logo-less hoodie. She looked like a low-fat black and
white cookie (a line he used every time she wore the outfit), and it was
endearing to see her stretch up to get some of the out-of-reach paper towels. Then he woke up from his stupor and volunteered to get the items
for her (why were the boxy and cumbersome paper towels always stacked
on the highest shelf?). Alex handed them to her, and she took them, dou-
ble-barreled, and put them in the cart. She looked cute carrying a super-
sized item, much the same way a little puppy looks cute lugging around an
oversized bone.

Sunny and springy as she looked, he could see why he'd approached
her back in college in the first place. Sometimes he realized he'd been in a
relationship with Caroline for so long that he almost forgot what his tastes
were like, until she went about inadvertently reminding him. She was cute,
bespectacled, slender, chipper and had spunk, the winning formula. And
being with her made him feel good.

She strode on ahead down the aisle to ascertain new culinary discover-
ies, while he turned the narrow aisle into an opportunity to stand around
and veg out. As befitting any co-dependent relationship, he divided his
attention between watching the cart and texting Kevin.

What's up, he texted.

A couple minutes later: *NM.*

Ahh, the glories of the modern era. Truly, a conversation that could not
wait until the work week.

A conversation that would probably be replicated several times over
the course of the weekend.

He felt another buzz and checked his phone. *Crack the case on Gloria,*

Sherlock?

He ignored this provocation.

But, as if the mere mention of Sherlock had an incantatory effect, Alex just happened to look up at just the right moment ... somewhere beneath his consciousness he espied a person and an image. Now, so quickly out of his vision that there was no way his mind was able to compute it and make visual sense of it. But still, a visual, rightly or wrongly, stuck out and took center stage in his mind.

Not convinced but curious, he pushed the grocery cart around the corner in pursuit of confirmation of what he thought he just saw. In flagrant dereliction of his honored stewardship of the groceries, he abandoned the cart — *just for a second*, he was already mounting his defense before the tribunal (of Caroline) — and hustled down the corner.

Into the valley of canned goods he ventured, in pursuit of what he thought he just saw.

The image he was after — the man he was after — was down at the end of the aisle, his back turned toward Alex. He had a red shopping basket in his right hand, a liter of *Coke* the only visible item. The man's face and body were practically buried in the canned beans on display before him. He stood still, motionless, as if paralyzed by the sheer plethora of options presented that could, potentially, fulfill all of his bean needs. But this man made no attempt to canvass the options; instead, he stared straight ahead, into the display. It reminded Alex of the end to *The Blair Witch Project.*

An ace in the hole to buy him time — two crouched elderly people at the other end of the aisle, bending over to examine the bottom shelf goods.

Thinking fast, Alex swung around the next aisle. Organics aisle, the province of the hip and able-bodied. He sped down it, thinking fleetingly that the man was staring so intently through the beans, toward this aisle, that maybe he could see through it and at Alex. But, as if the speed at which he hustled was too volatile for this thought to take hold, it disappeared as soon as he swung around the corner, now at the other side of the canned bean aisle.

God bless them, the elderly were still blocking the path. And the man in question — this middle-aged, thinning-haired white man — was still face deep in canned goods, his line of sight arched between the beans and the floor. So face deep, too face deep; he was hiding, like a freshman standing at a urinal next to a bully senior, just blank-faced, staring ahead. As if he couldn't be seen.

But Alex saw, and confirmed what he'd first espied: the man's bulbous, disfigured right ear.

>< >< ><

"Hey!" Caroline spotted Alex a couple minutes later in the original aisle. "I saw the cart but didn't see you! I feared you'd been grocery-napped!"

He shook his head and moved briskly, signaling 'come here' with two fingers. She got close to him and followed his pace.

"So, in that other aisle," he started, as she leaned in closely, *Puffins* cereal close to her chest, "in that other aisle, I saw this guy who worked at the abortion clinic I visited. He's very recognizable, has some ear defect."

"Oh, weird." She didn't know how to respond, and he couldn't blame her. Nonplussed was the appropriate response. He felt pangs of doubt and guilt, that he shouldn't have told her anything.

He wasn't going to involve her any further.

"It's nothing, I guess. Just weird coincidence."

"I guess. You're so crafty though, to track him down!"

He smiled. "You're so complimentary, you should come with a free drink."

"Oh you," and she flicked her hand in the knowing 'oh pshaw' way. He'd repeated that same play-on-words a fair amount throughout the course of their relationship.

He wouldn't mention any more of this Gloria business to her.

And why not?

(He'd been watching me, I know it...)

The anxiety he felt was answer enough.

>< >< ><

He found time during the week to stop by the Washington Heights Clinic. He felt it would put the matter to rest, somehow.

"Excuse me, you are Mr. Rampole's assistant, correct? I think I recognize you from a when I spoke with Mr. Rampole."

The middle-aged, thinning-haired, owl-faced man looked at him, hard. He was the only employee in this room. He spoke to Alex behind a service desk.

"Yes, that sounds possible. I don't think we met, though. I'm Garet Overton, I handle billing and other matters and generally assist Mr. Rampole. Do you need Mr. Rampole?" His voice was surprisingly sensual, a warm caramel baritone, even if his manner and words were punctilious and precise.

"No, well, maybe. I was just wondering, do you live in Bayside?"

His face maintained the same composed rictus. "Bayside, as in Bayside, Queens? No, I do not. Why do you ask?"

"Well, maybe not Bayside, but like, anywhere in the surrounding area, Auburndale or something?"

"No, not at all. Again, why do you ask?"

"Just wondering, I could swear I saw you in my grocery store in Bayside, Queens."

"Oh? No, sorry. It was not me. I've never stepped foot in that part of Queens. Wrong side of the wrong river. I live in New Jersey. I wonder, why you thought it was me?"

The man spoke as if he didn't have a brown root vegetable-styled mound growing perceptibly under his right ear. Perhaps that's the dignified, proper way of dealing with that, and Alex's eye-flicking gawking was just a product of him being, frankly, a juvenile asshole.

"Guess I was mistaken. It's a good area, underrated. Anyway, is Mr.

Rampole in?"

"No, he's not in today. Can I leave a message?"

Alex wondered if Garet's owl-like visage dissipated on the weekends, when he smiled or worked-out, read books or listened to music or got drunk or high or orgasmed. Garet didn't look like a man who did any of those things, but then again, just as his voice has been a surprise, people had dimensions and unanticipated depths.

"No, that's ok. Well, maybe let him know I stopped by, but I'll try and contact him later, when I have all the paperwork I need. Thanks for your time."

Garet nodded. "Have a good day. Sorry I couldn't be of more service."

So Alex left. What the point of this was, he didn't know, except he didn't for a second believe a word of what Garet said. Maybe he did live in New Jersey, that part was probably true, but Alex knew for a fucking fact that Garet, despite what he said, had been in that fucking Bayside grocery store.

>< >< ><

The next day, he got lunch with Kevin at Baja Fresh. Alex didn't like Baja Fresh, but it was serviceable. For Kevin, it was a big step up. Kevin had the diet of a feral dog; well, maybe not, because a feral dog would at least eat vegetables if it came across them in a dumpster. Kevin's diet was so bad that, at the ripe age of 31, his doctor, worried about the effects of such swill on Kevin's esophageal lining, recommended he temper his fondness for processed meats by incorporating a bit of fiber here and there. So Baja Fresh was a step in the right direction, albeit a baby step.

In other words, Kevin got his chicken burrito with a whole wheat wrap.

"So," Kevin started between bites, "how's the life of Alex, master sleuth."

"Uneventful. Except, one thing I didn't mention was that Gloria sort of admitted over the phone that something shady was going on. She was just like, 'do what you got to do.'"

"Really? When did this happen?"

"Like a week or so ago. Yeah. Also, and this sounds nuts, I know, but I know for a fucking fact that I saw this guy who works at the abortion clinic at this grocery store in Queens. Like, I'm positive. He has a very discernable feature, like, this fucked-up ear. And I went back to the clinic and asked him if he lives there or shopped there ever, and he completely denied it."

"Really? That really happened, and you really did that? Hmm ... that's interesting."

Kevin creased his forehead, like he was flexing his brain. This look of consternation was rare.

"Fuckin' philosophical Kevin over there."

"That is weird, though. That ... actually, I've switched sides. You've convinced me. There's definitely something shady going on here."

Alex, a little deflated by all the impasses he'd experienced, just shrugged. "Meh."

"You should try and get those HIPAA forms."

"Yeah, maybe."

They continued eating, about a minute of ambient mastication and push-and-pull of cold wind from the opening-and-closing front door.

"Actually, maybe you shouldn't?"

"What?"

"Maybe you shouldn't pursue this shit anymore. You know, maybe just, let it go. Kaye isn't making you. Kaye doesn't even know and wouldn't care. I don't know man, this shit like — I'm not sure if I believe you that that guy was actually in the grocery store, but, still man. I don't know."

Again, Kevin looked like he was trying to flex his brain. For a moment, Alex looked at him warmly and contemplatively. Kevin didn't notice. He was flexing his brain, his expression becoming more dour, more concerned.

"You should be careful about applying that salsa, right? Your throat and all that."

"Word, thanks." Kevin applied just a bit of the salsa, and washed down his bites with his large Coke. Alex stuck to water. Caroline would be proud, and he didn't need all that sugar. It made him feel sick, actually. Avoiding soda was one good trait he picked up before he even met her, but she certainly helped to reinforce it.

"You know what would be depressing?"

"Life?" Kevin responded.

"Word, but, no. You know what would be depressing? Like, imagine there was a psychiatrist whose job it was to go over the medical records of dead people to, like, determine their mental problems they dealt with during their life. Like, figuring out what pivotal events occurred in their life that caused or influenced their emotional problems, and then coming up with a treatment plan for them. But the whole thing would be worthless and futile because they'd already be dead. It's, like, what could have been."

Kevin nodded slightly as he gulped down the last of his Coke.

"Yeah, pretty depressing. Pretty stupid, too, but yeah, depressing also."

>< >< ><

The work day proceeded apace. While responding to emails, he dryly noted to himself that Keith Ortega had never called him.

He checked his personal email later in the afternoon, while nursing a late afternoon Greek yogurt and a Starbucks "Refresher." He'd gotten to a stage in his life where he was lax in checking his personal email. Most of his bills were paid automatically online, and if someone wanted to get in direct contact with him, they texted him or hit him up on Facebook or something. If he had waited a couple days, maybe he'd have missed this particular missive, especially since it had the tell-tale signs of junk. All CAPS, blaring, hyperbolic subject line, an unfamiliar sender.

PLEASE READ IMMEDIATELY APARTMENT NEWS

SORRY TO BOTHER YOU ALL. I USED THE APARTMENT EMAIL LIST TO SEND THIS OUT. PLEASE FORGIVE ANY SPELLING PROBLEMS AS I'M

NOT GREAT WITH WRITTEN ENGLISH.

MY DAUGHTER CAME HOME LAST NIGHT LATE IN THE MORNING
AND SAID SHE SAW A MAN ON A LADDER OR HIGH UP SOMEHOW TRY-
ING TO STARE INTO A WINDOW ON THE CORNER FACING THE STREET.
AFTER CHECKING, THIS IS THE HALLWAY ON THE 3E SIDE.

MY DAUGHTER SAID SHE YELLED AT THE MAN AND HE GALLOPED
AWAY. I DON'T KNOW HOW HE GOT AWAY EXACTLY IF HE WAS ON A LAD-
DER BUT SHE SAID THE MAN SOMEHOW RAN AWAY. I DONT KNOW IT
WAS DARK SO NOT SURE WHAT HAPPENED BUT SHE SAID SHE YELLED
UP AND THE MAN TURNED AND WAS GONE.

IVE CALLED THE LANDLORD MR. CHEN AND THE POLICE WILL SEND
OUT A CAR TO DRIVE AROUND AT NIGHT FOR THE NEXT WEEK. JUST
WANT TO LET EVERYONE KNOW WHAT IS GOING ON.

Caroline was also sent this email. A couple of minutes after that email
had been sent was her response to Alex: OH MY GODS ALEX, SCARY!! I
DONT LIKE THIS! WE TRAVEL IN TEAMS!
They were apartment 3D.
Another email from Caroline:
I'll be home later tonight. I have Zumba tonight! Shake it!
*Can you meet me by the LIRR tonight if ya not busy? I should be home
around 10 p.m. or so but I'll text you when I'm on the train. I don't like this!
I'll go to Zumba to get buff to defend us!*

>< >< ><

An aleatory pall was cast over the rest of the day, things and events drifting
by on autopilot. Last night, while Caroline slept, he whispered "I love you"
to her, mimicked lovingly her sing-songy way of saying it. He didn't know

why he thought of that now, unless to mentally ground his discursive, pan-icky thoughts toward something uplifting.

He gave no outward indication of these portentous stirrings, not in the idle follow-ups with clients or in the pursuit of his other mundane occupa-tional activities. Maybe if Kevin had had time to grab coffee, those feelings may have been cultivated and expressed. But when Alex stopped by his office, Kevin shooed him off in that odious Kevin way — batting the air to push him away like a cat batting a string — that grated so much on Alex's nerves. Sometimes Alex would return the obnoxious favor and play dumb while Kevin was on the phone and shooing him out — "Are you trying to tell me something?" — at which point Kevin's eyes would narrow and his features would become sharper and his air-batting became ever more der-vish-like. Alex didn't bother today, and just left with an "ok, whatever."

Alex left work around five and stood by the doors on the packed Long Island Rail Road train. In his mind, he was sitting, staring out the win-dow contemplatively, at the gray New York sky and the rows of bric-a-brac houses visible from the tracks. But in reality, this was rush hour, and since he'd barely made it on the train to begin with, he'd have to reconcile that wistful feeling with the rushed, packed and unpleasant scene before him: inconsiderate kids taking up more than their allotted seats with shopping bags, a harried mother sipping an open coffee practically waiting to be spilled, an oblivious businessman insistent on spreading out his newspa-per, neighbors be damned, and a whole mess of people content just to cram into the corners to get a moment of reprieve. It all took on a bloodless, weightless tone. Nothing tactile. He drifted through it, like a cartoon cat lifted up by the nose by the smell of a baking pie on a windowsill, until he'd drifted all the way home.

At home, he checked the mail. Some bills, some Broadway flyers. He remembered the last time there was an apartment-wide panic, about a year ago when a burglar had been caught in the apartment building adjacent to this one. There'd been a cluster of emphatic residents meeting-and-greet-ing, promising to look after each other and keep in touch. He hadn't seen any of those people since, or, at the very least, he hadn't been aware of seeing them since.

He made his way up the three floors without seeing anyone else. The complex was fairly new and well-lit, adding an anti-septic feel to the barren building. The soft pads of his shoes were his only accompaniment as he made his way up to 3D.

He looked out the hallway window — the same window that had been peered into, had been violated, he thought dramatically — only a day before. He saw nothing but encroaching darkness and the perspective-diminishing glare of reflected lights and his own hazy, evocative reflection.

His front door opened with an unusual creak. He flicked all the lights on, and here he was, in his nice (by New York standards) one-bedroom apartment. It was a nice building, an advantage of living out in the less popular, eastern nether regions of Queens. Off-white, clean walls, a small dishwasher (an amenity coveted in New York), a silver shiny fridge festooned with wedding invitations, Caroline's recycling chart, and various magnets from their travels together: an orange and black silhouette of a witch from Salem, Massachusetts, a tomato pie magnet from Asbury Park, New Jersey, a "Welcome to Milwaukee" magnet from when Alex visited Caroline during her Midwest work training.

Like always, Caroline's shoes were clumped up by the front door, their measly shoe rack not equipped to handle the shoe outflow. He walked toward the computer in the living room, past the pots and pans underneath their shelves, past the dinner table with its lived-in scratches and covered with candles, cups and a blender they never used, past the sad coat-choked chairs which they always planned on dealing with whenever they were going to have company. Here again, the blue leather couch, *Time Out New York, New Yorker, Glamour* and *Bust* magazines on the arm rest; the book he was reading, *Istanbul*, with its own place on the foot rest, looking crisp and regal by comparison.

He walked judiciously around the junk on the floor, filled a mug with water — an orange Salem mug with black cutout images of black cats and

witches — and watered their little eucalyptus plant that Caroline had gotten some time ago.

He turned on all the lights, including the lights in the bathroom and
bedroom. He found the humming whirl of the bathroom fan comforting.

He sat on the blue leather couch and put his feet uncomfortably atop
the ottoman, perched atop all those magazines, deathly concerned with
not toppling any of them over. Still, calm. Sane. He kept still for reasons
unknown. It was just him and the hum of the bathroom. His ghostly shadow was reflected back at him in the black television screen.

There was a cardboard box by the garbage that needed to be recycled.

Caroline would be at the train station around ten, he remembered, and
he'd walk her home from there.

Atop the lived-in table was a brightly colored plastic bag of cashews.
How long had those been there? Did cashews go bad?

Silence.

Next to the cashews were loads of tea bags. Caroline loved tea; she
particularly loved swiping them from hotels when she traveled. Jasmine,
Earl Gray, Peppermint (*good for stomachaches*).

Someone outside, down the hall, unlocking, opening and then closing
their front door.

He missed Caroline but for some reason was glad she wasn't home yet.

A black hanger was jammed in the top crevice of the living room closet.

The whirr of the bathroom fan, the faint tinkling of distant traffic.

He walked in silence to the bedroom. Same mess, same mound of
clothes on her side of the bed. Same piles of perfume on the nightstand,
same humidifier and fan in his corner, a single brown sock there on top of
his sole pair of jeans, by the refuse of work shirts he intentionally crumpled as his impetus to get them washed.

He clicked the bedroom light off, then on, then off, as if that'd change
something.

It didn't.

He kept it off and went back into the living room, closing the door shut behind him.

He ferreted his phone out of his pocket, saw a text from Brian, a text from his mother, and that mysterious symbol that meant voicemail. He should go outside to call them back.

He intuited something slinking behind him and, before he knew what to think of it, he looked over his shoulder.

And looked up.

Depths beyond eternity.

He looked up at what looked back down on him.

There was the flash-bang panic buzz of instinct and imprinted cell memory — a crystalline shadow image of Nosferatu's silhouette sliding across the room — except when his cell memory reconciled that image with the image before him, it was modified to reflect the hooked shrimp-like curl standing upright before him on its butterfly tail, and just this detail alone left him with the realization that there was no point in trying to discern the details of what stood before him.

They'd died of heart attacks, he remembered the newspapers had stated. An ersatz image of the dumpster behind the Washington Heights Clinic — of course the whole surrounding area had been well-kept and maintained — but now an image of a bloodied dumpster behind the clinic, mudskipper shapes inching toward it.

He looked up at the bisected, colorless mouth, was unable to determine where the mouth ended and the face began, but it made no difference, as there was nothing there, no spark of intelligence or critical thinking skills or relatable emotional experience writ large anywhere across this face, or if there was, it rang at a tenor he could not detect. The bisected, soft fangs of shrimp-like flesh vibrated softly, in some synchronized way, and, some-how, this was happening in the same world where Caroline was taking her Zumba classes, where he could reach out and grab a brightly colored box of cashews off his messy dining room table.

He almost, beyond logic, turned to the cashews, just to close his eyes and open them up and pop a couple in his mouth and pretend like nothing was wrong. Wanted to look up and watch saved episodes of their favorite shows. Wanted to apologize to Caroline for nothing in particular, maybe just hear her voice. In between these desires he closed his eyes and witnessed a silent movie of his own imagining, of Mr. Rampole and his assistant chucking little pieces of freshly-cut fetus meat down a pipe to the squealing delight of rubbery little creatures the color of a full moon, while their larger brethren flopped and squirmed and swam up to pledge their loyalty before those who provided them a feast of soft tiny little legs and limbs and offal.

Curling around and over him, tight. He thought of a newspaper, maybe one that stated somewhere, "they'd died of heart attacks," or reported on the unusual substance found ensconced between the arteries of the victims' hearts.

He would die, too, and he pictured his soul lifting out of him and inhabiting the pages of the newspaper.

An "O" formed around him. Bristles like horsehair and wet shoelaces on his face, half-cooked pasta on his head and the back of his neck, vice-like snapping on his thighs and between his legs, and he didn't need to see the two dried-raisin eyes on fleshy toothpicks and stalagmite crustacean face to understand why it ate only the softest and most delectable fresh protein, or to comprehend its full length to understand why it'd been mistaken for a ladder for whatever overseer it'd been carrying.

They'd died of heart attacks.

He didn't feel any pain in his chest or anywhere, really, though he felt like he was rolling, as if in a tire, but he no longer trusted his senses. Now the feeling of a horsehair bristle the size of a chalkboard eraser pushed down his mouth, rolling, in a hamster wheel, pink lungs cross-cut with sharp quills, a wetness in his chest, then slack, rolling, no one to pick up Caroline at the station, text message and voicemail left unanswered, remembered the day he first noticed Caroline at school, rolling now, an object out for — goodbye, no, please — the trash.

He turned without thinking and propelled himself out the nearest win-

dow. It gave way without shattering and he fell out of it, almost like a parcel through a slot, and fell the three short floors in an undignified sprawl,
the brunt of the impact bearing mostly on his outstretched upper body.

He thought there'd be concrete and a quick pullback and the snap of
his neck and the flight of his teeth, but by the grace of Heaven Above he
landed on a patch of rough grass around the apartment building. Thank
God. Thank God. If they'd lived in a neighborhood closer to the City, this
would all be concrete. Thank God.

He was in aching pain and fearful of moving, for fear of finding out that
he was immobilized.

He turned his weary body on its back, so he was looking up to the stars.
His left elbow was in rictus; he grimaced as he felt the sheared-off skin of
his elbow, but he could still feel the pain in the joint, in the bone ... so it
wasn't broken. He bent it oh-so-slightly and squeezed his eyes shut in pain.
He didn't think the jump had been far, but *by God* he hurt.

He was looking up toward the stars.

He was being looked at by the inhabitant in his apartment.

There was a prolapsed moment of great calm, when Alex looked at
it, and it looked at him. There were no words, other than some kind of
understanding in Alex that what he was facing-off against was, in some
undeniable way, rational and calculating.

The elongated brownish stick of an upper body retracted back into the
apartment.

He rolled over onto his stomach and kept his face pressed down
against the ground. He remained motionless. There was no one else outside in suburban Queens. He let destiny overtake him; he had no survival
instinct left, no false hopes or grand ambitions other than to just sit here
and ignore the pain radiating through his body. He didn't want to look up,
for he feared the moment he looked up he would be looking back into that
abominable spasm of a face, and confirming the futility of trying would be
more painful than anything to come. His only reaction was involuntary.
He coughed violently, ropy phlegm, first on the ground and then into his

hands; only when he rubbed his fingers through it did he feel the grit of slender, impossibly-sculpted cilia-like fibers.

He rolled over, thinking that maybe he'd inadvertently choke to death on his own backwash but not caring. Let death take him. Let him die without an inventory of everything in his body that was wrong, broken or contaminated.

Caroline.

No, Caroline. Caroline Caroline Caroline.

Caroline Caroline Caroline Caroline Caroline,

How could he be so fucking stupid?

No.

He took the phone from his pocket and turned it on, please be working, please be working. He didn't remember it being off but no matter, thankfully it turned on.

Now, a complete reversal of priorities. He had something to live for.

He got up and ambled toward the street, calling Caroline. He hobbled in a painful shuffle – his running speed had always been lacking, and it certainly wouldn't help to have it reduced so dramatically. Now he was thinking, strategizing: caring.

Her phone was off, just the voicemail, she still must be in Zumba.

"Caroline, it's me. Don't go home. Please. Just please, don't go home. There's a … a gas leak at home, a terrible gas leak, it's not safe at all. Please, just promise me you will not go home. Call me immediately. Don't go home, and you have to call me. Stay at a friend's house tonight, I will be alright, I … don't be scared, I need to take care of something. Call me.

"I love you. I love you more than anything in the world. Don't be scared, sorry I'm just... I'm just freaking out." He absentmindedly signaled a passing borough taxi; being so far out in Eastern Queens, the taxi-cab driver was probably starting his shift and en route to more profitable destinations. The car slowed down and he got in, still on the phone.

He tailored his voice to make it more benign and placid, the way he did when he realized he'd become too excitable or had spoken out-of-turn: "I love you. Don't worry. I will see you soon." He wanted to end on that but it wasn't in his nature not to be careful. "Just please, don't go home until you speak to me."

"Skillman Street and 46th Street, Sunnyside," he told the driver. Kevin's place. Alex had never actually been inside it – that's Kevin for you – but he knew where it was. He took a couple of minutes to catch his breath and looked outside the cab, just to see if there was anything out of the ordinary. Any minute he predicted a swinging pendulum-like shape dive-bombing through this poor man's side window, burrowing its frenetic face into him, tears and rips and spurts, car accident, disfigurement, looking up at that impossible face, waiting for death or something worse. He focused on the overwhelming heat in the car, as if to burn the vision out of his mind, and texted Kevin an advance warning. He thought better of that and called, also.

Kevin answered, by his tone blithely unaware of the text.

Alex told him he needed to come up, it was an emergency.

"Dude, what?"

"Just put some pants on and let me up. It's important, please, I'm literally begging you."

"If Caroline kicked you out of the house, that's not an emergency."

"Dude, fuck you. It's not that. By the way, that would constitute an emergency, anyway. But it's not that." He could easily get lost in the palliative of bonhomie.

Kevin gave an exaggerated sigh and gave him the address and apartment number.

"Be there in about 5 minutes. Turn off the internet porn and buzz me in."

The driver gave a knowing, jovial look at 'internet porn' and gave a hearty smirk-and-snort.

He paid the fee – in cash, it felt smart to do that, no record, he thought but didn't want to admit. (*Use the Blue Card!* He thought instinctively of Caroline's voice whenever he used cash: *Sorry, Honeypot. Next time.*)

He buzzed up to Kevin's apartment. There was far more street life in Sunnyside. It was a popular, near-Midtown neighborhood in Western Queens, a lot of new development, popular bars, the foodie-approved, appropriately-named restaurants *Quaint* and *Salt and Fat* just nearby. He felt safer here. An iota of tension dissipated from his gut. He didn't like Kevin's lag time in responding to the buzzer, but Kevin eventually buzzed him up a couple moments shy of straight inattentiveness. But after he opened both sequential doors to the building and was heading up in the elevator to the fourth floor, he didn't care and was nothing other than supremely grateful.

He called Caroline again, and again it went straight to voicemail.

Kevin propped the door open for him, face registering his usual impatience.

"You're lucky my roommate is out of town."

"Roommate, shit. I didn't even think of that."

"What, you think you were moving in now?"

That makes sense, the apartment was recently updated and rehabbed: Kevin would have to be forking over most of his salary if he lived here by his lonesome.

"Fuck man."

"So, what's the deal?" Kevin walked over to his couch. There was a paused DVD-screen on his impressive television. *Throne of Blood*, read the title, the cheap title at odds with the austere black-and-white visuals.

Alex pointed to the screen. "*Throne of Blood?* Sounds too low-brow for you."

"Dude, Kurosawa, man. I've never seen it. '8.2' rating on IMDB. I'm almost done with it, that's how good a friend I am. I paused this for you."

"Hold on." He walked into Kevin's bathroom and closed the door.

"Great now you're shit-" he heard until the closed door muffled Kevin's protests.

He peed and flushed. He always wanted to see the inside of the noto-riously fussy-Kevin's bathroom: what bathroom could be pristine enough for Kevin?

"So that was your emergency?"

"So," Alex began. "Don't you see that I'm basically limping? I was attacked at my apartment, and I was attacked because I was looking into the Washington Heights abortion clinic and Gloria Hernandez. They were paying her, and other people, to have abortions at their facility. I'm not sure why, I'm not sure what they do with ... them, but I'm positive I'm right. I think some of the mysterious deaths – those Christian leaders having heart attacks, I think they are somehow related. I think they, they are running this operation, killing off their enemies, I don't know exactly why."

"You were fucking attacked? Are you serious? In your apartment?"

Alex had been operating under a delusion. A delusion of safety. As if Kevin's questioning was a doomed clarion call, a smelling salt, the honeyed sanctum of Kevin's apartment drained of color, drained of security.

He said nothing.

"Dude, you were seriously attacked? In your apartment? Where's Caroline? Call the police man!"

"I ... can't."

"You can't? You say they are killing people? Seriously? Why are you bringing this shit to me, man?"

He tried to explain how he wasn't sure exactly who it was who attacked him.

"I can't go back home, I can't go back to the office, I need somewhere to lay low, I'll get out of here ... as soon as I can, I just thought you... you would understand."

"Dude, if what you are saying is even remotely true, you need to call the cops immediately."

He covered his face, in tears. "They'll never believe me. I have no proof. It ... gets weirder. It gets worse." So he tried to explain, tip-toeing around the truth. He was attacked by some kind of freak, he explained, lying, as crazy as it sounded it was much more grounded in any understood semblance of reality than the truth. "Just let me wait here until I get in touch with Caroline, then we will leave, we will get out of here. I didn't mean to get you involved in this. Just ... this is far deeper and far worse than I could have ever imagined."

"I told you to chill with that sleuthing shit."

"And the worst thing is I don't even care. Morally, I never really cared too much. So what, Gloria and her abortions. Who fucking cares? I made myself care. I should have just minded my business, like everyone else. No one really cares. I just wanted something to do. I wanted to feel like I was doing something, well, like I was doing something productive. I'm so stupid.

"They tried to kill me, Kevin. They tried to kill me. For real. I'm not fucking around. They tried to kill me. What have I done? I put Caroline in danger. I need to take her away from this."

"Dude, it will be okay." Kevin walked to the countertop, feeling utterly alone and directionless as he filled a cup with water.

"Why won't she pick up her fucking phone?" Alex texted her again and called; again, just the voicemail. She should be out of her exercise class now, maybe she was on the train and wasn't getting service, no, that was unlikely, she was probably just being absentminded, her phone all the way at the bottom of her purse, not even realizing it wasn't on ....

"And what about me, man? What the fuck am I supposed to do? What if they trailed you here?"

"No ... no one trailed me, I'm positive," Alex spoke as if he were an authority on the matter, as if he had anything to offer except blustery conviction, hope and assuagement.

"I need to think for a second." Kevin put his water on the table — *he never offered me any*, Alex thought to himself, hopefully just a product of typical Kevin selfishness and nothing more, he could hardly tolerate the idea of a growing distance between them, *this is a lot to put on him, stay calm, he's doing you a huge favor* — and Kevin turned on a noise machine in his bedroom, then turned on the faucet in the bathroom and closed the door.

"Let me know if you need anything," Alex called from the main room, which sounded immediately weird, but he felt he should say something assuring. He should have walked right into a biting Kevin retort, but it never came.

Alex texted Caroline again and stared at his phone, waiting for a call, a text, anything to make it spring to life with news. He needed to make sure that Kevin had Caroline's number, in case his phone died.

Several minutes passed. The DVD menu lapsed to a black still-screen due to inactivity. The faucet and noise machine continued without interruption.

Several more minutes passed.

"Yo Kevin," Alex sidled up to the bathroom. "Yo, Kevin." *Yo*, listen to him, he didn't speak like that with anyone except Kevin, and he spoke like absolutely nothing was wrong, like they were going to crack wise on Kaye or some of the hippie-dippies they worked with.

"Yo, Kevin," and now he rapped hard on the bathroom door.

No answer. He tested the knob and it was locked. He turned the knob as hard as he could, wanting nothing more than to have Kevin yell at him and kick the door closed. He forced the door open as far as he could and it wouldn't completely give, but it was enough to see crumpled legs and a shape draped over the tub. He continued to force the door open, shaking the lock, for nothing, for no reason except it was something he did, until the door definitely lodged shut, an unacknowledged finality to it.

He backed away from the bathroom door slowly.

The bathroom door opened.

He turned to run for the front door and saw a shape run through his legs — the closest understanding he had was imagining a dog running through his legs, but no — and its parts curled and spread out before him, extending at least a solid foot above him, a sculpted vicious flower of precision, raisin eyes that looked feeble and weak (*go for the eyes*).

Alex backed up slowly, palms up.

"Listen to me, I know you can understand me. You work with … people.

You work with people, there has to be a way you can understand me."

He kept his hands up, thumbs locked together as if making a fan. He rotated his hands back-and-forth, as if cradling a pot of water, doing anything he could to communicate complete and utter supplication.

"I can help you. I work in social services. I have access. I ... I can help you. Tell Mr. Rampole, Mr. Overton, the man with the ear "— he pulled an imaginary distended ear — "anyone, whoever you work with, I can work with you. I can help you. I can protect you. I don't care about whatever they've been doing."

The creature tracked his movement; for every step Alex took backwards, it took an equal step forward. But it hadn't killed him yet.

"Just please, don't hurt Caroline. Just leave her alone. Tell your bosses, I'll do anything, I'll do anything you want, anything you say, just please don't hurt her."

He said his piece and tucked his chin into his chest and closed his eyes.

"Please. I'll do anything. I'll do anything. Just don't hurt her."

It made no intelligible sound. But it didn't rush him, either. He refused to open his eyes and let himself anticipate the moment of his death, but from what he could tell, it wasn't moving.

"Please," he said.

He kept his eyes closed, pleading in vain, for the death that never came. Instead, it spoke to him of people to meet, fealties and expectations to be kept; and instead of the release of death he instead was left with the growing unease in understanding he had only himself to blame for this new imposition.

Big with the Past, Pregnant with the Future

THE LEGAL TABLOID *Above the Law* was going to have a field day with this story. Can you imagine it? The Admissions Office of Yale Law School — the most prestigious law school in America — through some incalculable mishap accidentally mass emailed the entire law school the admissions materials of every recently admitted first-year law student whose last name started with "M" through "Z."

Michael learned about this mishap via three text messages, all arriving in quick succession, from three different first-year classmates.

The last names of these three friends? Flaum, Heckenlivy, and Kahl.

Michael's last name? Washington.

Shit.

Flaum, Heckenlivy and Kahl were his friends, but like all Yale first-year law students ("1Ls") — and, really, like all law students at top law schools — they'd been immersed in a hyper-competitive culture where the most minute advantage, no matter how lacking in real world significance, was internalized as the basis for their self-worth. Why, of course, these worldly and sophisticated students knew that, in real terms, scoring, say, two points higher on the LSAT than a competitor was reflective of nothing but luck or a particularly good testing day, and held no significance whatsoever outside the conveyor belt of legal academia. Of course that's how they'd react if the issue was ever brought up.

But, of course, the issue *didn't* come up, because the system was so thoroughly internalized by all of its participants. So, of course, if a Yale 1L met up with a friend who went to a respectable school outside the Top 14, but yet was still a school blessed with all the rarified trappings of privilege — say, a George Washington University or Vanderbilt University — then, why of course, they could both agree that the whole system's obsession with GPA and LSAT scores was terribly silly. Both students could recount the sordid reasons for this sorry state of affairs, how LSAT scores and GPA were the two most important metrics governing school rank, according to *U.S. News and World Reports*, so top law schools prioritized these two markers beyond reason in order to keep their ratings high. Both friends could laugh about the whole ratings schema and how it had nothing to do with the quality of instruction, as each first year student in every law school read the same inapplicable horseshit taught to them by the same highly-credentialed idiots who never practiced law in their lives, whose method of instruction was the same outmoded Socratic Method.

See, those two hypothetical friends could agree on a lot. But here's the rub: the friend at George Washington University would be bringing this up defensively, to feel as smart and accomplished and deserving as his Yale friend. And the Yale friend would nod to all this and agree, but never lose sight of this important distinction: at the end of the conversation, he'd still be at Yale, with all the accoutrements and advantages that distinction entailed.

And, of course, The Yalee was better and more deserving. Because here he was, at Yale.

This was the culture Michael and his classmates were part of. They all went to Yale; they were all on the same exalted pedestal. But when you've been marinating in a culture that prioritizes pointless distinctions that serve only to make the distinction-holder feel superior, the release of these admissions materials, this veritable mother lode, the alpha-and-omega resource collating all such pointless distinctions ... could any creature immersed in this system really be faulted for taking advantage of this opportunity to spy on the merits of their friends? Who wouldn't take advantage of this ideal one-way mirror? All the big questions could be answered! Who had been admitted with a lower GPA or LSAT score? Who had concocted the most overcompensating treacle of an admissions essay? Which scion of plutocrats had presented him or herself as Mother

Fucking Theresa? In short, there was no doubt in his mind that his good buddies Jason Flaum, Brian Heckenlivy, and Cindy Kahl were poring over his admissions materials and sizing him up.

He'd been about halfway between the campus and his apartment when he received the texts (which had all arrived within two minutes of each other). It was only November of their first semester, and school had only been in session for about two months. Ahh, Yale Law School: so confident was Yale Law School about its pedigree that they didn't even have grades for their entire first year. (Yale Law School, ladies and gentleman! The hard part is getting in!). He was surprised their transcripts weren't fucking gold-plated.

Still, despite the seeming camaraderie and good-tidings this system was intended to generate — and the change in priorities among his classmates; Jesus Christ, they couldn't even compete over grades! — as are moths to a flame, so are law students to envy and resentment. Law students coasted on a steady stream of mean-spiritedness; blocking the channel only caused it to spray out forcefully in different directions.

And one such noted purveyor of this resentment and mean-spiritedness was Keith Mullins.

Michael, as innocuous and modest as he tried to present himself, was recently made one of Keith's prime targets. For Keith had dubbed Michael as part of team Triple A: the Affirmative Action Admits.

Do you know how politically correct Yale is? Here was a school that withdrew a moot court problem involving a hypothetical heterosexual father and a hypothetical lesbian mother for fear that students having to argue in favor of the father could be "psychically damaged" from the experience. Here was a school where students boycotted a professor who refused to use the word "Chicano." For Keith to express any opinion that could arguably be interpreted to be disrespectful to the institution of affirmation action was, to put it mildly, extremely ballsy and bordering academic suicide.

The tension between Keith and Michael — and really, the tension between Keith and everyone at Yale — escalated dramatically about two weeks ago, when Keith sent everyone on the 1L email list an article from *City Journal* about affirmative action. This article discussed the mismatch problem, or the allegation that black and Hispanic students admitted to competitive colleges with substandard test scores were far more likely to fail out, drop out, or choose less challenging majors. The article only briefly mentioned law schools, but argued in passing that black and Hispanic students admitted to competitive law schools with substandard GPAs and LSAT scores were far more likely to fail out, drop out, graduate into the lowest quartile, or fail to pass the bar altogether. The author also argued that legal academia's obsession with bolstering the admissions rates of blacks and Hispanics to appease *U.S. News and World Reports* prioritized race over more pertinent classifications, such as economic class. As a result, the article argued, the black and Hispanic students admitted at top law schools tended to be economically privileged and academically deficient: the worst of both possible worlds.

The social punishment for Keith's transgression was swift. Keith was deemed an insensitive asshole, a racist, and far worse. Various minority associations expressly questioned whether to report him to the Diversity Commission for knowingly creating an inhospitable academic environment. Ever since, Keith's resentment toward his classmates was obvious, writ large with every suspicious, hurt glance.

It was too bad, because Michael had kinda-liked Keith, or at least respected him, and Keith had been nice-enough to Michael, at least at the pre-semester receptions. But then again, maybe Keith didn't know Michael was black.

Michael was very light-skinned — Ice-T light-skinned — the product of a black father and a sallow pale white mother who must have shared distant relations with Casper the Friendly Ghost. So if Keith harbored any racial prejudices, it may not have mattered, because it's quite possible he didn't even realize that Michael was black.

Keith hadn't done much to endear himself to his fellow prospective classmates at those pre-semester receptions. Keith had been too probing with his classmates, and his mood perceptibly soured when the life histories of his classmates all seemed to present the same narrative: Ivy League or equivalent liberal arts undergraduate program, maybe a year or two stint in the Peace Corps or some other pleasurable year or two of "time off" or "funemployment," and a fair amount of students with lawyer or alumni parents. Even the same well-heeled locations kept popping up: Upper East Side, Manhattan; Montgomery County, Maryland; Newton, Massachusetts; Orange and Marin Counties, California; obnoxious parts of New Jersey and Long Island and Connecticut. All well and good, and all to be expected.

So Keith may have come off as ornery and spiteful when he managed to smuggle details of his lower-class upbringing into practically every conversation, cementing from the outset his personal narrative that'd become his ossified stock-and-trade. Son of a bricklayer (when he didn't know what the Dalton School was; "what do I know, I'm just a bricklayer's son"); his true-blue Chicago roots ("You're from Chicago? Me too," began some unfortunate classmate. "What part?" Keith asked. "Highland Park," answered this unfortunate classmate, marking himself with the geographical equivalent of a top hat and monocle. "Oh. I'm from South Chicago. You know, Chicago-Chicago."), and so on and so forth. The irony, of course, was that this salt of the earth narrative was Keith's distinguishing feature that entitled him to a sense of superiority, grounded bizarrely in a sort of anti-elitism elitism.

Even while Keith was in full rampage mode, he was at least pleasant toward Michael. Michael had an ambiguous background, his hometown wasn't one that Keith linked immediately to a lifestyle of unexamined privilege, and Michael knew a factoid or two about the Pullman strike and Chicago labor history. And in turn, Michael admired Keith's chutzpah. Michael was especially amused at how Keith would bait some environmentally conscious student by talking about his appreciation of vegan food, and then when that unsuspecting student would talk about some fancy-sounding dish, he'd take the wind out of the conversation by proclaiming his choices had nothing to do with such effete, luxury tastes, but were merely the result of him growing up as a child being unable to afford animal protein.

Who knows why Keith decided to send out that article? He was a smart guy, and must have known he was ostracizing himself from his classmates in one fell swoop, one click of the mouse. Who knows? Maybe Keith blanched a bit when he noticed that the female students — almost all of them younger than he — gravitated toward guys like Michael; articulate, bleached-out minority boys, acculturated enough to belong but still exotic enough to be attractive. So maybe this was all stuff Keith noticed; then again, maybe not, or maybe this was all exaggerated inside Michael's head, and was nothing more than a sounding board for his own insecurities and doubts.

He and Keith could probably sit down and get along, if they really tried, if Keith hadn't been so chastened by his swift rebuke that it was doubtful he'd extend any olive branches anytime soon. Although this was anathema to admit, Michael was more hyper-aware of the sexual opportunities his race afforded him than any jealous racist could ever be. These opportunities always came about thanks to "open-minded" white and Asian college girls pre-programmed with the belief in black "alpha male" masculinity. That Michael wasn't particularly well-endowed, or didn't present himself as some symbol of black male virility, hardly seemed to matter at all.

As a little joke to himself, whenever he suspected any of those girls was picking him up based solely on his race, he'd divert the topic to books. *Look how well-read this Negro was! Why, maybe they could even take him home to Daddy!* He'd lie and tell them his favorite book was the *Invisible Man*, by Ralph Ellison. Oh, they recognized that, maybe from some college reading list. Ooh, Afro-centric! In the *Invisible Man*, one of the female characters was a naive white woman who objectifies and reduces the main character, who is black, to a crude Mandingo stereotype in order to fulfill her sexual fantasies of being savaged by a black man. Perhaps those girls has been absent from class when that character had been discussed.

>< >< ><

Back at his apartment, Michael wondered about how Keith would view him after reading his admissions packet. It was all here. Maybe he'd be exonerated from Keith's resentment? His LSAT score was a little low, but his GPA was about-right, he went to a good school, had undertaken a challenging major, had strong personal recommendations.

But who was he kidding? Everything came down to that admissions essay.

Michael wasn't proud of it. Not at all. Maybe he'd once been proud of it, when he felt the world owed him something, when he'd been a bit more rakish and rapier-like in spirit. But maybe ... since he'd been willing to profit off his personal story to get into the law school of his choice (and the college of his choice, and ...), maybe getting Keith back in his good graces could be just another accumulated benefit of what he revealed in his admissions essay.

>< >< ><

Michael had been twelve years old. He walked into his living room; more accurately, he was in his living room. He doesn't remember walking in, or how he got there, or why he walked in, he just remembers being there. The room was unusually bright and well-lit — maybe it was midday and the windows were open, or maybe it's just an imaginary lens flare, his memory setting up the scene. There was no way to know for sure, because his memory was his only reference point.

He remembers a long, rectangular marble table. In his mind's eye, the living room shrunk to the size of the table, and he floats in and sits down. To his right is his father, Charles. Physically, Charles looks just like how Michael remembers. He's thin, caramel-colored, his minor facial blemishes — what he always called his freckles —looking dark and angry. His haircut is short, military-style, his face shows the mild creases that come with creeping age, but he looks healthy and fit, physically strong.

But something's different. Charles — Father — was the only authority figure Michael and his younger brother ever had — their mother had died long ago — but he doesn't look like an authority figure anymore. He looks tired and expectant.

There's a man sitting across from Charles, and Charles is crouched, hunched over, forehead level with the other man's chin. The other man is animated, and as he talks and gesticulates and seems to get bigger, Charles folds and nods until his stance seems to form a backward capital "C."

Michael was that rarest and most coveted academically accomplished minority — one raised by a single black father — but it was a testament to the power of the details he included in his academic admissions essay that he never even felt the need to mention that fact.

This man who sat across from his father ... he never revealed his name, but there's no doubt in his mind that his father knew who he was, and that this was one exchange of many. He was a white man, that he remembers, and he has the impression that the man is long and tall, in a spindly way. The details of his face ... details isn't the right word, because there are no details, just impressions. Sometimes, he pictures him as a man with wild, flaming red hair, but that can't be true, because that requires a degree of ostentation foreign to this type of man. In another survey — another attempt by his mind's eye to recreate this man — he pictures a well-dressed pallid skeleton, which was accurate in capturing the man's angled slim build and something about his precision. Something about the precision and structure of bone captured the ineffable gestalt of this man who sat across from his father.

"Sit down, Michael," the man said, but how the scene played out, Michael was already sitting.

Michael's little brother, Andrew, aged five, sat next to the man, with an oversized spoon and a full bowl of his favorite soup, chicken noodle. The bowl was still full but not steaming. Andrew was holding the spoon and licking his lips, bobbing back and forth trying to stay comfortable in his chair, his attention passing between both this strange man and his father, but his fascination clearly belonged to this strange man.

Michael had no way of knowing or verifying this, but he felt that only that strange man was capable of giving his baby brother the proper authority to start eating his soup.

"Glad you can be here with us. Are you glad, too, Andrew?"

The little boy nodded as little boys nod, nodding not only his head but his entire upper body.

"Good, good. Are you glad he's here, Charles?"

"Uh huh, I am." Charles turned toward him. "Glad you're here too, Michael. Glad you could make it here, uh huh," but his attention was divided and as he spoke his eyes kept flitting back toward this strange man.

Now the man was looking directly at him, and Michael could see his eyes, the only detail he knows — knows with every core of his being — that he remembers absolutely. The man's left iris is black, a deep rippling black with sweet, inviting light undulations, and in the center is a light blue star. The man's right iris is also black, a deep rippling black, undulating and breathing, this time in the middle is a red hammer, or maybe a red bull, something red and spiked. The man knows people must be fascinated by his eyes, so he locks eyes with Michael for what feels like several minutes, until he begins to nod slowly, perhaps thinking to himself, yes, the boy understands.

As the man stares at Michael and nods, his left hand gently directs Andrew's face toward the lukewarm bowl of soup. The top layer of the little boy's face becomes submerged, and the boy stays motionless for a couple seconds, until his little right arm signals resistance and bats out like a playful little kitten. The man softens up and lets Andrew come back to the surface. The little boy is smiling and giggling and clapping in his uncoordinated way, and the man lovingly mimics the little boy's clapping. "Did you like that?"

"Again!" Andrew shouts, and, used to having his excited outbursts rewarded with *oohs* and *aahs* and affections, looks around at Michael and

Charles for adoration.

"Again?" the man asks.

"Again!" and his little brother claps harder and leans in, giggling, oily chicken broth smeared across his face and nose.

The man guides Andrew's head back down — his hand seems strangely fitted to the little boy's skull, somehow reconciled to it, as if his hand had been molded to an optimum size for manipulating the heads of compliant little boys — and again Andrew is immersed in his lukewarm soup. He's blowing bubbles in it now, and a there's a telltale noodle flopped over the side of the bowl.

Charles looks on, but he doesn't blink and isn't enjoying any of this. Michael had never seen such resignation and capitulation. If Charles had been opened up, there'd be nothing but a shrill lonesome whistling.

Andrew was back above the surface of the soup, clapping.

"He likes it. Doesn't he, Charles?"

"Uh huh, he likes it."

Those undulating multicolored eyes and that smile; there was nothing inherently noteworthy about his smile, but there was a fearful symmetry there, an indication of something, that with more time or more experience or more knowledge, Michael could discern some relationship of significance between the contours of that smile and those eyes.

>< >< ><

And here another scene, back again in his house, some short time later, still a twelve-year-old boy. There is the ambient noise of something crisping, the sense of being enclosed by logs burning in the fireplace, the rasping lick of heat and fire and curdling and warmth, but there's no source that he's aware of. There's a closed door — the room he shared with his little brother, and he wants to go investigate — and he's in an impossibly long, narrow hallway.

He's looking down this long hallway and there's an intimated shape at the end, a suggestion, but now something is lumbering toward him, now past him. Halfway past him, staring. He has a sense impression of some combination of an elephant and a giraffe, something about the bulk, the thickness, protrusions he can't see and a triangular shape stretching out above him.

He can't reconcile these senses and shapes but he comprehends what he is dealing with. It's some version, some essence, of that man from the living room.

He remembers a feeling of immensity. At that time in his life, he associated it with big trucks, where the driver had to check all his mirrors, look behind him, engage in a whole drawn-out process in order to back out. *Beep Beep Beep.* That's the feeling he had; that this huge, complicated thing was moving past him, and that a whole series of behind-the-scenes operations were being undertaken to grant him the courtesy of stopping this towering thing.

He dreams of a moment when it speaks to him but he can't hear what it is saying as a result of some clangorous din, and that inability to hear this missing information jolts him from unconsciousness and makes him aware of something worse.

But that never happened. He knows what it said.

It turned toward him — there was an end to it, and that's where the face was, the same face with the symmetrical smile and the blue star and red hammer of an eye — and it said to him, without looking at him, "Your father is dead. As you assumed. I'm taking your brother with me. I don't owe you an explanation, but just know that I deserve this. Your father did this to himself. You should be grateful to me for this."

And then it lumbered past him, with that marked gait, hobbled somehow, like a giraffe with the bulk of an elephant.

His father was dead. That'd been accurate. How he was killed was extreme and the cause of much consternation, but there was nothing so extreme that couldn't be explained away by normal means. So the murder of his father and abduction of his brother were investigated. Michael told the authorities what he could, about the strange white dapper man with intense eyes, but he knew nothing beyond that. It never went anywhere, and signs and articles and pleas for the community to look for his darling little brother continued unabated.

He can still throw his brother's name into Google and still find sites and information about his abduction.

That last fact, it's true. He can still do that. That's something that made it into his personal admissions essay. That, his father's death, the aftermath, of growing up with godparents ... all of that ended up in his admissions essay. He even had something cute in his admissions essay, something about how he wasn't telling the full story because it was too painful, but was just presenting the material facts descriptive of his experience, just as trained attorneys need to be able to understand and present the key facts of a client's case, blah blah blah... .

Thanks to these leaked emails, he had his admissions essay right in front of him but he refused to read it again.

That's not how he felt at the time he wrote it, right? He'd presented his feelings, his anguish, his adjustment process — the process of living with godparents, of never getting to see his younger brother growing up, how it affected him, enraged him, molded him, inspired him — all that, he told himself, was presented truthfully and honestly, and to omit those experiences and feelings would be tantamount to libel, because that was the experience which formed him most as a person. He omitted facts that were unhelpful — facts no one would believe, facts that would have him labeled as delusional or crazy — because he knew there would be nothing to gain from sharing them. He couldn't share any of it, not even any explanations for the quirks of his that people found perplexing, such as why he couldn't stand the sight of elephants or giraffes or even whales, for watching them languidly drifting past him, even through glass at an aquarium, made him feel tiny and helpless.

"You should be grateful to me for this." That's what it'd said to him. Those words vexed him, mocked him, wrenched him, cut something deep, deep, deep inside him and twisted. He had no indication of what that meant, but surely it wasn't some mocking prognostication, some goading about how Michael would end up basing his identity around this incident, how his sweet little brother would be the beneficiary of indescribable suffering and he'd be the beneficiary of unlimited academic opportunity ... no, surely, no.

But he had nothing to go on, no way to guide him, nothing to do, no connection or no understanding, so on those endless creaking nights when he'd submerged all his tormenting thoughts, that one phrase always slipped through his mental armor. He'd spin it over in his head, and the curse would work its magic and remove all hope, for then he couldn't even take pride in his accomplishments or achievements.

"You should be grateful to me for this."

>< >< ><

He saw Keith the next day while heading to their 11:00 a.m. *Property Law* lecture. They met eyes and didn't speak or signal or indicate to one another, and he couldn't read Keith's expression at all, though there was some expression — something — there to be interpreted. A broker of peace, perhaps.

"You should be grateful to me for this," the man with the colored eyes had said to him.

Soon Enough This Will Essentially Be a True Story

IT WAS THE easiest thing to do, so she did it.

Click, and she was entered into another Goodreads giveaway. She'd entered about ten giveaways in the last couple of minutes, just entering with nothing more than a click, to win whatever seemed even marginally interesting: meaning something dark, something weird, something bizarre. *Click. Click. Click.* If anyone ever wrote a biography about her, they'd have to come up with different words for "click."

Here was a Penguin re-issue of some Edgar Allen Poe Stories, stories that were available for free online and that she already owned, but she didn't see any harm in entering the giveaway, anyway. It was just a click away. *Click.*

Give me Convenience or Give Me Death, the band the Dead Kennedys had named their compilation of rarities, their dig at 1980's consumer culture. That album was released back in 1985, years and years before she was even born.

What had they been satirizing, mail-order catalogs? What was that in a world where she canvassed a digital aggregator for free books — free books provided by authors so eager for readers that they even paid their own shipping costs — while simultaneously pirating four albums off Soul-Seek and skimming through her friends' online pictures of food shots and exaggerated expressions.

Give me Convenience or Give me Death, indeed.

She checked her Goodreads tally. She'd entered about fifteen give-aways, thought, well, this is enough empty-minded clicking for one day, and logged off.

It was about 2:30 p.m. on an unassuming school day. Karen was home alone in her room, had been for approximately an hour. Ahh, the perks of being a high school senior. If you couldn't set yourself up with an easy-peasy schedule, they should demote you back to freshman.

So much free time, yet her room, still so messy. Maybe she'd spend her afternoon conquering "Heap Mountain," as she and her mother dubbed the lump of clothes, accessories, books and accumulated detritus that gathered around her bed. Her mother would be pleasantly surprised and impressed, and that would be her strongest reason for doing it. But still, she didn't. No reason why not. She should, she wanted to, but she didn't.

Her rickety old phone buzzed. She checked the text.

Yo Yo Bee-yotch, swingin' by. It was Rose, her best friend and hetero-life partner. Karen was impressed that Rose had bothered to spell out *Bee-yotch*, put in the little hyphen and everything. That's the type of care and dedication that makes someone a best friend.

Coolio, in the lair, astride Heap Mountain. Stop in, she texted back.

Good thing she didn't get started on cleaning up her room, she would have been interrupted anyway, she fake-thought. Getting to work on stabilizing Heap Mountain remained the insurmountable task. That's because Heap Mountain never updated – it was always the same. Maybe if cleaning incorporated clicking.

She went on Songza for a dour-but-upbeat music mix, and on came "Crawl" by the Alkaline Trio. She bobbed along, keeping rhythm.

She uploaded her just-finished Goodreads review. It'd been almost 48 hours since her last update. She was in the top 20 in the United States on Goodreads for her prolific and well-"liked" reviews (literally: the algorithm that ranked reviewers depended on how many people clicked "like" on her reviews). ("Yeah, top twenty reviewer. At twentieth," she imagined Rose saying, something she'd probably said in the past. "Still the top twentieth," she imagined shooting back, gleefully).

She was damn impressed with herself. Top twenty for the United States was an achievement. There was a lot of competition; America created the online marketplace for attempts at attention-getting. If she were in Latvia or something, she'd certainly be taking the number one spot.

Hobbies were getting more and more niche. Posting online reviews on Goodreads was hers. She posted the review and closed the website, with the full knowledge that she'd be back online in about ten minutes (or one minute, who was she kidding) to see how many likes, tweets and comments she'd amassed.

"Crawl" played again. She set it on repeat. She was like that, she loved hearing the same thing, refreshing the same pages, whatever controls the circuitry of satisfaction and pleasures, well, that was what got her off.

Fifteen minutes, five refreshes, eleven individual comments, fourteen likes, and two profile picture changes later, Rose arrived.

"'Can't believe how strange it is to be anything at allll,'" Karen sung along with Neutral Milk Hotel, another repeat favorite, as Rose came into the room.

"Hola, hola." Rose came to Karen's house to-and-fro and as she pleased, essentially another family member. "Damn, still good ole Clutter Island in here, I see. You didn't lie."

"Yup, and still can't get Leonardo DiCaprio to sign on."

"Well, in his defense, you're no Scorcese."

"Not yet."

Rose leaned in and looked at Karen's Goodreads page. "Raped by the Raptor," she read the title of the book Karen had just reviewed off Karen's computer screen. "Sounds like another Karen-approved classic."

"Actually, it's 'Raped by the Reptar.' Learn to read, beo-otch. It's Rugrats fan fiction porn. Rugrats is this old kids' cartoon."

"Jesus Lord, you keep sinking lower and lower, don't you? Damn, Karen, you never cease."

"Don't hate the player."

Karen pointed her cursor over a comment that a fan had just left in the last minute or so and read the comment aloud: "You sexy goth librarian you, you never cease to amaze us." She turned to Rose. "See, my fans agree with you. I never cease to amaze. And my fans are legion."

Rose laughed. "That's awesome. Great minds think alike. Serendipity, it must be." Karen replied to the comment, noting her friend Rose had just said the same thing, and clicked 'like' on her own comment.

Karen liked being called a sexy goth librarian. Goth librarian was not exactly the look she went for, but was somewhere in the wheelhouse. She didn't see herself as sexy: she instead focused on the fifteen pounds or so she felt she could afford to lose, if only clicking was exercise and cookies and ice cream didn't taste so damn good. She had natural dark hair, which she kept pulled back; well-curated outfits of dark colors, tight-fitting enough to suggest the chesty body underneath, which she knowingly accentuated with pendants or necklaces to lead the eyes to the fun parts. Her current profile picture was appropriately gothic and decked out for Fall, the lower part of her face covered by red-and-orange crumpled leaves she held up for the camera, only her arch, sharp eyes and angular lashes visible. And the picture showed off one of the best things about living in Rhode Island: damn good Fall foliage.

She received a new message on Goodreads.

Mhmm why you hiding behind those leaves lol, you're too pretty for that. Maybe put the leaves between the boobs though, that may work better for Fall lol. Groan. On a good week, half of the comments she received were sexualized come-ons, always replete with the 'what-me?' LOLs, as if dropping a LOL or JK in a comment completely nullified sexual obnoxiousness. The same guy — profile picture showed an avuncular older man with well-styled white hair — had left a couple comments before, some of them substantive and constructive. She only responded to those worthwhile comments. Eh. She didn't want to ignore him and lose a follower, but still, eh. She oscillated about how to respond.

Two more messages popped up.

The first message was from the same avuncular older man. An apology of sorts. *LOL sorry I didn't mean any offense, just ignore that, I'm an idiot sometimes.*

Whew, problem solved. *No prob :)* she replied.

The second message.....

"OH SHEET," she bellowed.

She won a Goodreads lottery, which meant she'd get a free physical copy of the book she "bid" on. She usually only read physical books if she won them; with her reading interests, the books were usually free or, at most, 99 cents for a Kindle copy. Not many authors or publishing companies would bother to physically produce copies of the gems in her collection, which included such classics as *Mounted by the Monster*, the related but far more offensive *Mounted by My Masta; I, WhoreBot; Vampire Fuck-Fest, The Only Crosses We Respect Are the Ones That Go Inside Us;* and that beguiling story of star-crossed lovers, *The Maiden and the Deer Gods.*

She actually did read some respectable fiction, non-fiction and the like, but those reviews took longer to prepare, and the Goodreads metrics prized quantity. She absentmindedly ended up becoming the ascendant genre erotica reviewer on Goodreads. She was listed as a favorite reviewer on the "MonsterErotica Chat Group," and every related review had a guaranteed fan base of at least 500 pairs of eyeballs. The competition was always nipping at her heels, churning out reviews that were barely more than click-bait gifs and look-at-me meta-hipsterism. The genre she was reviewing, of course, was largely fatuous trash, but she made an effort to separate the wheat from the chaff. I mean, there's something to be said about trash *done right.*

She read up on the book she'd won. *The Ardent Aardvark Who Fucks The World, and Other Stories, by the Obviously Pseudonymed KatMandu.* That was the whole title, which included the author's name for whatever reason. And literally, that was the author's nom de plume: Obviously Pseudonymed KatMandu. The author's profile picture was of a grey-and-white tabby cat wearing wide-framed wire glasses, donning a Photoshopped, squiggly-black line of a smirk.

She read the book's description:

A serial killer who only targets the most deserving victims: people who don't turn off their phones in movie theaters. An unloved Aardvark who,

*frustrated that his species is unknown to the wider world, becomes what-
ever he imagines himself to be. A tree who rapes a shrub: only to become
America's Sweetheart. Ellen Page's boobs that were digitally created
for that video game gains sentience and haunts her dreams - with sexy
results. Plus, Katy Perry and Taylor Swift dyking it out and blowing a
bunch of dudes while Ashton Kutcher gets set on fire.*
All this and more, finally in one place.
*For the first time, after much demand, KatMandu's surviving stories have
been collected in one anthology.*

Not strictly Monster Erotica, but the type of wallowing genre so-bad-
it's-great Kindle-bred trash that should make for a decent review. And, she
had to give credit where it was due, this guy (well, maybe not a guy, but let's
play the odds here....) took the time to self-publish the book in a physical
format. That boded ... not well, but at least meant something. Perhaps this
author put a little more tender love-and-care into his creations.

"Oh man, this one's a winner," Rose leaned in, her long neck and limbs
crowding out Karen's view of the screen.

"You just like it because it's written by a cat." Karen pointed to the
profile picture. Rose was lithe and cat-like, naturally dark-haired and with
soulful green eyes, and many a Halloween she'd donned black tights and
black-stub earrings and gone as a cat, a good I'm-pretending-to-be-lazy-
but-this-only-works-because-I-can-sorta-pull-it-off costume. "Mreow,"
Karen play-scratched at Rose. Rose hissed back, impressively. She'd had
practice.

Goodreads provided the participating author with the addresses of the
contest-winners. The author would send out the physical copies, and then
verify electronically that the copies had been sent.

Within 5 minutes, Goodreads sent her another automated message:

"Congratulations! We are happy to let you know that [Obviously Pseudonymed KatMandu] has sent out your contest copy! Happy Reading! You
are encouraged to write a review, but it is not mandatory."

Damn, this Kat was an eager beaver.

Another email arrived.

Subject line: Straight from the Kat's Mouth.

Karen! Thanks for submitting to my contest. And even better, thanks for
winning! You are a review rockstar, even if you didn't win I would have sent
you a copy anyway!

I knew you had it in you! Holy Meowzers, you live in Rhode Island, too. I
hope you love the book and we can drink Del's and 'Setts and I can eat your
clam errr we can eat clams together! Hope you like it, it's my life's work! I
sent it out via Amazon Prime.

And remember.....MEOW!

She responded kindly and enthusiastically, ignoring the clam comment
(par for the course) and electronically high-fiving him on his love of Del's
and asking him where he lived in "Lil Rhody." She sent him the usual dis-
claimer — that she had a bunch of other books on the reading queue, so
a review may not be forthcoming anytime in the near future — but she
would definitely make sure to get to his book in due time and post an honest review.

"Hahah, oh man, what have you gotten yourself into?" Rose asked as
they got ready for the night.

"Just another day in the life."

>< >< ><

They were going over to Justin's house. In shocking-yet-related news, Justin's parents were out of town. This was going to be a low-key affair, a
couple of friends over, drinking whatever cheap and/or tasty alcohol they
could procure, probably end up streaming a movie and pigging-out on fast
food. She and Justin had a little on-again/off-again thing going. They'd
been friends since Junior High, and undoubtedly, as she joked, allowing
Justin to put his penis in her mouth on a few choice occasions only heightened the bonds of their friendship.

He was sweet, and she suspected he was a little infatuated with her; since guys are obsessed with their dicks, she reasoned, Justin may feel weirdly indebted to her, or maybe he just would have felt that way toward any girl who helped him satisfy that most incessant, perennial craving. But she liked that he was too shy or sweet (or both) to ever make any moves on his own. She was in control. He was so understanding, sweet and ... is grateful the right word? Maybe, but she liked it. She liked having his penis in her mouth, and she liked when he satisfied her, too. She straight-up liked it and wasn't afraid to say so.

And God bless Rose, her wing-woman. If Karen could take an informal poll at school, she imagined most people would think Rose was the more sexually active of the two, probably because Rose just *looked* more sexual — taller, leaner, more svelte of face and form. But in fact, they'd be wro-ong; Rose had the sense of humor of a sailor but the chasteness of a school chaperone. The most salacious thing she'd ever had in her mouth was a chili cheese dog.

Funny, you can't win: too much sexuality, and you're a slut; too little, and you're a cock-tease. Rose had been burned by guys who dated her a bit and then cast her off after she'd do nothing more than kiss and feel. Maybe they thought she didn't like them, maybe their pride had been hurt, who knows. Karen and Rose talked about this at length — they'd talked about everything at length, and Rose had no moral or religious objections to sex ("and, appropriately, no morals or religion whatsoever," she'd once quipped), but just didn't have the desire to get embroiled in sexual high school politics and never found a guy worth the risk. Poor Rose, she was actually eager to experiment, to know and give pleasure, but these local scrubs weren't fitting the bill.

Someday.

>< >< ><

After they'd gotten ready (which meant looking a bit more sex-ified than usual, but without doing anything that brought obvious attention to their efforts), they made their way downstairs.

"You want food? We got pizza left over from last night," Joan, Karen's mother, offered as they were making their way downstairs. The one set of stairs in the house ended across from the entrance to the kitchen; in other words, when you went down the stairs, the kitchen would be directly before you. You had to turn a left from the bottom of the stairs and turn the corner to head out toward the front door. If Joan needed to talk to Karen, she made sure to be centrally-located in the kitchen. Whether Karen was coming-or-going to her room upstairs, she had to walk past the kitchen.

"Is that *my* Karen wearing perfume?" Joan asked as she opened the refrigerator. "It smells like...flowers! You smell like flowers! Not grave-stones—" (at this Rose doubled-over with laughter) — "or something weird, but flowers!"

"No, it isn't perfume. Mom, you know if that day ever comes, you will be the first to know. And by the way, if you know of a gravestone perfume, then I don't need to tell you what I want for Christmas this year."

"You're not?" Her mom came over and sniffed at her neck and hair while Rose laughed. "You smell nice, though."

"Must be all the patchouli I bathe in."

"Must be," she said as she whipped Karen playfully with a dish rag.

"Ahh, assaulted by my own mother! Rose, you're a witness!"

"Oh shush you," Joan continued, emptying out the fruit drawer. "Are you sure you don't want to bring a fruit or anything? You didn't eat yet! Eat something good, at least. Or you two could not go out at all, it might rain tonight, you know?"

"Eat something good, like pizza?" Karen asked rhetorically.

"If I was your daughter, I'd love to stay at home and eat pizza," Rose brown-nosed.

"Oh, I know that, Rose. They must have switched you two at birth."

Karen played at exasperation. "She hits me and then wishes she had a different daughter. This is what I live with."

"Oh boo hoo, call me when you come back. Be safe. Don't drink and drive, ok Rose, you promise me? And even if you do drink, call me, I can pick you up."

"No drinking and driving, got that?" Karen told Rose. "She didn't say anything about doing crack and driving though. Loophole!"

"Oh look at you, future lawyer over there," they heard Joan as they made their way out toward the door.

"Haha, yeah, right. The closest I'll get to being a lawyer is suing your ass if you try and kick me out of the house!"

"Yeah, let's be honest here, future lawyer's assistant, at best," Rose added as she put her arm around Karen. Karen gave a cheeky Cheshire Cat grin.

They made their way out to Rose's used Civic — Stanley Civicus, they'd named it — and took off.

>< >< ><

They had a fun night. Technically, Rose violated her promises to Karen's mother: she both drank and smoked pot, although she only had one beer — purloined from Justin's parents — and only a couple tokes, but there was at least an hour gap between her indulgences and when she drove Karen home. Karen outdid her, smoked pot and had a couple of mixed drinks, mixing together whatever was available. Some vodka-ginger ales, why not? There were eight people there in total, and a fun time was had by all. They couldn't stay out too late because it was a school night and they both had quasi-curfews.

Her mom would be pleased: they ordered pizza. They watched some cheesy softcore pornified horror movie and just hung out. She spent a little bit of alone time with Justin, just playful chatting, knowing flirtations. She was proud of one of her evocative lines. She told him about the book she'd just won on Goodreads, written by a supposed cat, and how she looked forward to reading from a pussy. "And maybe sometime soon you'll enjoy eating from a pussy," she stated dryly, no unusual intonations, both of them responding with exaggerated Oh-shit faces.

"That a promise?" he asked.

"Haha, well if it was a super promise, like no matter what, then that'd be rape my boy. Depends how I feel at the time. But, ya know, keep your calendar free, is all I'm saying."

She came home fifteen minutes shy of her curfew, and enjoyed a deep sleep.

>< >< ><

After a drama-free day at school, guess what awaited her at home.

"Another one of your junk packages," her mom informed her. Her mom was supportive but perplexed by her daughter's chosen hobby. A generational thing, she thought, that she just didn't get. She didn't get a lot of modern things, but at least with most modern things, she could understand how someone could conceivably enjoy something, or what they were supposed to be enjoying about it. These books Karen got were just outrageous junk, attempts to shock.

"Oh shee-it!" Karen grabbed the package and noticed the return address. "Woah, this guy lives in Woonsocket. He's next door!"

"Better give him a good review!"

"He could be huge one day! I could be launching the career of a hometown hero!" Of course, they both knew that no one got famous writing the shit that Karen reviewed.

She opened the manila packaging and, what could she say, she was impressed. The book was a handsome and hefty trade paperback. She checked the back of the book — geez, 200+ pages, although she did note the text was probably size 14 font. This couldn't be cheap to produce.

The cover was of ....what was it, exactly? A black cartoon dildo juxtaposed next to a picture of a strange animal that looked like a wooly quadruped with a pig-like snout. The animal picture was ripped right off *National*

Geographic website. How'd she know it was taken right off *National Geo-graphic* website? At the very bottom right of the image, she could see the crunched-font copyright.

What the hell is the... ahh, this must the eponymous aardvark. The title of the collection and the author's stupidly long nom de plume were both spelled out in the same garish, splattered-paint font.

She loved, loved, loved new trade-paperback books: the almost bio-mechanical smooth feel of the covers, even the smell of the pulp paper. She clutched the book and ran into her room like a dog absconding with a biscuit.

She opened the book to a random page, just exploring it. *Ashton Kutch-er Slaughter Dance Party*, read one title. Brilliant. This book was going to be a hot tawdry mess. She updated her Goodreads page and added this book to her "Currently Reading" list and dove into the introduction.

The ASPCA states that 1.4 million cats are euthanized each year. I was supposed to be one of those cats.

Quite the lede.

Alone, abandoned, no cat mommy to call my own (my siblings ate her upon birth), all selected for adoption. Despite this rap sheet, I had one loved one in the shelter system, my cat man and main squeeze Cuddly Malone. Life is never easy: he ended up doing 25 years in the State Pen for loitering in litter boxes and aggravated rape.

With no one to fend for me, I fended for myself. I taught myself to read. To write. To feel. That's when I was no longer just a cat. I was....A Kat, which is like a cat but with a different spelling that would impress other cats if they knew how to spell. But they don't. Only kats can. And I'm the only Kat.

Okay then. She was used to this type of gonzo-style myth-making. How long did this introduction last? She skimmed it and felt fatigued. Jesus, fifteen pages. She skipped five pages of it and found more-of-the-same, with all the standard non-titillating attempts at titillation, violence, non sequiturs and spot-the-references that she half-feared / half-expected.

Ashton Kutcher adopted the author at some point, then peed on him and returned him, with strict orders to be euthanized, that's why he's targeted in one story, et cetera.

She turned to the story that seemed the most promising, i.e. like an actual real idea: the story of the serial killer who only kills people who use their phones in movie theaters.

It was two lines of set-up and all "pay-off."

It was in some super hero movie, does it even matter which one anymore? You texting whore, you don't think this money means something to me? What kind of fucking sociopath are you? I paid for these tickets. Do you really not realize how annoying that light is? Really, is that possible? Is that humanly fucking possible? Or do you just not care? Your thug boyfriend isn't here to protect you, he's gone to take a shit instead of listening to the shit coming out of your mouth, I thought as the knife went through the stupid cunt's throat, rivulets of blood flying like my future ejaculate when I'd fantasize about this later with a toaster up my ass. I crushed her dainty fingers with my free hand, breaking her stupid fucking expensive nails, too. I did a 360 around her neck with the knife like I was wrapping a Christmas present. I popped her head off like a pie top and put her beaming, blaring smart phone into the stump. Her orifices lit up like a fluorescent jack o-lantern. A jack o-lantern... of death!

She skimmed the rest of the story, sighed, then listlessly skimmed some others. They were all tiring and unengaging, all pretexts for hate-filled violence, perversions, and shoehorned wackiness. It was boring and tepid.

She put the book aside. Oh well. Non-fiction was her go-to palate cleanser, so she fired up her Kindle and returned to her book on the missing colony of Roanoke. It was well-written and informative and her mind felt lubricated, that in-the-rhythm satiety when your brain is engaged in worthwhile discourse.

>< >< ><

She thought nothing of the Kat book until two days later, when she received a message from the author on Goodreads.

Hey, it should have arrived by now. Did you get it? Let me know when you did. Is there any way I can get you to read it sooner? Any way at all...... Kitty treats!

Ugh.

I got it, thanks! Might take me a while to read, but I will someday. Thanks! was her response.

>< >< ><

She hated writing bad reviews, although she did it if a book was unbearably twee or pretentious, in which case she could be scathing. Despite all the shock factor, Kat's book was typical run-of-the-mill, boring gonzo stuff. Not very well-written, interesting or clever. In the pantheon of trashy smut, it was no *Raped by the Reptar* or *I, Whorebot*.

Karen hoped he'd just forget about it, but that wouldn't happen. Writers — even junk writers, perhaps, *especially* junk writers — were incredibly egg-shelled. Realistically, she hoped to just never write anything about it and that he'd pick up on the hint. If that fails, maybe just a two-star review and just saying it wasn't for her. Short and sweet.

He responded the next day with an *ok* and she didn't respond.

Before class started, she uploaded two new reviews, including a detailed, four-star review for the Roanoke book she spent all night reading and a three-star review for *Dive Into Me*, a short story smut-thriller that actually took a little time to develop its main two characters. After uploading the reviews, she tortured herself in the gratifying way she always did, by not permitting herself to check on the status updates and comments the reviews had accumulated until she returned home from school.

>< >< ><

Finally, the school day was over. She met Rose in the school's parking lot. Rose drove her home almost every day — they had the same extracurricular schedule (meaning: they participated in no extracurricular activities), so the timing always worked. Karen's mom was working late, so naturally they got a little bit high, shielded as they were in the cramped, fenced-in pocket of a backyard.

Karen and her mother lived in a single-family detached cottage-style home, typical for their neighborhood. She called the neighborhood homes Snugsies, each a small cute little house for a small cute little family in the smallest, cutest state in the country. If either of her neighbors ever saw her sneaking in a little reefer with her friend, they never said anything to her mom about it, so she was thankful for that. She was respectful enough to be discreet about it, though. She had that going for her.

Nice and pleasantly-baked — well-done, they called it — Karen and Rose moseyed in from outside, through the Snugsie little kitchen, up the stairs, into her bedroom, the snuggiest room in the whole snuggy house.

"Snuggles," Karen said aloud, in reverie.

"What?" Rose asked, eyes dimmed, feeling pleasure in nothing more than the act of speaking, the pleasure of existing.

"Check this out!" Karen pulled up her Goodreads account.

Rose checked it out. "Ahh ... too ... many ... comments ... cannot ... process."

Karen alighted both hands in victory. "Oh shee-it." She'd racked up a bunch of comments and likes on her last review. She opened her inbox. Somehow, the message from KatMandu was the one that jumped out at her.

I take it no progress on the book yet. BTW are you rich?

Karen groaned loudly.

"Hah I guess his book failed to deliver."

Karen reached for the book in a stupor and tossed it over to Rose. "Take it, you can ghost-review it for me."

Rose strained to read in Karen's half-lit room.

She read aloud from a passage: "And I made sure to use the edge of my sharpened blade to pop out the clit, the juiciest and most delectable morsel. All was well, as I just ordered in a new shipment of cocktail sauce. Clits: the successful man's oysters."

"And that is eeee-nuff of that," Karen said in a sing-songy cadence.

"Yeah, definitely. Yikes. Fail. I mean, I don't think a cat could even use a knife?"

"I know, that's the real problem with it, right? Why else do cats have claws? But seriously, it's all like that. True fail."

Karen fired off a reply, saying something like: *I'm the richest girl in my entire rich town, shoving my riches in everyone's face. I mean, who isn't jealous of the daughter of the overworked single mother who is always afraid of getting laid off from the hospital. I feed off that shit. Cower before me mortals! Serve me my hamburger helper. And no I didn't finish your book, sorry, I just can't now. Best of luck, go Bruins, Go Sox (the Rhode Island ones).*

She turned off the computer and chilled with her friend, which was all she could ask for.

>< >< ><

She woke up the next day fully-rested. She changed most of her clothes but kept on the same black cat socks, just 'cause.

It wasn't until she checked Goodreads that she officially woke up. She was excited. She had eight messages.

Except all but one were from you-know-who.

Okay that's fine I don't think you had to give me an attitude, I just felt like you had a rich girl attitude is all. I think it's rude to accept a book and not review it as soon as possible but it's ok, just do it whenever.

The other messages all tended toward indignation.

Btw I paid to send you that book out of my own pocket not to make you feel bad but it's the truth, I don't make any money doing this, i do it for the fans and for the love of it. People think its all a joke but its not, I take this very seriously.

How do you respond in the face of seven messages, most of them sent between midnight and 4 am? Answer: You don't. Ignore, bye bye!

It never even occurred to her to conduct a deep-dive of his profile page on Goodreads. The background of his profile page was overlaid with the same tabby cat as before, with the same gash-of-a-Photoshop style smile. She scrolled down to see some of the recent posts.

Another bitch ignored me, whatcha gonna do, back under the kat house.

Going out for the evening, started another post. Under the heading was a picture, shoulders visible, of him wearing a brown paper bag on his head that looked tightly soldered on. The bag reminded her of when she had to wrap textbooks in brown paper when she was in elementary school. There were drawn-on angular black-marker triangles for cat's ears and a roughly-drawn black circle — a mini-head for his head mask — with black rows of triangles, presumably to resemble chomping teeth, if you were a lenient parent of a particularly lazy and artistically untalented child. He was raising his arms and, from the color and appearance of his hands, she pictured a lean, wiry white man in his thirties.

One other image actually made her do a double-take. Most of his face wrapped in sheer saran wrap, with him making a malevolent O-face with just his front top and bottom teeth visible. The saran wrap added an alien viscosity to his appearance that was, given the intensity of his look, pretty damn frightening. She could see his brown eyes, his brown, longish hair, his thin brown eyebrows, his other dominating masculine features: slightly protruding forehead, long neck and pronounced Adam's apple. He was white and in shape. His face was even kind of cute, if taken out of all other context.

With a free hand, he was pulling a tuft of his brown hair. Viciously. The angle, his face, his partially-closed eyes, all made the distress plain to see. This was, uhhhh, suffering for his art?

Someone I really respected gave me a shitty review. Fucking all. Feel like shit now. Need to suffer through it and keep going, read another post, which had some "likes" and semi-literate comments encouraging him not to get too down and to keep "persvering."

She didn't like looking at other reviews before she did her own, but since there was frankly no chance in hell she'd be reviewing this guy's book anytime soon, she allowed her curiosity to get the better of her. Shocking — largely confused and irritated 1-and-2 star reviews, with some surprisingly eloquent five-star defenders lambasting the masses for not getting the satire or being too politically correct and squeamish.

How can you not love a story where a dog-version of Zoe Deschanel is the bad guy who goes by Zoey Daschundelle? Seriously, people? Get a sense of humor. It's satire. It's making fun of your superficiality, your obsession with celebrities and taking it to its most outrageous extreme. So it's ok to commodify female sexuality, to pretend to be a nation that hates violence but glorifies bad-asses and superheroes? Well, this collection is brave enough to take it all to the extreme, to throw it right in your face. You can't look away. This is the underside of America, all the concealed psychosis laid out for all to see. Nowhere to hide. This is your principal furtively masturbating to the high school yearbook. This is your beloved father figure taking bribes. This is genius.

Karen made one last attempt: she read — all twenty goddamn pages — of the above-referenced story, and, no no no no no, not for her. Or anyone. But particularly not for her.

She perused the rest of his profile absent-mindedly, eager to log off. One other picture stuck with her. An open refrigerator, top shelf full of Narragansett Coffee Stouts. *God bless Rhode Island and fuck all the haters, only Nassets and Argonauts, straight from the source, can inspire my mind,* read the caption. So, claiming he was from Rhode Island wasn't just fronting — as low-stakes as Goodreads seemed, sometimes authors pretended to have something in common with a reviewer to try and curry favor.

He did live in Rhode Island, apparently.

Unfortunately.

The last of his eight messages read:

Fine, actually I tell you not to read it, you aren't worthy of it or you are not the right audience for it. Or, in other words, fuck you rich girl! Stupid whores I don't mean literally whores but people like you just goddamnit fuck it if you aren't going to be supportive then fuck it. I'll always have Scarlett Johannson and Gillian Anderson and a million other beautiful woman to inspire me. Kats get all the pussy you know. Sorry if that was harsh but I need to be honest.

Her response wrapped up her feelings nicely:

Please do not ever contact me again.

Already a little jittery with nervous energy, she sent out a text to Justin, inviting him to come over on Friday night from around "10 p.m. to ?" The (?) was to add to the mystery, but really he had to be gone by 2 a.m., because that's when her mom's double shift ended and he'd have to high-tail it out of there way before she got home.

Might as well transfer her nervous energy into something productive, she figured.

It took Justin a while to respond — playing it cool, she figured, although cool was the last word she'd use to describe him (and that was a compliment), but he accepted the invitation amidst a flurry of coy emoticons

They were on (*like Donkey Kong*, she added unconsciously in Rose's voice, as if they were linked up telepathically, *get out of my mind!*). Two days away. Yeah. *I'll make sure to shower that day!* she texted him when he confirmed that he'd come over. *Ewwwwww*, he responded, *but even if you don't you know I still WUB you.* She sent back a blushing emoticon. They never said anything about love; maybe that's why he went instead for the satiric misspelling. If she responded positively, maybe he'd work his way up to "luv" and more and more permutations until he got to the real thing.

Maybe she should have stopped him. Maybe she would. She morally should, it was the right thing to do. She did like him a lot, but they had to be realistic, what with college and everything right on the horizon. Maybe talk about it in person. Texts were not the medium for nuanced explorations of affection. But for now, she liked the inherent promise of protection and trust embedded beneath that unassuming goofy text.

She spent the next day blazing through short fiction and uploading some other reviews. The last piece she reviewed deserved three stars for its title alone — *You Spit out my Coffee like you Spit out my Seed* — and, as she declared in her review, for including the following sublime passage containing the typo of the year.

The burly barista raised his head and released a yawl of his own, as his cock tensed up inside her, ready to explode. "Ironic, you're a vegan who needs my meat to live," he teased Candy, the cute new hire. "Mhmm, I can't wait to unleash this new product. Small batch, limited release. Only available here," he said, and pointed to this throbbing balls. His thick cock twitched inside her. She felt it contract and spurt hot liquid deep into her worm.

Her worm! Classic. She let the likes and comments accumulate as she pored over he-who-shall-not-be-named's Goodreads profile. Recusing herself from the obligation of reviewing his work was freeing. She now took an almost anthropological interest in this guy. She was fascinated. It took a lot for her to block someone on the site: hell, she didn't think she actually blocked anyone before, and half the messages in her inbox were lewd inducements. If she could be assured he wasn't bat-shit insane, she'd want to interview him.

His profile page was filled with so much rambling, so much...confused anguish, juxtaposed and interspersed with these fucking cat-and-celebri-ties references. *The fuck fest, birth, death, and birth again of Kitty Perry*, began a recent blog post of his that caused her eyes to glaze over. Jesus, what a sordid little world she stepped into. KatMandu evidently had a particularly nasty streak of engaging in vindictive flame wars with hostile reviewers, which perhaps accounted for the downtick in takers for his col-lection. She saw online another contest of his, offering three copies of his collection with only 38 current bidders.

>< >< ><

"Holy shit," Rose said. It was Friday around 4 p.m., and Karen and Rose were chilling, planning on grabbing dinner and chatting about Karen's night to come. Rose was surfing the psycho's Goodreads page. "I am fascinated. I want to subscribe to his newsletter. He is crazy. He is a work of art. If a car crash could turn into a human being and write, it'd be him. If he is obsessed with cats, why is the book named after an aardvark?"

"I never read enough to find out. My loss. I imagine there is some stupid coda or post-script buried in the back, something like 'haha you stupid faggot you read all this and there's not even an aardvark story.' Some things should just remain mysteries."

"I'm borrowing this." She flipped through the book, put it in her school bag and returned to his profile page. Easier to put it in her school bag than keep it on Karen's desk, where it might get swallowed up by the voracious clutter.

"Make sure to read the story about the unlucky guy who shits out melting crap-babies!"

"Oh, as if you needed to tell me. I wish we still did book reports in school." Rose shook her head in something like befuddled awe as she pored over his profile page. "Is there a way to get access to his Goodreads page without actually signing up for Goodreads? I'll admit it, I'm hooked. He actually might be cute, or cute-ish, hard to tell below all the crazy. He promises a big announcement tonight. I'm not embarrassed to admit I'll probably look online to see what it is. Okay, so maybe I am a little embarrassed."

"I'm sure he'll be blocking you from Goodreads soon, Sally Stalker. Come on, let's go." They were going out to Rizzo's Fine Italian, about twenty minutes away, which, despite the chintzy name, was actually pretty good.

"Are you going to wear that tonight?" Rose asked with a trace of friendly skepticism.

Karen wasn't one to get insecure, especially not about fashion, but she wasn't a robot, dammit. "What's wrong with this!?" She wore a tight-fit-ting, soft black sweater with a singular, oversized button at the top as a flourish, paired with black skinny jeans. "I think he will find it hot, tight-fit-ting." She leaned in mock seductively. "Should I have more décolletage?" she pronounced in a husky sotto voice. "He's seen my boobs before; he'll want to unwrap them in this. Don't deny him his fun!"

"No, you crazy person," Rose spoke as they made their way from Kar-en's room, down to the living room, toward the door. "You wore that shirt this week. I remember it, you slob. Aren't you trying to get sorta-laid tonight? Up your game!" Joan had already left earlier this afternoon for her double-shift, so they were free to profane and slut-talk all night.

She shrugged. "Eh, he's a guy, I doubt he noticed. Shee-it, I don't even remember." She wouldn't admit it now, but she resolved to change when she got home.

>< >< ><

Rizzo's was in fine form that day. Karen got the penne vodka, which always sounds fancy but totally isn't, Rose got the veal cutlet ("you heartless bitch," Karen teased), and, as Karen was prone to saying, a good time was had by all.

It was around 8:30 p.m. when they got back to Karen's house. She wished she'd left a light on — she always hated returning to an entire-ly darkened home. She was glad Rose was still with her, even though, of course, she'd have to skedaddle soon.

They went into the house and turned on all the lights. The old home groaned, all its organs hissed to life as Karen adjusted the temperature.

"Soooo ... do you want me to leave now for your little date? Does it take some time to prime your vagina up or something?"

"Just blowing the dust off. Easy-Peasy. Hah." Karen mock-dusted her shoulder.

"I think it's probably more like," Rose began, and blew hard on one hand while using the other hand to convey massive amounts of dust flying up into the atmosphere.

Karen laughed, said "yeah right," and then there was a brief silence. Karen, for some reason, felt a twinge of sadness, something about the dark quietude of autumn. She was so over this cold weather bullshit. Everything looked so sparse and dead. She didn't admit this much, but she hated being alone, especially when she was waiting for something to happen. The night had a way of settling uncomfortably upon her. She was glad she wasn't alone.

"Nah Rose, it's you, you stay. If it was anyone else, I'd tell 'em to leave. But you, c'mon Rose, you ... you can stay. Stay until like 9:45. Psych me up." She thought about asking what the rest of Rose's night might have in store, but didn't.

Rose plopped down on the living room couch, feet up on the ottoman.

Karen wanted to pass this off as nonchalantly as possible, so as not to give Rose the satisfaction. "So, I'm going to go upstairs for a couple minutes."

"To change?"

"Yes, you bitch, to change. Are you happy?"

"Ecstatic."

With that, Rose pivoted her feet from the ottoman and took up the whole couch. It was a small couch — only intended for two, after all — and Rose's long legs peeked over the side. She whipped out the damned book and adjusted the light behind her.

"Take your time, this will keep me company." Rose held the book before her with outstretched arms and gave the book a deep sinister voice, jostling and spinning it as if it was possessed, as if its demonic voice was so powerful it caused the whole book to quake: "Bwahahah, fear me Karen, fear me!"

"Cute. Have fun with that. Any suggestions, by the way, on what I should wear?"

"Your purple dress that shows off your rack."

"Noted." That dress had a funky odor to it that needed to be addressed. Probably a pass.

Karen made her way upstairs to her bedroom and looked at herself in the mirror. Hmm. She liked the way she looked in tight sweaters. Goth librarian. Hmm, maybe just a different sweater. She was something of a sweater-head.

She checked her phone to see if there were any messages. Nope. She plugged it with the charger by the bed ("the power juice") and debated whether to text Justin, just to make sure he was still coming. She hadn't heard from him in a while. She relented, texted *see you soon at 10 p.m.* and then was ashamed, deeply, deeply ashamed. Patience, dear.

She took her sweater off, exploring how she looked in her plush purple bra. Should we wear a purple sweater over it? With black pants? Yeah sure, typical, but for a reason. Hmmm.

>< >< ><

Rose wished the lighting in the living room was better. There was a standing lamp and two less-than-optimal bulbs on the ceiling that emitted hazy, dirty light. Why do dim bulbs even exist anymore? She knew so little about technology and science, she thought to herself, that she could read about an "amazing discovery" on one of those clickbait sites that just described the operation of a standard light bulb, and she'd probably be amazed and send it around with the subject line "Science is Awesome." She laughed to herself and thought about how to explain the thought to Karen.

If Karen was around, Rose would probably stay reserved and not allow her mien to register her unease with what she was reading. She'd just joke it off, be flippant about it.

Karen actually gave out her home address to this psychopath?

The smell of his inner organs made my cock hard. Knowing he was dead, that they were all dead. My cock got fully hard, and like usual I got momentarily dizzy because as I mentioned before my cock is like 10 inches. My super cock folded onto itself in a cork-screw like Tigger's tail and I used it to bounce up and down. Cats don't yell at the moon, but holding that faggot's intestines called for something special. Sproing Sproing Sproing. I bounced on my cork-screw dick, which pounded a deeper and deeper hold into the earth with each bounce. I wrapped the intestines around my neck like I was Jake the Fucking Snake and it was 88 (and other things that kinda of rhymed). I put a warm piece of the offal under my balls because that felt nice and fuck it this was my time to shine.

There was a little footnote next to "faggot's intestines" which read: *As I mentioned to those who don't listen, I don't have anything against gay people. My cousin is gay actually but I like the way the word sounds and I like pissing people off.*

Scanning the book would become her new M.O. She wanted to find that damn aardvark story.

>< >< ><

Karen, still in her purple bra, kept quiet and listened to the sounds of her house. Been a couple minutes and Justin had never responded. *Don't be like that, c'mon.* She pretended to just be killing some time online but also hoped he'd affirm the plans in the next couple of minutes. He was the eager horny one, after all, i.e., the guy.

Naturally she went to Goodreads, and it was only a couple of minutes until she ended up on guess-who's profile. That was the gift she'd gotten from all of this. She'd always have the crazy psycho KatMandu to cyber-stalk. The tables have turned mofucka!! When the lines of communication were open, he'd been kind of scary. Now that they were officially closed, tracking him became fascinating.

He had a new post.

You pretentious assholes will like this, it's a prose-poem. It's my first time doing a prose-poem so bear with me. I'll probably (read: definitely) be gone from Goodreads and life itself (is Goodreads life itself?). Just remember whatever they say about me isn't true, unless it's a positive thing and then it's definitely true.

And by the way, my stories will, from now on until forever, be free on Kindle and Nook and all that other shit. That's so I can profit off my crimes, at least in terms of exposure. And if they get removed from the online places just know that I'll soon be famous and I'm sure they'll be available to find. I have Dylan Klebold's story on my computer, for example.

So anyway, here goes:

Your Mommy worked at a hospital,
What rhymes with hospital?
Unstoppable.

Note I say worked, past tense
Too bad for Mommy, you were dense
The work I showed her was too intense
Now there's nothing left of her but stench
But stench? Butt stench.
Plus I pissed down her throat and it spilled out the slit.
Mommy said she loved you!

And there was a picture of him, this time in a flinty matte cardboard mask with holes cut out for the eyes. She could practically see the double-duty rubber band around the back of his head which held up the mask. A dot nose with three curved lines on each side for whiskers and a frenetic "O" of a mouth were drawn on in what looked like blue pen. She could see two blue triangular shapes on his head. Ears, she presumed.

It was obviously a selfie. From the looks of it, he was taking the picture with his right hand. He was leaning into the picture, and his face took up the right side of the frame. He offered his upturned left hand to the camera as if in supplication. It was thoroughly covered in what was intended to be blood. It's like he dipped his whole left hand and even part of his arm in red, clotting paint.

There was something else in his left hand, but it was too low-resolution to really make it out. It was rectangular and silver, reminded her of a Monopoly piece. Life experience told her it looked like a name tag, like her Mom wore while she was on nursing duty.

The picture looked like it was taken inside a car, she figured. He was leaning on seats.

The post was time-stamped at 7:23 p.m. Posted today. She checked her phone. No response yet from Justin. It was 8:54 p.m.

She had the urge to text her mother, something simple, something both loving and friendly, but didn't. She wanted her phone charged.

She popped open her bedroom door and yelled down the stairs: "Hey Rose. Rose! Come up here for a second. I'm in a bra, you're in luck, c'mon up here!"

No response.

She hated the stillness in the house. She moved and shifted just to feel some activity, get her blood moving, as if her heart wasn't already beating out of her chest and she was doing her best to ignore it.

"Hey Rose!" She made her way downstairs without turning the corner. She peeked around the corner because she was still in her bra, even though she had no shame about it whatsoever and usually couldn't care less. She could see the empty kitchen before her and, through the kitchen's glass window, the pocket-sized backyard where they'd last gotten high.

She felt vaguely nostalgic and then, vulnerable. She should go change but wanted to hear Rose's voice first.

She turned the corner, entered the living room and saw it was fully-lit, Rose sitting and reading on the couch.

"Yo, what's good," Rose looked up at her. "Nice ta-tas. Save 'em for tonight."

Karen entered and bore witness to an alien visage. Rose was talking casually and normally, as if there was supposed to be someone standing

right behind her, like it was no big deal, like Karen was the crazy one for
holding her breath and wondering what in the fucking hell was going on.
Karen froze, waiting for an explanation, not processing exactly what she
was witnessing.

"Rose! What's going on?"

Rose looked at her quizzically, still imbued with her usual sass. She
couldn't parse the sheer bewilderment that was Karen's face. She followed Karen's eyes and turned her head around, looked up to see what
was behind her.

Her widened, dinner-plate eyes. Shock. Shock. *She was shocked and
there was no explanation.*

A figure in cat ears and a paper plate mask.

"Kare-"

A serrated blade plunged into the area where Rose's neck and chest
met.

What came out was only a muffled gasping wheeze mixed with gar-
gling. She reached her hand out to Karen, her expression raw panic.

She fell backward onto the couch, almost in the same position she'd
been in when she'd been just killing time reading.

He raised the bloodied knife in the air and brought it down squarely
through her neck, with such force that it pierced through her throat and
came out the other end, burrowed deep into the cushions of the couch. The
masked man steadied his left hand on Rose's shoulder and jerked the knife
out of her neck with his right.

In that instant Karen noticed so many things, all fighting for primacy in
her brain, overwhelming her. How the torque of the knife-pulling had two
distinct motions — first removing the knife from the innards of the couch,
then removing the knife from the gape of Rose's neck. That he was wearing
a light green — almost puke green — down jacket, with the hood halfway
up. *He didn't pull the hood up so I can see his cat ears.* He was a bit taller
than she expected — taller than 6 feet, maybe 6'2", definitely much taller
than her, and built lean. He stared at her from beneath the paper-plate

mask, and she couldn't see the details of the mask *but who fucking cares*, why was her brain trying to see it, *run, run, run*.

While never breaking eye contact, he lodged his left thumb into Rose's pulsing wound to tear it open even more. He did it casually, with no sense of urgency, like he was feeling for change under a couch cushion. Her brain filled in the sound of Velcro, of cheap leather, tearing.

The enervating compression of her nerves was over. Karen turned on a dime and ran toward the kitchen behind her. Her legs got the better of her and they quite literally galloped over each other, tripping her up and sending her gliding toward the floor, but she caught herself and pressed on. Five long strides and she was in the kitchen.

She reached toward the wall by the refrigerator, in almost phantom-panicked hallucination, imagining her grandmother's heavy corded phone she could use to smash him over the head. But that phone was long gone, a product of another time, an innocent unfathomable era now. *No phone, not a weapon, phone upstairs, think, think, think.* Interspersed through the explosive panic was a flat memory of her mother talking on a phone in the kitchen, something jejune, cruelly bobbing up from the swamp of her memory as if it was something noteworthy. Snap out of it, focus. *Get a knife, a pot, a weapon.*

He was running toward her, briskly, muscularly, with grim efficiency. When he crossed the threshold of the kitchen he pounced in what could only be described as a delirious skipping. She evaded and jolted open the refrigerator door on instinct. He ran right into it. He made a noise that she recognized to be artificial, insincere. It was almost a laugh, an exaggerated joke-noise, as if he was just nothing but a lighthearted buffoon. The effect was disorienting, as she was still in shock and some part of her wanted to pretend this was all an act, not real, that there was someone watching this about to yell "Scene" or "Cut" and put an end to this. He overcompensated for the abrupt, painful disturbance in his movement and fell forward, landing partly on the kitchen table. He cursed, sharply, in a way that punctured illusions and fantasies of mercy.

Karen frantically opened the utensils drawer next to her for a cooking knife. She grabbed her mother's fancy Wusthof cooking knife and turned toward her attacker in double-time.

She turned just in time. He was running at her as if he planned on tackling her but stopped just before he did, flexed his knees to mimic a strike, and then swung high. His feint worked; she'd instinctively taken firm root and readied herself to handle the tackle and stick him with the knife, and processed the newfound need to duck too late. Instead, as if a compromise, she dodged her head backward but not far enough, a cruel notch of the serrated blade caught a meaty chunk off her left cheek. It tore effortlessly and the gore flowed down her face like it was actively fleeing from her — in the span of a few seconds the blood was flowing down her face and pooled in the crevice of her clavicle, sticky and hot on her exposed flesh.

His left palm pawed at her left cheek sharply. His knife careened back toward her face in a backward slash. She ducked and thrusted her hand forward, stabbing with her knife, which, thank God her mother had always kept sharp. *Mother mother dead mother don't let the knife go dull on the pots and pans* and he was quick (*like a cat quick like a cat*). She wasn't sure how he'd parried the blows, but he had. She slid back to gain some distance from him.

They stood off from each other, him pivoting and feinting, her eyes locked on his movements, both holding their weapons in their right hands. He held his knife firmly, resolutely; her hand was too choked-up on the handle. Ludicrously, she copied his knife-holding, intuiting he knew more about this than she.

They were only a few steps apart, or perhaps one hard lunge. Her entire body was an electrified pole of nerves, squaring off; and just before he made a decisive move toward her, she reached her free left hand behind her, felt a pot, and launched it at his head.

She was a good throw and if he hadn't ducked, it'd have conked him square in the head.

As he ducked, she bolted past him. *God let Rose be alive and be here to help me kill him,* but she knew, just knew, that there no longer was a Rose, just a sticky long lumpen shape on the couch.

Upstairs to phone lock the door call police run straight out the door run to the neighbors get help rocketed through her brain in the short span of her sprinting. The stairs were closer, just outside the kitchen, so she ran up them in galloping leaps without thinking, on instinct, no time for consideration.

She was halfway up the stairs until it seemed as if gravity itself upended her. She fell hard on her chin. He'd caught her by the foot and pulled. All she thought as she fell was *please don't let me kill myself with my own knife* but she didn't, it remained under her control in her right hand, which she'd intuitively extended away from her body.

She turned to kick and the leverage was perfect — she kicked him, crunch, directly on the bridge of the mask's nose. He was caught off-balance and rocketed through the air down the length of the stairs, landing squarely on his back without hitting a single stair to break his fall. *Please god let him land on his own knife and impale himself* she thought as she turned and ran up to her room, slammed the door and locked it. It only had one lock, one of those door-knob locks that prevented the knob from turning.

She pushed her desk, computer and all, to add heft to the locked door. She put her dresser on the pile, too, all her junk. *Locked door, desk, dresser, Heap Mountain.* He couldn't possibly hack through all that, force that all out of his way.

The phone, where was my phone? She felt in a panic for her phone cord in the wall and followed it to its end. No phone. Must have fallen off in the scramble, swallowed by the Great Heap. By some miracle of heaven her lizard brain detected a sharp bluish light under the mass by her locked door, forced her toward the object and yes, it was her phone.

It was already on. She unlocked it and dialed 911.

"I am calling the cops you fucking … you fucking maniac!!" she yelled, without thinking.

Maybe he didn't know you were in your room and you just gave it away, she thought in a half-second of fear, but his voice from the hallway made it a moot point.

"You were already in a bra for me, you were ready for me!" His voice was high-pitched and squeaky, a nightmare Mickey Mouse. "Nuts for you! I'm going to go fuck your dead friend and leave. Bye bye don't write!"

"Help me, there is a murderer in my house, he has a knife, he killed my friend and my mother and he's trying to kill me," she spoke urgently but coherently to the operator on the other end of the line. She gave her address, the most important information she knew to give. Again and again, she gave her address.

Help was a few minutes away. It was a turning point for her, and she fought the build-up of mucus and tears. *Help was on the way. Help was on the way.* She put on her purple sweater and the moment it took to do that was agony; she made the dispatcher keep talking, couldn't pry herself from the sound of salvation for even the moment it took her to put on the sweater. Her sweater being on felt symbolic, relief, comfort.

"Boyfriend is here!" she heard from the hallway, again in that insane nightmare parody of what a crazed Mickey Mouse might sound like. This time there was a little strain to the impersonation; there was a bit of an underlying baritone, what was probably closer to his regular voice, maybe for effect, maybe for volume. He course-corrected in what he said next: "I can't wait to meet him," he said in a yippie-skippie screech that could break glass.

Still on the phone, she opened her blinds and looked outside. There was a car, headlights on, pulling into her driveway. She now realized the red flashing light of her phone, which signaled she'd received a text message, but she didn't dare do anything to disconnect herself from 911.

She opened the window inartfully. Something about the cool night air made her feel sick. She almost threw up, but held her composure.

It was Justin. He was still in his car; the top floor of her house wasn't too far off the ground and she could see him perfectly fine. There was Justin waiting in the driver's seat, maybe tapping the steering wheel impatiently, maybe consternation across his face; no way to tell, intuition filled in the visual lapses. He was definitely reaching for something, probably his cell phone to call her.

She waved her hands and yelled. "Go, Justin, get out of here, run, get out of here." She banged loudly on the top interior of her window. At no point did she contemplate leaving the sanctity of her boarded-up bedroom. That would be suicide, tempting fate. *Please hear me please hear me.*

She continued banging and yelling. *Please hear me please hear me.* "Justin, drive, get help! Get out of here!"

There was pounding, a tilting almost, of noise in the hallway behind her, something or someone running at full speed. *No Justin please God don't come in here* but no, it wasn't him, he was still in the car. She tucked the thought away.

The window was now raised all the way. She made a funnel with her hands — still holding the knife, which she kept jutted outward away from her body — and yelled with all her might. "Justin!" She felt her phone vibrate again and knew it must be him calling, but she refused to hang up with 911. She was staying on the phone until help damn well arrived.

She felt the sense-impression of kinetic motion and an explosion of panicked, frayed thought. She was barricaded in this room, he couldn't get in. *Think. Stay calm. Let him run around, try and scare her, psych her out. Why didn't she hear him outside her door? Where was he?* She didn't see him by Justin's car, didn't see any shapes running outside.

She thought to grab something from her desk and throw it at Justin's car to get his attention. Justin was at least smart enough (or cold enough) to stay in his car.

Her mind was still racing a mile a minute, and she couldn't put her mental-finger on it, but there was something she was overlooking.

I love you Mom, a deep welling sadness opened up within her chest. *Rose, I love you too. Please don't let him be desecrating their bodies. Or my*

Mother's room

Mother's room, something about Mother's room. Location. Rooms faced the same side, windows faced the same side.

She leaned out the window slightly and looked toward her Mother's window. A faint but conspicuous light was on. A desk lamp, she conjectured. She panicked again, looked down in a panic, *what if he's down below, throws a knife up at me*, she escapes only to die carelessly, a knife flung into her throat.

Out of the corner of her eyes she saw movement and a human-shape, with awkward determination, launch itself toward her.

He'd been lurking in the windowsill from her mother's room.

He wasn't at an angle to leap directly into her room; he came from the side, but both his hands were flailing, a whirlwind of movement, and his free left hand grabbed wildly at her hair and latched on. *Gravity should be pulling him down, taking him away,* but between his fistful of her hair and the insane, rabid contortions of his body, he was getting a foothold.

She pushed his face down, going for the eyes, but his face was wrapped in something like padded paper, almost like a reinforced diaper. She reached to gouge his eyes and hooked with her thumb, but felt only this bizarre material that gave no clues as to what she was touching. He held on and she saw his knife come down and registered she should do something but it was too late, it pierced through her sweater into the blubber of her upper left breast and she screamed. She was going to die, to have her heart ripped from her chest in full view of the street, in full view of Justin, in full view of the police, she had done everything right only to fuck it up when help might be arriving in just a few minutes, pulling defeat from the jaws of victory.

She bled and cried, for her, for Rose, for her mother, for everything that was cruel and evil.

He pulled back to strike again, but she grabbed his right wrist and pinioned it to her chest. She felt one of his digits invade the cut in her chest, the open, sacred space of her body, one digit, maybe two, like he was doing nothing more than ripping a blockage out of a stubborn drain.

She propelled herself forward out the window. He intertwined with her and fell too, positioned right below. She pushed his hand out of the way but feared beyond all fear that she would land straight on, be impaled, by his knife. *No.* In those fleeting moments, thinking nothing of the pain that would greet her upon impact — *grass and pine chips will break fall* — she thought only of the logistics of bringing her knife down into his head as if she were slicing nothing more than a block of cheese.

There was the crunch of their bodies and a profound dislocation and disconnection. The relationship between her right leg and the rest of her body had changed; it felt like it crumbled into itself, that she was now somehow no longer bipedal. She couldn't move it.

He was still beneath her, groaning and kinetic, alive, but operating slowly. She had largely used his body to cushion her fall.

She heard sirens in the background and the rumble of approaching vehicles. She heard the click of a car door open and the slam of it closing. Justin's voice, yelling her name, for several moments, getting closer. She rolled over, blotting out the world, catatonic. *Tharn*, she thought, a fantasy-word she read in a children's book, used to describe rabbits that became so paralyzed with fear and anxiety that they'd stop moving, stop functioning. *Tharn.*

Justin rushed down toward her, taking a knee. She felt his hands on her shoulder, helping her up. She registered that his knee partially-landed on and pinched her nose, one of those sharp-frustrating pains that might be funny in other circumstances, klutzy uncoordinated Justin.

Justin lifted her slightly to her side. "Karen are you —" and next thing she knew there was a horrifying squishing noise and an abortive inhalation. Justin, still on his knees, looked up at the sky and landed on his back, a knife lodged securely in his gut, up to the hilt.

Not my knife. Not my knife. She flexed and pumped her hand, yes, her hand was not broken, she could feel it, yes, she'd locked her fingers tight, yes, she was holding her knife.

Rose's murderer had rolled out from under her in her daze and shoved his knife into Justin's gut. Her mother's murderer was pushing his knife deeper-and-deeper, putting his whole body into it, as Justin, poor Justin, gasped without sound, the only sound the barely-perceptible wet suction of Justin's gut wound being torn further open.

She screamed, lunged, grabbed the psycho's shoulder and twisted him around, where he sprawled onto the ground before her. Her probing fingers felt a wetness that she knew came from his body, from an injury he must have sustained from the fall. Nothing, that would be nothing, a papercut, nothing compared to what she had planned for him.

She was screaming.

She thrust the knife from behind her shoulder, stabbing down, down, down into her tormentor's face, pushing him down, down, down, down into hell. The blade went straight through the waxy padded-paper covering his face. She stabbed again, and again, and again. The tip of her knife intuited a slit for eyes, and she took the blade by the hilt, steady with both hands, and raised it to the sky — malevolent thoughts of how the Aztecs ripped out human hearts — and brought the sharp blade straight through his eye, straight through his head, into the yielding earth. She stopped only because the knife was stuck, a railroad spike.

Karen folded upon herself, passing out, worrying crazy things about her vanity, being cold in only a bra, then, before losing consciousness, remembering she was wearing a sweater. She wanted to reach out to Justin, touch him, help him, but she couldn't. *Tharn.*

There was the great rushing of bodies, swarming and sirens, and she didn't exactly pass out but was somewhere else when she was put onto a stretcher and lifted like soft magic into the back of an ambulance.

>< >< ><

The following months were ... not a blur, no, that wasn't right. How to describe it. It's like she'd been placed on a gentle raft bobbing down a slow-moving but implacable river. Where she'd end up, she didn't know. How she ended up there, she couldn't conceive of. Where she had come from, the story of her bygone days, she could still see dimly, but each day the reality of her new situation became less and less deniable. She held onto her memories of her mother, her memories of Rose, and amplified them, magnified them a million times, took intentional chunks of time to do nothing but think of them, as full, important, sacred human beings. Mythic totems, almost.

Turns out that neither she nor Rose had thought to lock the front door, a fact mentioned ad nauseam by anonymous social media commentators. *But why would she, it was a safe neighborhood, people make mistakes*, God, she'd imbibed the social media discussion threads so thoroughly that she replayed them in her daydreams.

Her injuries were relatively minor. She'd fractured her right leg jumping out the window and was left with two deep scars, one on her breast and the other, the more garish scar, on her cheek ("quite the badass," she imagined Rose would say). She hated the scar because it reminded her of nothing but abject cruelty— the serrated crocodile's teeth of that knife left her cheek ridged, looking like plowed Earth. It served no purpose other than to disfigure and destroy.

Justin recovered relatively well. He too, had a ghastly scar, though it always remained hidden under whatever he wore. He did, however, walk with an almost-truncated gait and had to reconcile himself to a host of abdominal and intestinal problems.

She and Justin kept in touch but rarely saw each other for reasons they never fully explored, although to Karen the mention of his name was concomitant with flooding waves of shame, guilt, and anguish, and no doubt the sentiment was mutual.

She also did her best to avoid — as much as she could — the history of Geoffrey Melville, a.k.a the Obviously Pseudonymed KatMandu, or Geoff the Shotgun Shell, or Geoff the Whirlwind, Destroyer of Cities from New York to Berlin: he suffered no scarcity of nom de plumes. He had more nom de plumes and online aliases than publication credits ... more than anything else, really.

She resisted poring over the BREAKING NEWS articles and trashy tabloid spreads that brought news reporters to a frenzy, but one can only resist so much. For there were always dark nights of the soul, where you have too much to drink and you binge and you indulge, for no other reason to quell your curiosity or to smother vexing feelings of anxiety and uncertainty.

So she read up, bits and bobs, never finishing a full article about him. He was 34. He lived in a small studio in an unappealing part of Woonsocket, Rhode Island. He was estranged from his family. He had idolized his older brother, but the affection went unrequited. He worked on-and-off as a custodian and as an air conditioner repairman. Colleagues called him a good worker but erratic, and he'd inevitably get fired for talking back, tardiness or just plain no-showing.

He kept an intimate journal that spoke of nightmarish things. He vacillated between mild self-deprecation and intense seriousness. He firmly believed he was destined for better things. He was bilious toward people who rejected his writings or dismissed it as juvenilia, and dropped friends who questioned him or gave him unsolicited writing advice.

At some point in his journals, he resolved to kill, in a wild, elaborate and hysterical way. He died wearing a mask made out of diaper. He took selfies with the corpses of her mother and Rose. She saw one of the latter, just for a second, on a terrible website called *Best Gore*, where he stared ironically dead-faced into the camera, as if he didn't know the tendons and viscera of her beautiful friend's open neck was fully on display just above his shoulder. And her face, God her face, cadaverous, still beautiful, always beautiful, but those dead sunken eyes, the radiance of them, gone.

She'd looked at the picture for a moment — the picture had been labeled as *The Crazed Kat Killer's Last Selfie*, but the website hadn't mentioned that there'd be a corpse in the background (but perhaps a website calling itself *Best Gore* didn't hold itself to the highest journalistic standards, phantom-Rose would have said) — and oh God no, never again.

He had typed a long-winded suicide note where he looked forward to better things. The letter became irreverent and manic whenever it risked seeming treacly.

>< >< ><

As promised, he'd uploaded his story collection to various marketplaces and offered it for free.

One night, over a year later, she looked up the collection online and found hundreds of ratings, reviews and discussions. On Kindle, it was one of the top 50 most downloaded items in the free anthology category. There were links to Reddit and 4Chan that she left unopened. There was even fan art.

She ignored it, she pretended otherwise, but it was there.

There was a whole universe that'd been created, that clicked and churned ceaselessly.

I'm A Good Person, I Mean Well
and I Deserve Better

ROBIN LOOKED NICE tonight. She was dressed in an effervescent dress that, while not tight-fitting, at least acknowledged the appeal of her petite form and hearty bust. She had applied a little bit of make-up and eyeshadow, too. Bryce preferred the au naturale look, but the eyeshadow gave her a hint of an edge, a little sass. She had pretty eyes, and the eyeshadow feminized her, tilted the appeal of her androgynous vulpine beauty back firmly to the feminine side of things. Her hair was done the usual way, pinned-up in the back, which he liked. He liked the crook in her nose, the nose that most girls (her included) probably grew up feeling ashamed and insecure about. An asshole could say it looked a bit like there was an extra bone in place of where the cartilage should be. But everything about her was decisively cute, and her nose was that kind of charming imperfection that, in their brief foray into dating, he'd firmly identified her with and maybe even fetishized a little bit.

She wore rouge lipstick, noticeable but modest. Red was the color of lust, he'd read in an article, and that bode well of her interest, he thought. That, and that she agreed to a fourth date with him, this time an unabashed date, a full meal and everything. But he tried not to get too ahead of himself. That was emotionally dangerous. His mind was always analyzing the odds. Rouge and a dinner date. Good signs. But this was an unusually early dinner, 6:15 pm, more befitting of the senior citizen early birds than a couple in their mid-thirties. And they were the earliest of the early birds — there were literally no other guests, and they'd arrived at the weird liminal phase where the wait staff were still setting up a bit and were resentful that you cut down on their time to prepare. But maybe he shouldn't read too much into the time, maybe she just liked eating early — hell, he liked eating early — but his mind refused to turn off, always the dating thresher, churning in input and spitting out conclusions.

He met her there, which was always a smart bet. Don't want to waste needed conversation talking points on the pre-dinner repartee. That's time you can't control — imagine having to wait for a table for an hour and spending all that awkward, uncomfortable, impatient time together.

So he was already there when she arrived, sitting at the table. When she arrived, he bounded up and pulled her chair back for her. It was simultaneously genuine yet ironic, which was a fairly good description of how they both had separately represented themselves on their *Kettle of Fish* pages.

"Ahhh, what a gentleman," she smiled, ironic in her use of gentleman and what a hoary cliché pulling out a lady's chair was, but genuine in appreciating his interest and his effort, at least, to impress. "Pulling out all the stops, are we? Watch out!"

"Hah, you know it."

They made small talk for a bit and he pointed out the drinks menu. She perused it and he didn't say much. Let her read it, he thought, but that was displacement. He just didn't know what to say. That was one of his bigger fears: not saying enough. He felt he was an interesting person, but too often all that interesting stuff was buzzing around in his mind and he didn't let it out. Dating and sharing and intimacy didn't come naturally to him; he didn't feel comfortable with it until he knew he wasn't being judged, that he was loved and appreciated. In a sense, he put the cart before the horse: he needed the adulation, and then he felt comfortable with the sharing intimacy; that women expected sharing, intimacy and the connection before the adulation was a fatal lapse in his emotional sequencing.

"Did you know" — oh boy, goddamn the man who begins a conversation with "did you know?" or "know what's interesting?" — "that the word 'Jeep' comes from the abbreviation used in the Army for the General Purpose vehicle, G.P." She worked as an analyst for a car company. "Yup, you can take that fact into the boardroom."

"Promotion, here I come!"

"Hah, yep. Thank the Internet and a slow day of work."

He had to be careful. Dead air tended to turn him into an Interesting Fact Generator. Could be good for a cocktail party, but no girl wanted to fuck the human embodiment of Wikipedia.

"Well," she drawled. "Let me one-up you."

"Okay, okay, I'm game, let's hear it."

"So, you know what the 'Q' in Q-tip stands for?"

"Nope," he said with metaphorical open arms.

"Quality," she said, throwing up her hands like a rap baller.

"Well look at that."

The drinks came and, this was pivotal, after she went in for her first sip after they cheers-ed, she smiled upwardly from her drink at him in a way that froze his insides and made his heart stop. Inadvertently — it apparently not being enough that she agreed to a fourth date — he'd subconsciously been dedicating mental processing power to monitor all the signs she was into him. Hair teasing, forthcoming laughter, steady eye contact: running the metrics behind his eyes like an undercover economist. But he needn't worry. That look sealed the deal. It was a look of joy, of the pure sensual pleasure of enjoying another's company and being open to the electricity of good companionship. It relieved him and unnerved him. He wished he could change his reductive thinking — she was a human being, a great human being, for God's sake, he should stop with these objectifying comparisons — but all he could think was that he was a dog who finally catches the car and doesn't know what to do with it.

He wanted to tell her that he really liked her, and that he wanted to save this moment in time in case something went wrong later in the date, so he could backtrack to this moment and start again. Like the beginning of a stage in a videogame and he'd stocked up infinite lives. Of course, if he said that, he'd fuck everything up, and, accepting the logic of his own premise, would have to jump back in time to right before he said those words.

He sipped his cocktail — gin and bitters and lime and sugar and a fancy name that added $5 to the price — and he liked it but that didn't even register because he was acting like drinking was something that just got into the way of talking.

"Know what else is interesting?" He said, kicking himself mentally for it — he hadn't even swallowed fully before he started.

"No, tell me," and he detected a less enthusiastic reception than before.

"Well, I don't want to just spout out interesting facts, but bear with me, this one is interesting."

"Raising the stakes. You better deliver," and she leaned in in such a way that the menu pressed against her dress to make a steeple of cleavage. He never averted his gaze from her eyes. It was just a lovely detail he noticed in his periphery.

"Well, do you know that they never toast in Hungary?"

"No."

"Well, and I don't know if this is true, but it's what I've been told—"

"Duly noted. Told, you mean on the streets?"

"Yes, of course, the streets, the streets are always talking about Hungary." He was performing that weird obligation to generate witty repartee, and he found it a little bit annoying and disruptive when she joined in. This was a solo act. He was doing his best to even remember the factoid, which was hazy and half-remembered. Was it that they only didn't toast over beer? Eh.

"Well, after the Hungarian revolution against the Hapsburg Empire in like, the 1850's, the Austrian army leaders executed the Hungarian generals, and they celebrated it with a toast. So, from then on, Hungarians never toast when they drink beer."

"Interesting, interesting." She made a face that registered her appreciation, like she was storing the information. "What was the Hapsburg Revolution?"

He sipped and shrugged. "I don't know. If they want me to know, they need to tie it in with some beer or food-related fact or something."

"Obviously," she smiled.

The performance ritual of repartee was draining his mental battery. It's interesting, how things are considered mildly unpleasant, and then something comes along to drop the end out from under you and make things so much worse. Here he was, juggling being charming with a mild headache; his mild self-hatred of his dating game-playing and his wavering about whether dating as an activity was even worth the effort; his desire just to declare his affections for her and move onto the next steps; and all the other tests to his endurance, when ... the bottom fell out.

The mysteries of the human body. There's a nesting fullness you feel when you need to move your bowels, but that's usually the key — fullness. A fullness, like a shifting tractor trailer. There's weight there. Not this. This was a water hammer in a sewer pipe. This was a 7th grade Earth Science lecture on potential to kinetic energy. This was his asshole puckering up with flop sweat in the midst of turning into a swamp. This was the type of shit you fooled yourself into thinking you could control with the proper positions you assumed and the seasoned contortions of your asshole, but in reality you knew it was going to come out hot and burning and for a second you'd think, Jesus, what have I been doing with my life?

His stomach gurgled. He kicked himself for his early-, mid-, and late-morning coffees, for those unneeded shots of vanilla-hazelnut-flavored chemicals he'd added to them. The sour sludge inside him turned his hunger off like a light switch. There's that pyramid of needs. Hunger, water, those are on there at the bottom, the base of the pyramid. Young guys will act like sex is there as well. Look lower down, in the footnotes section. There's a caveat: "The need to shit rules out all other needs."

He yearned to return to the gentle patter of conversation he'd established. Like an old man on his death bed, how foolish he was for not realizing how good he'd had it not so long ago.

He was a strategic man by nature. Especially where something important was concerned — a job, school, a significant other — he had the tendency to break down every action into a play-by-play like a coked-out John

Madden, until it was usually just him alone and a trusted friend hashing out and debating what exactly happened, long after the opportunity came, went or passed and everyone else had moved on.

One of his long-standing life hacks: never go to the restroom before you order food. This didn't just apply to dates. It's inefficient, and the other party will be impatiently waiting for you to return and be doubly attentive to the passage of time.

He resumed saying something, under the quixotic delusion that he could flag down a waiter and put in a food order before he had to take the bathroom out of commission.

Nope, there'd be none of that.

"I'll be right back," a line which, if their relationship survived some length of time, was destined to become an inside-joke euphemism.

He retired to the restroom before they even had gotten dinner menus. *Before they had even gotten dinner menus!* He thought of that word, *retired*, and it seemed apt, because after this he'd have to take a nap and perhaps retire from ever showing his face in public again.

He navigated his way to the restroom, a couple members of the staff intuiting the urgency just beneath the placid mask of his face and pointing him in the right direction

Le Latrines, the sign on the door read, complying with that unwritten rule that every restaurant above a sufficient level of hipness was required to have some whimsical name for the place where people pissed, shat, farted, ralphed, applied and re-applied make-up and maybe did coke.

He twisted the knob on the door and it didn't turn. Oh god. Oh god. Occupied. And it's only one stall.

One stall, for every man, woman, and child. Providing one unisex stall should be a crime against restaurant design. Under almost all circumstances, he wouldn't have the guts to shit in a unisex stall, only allowing himself to pee and maybe later squeak out silent farts at the dinner table if the pressure got too bad. He could just never bring himself to defecate where there's only one unisex stall; the pressure was just too much for him. He'd immediately imagine a line of innocent, angelic American Apparel models lining up right outside.

He remembers his own traumatic experience, at a Barnes & Noble many years ago. Barnes & Noble must have known that every customer secretly resented it for some reason or another, and tried to appease them by providing a separate bathroom for men and women. But not the Barnes & Noble he'd ventured into. No, not that Barnes & Noble. This must have been a closing Barnes & Noble, where management said "fuck it, we'll show these ingrates, make it a unisex bathroom."

He'd never forget the look on that beautiful woman's face after he came out of that Barnes & Noble bathroom — her pixie-ish dirty blonde hair, her button nose, her button-up shirt that looks so cute on girls of her type, her angular cheeks, flush with rouge, the nose ring stud, that little indication that in other circumstances she'd be cool and understanding and open-minded — and that, that unconscious twitching of her nose, that look of dread and embarrassment and shame that registered knowing that this filthy creature in front of her had just befouled the space she was entering, a creature of honeyed charms and fairy dust entering a labyrinth of emanations bespeaking pestilence and contamination.

He twisted the knob before him, again, and ... it opened, albeit slowly, with another person opening the door on the other side. She was trying to twist the door open from the other side at the same time and they'd been working at cross purposes.

"Sorry about that," he nodded and slid past her.

"My bad." She wore flannel and had night black hair. Other than that, he couldn't see much of her, but she seemed nice and big-hearted.

He made his way in, and, lo and behold, he was wrong in his estimation. There were actually two bathroom stalls! One with a ... what the fuck is this? There was this trend in restaurants to convey the crucial information of MAN or WOMAN through quirky signage. That may have made sense at certain themed bars; if you see a male pirate or a mermaid on the bathrooms at a seafood restaurant, well, that's pretty intuitive.

But here. One room labeled Mars, with the Mars symbol — a circle with an arrow pointing northeast in red — and another door labeled Venus, with the Venus symbol — a circle with a cross below it — in light blue.

God, he had to be a fucking astrologist here in order to take a shit. Which was which? What other purpose is there of signage than to be clear and direct? Literally, the point is to convey a message clearly. That's why a STOP sign reads "STOP," instead of representing a cleverly illustrated parable of a before, present, and after situation.

Venus rhymes with penis? Could that be it? No, he felt that the jutting arrow was a proxy for the penis, and even if that was wrong, society still felt comfortable gendering colors, and light blue usually denoted the feminine.

He tried Mars, and it opened.

His asshole almost gasped in release upon entry. There was an undeniable rush, a dampening of the back of his underwear. Why? Did his body just think that when the button comes undone and the pants come out, it can just spray shit everywhere like a fire hydrant? Mind over matter, mind over matter. His bowels protested with each second, and in the anticipation of impending release was an unspoken euphoria and satisfaction that society dare not name.

>< >< ><

Alexander, he decided. He would call himself Alexander. It made him feel smart and cultured, and tales of conquest and adventure were the only things he ever enjoyed about high school. Alexander the Great had conquered, like, the entire known world at the time. Just went on in and rolled all over people. That would be his inspiration.

He took long, reflective pauses as he walked the several miles in the fading natural light toward the Deer & Fox, as befitting a conqueror debating his options. He put his fingers to his chin, softly stroking a beard that was not there, just staring off into the distance. One second, five seconds, or thirty seconds: it made no difference, he wasn't actually thinking anything. Just assuming the position.

He crested the hill overlooking his destination. Alexander, formerly Steven Acevedo —the unloved, overworked and underappreciated former line cook at the Deer & Fox — prepared to stride into battle. Let the history books forget how he arrived this day, the undignified means of last resort: literally walking several miles along the shoulder of Route 6. Let the royal decrees leave that out: Steven's broke ass seeking his revenge on foot, all those cars full of spoiled housewives giving him dirty looks because walking in suburbia is for poor people and because God forbid this town have a working bus system.

Steven's car had been out of commission for over two months now. His car troubles were a source of inexhaustible amusement to the rest of the staff. "Is his car back on the road yet," someone in the kitchen would ask, as if he wasn't right there. "Close," someone would reply. "It's in the driveway." Even the people who didn't speak English would join in on that. It was a joke to everyone, from the manager — who is supposed to be fair and impartial, who is supposed to put a stop to that sort of harassment; and maybe if you fucking paid me a little more I'd have the car on the road and be able to make it on time — to the pretty hostesses, to the others in the kitchen who were supposed to be his family.

He'd laugh off the jokes at first and tease back, but he wasn't good at it; he was too transparent, it was obvious how much it burned him up. He'd liked working as a cook, he read books about the industry; there was supposed to be a sense of camaraderie between all the staff. And he'd been there longer than most (granted: there was a high turnover), but there didn't seem to be enough deference; a couple of people teased him and all the new guys thought it became the thing to do, the bypass for bonding.

And then, to think, all the people he'd bum rides from quit or leave town in a matter of weeks, and he has no way to get on time other than the impossible, terrible bus system, and he's late enough times and he's fired, just like that. All those motherfuckers still talking about him, no doubt. He doesn't have anything: no education, no family, no nothing, except that job. And where were they? They were supposed to be family, right? They sweat together, hustled together, bled and burned their skins together.

And he was good at it, goddammit. As much as everything about it sucked, he loved that place.

He looked down at hands outstretched before him and watched the forms take shape. He had what appeared to be an undulating baseball poking out just beneath his skin, cresting and falling like a lapping wave. He pivoted and flexed his sore right thumb. Black mist sprayed out with each flex. It reminded him of a cartoon choo-choo train belching smoke. It even made a faintly audible gusting sound, like a stuffed nose on a winter's day. He didn't know if he chose to make that noise, willed it, or if whatever was allowing him to do this had access to some remote memory of a cartoon choo-choo train and fashioned this to amuse him. He didn't care, really.

He'd woken up one day having already come to terms with it.

He'd been fired ten days ago. He'd spent the first weekend getting drunk and feeling sorry for himself, cursing himself, cursing this place. Monday, he found himself instinctively waking up for his morning shift, as if he needed to be somewhere.

Then one day that week he looked in the mirror and saw one of those composite posters looking back at him. There are those posters, he didn't know how they were made or how to describe them, but those posters where one larger identifiable image was made up of several smaller images of the same person in different poses. Half the time, the subject of the poster was Bob Marley, for some reason. He didn't know why.

Well, that had been him one morning. Except the smaller images weren't him, but a shoulder comprised of egg-shaped black orbs, beady eyes of succulent blueberries, a tornado of angular, writhing shapes for a torso. He had opened his mouth in surprise, convinced this was a dream but still playing along, and his tongue was an oversized squamous brick yet still somehow fit fine in his mouth. Tendrils of thick grain — cookie dough, he thought — pushed their way out from under his nails, flapping a bit like Spanish moss in a breeze. They extended down to the grubby floor of his basement apartment. When they reached the floor, the tendrils flowed back upward, unseen, through his fingers, burning a bit like fluid through an IV tube, traversing through canals in his fingers and arms he never knew he had, or never had before.

That morning, he'd made five strands of finger-dough rise up and vibrate like slithering snakes. The egg-shaped black orbs underneath his shoulders bore no faces but he knew they were directing their attention to him. His nails painlessly burst open with appendages the color of cobalt, the shape of carrots, the texture of glass. Then they retracted and his old nails were there again.

The constituent parts of his new body had explained everything to him. They'd done that trick with his nails because it knew he'd think it was cool. It'd made him feel comfortable. Wolverine, bitches. Snchict!

Sometimes dreams do come true.

He stared at the restaurant. Kind of pathetic, he thought, all this power for such an unworthy target. In movies, to show a character is good, mature and above-it-all, the character will have the opportunity to take revenge and get his justice and then, nah, pass. Like, saying "you're beneath me."

Like anyone would do that. That's why those are movies, and this is real life.

Two pillars of crooked bone protruded up out of his shoulders, tapped three times — click, click, click — crossed each other like whirling scimitars, and popped back into place. That was cool, like he was a super soldier or something, a samurai.

He wanted an adjustment to his face, something to scare the shit out of people right before he killed them — wanted his mouth to spread out like the wings of a manta ray, little suckers and teeth embedded into his checks. But he couldn't will that, for some reason.

He went down on his knees like this was the culmination of a life-long quest, like he was nothing but a modest servant fulfilling the calling of a higher power, seeking to set order to a universe gone wrong.

His elbows shook and clicked and chattered like they were filled with rattling dice.

This was going to be great.

>< >< ><

This was going to be awful.

He forced himself to complete the task as quickly as possible. There wasn't even that dreadful couple of seconds of anticipation, when the bathroom door closes and the other occupants enjoy their last seconds of calm before the embarrassing multi-tonal timbre of horrific noises. Between the time he closed the stall and the time he started, someone listening in from outside could be excused for wondering if he'd even had time to take his pants off before the wholesale slaughter began.

His cacophony of embarrassing bathroom noises right now were bad enough that he wanted to ask his father about stomach problems running in the family. It sounded like an old man coughing up his soup.

Oh god, what relief.

He didn't even look in the toilet afterward. That was a first. Maybe that signaled something, growing up, step one into overcoming his weird phobia and this obsession of his. The bowel movement had gone on for so long and with such intensity that he half-expected the contents to ascend vertically and carry him straight up to the ceiling, like Scrooge McDuck astride his overflowing lucre.

With his bowels released, he felt a dormant gurgle of hunger pangs, as if the body stored pre- and post-digested food in the same area. Pro tip to remember: whatever you do, do not, under any circumstances, come out of the bathroom and mention that you have just become hungry.

He made sure he was as clean as possible, which accounted for his excessive flushing. There were certain tips and tricks he lived by. One of them was a commitment to being a devoted over-flusher. He flushed so much whenever he used the bathroom that he worried that one day some environmentalist would overhear him and accuse him of wasting water ("fuck off, go after someone who uses a humidifier," he already had his riposte prepared). Better to be safe than sorry: the only thing worse than having to be occupied in a toilet stall on a date is to be identified as the person responsible for clogging the toilet. He always flushed post-movement, and then after every 2-3 toilet paper deposits. He figured that should be common practice, though more often than not someone sharing the bathroom with him when he was washing his hands at the sink would give him a sideways glance, borne of curiosity, of this unassuming man who deemed it appropriate to flush 3-4 times. What horrors had taken place behind those closed doors, he imagined them thinking.

He could nod in agreement with his Green friends and "like" articles online about the need for conservation, but a small plot of virgin Amazonian rainforest was torn asunder for the exclusive use of his asshole.

Oh my god.

He felt the expected stimulus one expects while wiping. But outside his ass, not inside. There was a sensation that should not be. While parting his matted posterior hair, there was, enmeshed within and between, the tactile sensation of plowing through a nugget of hot mud. No, no it can't be. The human body could not allow this, no matter how hairy or overgrown he was back there. Millions of years of human evolution should provide for, at the very least, the human body not providing its own hair hammock for feces to rest in.

Oh my god.

This date was over. It just had to be. How could he recover from this? And no matter how diligently he worked at cleaning himself, could he ever be sure? Any time she wrinkled her nose or smelled her entree, could he rest assured that she was not aware of the rancidity wafting between them? How many times would he need to check his feet to make sure no feces-encrusted toilet paper dangled from his shoes? Or — God — worse, that there were no smelly remnants on his clothing.

It wasn't fair. They were so aligned. It couldn't be, it's just not fair, that this was to befall him on this day, on this date, with this woman, who otherwise should be so perfect for him. He was a good person who tried; he was good-looking, 6'3", broad-shouldered and well-groomed.

But this was unrecoverable. This was a dumpster fire. This was shitting the bed.

No, worse — shitting yourself.

>< >< ><

Hoodie up over his head like a cloak, arms outstretched in the middle of the dining area. Alexander stood between tables; a server he didn't recognize leaned to the right carrying a jug of ice water. He intuited that she rolled her eyes as she made her way around him, made a vowel-less expression and a face reading "some fucking people," that insta-expression that servers made whenever they were briefly interrupted in their duties, that immediately dissipated as they continued their mad scramble dash that was the dinner time rush.

"Sorry," he said meekly, instinctively cowered, and immediately regretted it.

"Excuse me! Everybody!" he bellowed. "Everybody!" he called out again, this time pointing down at himself while he spoke, as if it wasn't clear where the focus of the attention should be. "Every...BODY! Errr ... Now that I have your attention ... In our life and times, there comes a time when enough is enough. Where there's only so much you can take...."

>< >< ><

"Ohmygod, ohmygod." He scrubbed at himself, that hopeless scrubbing you do when you get a fresh stain on a new white button-down and you know it won't work but just hope it does, this time. He even ran out and dotted toilet paper with sink water. He was, quite literally, rinsing his ass out while on a date.

>< >< ><

The restaurant-goers looked at Alexander blankly. Some checked in for the beginning of his spiel, concluded it was something they wanted no part of, shook their heads and went back to their meals. *Crazy panhandlers in restaurants now?* Others kept their gaze, curious but hesitant. Other tables chatted excitedly about the upcoming, unexpected show.

"Only so much you can take. This place, this restaurant, it's treated me so badly. So, so ... unjustly."

"Save it for Yelp!" a girl's voice rang out from the back.

Laughter.

"Quick, someone get that guy a refill," someone else shouted from the same vicinity, his joke not landing as well as the Yelp Girl's.

Alexander paused, then continued. "How much injustice, how much embarrassment, how much wrongness, is one person expected to take?"

"So what he's asking is — 'who's coming with me?'" More laughter. He heard competing laughter and interpretations from the audience, some people repeating the line in a Jim Brewer space-cadet haze, others adopting the original version's pathetic, intense neediness.

"What justice is —" He felt overheated and small, pathetic even in his moment of glory.

>< >< ><

Bryce continued to clean himself off. He disentangled some small pebbles, shards of sharp crustifed shit that reminded him of cleaning out specks of glass from a broken light bulb. Had there been times when he felt discomfort while sitting, thinking maybe he was sitting on his keys, when in reality it was the gravel-like friction of accumulated shit debris? Could such a thing be possible? Could it be possible that he was someone who showered every day, made reasonable efforts to live up to basic standards of hygiene, yet found himself in such a situation?

Come to think of it, anal hygiene and cleanliness is something no one ever taught him or talked to him about. He remembers being a little boy and complaining about being itchy back there, and his mother explaining how you need to make sure you're clean back there, otherwise the "stuff" (as she called it) back there will make you itch. Were there other life lessons he didn't know about? Should he be clipping himself back there, much the way some men clip their pubes? Should he get a dedicated razor?

>< >< ><

No one laughed, no one catcalled anymore, not after he covered his face with his hands, gnawed on his fingers, and spit and flung wildly as much liquid outpourings as he could.

The response started as laughter and coursed swiftly into horror. "Jesus Fucking Christ," someone said.

"Manager, manager, someone get the manager! This isn't funny, I'm having a pleasant meal, this isn't the time for ... this performance art," someone stammered.

The restaurant had windows that allowed some of the remaining natural light to stream in. On the upper corner, where the ceiling met the wall, hovered a red, humanoid creature. It made its entrance without fanfare, without acknowledgment. Just slowly, someone spotted it, and pointed it out to someone else, who pointed it out to someone else, until the restaurant was abuzz with excited chatter and cackles, but of the kind that is obviously tense. A loud scream or shriek would put people over the edge.

"Ahhh, ladies and gentleman and assorted assholes of all types, our first guest," Alexander stretched out his hands like a celebrity television host. "For my first trick, a blast from the past, a special guest from *Ghouls and Ghosts.* I'm sure some of you stupid hipsters remember that game, right?"

The creature was just there, as if treading water, but in the air. It stood maybe four feet tall, but that was hard to tell as it was not standing upright. It had deep red, rough skin, with light blue bracelets on both ankles and on both wrists, and oversized gray bat wings, the breadth of which probably matched the creature's height. The color coordination was odd and unexpected and was the subject of a couple quick observations and jokes. What also caught everyone's eye was its nudity — other than those bracelets, it was entirely naked, yet it had no discernable genitalia, but only a rounded nub, like a Ken doll.

It moved, but inorganically, in a pattern. Its short, hooked arms and legs kicked in-and-out, its wings flapped rhythmically, but there was absolutely no variation in the pumping neither of its limbs nor its wings. It was on auto-repeat. And it just hung there, in space, with no whooshing of air or sound coming off its flapping. Its face was rough, its mouth a perplexing gash somewhere between grimace and smile, and its nose was bulbous and uncomfortably hooked. It just stayed up there, pumping its limbs, pumping its wings.

Someone clapped and hooted. "Yeah!" a crowd of guys yelled.

"Do Mario next!" a girl who knew nothing about video games yelled, the equivalent of yelling "Free Bird."

"Bowzer!"

"Bowzer!," Alexander yelled back in a pitch and intensity that was all wrong for jocularity. "What else do you retards want!"

Somehow, more than the grisly display and unexplainable creature flying overhead, the use of the politically incorrect term 'retard' did the most to signal to the crowd that something was dangerously off-course.

"So if you remembered, when the knight in *Ghouls and Ghosts* got hit, his armor would fly off! And when he got hit without armor, he turned into bones. Let's see what happens if one of you morons gets hit."

The red demon assumed a sitting position and floated in the air, moving horizontally toward the center of the restaurant, still well above all the diners. This was too much now, and a huge exhalation went out from the crowd, now could be heard "oh my gods," and loved ones clutching each other tighter to reveal that they were scared, this was no longer fun or funny. The creature's expression never changed. It moved its arms in a robotic, almost jaunty fashion, and swooped down in an arc like a pendulum.

Still flying, but now at ground level, people shouted and shrieked. Some were stunned and confused at how, despite being closer, they could not make out much more detail about this unwanted guest. It hovered close to the ground, in a straight uninterrupted line, as if it was taking off on a runway. Then its direction arced, as if it was taking off to the ceiling again.

It made its way toward a table of three, and it collided with the unfortunate, most smartly under-dressed hipstery kid of the bunch. Most people instinctively averted their gaze from what they suspected would be the undignified, chaotic crunch and tumbling of bones and bodies. The creature didn't even register the collision, the arc of its flight completely unaffected.

The poor kidult, though, registered the blow, toppled backwards off his chair, and quite literally exploded into chunky fragments. Tables overturned, the red sauce in the pasta appetizer got a new thickener, the drinks new bloody garnishes.

"AND SO IT BEGINS!"

Alexander worked himself into a frenzy, a rabid dog. No, worse than a rabid dog. He contorted his back and his joints, head-banging, a man in perpetual spasm. He gnawed and raged, tore and ripped. A substance the shape of bologna and the consistency of caviar extended out from his breast. He torn it out and threw it to the horrified onlookers, where it somehow splattered, shattered and rolled into four separate pieces, their momentum never stopping, picking up speed, the velocity of their movement the same whether it rolled or used its still-growing but still powerful lunging legs. *Four pieces of sentient, Spam-like meat,* Krystal thought, the only one of her party able to process what was enveloping before her. But those thoughts were gone when the creature was fully upon her, squishy and suffocating, and there was nothing sharp about it, then unbearable pain and her top half skidding along the greased floor, recognizing her separated lower half by the tight Theory jeans she'd just bought yesterday.

A star-faced mole jumped atop the sentient strips of meat and hissed.

It dipped the prongs of its face into her bloodied wound and, contented, it scampered off to further its feasting.

More and more of his minions were assembling. An army. *An Army of One,* he thought, and that seemed right, since they originated from within him, from the pieces he tore off himself, from the sheer determination of his iron will. A floating pineapple of eyeballs. The star-faced mole: that was an inventive one. A McDonaldland Grimace in a Viking helmet. Head crabs.

Bodies ascending and descending and dividing into uneven quarters. The chaos and abandon was too much and too unplanned — he wanted to hold some of the chaos in abeyance, understand exactly what he was working with, try and plan certain punishments for certain people. Truth was, he just acted; he had no idea what he would be conjuring up. Hell, he didn't even initially plan for any of the customers to get hurt, it just happened; a sentiment he'd accepted as he stared at the fresh corpse of a hipster beardo, eyes-bugged out, a white gelatinous square the texture of tripe wrapped tightly around his mouth.

Why did he feel bad, of all things? He should move beyond that. That should be beneath him. Morality was for other people.

Out of the corner of his eye he recognized Manny, the head chief, bolting straight out from the kitchen and toward the front doors.

He extended an open hand toward his closest minions — dark-brown, round creatures the size and shape of bowling balls, covered in cross-cutting, viciously sharp quills. They even rolled like bowling balls. Three of them were rapaciously chewing on what, at some point, had been a face. In a moment of accentuated detail, he saw one cleanly chomp off several fingers from a disembodied hand, make an awkward face following the crunch of what must have been a wedding ring, constrict its face as it made a hearty swallow, and reveal what may have been a smile.

"Critters," he called them unthinkingly. "Attack!" And he pointed at a fleeing Manny. Manny turned back for the briefest of moments, saw the finger directing the attack upon him, and resumed bolting, emitting something like a guttural yelp.

The creatures continued their chewing. The three of them formed almost a triangle. They shook while they ate like gulls imbibing live fish.

"Attack!" he directed again. The creatures continued unabated and undisturbed.

Even among the ruckus, Alexander heard a loud smack and knew it was Manny, falling hard. His vision was obscured by booths and tables, but he distinctly heard Manny yell, a yell that lessoned in intensity and volume until it sounded like it was coming somewhere more remote, maybe underwater. Alexander adjusted his position to see what had happened, to find a hazy outline of Manny, visible through the translucent sheen of whatever jellyfish-like creature he'd disappeared into. The creature sat with the repose of a giant toad, even as protesting hands pushed tiny stalagmite-like ripples through the base of its head. A few seconds later, some adjustment, and ambiguous motions later, the movement stopped, the mass of what was Manny subtracted, like sand from an hourglass.

Luck smiled upon Alexander. How could he be in the wrong, when everything was now so right, when fate convened to give him these powers and make sure his harassers got their just rewards? He'd commend that creature, promote it somehow, even though he knew not what that meant and feared they cared not a whit for or about him.

He saw a tall blonde girl outside the restaurant, looking in, pounding on the glass, sheer terror and desperation on her face. She pounded, and lost resolve, descending for a moment into a crescendo of tears as her friends were digested before her.

"Get her!" he yelled as a general command.

If there was any discernable change in the arrangement of the battlefield, he was unaware.

"Get her. Make sure she does not escape!" Somehow, the woman outside clued into what he was saying or directing, and ran.

She escaped out of sight.

"Get her! You let her escape!" He pondered how many other people had simply escaped, and concluded it must have been many. This was chaos, and he and his minions appeared to be on different wavelengths. He wanted swift, organized justice. They seemed content just being fed.

"More food. Food. In the kitchen. Plenty of food. Live food."

He hadn't taken a tally on how many of his minions had been wreaking havoc, but he suspected plenty had left the restaurant already to satisfy their own devices. There was certainly less commotion than when he started. He looked for the star-faced mole — that was his favorite, the one he was most impressed with — and couldn't locate it. There were panes of broken glass and open doors. As to make the abandonment all the more obvious and embarrassing, there was a green, viscous trail way of slime leading from the center of the dining room straight out of the front entrance.

The Critters were still here — one was face-deep, or perhaps body-deep, since the entire creature seemed to consist solely of a face — its *Sonic*-like quills cresting out of the inner cavity of a corpse like a chest-shark. Another sat on its haunches, its stubby legs sticking out, not a care in the world, perhaps even vibrating as it burped through its meal.

He walked closer to the Critters — they for some reason becoming his lodestar — a feeling of oppressive ineffectuality gathering in his chest. He accidentally kicked the soft frame of an over-sized slug. Its delineated head raised and twisted 360 degrees; its head was that of a horrifyingly real, too-scaly and too-green *Hypnotoad*. Its head lowered down and it ignored him, though a weird ambient slushing noise emanating from its midsection became temporarily louder.

He feared it would strike him. He tried to look casual and avoided eye contact.

What have we here?

Wedged in the corner underneath a table, where the booth meets the wall. A quivering, shivering young lady. Well, not that young, more like youngish, maybe in her thirties. He assumed a squatting position, reached underneath, felt the firm, impressive outline of her lower body, and began dragging her out. She screamed and kicked, jamming one of his fingers. It took him longer to pull her out than it should have. He wrapped both his arms around her ankles and pulled, but she was stronger than she let on and held onto the edge of the booth. His minions heard the tussling and turned in his direction (with the exception of the floating pufferfish, which continued staring vacantly ahead, drifting listlessly).

He tugged hard enough, hard enough that her hands gave way and she slid on her back out from under the booth. He tugged so hard that he fell back, hard, on his ass, like an obese woman crashing through a lawn chair. Christ, he landed so hard, with such emphasis on his ass, he half-expected this was a comedy bit and he'd just landed in a pie or dog shit or something.

From her back, she launched herself forward and rained punches down on the bridge of his nose. With his hands now covering his face, she took the opportunity and bolted up and ran.

She shrieked, turned and surveyed the confusing, intimidating landscape. Overcome with nausea, sensory overload — soft round organs, bright streaky blood, violent, puncturing angles — and ran to the first opening that was unguarded. The kitchen.

"Follow her. She ran into the kitchen. Follow her, there is more back there. Food.

"But don't eat her. I want her for myself."

>< >< ><

Bryce looked into the mirror and sighed with a heavy heart. He checked his phone. Twenty-three minutes. He had been in the bathroom twenty-three minutes. What would overcome her first, he wondered, her hunger from waiting, or her repulsion about wondering what could possibly take him twenty-three minutes in the toilet. Maybe her revulsion canceled her hunger out? Wishful thinking. He half-expected to find out that she left. Maybe she thought he bailed. God, can you imagine that? Shitting for such an inhumanly long length of time that your date can rationally, plausibly conclude that it's more likely that you abandoned her than you were just fulfilling an unfortunate human need.

Maybe it'd be better if she did leave. Less embarrassing, perhaps, than going out there and seeing her face and coming up with some small talk to deflect the 500-pound floating piece of shit in the punch bowl.

He adjusted himself in the mirror and again liked what he saw. He looked good. This sweater fit him well. His skin was largely blemish-free, his recently shorn hair respectably stylish. He fake-smiled, sighed again, washed his hands like he was about to perform an appendectomy, and made his way out.

He left the Men's room (or whatever room he had turned into the Men's room), turned right, and pushed open the sliding door that connected the bathroom area to the dining room. He pushed it partway open until it moved no further. He pushed harder, and it made a little bit of headway. *Okay, be cool,* he thought. The odds of being stuck in the bathroom are pretty slight. God, can you imagine that? As if a twenty minute sojourn into shitting wasn't conspicuous enough, he announces his return by being publicly stuck in the bathroom? He retained his composure and tried again, simultaneously pushing the door and trying to wedge himself through the opening. The door snapped back a little when he transitioned his energy from the pushing to the wedging, and it socked him in the lip, as if throwing a quick jab. His nose and lip burned with that angry, unpleasant energy of an unexpected jolt, like when you smash your funny bone or...well, get hit in the face with a door.

God, can you imagine if I'm bleeding now? Imagine that? Gone in the bathroom for twenty-plus minutes and return BLEEDING. It literally made him laugh. Maybe that'd be for the best, maybe he could say he was mugged in there or something. Can you imagine launching a police investigation to save face? He laughed despite himself.

He kept his head down and made a beeline for where he knew his table to be. He didn't see her sitting where she should be sitting, and he looked down and his stomach burned and sank. *God, could it be possible that she actually did leave?* The burning in his stomach became a stabbing, sinking feeling of despair.

That idea didn't seem so funny anymore.

He slipped on an outrageous pool of liquid and went bowlegged, then slipped forward and went down, hard. He landed on his left shoulder, splayed out on his left side, and closed his eyes. He was in some kind of liquid: water, he assumed. But it smelled bad, almost copper-like. Toilet water. Imagine that. *Imagine I shit myself, spent twenty minutes in the bathroom, bloodied my nose on the door, and then fell in fucking smelly water in front of an entire restaurant. Kill me.* He closed his eyes. *Just let me fucking die here. Let me close my eyes and never wake up.*

No one rushed to help him up, he didn't hear any exhalation of energy from the restaurant-goers, no "whoops" or "ohhhs" or anything. Perhaps they were all in stunned silence, mortified on his behalf.

He turned to his side and looked into what, yesterday, may have formed the base of a perfectly acceptable face. Plucked from its roots, it was now a garish lopsided curlicue of bone, teeth and sinew. He jolted and shot out a hand and my god, the texture of the thing, it was emulsified, the base of it stayed put and sunk into itself. He screamed, stood up —;

and saw all that was before him.

He said nothing, and stared. Somewhere in the back of his mind, in the smarter part of his subconscious, he recalled a quote. One death is a tragedy, a million is a statistic. All this, laid before him, all deathly silent but there, all there, all these people and their derivative parts. The thick wire framed glasses of a guy he recognized had been sitting next to them. Several such glasses, actually; Clark-Kent styled glasses had obviously been popular at this hipstery-eatery, there were so many varieties: broken ones, bloodied ones, some still dangling from faces. He registered the gallows humor but didn't laugh. He just turned back around. He wanted to slowly walk into the bathroom and blow his brains out, but he didn't have a gun and he couldn't move.

He looked back over his shoulder. A green, hulking creature, gait of a gorilla, all strong shoulders and long arms, dragged the relatively well-preserved corpse of what appeared to be a teenaged boy. The creature dragged the dead boy to a certain, inexplicable point, and then, with three-foot arms outstretched, launched him up over the banister to the top floor of the restaurant. There wasn't the loud thud you'd expect, but rather a soft bristling of vegetation, like the body had landed in a nest.

The creature lumbered across the room, in no rush, to do the same with another body.

"Robin," he called out. "Robin! Robin! Robin, are you here!?" If he'd thought about it rationally, he wouldn't have done it. There was no doubt this creature was already aware of his presence, and with that strength, could easily snap him in two.

The creature registered his presence for a second or two, and then dumbly continued its task. It had a simple, unamused simian look.

"Robin!" he yelled again, this time pivoting in place to yell it across the entire dining hall. "Robin, are you here!?" He heard a loud cracking pop from outside, the sound that Hollywood told him was a hand gun.

Jesus. Somehow, the sound of something so concrete and familiar — Thank you Hollywood, and God Bless America — brought him back to reality. He scanned the bottom floor as comprehensively as he allowed himself to, and saw no sign of Robin or her clothes or anything else identifying. His search became so frantic that, instead of regarding with a sense of wonder the oval slug possessing the face of a monstrous toad, he thought of it as nothing more than a fat, wasteful impediment, an inconvenience.

Maybe she ran away, maybe she got away. He walked toward the closest door, which opened to a hallway which led to the kitchen.

>< >< ><

"Did you ever see the movie *Critters*? Well, did you?"

She nodded, the nod of a trapped victim buying time with a terrorist. She was pinned in the corner, surrounded by this bubbling facsimile of a man, supported by his flanking fan of four vicious-looking, squat creatures. They did look like the creatures from the movie *Critters*. That was the first thing she thought of, too.

"'Crites,' they were called in the movie. They look just like them." Alexander pointed this out to his captive audience. The creatures chattered and stood there, their small limbs and tiny hands folded, their large mouths, row-after-row of sharp and grinding teeth, their cherry-red cat-like eyes.

"Are you a Crite?" he turned and spoke to the nearest creature. "Are you a Crite? Is that where you came from, is that what you are called? I loved that movie as a kid. That has to be what you are."

None of them seemed to respond, maintaining their deathless, voracious gaze. The only difference among them was one of them breathed with a heavy wheeze.

"Someone call the prop department," he joked to no one.

He turned back to face her.

"So what do you think of all this?" he asked her.

She shook her head, unsure of how to answer, but knowing that she had to keep the conversation going. The more he viewed her as someone to talk to, the less likely he was to kill her. It was hard to look at him; the area around his lips looked like bubble wrap fashioned out of pastrami.

"I'm trying to identify all the ... monsters, I guess, that are here. I think I saw one of those plants from Super Mario Brothers before, you know, those red-and-white plants that come out of the green pipes? That was cool." He smiled, and it was horrible, a mass of bleeding caviar rearranging itself into a human expression. "I feel my face changing, and I'm happy about it. I wanted to change my face, and I feel like it's happening. I'm getting stronger, it must be.

"I don't understand why it's so gross, though. I don't like that. Why does it always have to be gross? Why can't it be something beautiful? I can't even see it, but I can just tell it's gross, the way it feels."

He looked down at his hands. They were wider and broader than human hands should be, and it was harder to demarcate the separate fingers. There was a hazy filament of hair catching the light.

"What should we do, guys?" he asked the four Critters standing behind him. Funny, they looked like cheesy props, almost; they looked flat and unreal, like projections on a screen. They didn't seem fully-textured, like there were important details missing, like how they smelled — that's right, come to think of it, they didn't seem to have any discernable smell.

"Even when my fantasies come true, I'm not in control, I guess." His face had changed so much that his expressions weren't readily classifiable. "So, what should we do? To be honest, I don't really want to kill you. I only wanted to get revenge on the people who worked here, and not really, I don't know. I think I just wanted to scare them. I wanted to scare the manager but I didn't even see him today. I don't really know what to do, to be honest."

She nodded slowly, as if she was his confidante and was really objectively weighing his statements. "I understand. It all got out of hand. It's not your fault. You didn't want any of this to happen.

"Can ... can you let me go? I won't tell anyone, I promise. No one would believe me, anyway."

"No, I'm sorry, I can't do that. I mean, I understand what you are saying, I do, and no one would believe you, but I imagine the police are already on their way, and they'll believe what they see with their own eyes."

"You ... can't ... yes, you can do that. But just let me leave."

"No, I'm sorry," he said, but slowly, with the weighing gravity of a henpecked father deciding whether to let his kid borrow his car, like he was asking for forgiveness as the subtext of his refusal.

"Then ... what are you doing with me here."

"I, I don't know. I like you being here, I guess."

He took a step closer to her. He was perhaps a foot away now. "I don't know, I don't plan on, like, I don't know. I like your company though. Do you think maybe you could take your shirt off, actually? I don't know, it might cheer me up or help me think."

She swallowed hard. "Wh-at. I. I. If I do, do you promise to let me go?"

Her attention turned to the entryway and she almost shouted with excitement. There stood Bryce. He just stood there, in plain sight, as if he came to a threshold after entering the doorway and couldn't come any further. He was surveying everything he could — this horror show before him, and the structure of the kitchen he found himself in.

Bryce was bad at estimates, but he was maybe six feet away from them, and felt the heat of boiling water and active pots and pans. Underneath torn vegetables, he saw metal shapes. Hopefully, those were knives.

It took an additional beat for the bubbling mass that was Alexander to turn and face him. He looked disappointed and the air was tense with something other than murder, as if Alexander was an ex-boyfriend trying to keep his composure and sizing up her new lover.

As if on cue, another person-of-sorts joined them in the kitchen. From another entry-way — this one leading from the cold storage room — came another form, making its entrance known with a sound approximating wet towels dropping on to the floor. Its entire aura was imbued with stagnant water — even when it wasn't moving and stood there, staring, there was the sound and scent of tepid water, of slipperiness. It stood about five and a half feet — not particularly imposing — on two webbed feet, with its webbed hands extended slightly horizontally, as if planning to give someone an exaggerated hug. The details of its body were scarce, except that it shone a sickly form of green and its body was slick and long, almost like a seal. The details of its face were even worse, almost as if Bryce needed prescription glasses in order to understand what he was seeing. The face was vaguely humanoid, there were lumpen masses that might have been tentacles, but it was too indistinct to make out. There didn't seem to be any mouth.

Alexander pointed at the new visitor. "'Zombies Ate My Neighbors.' It has to be, right?" He wished he'd actually seen *Creature from the Black Lagoon*, because he knew the fish monster from *Zombies Ate My Neighbors* was inspired by that movie. This was a poor, low-budget facsimile. "Man, I haven't played that game forever, but it has to be."

Bryce seized the opportunity. He grabbed the nearest pot by the handle and lifted it high over his head, ready to bring it down like a hammer. It was heavier than he expected, and the lid fell off with a heavy clunk and narrowly missed his foot. As he arched the pot over his head, he realized why it was so heavy: it was half-filled with boiled water. Miraculously, he lifted the pot fast enough and tilted it just so the water emptied out harmlessly behind his head, although he felt steaming water residue on the bottom of his jeans. Still moving on impulse, he leaped toward Alexander and swung the pot down as hard as he could on top of Alexander's head.

Bryce hit him square on the forehead. The impact wasn't as dramatic as he expected — there was the forcible collision with bone, but also something softer, bone wrapped in marshmallow. Still, Alexander went straight down on his back.

The Critters retained their look of voracious detachment, their mouths still open, their cat-eyes still frighteningly red yet immobile. Then — thunk — Bryce felt a reverberation through the pot. A cruel-looking quill was vibrating, half-deep, into the metal. Jesus, he'd gotten lucky again — if he hadn't been holding the pot at around face-level, that quill would have gone straight through his windpipe.

One of the Critters changed its position and was back on its hind legs. So that was the fucking bastard culprit.

"Fuck you," Bryce screamed, this time swinging the pot like a tennis racket at the big wide target that was this Critter's face. Now that was satisfying — the impact literally lifted the round fat ball of quills and teeth off the ground and sent it on a curving trajectory toward the stovetop.

The other three Critters hissed and growled and made high-pitched noises.

Womp. The fish monster lashed out at one of the Critters with its claws, and one swing was enough to take it out. It followed up with three, identical strikes on the now clearly-dead Critter. It now looked at another one, but its facial expressions didn't change, and its movement was rote and almost mechanical. It swung its arm back again to make another horizontal strike, and as insane as this all was, Bryce could not help but realize that this strike looked identical to the previous strikes, as if this creature had only a certain range of programmable actions and was doomed to a life of infinite repeats.

A quill flew into the mid-section of the fish creature. It flinched and flashed white for a brief moment, and continued moving forward. It was struck with two more quills and it flopped down and died, in a surprisingly efficient and unlabored death. One second it was marching forward, then it was down on its back in a heap, and then it was simply gone.

But that was enough time. When the firing Critter turned around, Robin was already upon it with a sharpened kitchen knife. She sunk the knife into its fleshy stomach. Again, and again, and again, she plunged her knife, and the screaming was almost intolerable, so reminiscent of a pleading, wounded dog or tortured cat. Bryce felt almost sick to his stomach, as if they'd just done something unrepentantly inhumane.

She stopped stabbing it only when it rolled onto its back like a cartoon tortoise.

The last Critter launched itself at Bryce. It made no gestures that indicated it was about to leap. It was just suddenly in the air.

It bit hard into whatever its teeth came in contact with. Unfortunately for it, that whatever was Bryce's trusty hammer-pot. The Critters looked almost like giant brown Koosh balls, and this one played the part as it soared through the air. It landed with aplomb against the industrial-strength refrigerator door.

The creature took a moment to regain itself, then shook itself into convalescence. It bit at the air for whatever reason.

Robin ran beside the struggling creature, kicked it toward the refrigerator door, and slammed the creature between the door, again and again and again, to the point where she was actually able to close the refrigerator door fully while the top part of the creature thrashed and chomped futilely, emitting the same disturbing, dog-like shriek of its stabbed brethren. It spasmed a couple of times, and when the door opened back up, there was a pool of green blood and a distorted mass of gore between its stubby legs and the rest of its body.

Bryce ran over to Robin and pulled her back from the refrigerator. She relaxed in his arms for a moment, then grabbed the pot — now substantially dented — and ran over to the Critter that had first shot the quill at them and which Bryce had subsequently punted across the room. It lay prostrate on its side — from viewing just the fuzzy back of it, it was almost cute, its back looked like an innocent wooly brown bush — but such concerns didn't slow her down at all: she smashed it, again, and again, and again. Three times she smashed it, until she was sure it was dead.

"Robin, I'm so glad you're alive." He ran toward her and noticed that — that green fish creature, it had been here before, right? Where could it have gone? It was gone, just disappeared.

"There — there was a green, fish-like creature-thing there before, right?"

"Right, you're not crazy." She spoke slowly and deeply, catching her breath. Her tone was too brusque, not as warm and relieved as he'd like, if he had his druthers.

He held onto her back, coaxing and comforting her.

"Wait — there's still him ... ," she signaled toward the increasingly-humanoid form of Alexander. His forehead and the area between his eyes were deeply bruised and a lightning bolt scar ran made its way down between his eyebrows. Harry Potter, Bryce thought randomly. Under the bruises, the monster's face had become identifiably and unremarkably human.

"We need to make sure he's dead, we can't take any chances. He caused all of this out there. He's a monster, a literal monster."

"Agreed," Bryce nodded. He took the pot by the handle, hesitated, gave it back to her and took a butcher knife. From the way he held it, you could tell he didn't have a lot of experience cooking chops for himself. He choked up on the handle, holding it more tightly, resolutely.

"Ok," he said, and moved in closer to the recumbent body. Alexander was splayed on his back, arms spread on an invisible crucifix.

Bryce prodded the shape in the left rib cage. The shape groaned but did nothing else. This would be a lot easier if the guy shocked back to life or something, and he could get this over with in the heat of the moment.

"I think, I think he's out cold." Bryce knew that sounded stupid, if he were watching this on a movie screen he'd be screaming "fucking c'mon, man do it!" and then complaining loudly that the witless character was asking for it when things inevitably went awry.

"No. We can't allow him to escape. He needs to die. You saw what he did. He killed all those people. He was going to kill me. He was going to rape me, even. He caused all these ... all these things ... It's a fucking massacre out there." She stopped herself from breaking down completely but exhaustion was clearly eroding her.

"I know." He got down on his knees and straddled the body, chopping knife at the ready.

He didn't know how to bring the knife down. A hard *thwack* into the skull, as if it were a watermelon?

"Can you give me like, a cutting knife?"

She brought him a sharpened blade. *Used for fine cuts*, he thought, which took on a sinister connotation.

He put the blade to the bastard's throat. It helped to think of him like that, a bastard, a murderer, he killed all those people.

"You fucking bastard. You fucking, piece-of-shit murderer." No response. "You, you fucking killer, how could you?" He was speaking unnecessarily loud. Can't this guy wake up or move or something, so he could kill him and pass it off to himself as self-defense? He wished he had a gun, although he'd never shot a gun before in his life and wouldn't even know what to do with one.

"Do it!"

Bryce gracelessly pushed the blade into where the center of the man's throat should be. He envisioned a tactile slice, one quick slash, a controlled seepage of blood, and that's it. Misfire. He put only a quarter of the blade in and found resistance, grimaced — he was committing the throat-slitting equivalent of slowly tearing off a Band-Aid — course corrected and overcompensated, plunging the knife at an awkward angle. Blood sprayed wildly, the knife was partially buried and obscured, like he'd dropped the blade into a cooling cake.

"Aww God. He's dead, he's dead: he has to be dead." He stood up, covered in warm, coppery blood, the opening of the wound actively gurgling.

They stood there, both panting. Several wordless moments passed between them. It was over, he felt. This was a natural concluding point, the curtain to fall, the credits to appear. The weight of the whole day made itself evident, a feeling of nausea and frazzled disconnection came over him, and he fell to the floor. She bent down at first to maybe help him back up, but collapsed upon him in what became an affectionate embrace.

>< >< ><

Eventually the outside din made itself physical. They were soon being assisted by more police and emergency officers than he'd ever seen before. The conflict wasn't over, exactly, and he was oddly grateful for that. He half-expected everything to just disappear, and for the authorities to find just this hideously slaughtered disfigured body in the kitchen, the placid presence of undisturbed restaurant-goers undercutting his entire cockamamie story. That was selfish, he thought. It would be better if this was a dream, an unreality. Then there wouldn't be all these bodies.

There was a shoot-out that took place out of sight, and one shooting directly in front of them that was particularly shocking for being so abrupt and bathetic. That gorilla creature from before moseyed out from somewhere, spotted the officers and grunted. It picked up and threw a nearby body part at them, apathetically, as if following a pre-set program.

It went wide, wide enough that no one needed to dodge. One of the officers fired. The beast clutched its left shoulder with its right hand, pivoted, groaned, and slowly walked toward the officers.

Another officer fired, this shot low, around the groin. The creature repeated the movement as before: clutching its left shoulder with its right hand and groaning. Several more shots. The same movement, the same animation, and then the creature practically hopped backward to land on its back, where it outstretched its arms and its tongue and just stopped moving. Everyone stood, blinkered, and no one said a word.

A minute later, the beast was gone.

There was one other lasting memory that stood out to him. A burly, mustachioed officer was speaking animatedly with this hands, giving directions to his cadre. He moved his hands in a chopping movement while he talked, like he was doing the Braves Cheer. Suddenly, like a moray eel, a red-and-white spotted plant shot out of an unremarkable pipe against the wall, soundlessly chomped into his finger, and disappeared — finger and all — back into the pipe.

Bryce and Robin were ferried out amidst the commotion, and they never stepped into the Deer & Fox ever again.

>< >< ><

Robin breathed heavily and her breasts heaved metronomically. They showed nicely through what appeared to be a stylish, form-fitting white blouse. No, something more threadbare than that — he could clearly make out the contrast of the maroon bra she wore underneath.

The disfigured man reached out toward her. His face was orange, puffy and indistinct.

The man pulled Robin forward. Her breasts pitched upward from the force and jiggled vigorously as she stopped short in his grasp. He grabbed around her, trying to dominate her, get leverage on her shoulders. The man squeezed one of her breasts painfully. She pushed him away, and his fingers were crumpled up within her shirt, so when she pushed her shirt extended, exposing her deep décolletage.

Bryce's erection flooded full and sharp, pressing hot against his pants. It was his first glimpse of her perky breasts, but also not, because underneath the dream he registered that he knew what her breasts looked like, but there was something powerful and erotic about this sight, the thrill of a slip, the power and control of the image.

He charged and knocked out the disfigured man with one straight blow.

Bryce woke up next to Robin. Actually, next to her was not fully accurate — she was already half-up and getting ready for work. He only saw her back. His stomach sank and that was enough to know the vitality that radiated off her was limited to the dream world. The only thing that carried over from the dream world was his erection.

He laid awake in bed while she prepared for the day. He felt her staring at him impatiently to get up — they often tried to leave for work at the same time — and there was something satisfying in staying in bed for a bit, the slightest form of obstinacy he could muster without overtly riling her. The covers were still over him, and he rested his hand on his privates, the erotic elements of the dream still in mind.

He looked up at her brushing her hair. She looked back at him, looked away, looked back at him, and gave him a slightly annoyed look to show that she didn't see the point in breaking and maintaining eye contact. She wasn't going to give him a goofy or warm smile just because. She wasn't his cheerleader.

He groaned and got out of bed and let his half-erection jut out from his boxers. She didn't acknowledge it. He let it hang, untouched and unremarked-upon. He felt he was making a statement of some sorts.

It had been about almost a year since that defining date at the Deer & Fox. They'd lived together for the last six months, and they hadn't been physical with each other for the last two.

"I'm going to shower," he told her.

"Ok."

"What time is it?"

She looked at her phone, and said, in a phlegmy, impatient way: "8:30, no, 8:35." They normally wanted to be out the door by 9:00 a.m. so they could get in to work sometime between 9:30 and 10:00 a.m. They were running late.

"You don't have to wait for me, I guess."

"Yeah, I figured. I wish you would have told me earlier, I wouldn't have waited."

"I figured. Sorry. I can get in later than you though."

She made a testy sound. "I know."

She was already half-way dressed.

"I left two wheat bars out for you if you want to bring them to work. I bought some for us, as I don't have time to make breakfast."

He mentally rolled his eyes and revealed this by giving a sarcastic woe-is-me, okey-dokey head nod.

She maintained her frigid distance, zipped something up, and left the room. She was wearing a black bra and still needed to decide what to wear up-top.

He didn't want them to go to work like this, to leave and start the day on bad terms.

"Hey," he offered, as she came back in the room. Her chest jiggled a little when she stopped abruptly, and, absurdly, it made him feel bad about himself and what was becoming of their relationship. He hadn't seen her chest bounce of her own accord (or his) for quite some time now.

"Hey, what's going on with you?" That didn't come out right, at all, and it was dreadfully obvious.

No response. She had left the room. He heard the refrigerator door close. "Nothing is going on with me," she huffed when she came back. She was eating Fage Greek yogurt, the one where you mix the honey and yogurt. He could see the clump of honey on the spoon as she mixed it in.

"C'mon, something's up."

She positioned her shoulders defensively and sucked the honey off the spoon in a desperate, rushed way. Funny, he didn't know there could be so much emotion conveyed through yogurt-eating.

"C'mon, I don't have time for this shit. I need to go to work. Can we not talk about this now?" She usually didn't curse in reference to their relationship.

"Well, I'd normally let it go, but this has been going on for a while. You just called our relationship 'shit,' for one thing."

"Just … don't. Let's just not talk about it now, okay?"

"Okay."

She put the half-eaten yogurt down outside in the kitchen and walked to the closet to resume looking for a top.

He felt an intense, burning sense of aggrievement that manifested in his chest and shoulders. "Look, I want to talk about this. We always stop talking about things when you say so. We always go by what you say. You are important to me, this relationship is important to me, and I don't want to spend the whole day worrying about what's going on with us, I want to talk about it now."

"Look —" she started, her arms up as if she was literally stuck between a rock and a hard place and needed to wedge herself out. "I have a lot to do today, you know my boss has been a major bitch recently and I have a lot on my plate, and you can't stress me out this morning, and you can't make me late! Don't you understand that? Don't you get that? If you cared about me, you would not fuck up my work or make things so difficult for me!"

Oh no, here she was, getting worked up. She had a subtle way of shifting blame — now he was morally responsible for her inability to control her emotions and what effect that may have on her work day. And why was it that she could call her boss a bitch, but god forbid he say that she was acting bitchy?

"...and you always make me late, I make breakfast for you and wait for you to leave with me, but no more. I can't do that anymore, you need to wake up earlier, or let me wake up earlier and leave without you."

"Okay, okay," he said, extending his fingers out in a soothing, deescalating way. She was right about that, at least — he had made her late a couple of times, but he couldn't stand it when she made him feel morally responsible for stuff that was not his fault.

She was fully dressed now. He knew this was fucked up, but he had felt more sympathetic to her when she was half-dressed.

She turned back to him, last bite of yogurt in her mouth. Her expression wasn't good — it was largely frustration with a sprinkling of the heavy sorrow inherent in carrying out a dreadful but inevitable task, like taking the cancer-ridden dog to the vet for the Big Sleep.

"I can't do this anymore. I can't. I can't. I can't do this anymore."

"Baby, don't be silly." This was going nuclear. He'd thought about it ending, too, and there was excitement and freedom there, he knew, but no, he didn't want it to end, not like this, not now.

She shook her head, her eyes were closed and there was a streak of wetness along her cheek. "I'm sorry, I'm sorry, I just, I can't. I can't do this anymore. I'm sorry. I'm sorry. I just, I don't, I just don't feel like this is going to work."

"Baby, c'mon, let's just go to work and we can talk about this later."

"No. I'm sorry. I ... I just don't feel like I'm in love with you anymore."

"Baby!" he shot back like she said something wildly offensive and uncalled for. "Baby, you're just stressed, I'm sorry for bringing this up before work, it's my fault. It's my fault, you did nothing wrong, I'm sorry." Usually, taking the blame and appearing plaintive was enough to escape long enough for her to calm down so he could live to fight another day.

"No," she shook her head, eyes still closed. "I'm serious. I've been looking into getting another apartment. I have one picked out already. I'm sorry, I'm sorry. I should have told you before. I'm sorry, but I'm serious. I'm just not in love with you anymore. I've fought it, I've pretended otherwise, I kept telling myself I loved you. You are a good person, and I appreciate what you did for me —"

"What I did for you? You mean, saving your life? As in, I literally saved your life."

"Yes, I know."

"Look honey, let's just talk about this later, okay?"

"Bryce. Look, I'm sorry, but this has to be done. I'm sorry that this is the wrong time. But, it's not working out. I'm sorry, it's not working out. I need to go to work now, I'm sorry, but it's not working out."

"Baby, c'mon, you don't mean that."

"I know what I mean. I know what I am saying."

"You can't possibly. We love each other. I'm your hero. You say it all the time, why, you said it even, like, just last week, when I fixed that cabinet for you."

"Bryce ... I shouldn't have said that. I like to make you happy, I'm sorry I ... have been leading you on for some time, I suppose."

"I quite literally saved your life. I quite literally am your hero. There were magazine articles written about us. I'm a fucking hero. I literally did everything I could to —"

"I know, Bryce, I know. I appreciate everything you did for me, and —"

"Everything I did for you — you mean preventing you from being raped and brutally killed. That's what you mean, right, when you say that?"

"Bryce!"

He didn't know what angered him worse — her breaking up with him, or her pat formality in doing it. She was like an executive getting through a difficult but predetermined business decision.

"You have to ... we have to be able to work this out."

"I'm sorry, Bryce. I'm ... I'm sorry."

"I literally saved your life. I fucking saved your life."

"I know. I know, I feel terrible about this, but ... I'm sorry. I, just don't feel ... think I'm in love with you. I mean, I know I'm not in love with you. I'm sorry, I just, I just know I'm not in love with you —"

"You can't do this, after all I've done, after all we've been through — "

"It's not — it's not a judgment on you. I can't, I can't weigh the pros and cons of what you do or don't deserve based on what you did for me. This isn't a formula. I'm telling you, I'm telling you, I'm sorry, I have love for you, I so greatly appreciate everything you did for me—"

"Saving your life. Let's be clear about what I did. I literally killed a maniac for you, literally killed monsters — can you believe this, literally killing fucking monsters, risking my life to kill monsters to literally fucking rescue you, and this is how I'm repaid for it."

"Repaid? My love for you isn't a gift that you earn by achieving some-thing for me—"

Of course it fucking is, of course it all is, his mind screamed in protest.

" — you don't win me. I'm not the prize —"

"You said you'd never be able to repay me. Do you remember that? You said you would never be able to repay me, and that you would always be there for me. So I'm asking you, please — please — don't leave me. Let us work this out."

She breathed deeply, as if quibbling with someone pointing in vain to a contract technicality. And in a sense, he was, and he knew it.

"For everything I've done for you, for everything we've been through together, please, we have to work this out. I'm a good person. I'm a good person and I'm sorry, I try, you know I try to be good." He was crying, unmistakably and unabashedly.

"You said it — you promised me — that you'd be eternally grateful to me. That you loved me, that you'd never be able to repay me. So please, do this for me, repay me this way: don't leave me."

She didn't respond, not verbally at least, but she ploddingly shook her head.

"I'm sorry. I'm sorry. We can talk about this later, but I'm sorry. I'm sorry. I — I'm not trying to be mean, but I'm not in love with you. I'm sorry. It's not a thing I can work out. You are nice, you are a nice person. You will find someone else to be nice to, someone else to love. I feel like I could be anyone. You just want to be loved so badly, I feel it has nothing to do with me. You just want me to cheer you on, to hug you and treat you – almost treat you like a dog or something, like you are my son or something and I'm your biggest booster, your biggest fan. I just ... I just can't. It's not ... "

"I can't fucking believe you —"

"Don't! I can't do this now. I'm late for work, we can talk later."

"I can't fucking believe this is how you ... how you treat me. How you repay me —"

"Fucking repay you!?"

He made a strategic mistake, he knew. Whatever welling of sympathy he'd evinced within her was gone. The course was now irrevocable. "Again, I'm not your princess that you rescued from the castle. You don't own me. You didn't win me, so just stop it! Just stop it and act like an adult. And if you want to get all technical with me, and bring up every fact and detail from the past instead of focusing on how I've fallen out of love with you, then if I never met you, I'd never have even been in that restaurant to begin with."

"Okay, whatever," he turned around to head back into the bedroom. "Whatever, I can't believe you, I can't fucking believe you." He plopped back into the bed, the vertigo of sadness and uncertainty overwhelming him, seeping into the cracks of his rage. It felt better when these emotions were converted into rage, into indignation.

"I'm a fucking hero, you know that. A literal fucking hero. I saved your life, I literally saved your life, from god knows what, from getting eaten, from getting raped, from who knows. You had a different tune back then, let me tell you. You'd have been begging for me back then, and now, look at you." His conflation of pity and anger was mismanaged and received poorly, he could tell, and while he talked, she hedged, torn between consoling him and just storming out. She finally made a face of hands-in-the-air disavowal, packed up her work things, and said she was leaving and they could talk tonight. He noted with some inner sadistic glee that she dotted her eyes a bit as she left.

He didn't want to move out or have her move out. Things weren't perfect, far from it, but he liked the life he had with her, liked the feeling her had with her. He looked at her and saw the best of himself.

"I'm a fucking hero," he told himself again, this time into the pillow, in a sulking way he'd perfected throughout his life, in a type of self-pitying performance art. It felt good to repeat that, and what he had done for her was undeniable, it could never be taken away. It was an assurance into Heaven, into sainthood. He had always stayed faithful to her, even when the hero-narrative went full blast following the media blitz.

It felt good to be indignant and hate. People forget that. There was something soporific about it, anesthetizing. Bad feelings sunk inward and were expelled outward, leaving him cleansed. "I'm a fucking hero," he consoled himself again, burning up into the pillow. "I'm a good person and I deserve better than this. I deserve to be loved and treated better. I deserve to be with someone who appreciates me.

"This isn't how things are supposed to end."

Cthulhu, Zombies, Ninjas and Robots!; or, a Special Snowflake in an Endless Scorching Universe

THE WORDS AND wisdom of H.P. Lovecraft are best enjoyed alone. Nay, they can only be savored when alone. "What a man does for pay is of little significance. What he is, as a sensitive instrument responsive to the world's beauty, is everything," Lovecraft had written. His was a mind sensitive to rare and gentle things, an armament against the frothy nothings of the hour. An escape from machinery and modern inventions, an escape from the dictatorship of the uncultured, to paraphrase John Cowper Powys.

Yet, knowing all this, here was Malcolm. Here, of all places.

Malcolm walked among the crooked timbers of humanity in the vendor room for the redundantly-named Con of Cthulhu Convention. The closest vendor booth was SICK 'N PSYCHO, a horror-themed apparel line which had a whole corner display to itself. The booth was staffed by two white girls in their mid-twenties, both attractive in that gothic way, one with dark black hair streaked with purple, the other a red pixie cut. Their outfits were tight-fitting, form accentuating, and leg-exposing but were also black and featured nods to the occult and scary imagery, so they were completely and totally not beholden to the patriarchal fashion of the day. The furtive glances at their tits and asses were so totally unlike the same furtive glances afforded to other attractive girls who chose to or were forced to highlight their physical attributes at Hooters or other breastauraunts, but because here the male gaze also picked up flecks of the dark and gothic, their outfits were transgressive and challenging rather than tawdry and typical, of course. Lovecraftians who spoke the game of black abysses and cosmic futility gravitated around them, warming themselves on their false affections like Outer Gods to distant suns.

Malcolm perused the vendor's wares. CTHULHU, ZOMBIES, NINJAS

& ROBOTS!, promised one book, which had a cover image featuring zombies being crushed by Cthulhu's tentacles, robots firing plasma cannons at the roaring beast and a ninja swinging, Tarzan-style, across the protrusions of Cthulhu's face.

"What more could you ask for? I mean, zombies, ninjas, Cthulhu. Shit's got robots, too. Shit's got it all!" the red-haired saleswoman offered.

"Check this out!" one potential customer took the book and showed it to his female friend, both of them festooned with bric-a-brac buttons and accessories declaring their allegiance to Cthulhu and his large marketing empire.

Malcolm scanned some of the other books on display. *High Seas Cthulhu; Heavy Metal Cthulhu; Cthulhu Lives!; That Which Should Not Be, But Inexplicably Is; The Queef of Cthulhu: Transgressive Erotica; World War Cthulhu; I Fucked a Shoggoth; Cthulhumon (Gotta Release Em All!); The Horror From Bedford, Massachusetts; Pickman's Cable Modem; Aliens vs. Cthulhu; West Coast Cthulhu, Cthulhu-bunga!; Bunga Bunga Sex Party Cthulhu; Cowboy Cthulhu; ...* shall he keep going?

Yes, you piece of shit, he shall keep going. *C is for Cthulhu: the Lovecraft Alphabet Book ... Crimson* —, no the mind stops at *C is for Cthulhu*.

A Lovecraft alphabet book for young children? The mind reels.

On to the other vendors.

A t-shirt of a slumbering monster dreaming of earth, emblazoned with "Teach the Controversy!" (Malcolm could admit, that one made him laugh); the perennial Cthulhu/Dagon political stickers (*Why Vote for the Lesser Evil?*, which of course makes no sense because Cthulhu isn't evil in any terrestrially understandable sense, Cthulhu represents that which is outside our understanding of good and evil, but ha-ha-ha who cares about that?), another t-shirt that inexplicably read *Eat-Sleep-Cthulhu* (with green, vine-like tentacles around the word Cthulhu, natch!), a green Che Guevera shirt with Che's fashionable mug branching off into the type of tentacles that are redundant for anyone who's seen the Davy Jones character in *Pirates of the Caribbean II: Dead Chest Boogaloo.* There was other junk, too, like a Cthulhu ski mask or Elder Wear Panties, for the sexy minion in your life.

And don't forget the baby minions in your life! Why not a *Hello Cthulhu* onesie, with the iconic white kitty now green and tentacled; or a *My Little Cthulhu*, with an adorable pastel-green Cthulhu riding a rainbow, fluttering about with cartoon hearts; a Cthulhu Crossing sign, with the black outline in the diamond yellow symbol having a tentacle or a wing or some such; a Charlie Brown parody with a winged, cephalopod-faced Snoopy looking up at the sky atop a black, symbol-specked dog house, with a gothic, anxious kiddie Lovecraft as the Charlie Brown stand-in.

There were more. There were many, many more.

Cthulhu Fish, Pewter Cthulhu pins, Old One Sigils, Fighting Fishes logos for fictional sports teams. Approximately five trillion shirts identified with Miskatonic University, The Esoteric Order of Dagon, Dunwich, R'lyeh or Innsmouth.

Don't forget that gift for the practical Lovecraftian: a Mi-Go Crustacean claw-cracker, which did not even have the dignity to make Mythos-sense.

"Contrary to what you may assume, I am not a pessimist but an indifferentist—that is, I don't make the mistake of thinking that the resultant of the natural forces surrounding and governing organic life will have any connexion with the wishes or tastes of any part of that organic life-process. Pessimists are just as illogical as optimists; insomuch as both envisage the aims of mankind as unified, and as having a direct relationship (either of frustration or of fulfilment) to the inevitable flow of terrestrial motivation and events. That is—both schools retain in a vestigial way the primitive concept of a conscious teleology—of a cosmos which gives a damn one way or the other about the especial wants and ultimate welfare of mosquitos, rats, lice, dogs, men, horses, pterodactyls, trees, fungi, dodos, or other forms of biological energy." – H.P. Lovecraft

All throughout the weekend, Malcolm sat in on conferences on cosmic horror and indifferentism, the agony of existence, all these scholars and readers and writers praising — nay, advocating — for this man Lovecraft, for his insights into the true nature of the universe and his fiction's power to articulate the philosophy of cosmic indifferentism, and yet ... and yet ... somewhere in between cosmic indifferentism and the inherent futility of all organic life was room for children.

Lovecraft's supposed intellectual followers seemed to think there was no contradiction, nay, no contradiction at all in gazing out into the whirling vortex of meaningless pain, agony and suffering and thinking, sure, why not provide access to this experience for the next generation? What is this, *Against the World, Against Life, For Children?*
Did *C is for Cthulhu* contain this pearl of wisdom?

"It is good to be a cynic—it is better to be a contented cat — and it is best not to exist at all. Universal suicide is the most logical thing in the world — we reject it only because of our primitive cowardice and childish fear of the dark. If we were sensible we would seek death — the same blissful blank which we enjoyed before we existed."- H.P. Lovecraft

Sleep tight. kids!
Lovecraftians feted after their little minions, dressed them up like baby eldritch abominations for their fun and amusement, laughed and giggled and wiped the spittle off their worthless little faces while Mommy and Daddy played their meaningless philosophical parlor games.

"It must be remembered that there is no real reason to expect anything in particular from mankind; good and evil are local expedients—or their lack—and not in any sense cosmic truths or laws. We call a thing 'good' because it promotes certain petty human conditions that we happen to like—whereas it is just as sensible to assume that all humanity is a noxious pest and should be eradicated like rats or gnats for the good of the planet or of the universe. There are no absolute values in the whole blind tragedy of mechanistic nature—nothing is good or bad except as judged from an absurdly limited point of view. The only cosmic reality is mindless, undeviating fate—automatic, unmoral, uncalculating inevitability. As human beings, our only sensible scale of values is one based on lessening the agony of existence. That plan is most deserving of praise which most ably fosters the creation of the objects and conditions best adapted to diminish the pain of living for those most sensitive to its depressing ravages. To expect perfect adjustment and happiness is absurdly unscientific and unphilosophical. We can seek only a more or less trivial mitigation of suffering."- Take a Fucking Guess Who Said This

And Jesus, some of these people. They may have desecrated Lovecraft's cosmic philosophy, but they apparently took his invented Shoggoth's decorum and appearance as something to aspire to. These enormous, sickly, fat sloppy elephants that paraded around this convention were befitting of the climax of *Imprisoned with the Pharaohs. Hippopotami should not have human hands and carry torches ... men should not have the heads of crocodiles ...* men should also not exist without defined necks and the ability to work a washing machine.

What had he expected? Honestly, he imagined he would meet more souls like himself, sensitive to the majesty of the sublime, struggling with the angst of corporal limitation. Intelligent, searching people drawn to Lovecraft's life and work. Instead, he found a bunch of slobs and posers and idle dabblers who had taken up their hobbies after being unable to fit in with the mainstream, booted off the tree of respectability and hanging on desperately to whatever low-lying branch would support them. Had these people been born with normal dimensions, they'd be cheerleaders and football players or hipsters.

Worse, hipsterdom already seemed to have infiltrated Lovecraft, a miscegenation more horrifying than anything the great scribe had dreamed up. Lovecraft bars, Lovecraft beers, Lovecraft hoodies and beanies....

Malcolm checked his gear-operated antique watch. He had about ten minutes before the author reading.

"Cool watch man, where'd you get that?" asked a kid in his mid-twenties, decked to the nines in the newest vintage fashions: striped gray suspenders, tie, dark framed glasses and fedora, the result of a chimney sweep and a 1920's pulp detective barreling into each other at high speed and exploding.

"It's a family heirloom," Malcolm responded, in his high, piping voice.

"Sick man, I like it."

"Thanks."

Malcolm had some time to kill, so why not have some fun trolling?

"I can't believe all this stuff. Keth-oo-loo, is it? I love H.P. Lovecraft, but I had no idea he wrote short stories."

"Really?" the young man looked at him cock-eyed, but beamed with the opportunity to explain something pedantically to someone else at length.

"Yeah. I mean, I know him primarily as an essayist. His thoughts on culture and race are ... inspiring, I'd say."

"Inspiring!?" the man was beginning to fume with the joyous indignation of the SHOCKED and OUTRAGED.

"Yeah. I mean, don't you agree with him? Otherwise, how could you support his other work? I would argue that supporting a Lovecraft convention is a tacit support of the man's other, larger views, if you think about it. Cosmic horror, race, religion ...."

"I – I – his views on race are terrible, so outdated, there's so much more —"

"Anyway-nice-meeting-you-I-have-to-go," and Malcolm walked out.

Well that was fun. He left the hotel where the convention was being held and found a small coffee shop. He ordered an iced coffee ($4). He took out a wad of singles, pulled four out, and handed them to the barista.

"Woah woah, look at all those singles. Going to hit the clu-ubs." She elongated "clu-ubs" to make her reference to strip clubs obvious. She was a cute, affable young woman, a bit hipstery looking. Surely she was of the sort to dislike male chauvinism. It befuddled him what life circumstances or perspective would compel her to say something like that. The desire for tips, maybe? The sense that having a consistent moral outlook was outdated, that everything had to be ironic and frivolous?

He mumbled something, left a dollar tip, and left. Above the tip cup was a Cthulhu Plushie, holding a sign: "IA! IA! Cthulhu Fhtagn! Tip or Be Devoured!"

That plushie. His eyes narrowed and everything zoomed in on that plushie. Grumbling sounds, suggesting an encroaching storm on the soundtrack. Low tones of dread. Everything he resented about these people, about this convention, was embodied by that plushie.

He wanted to take that tip back.

He sat in the suite for the author reading. He couldn't recall the author's name and was unfamiliar with her work, but she was supposedly highly regarded as a fantastic weird fiction prose stylist. He knew what she looked like, however, and saw that she was standing outside the conference suite, talking to a man in a suit. A fan tried to get her attention. Malcolm couldn't hear what she said to her fan, but she put up her index finger dismissively without looking. The fan got the hint, his enthusiasm a little dampened, but waited dutifully.

There were about fifteen others in the suite. She entered the suite about fifteen minutes after the scheduled time (perhaps a minute for every waiting attendee?), explaining blithely that she had to take care of business with a publicist.

She started up a projector. An illustration of her, wearing a magician's hat, her fingers up as if she was reading an incantation (or shushing an unworthy fan) with illustrated ghouls and creatures of the night waiting around her with rapt attention.

Mild applause.

"I'm proud to say this story is slated to appear in Del Howison's *Prestige*

New Horror 19." (Miraculously, by dint of some cosmic kismet that even the Elder Gods could not fathom (as presumably nepotism is a wholly-human invention) the same roster of authors always managed to produce each year's best new horror.)[1] She paused, expecting applause, received a few beats of silence, then some tepid claps to fill the air. "Mr. Howison, the legendary editor, as you may well know, is the gold standard for quality horror and dark fiction." Undaunted, she then rattled off all the awards this story had won, many of them given to her by the same authors, committee members and assorted Lovecraft dickriders she'd been hob-nobbing with all weekend.

He doubted he missed much by ignoring her story. For in the corner he recognized one of the authors from yesterday's panel.

The author bouncing the little baby boy in his lap, the little baby boy rocking a Hello Cthulhu onesie.

The man with the by-all-appearances pleasant, supportive wife by his side throughout the convention, the one who took pictures of her betrothed making mock-horrified faces by all the Lovecrafticana around the convention. The man who had to dip out here and there to answer his important work calls, no doubt from his cutting edge smart phone.

The author that discussed Lovecraft as his greatest inspiration, described how exposure to Lovecraft's cosmic philosophy exploded the way his brain worked, put everything into a new perspective, how in awe he was of the man and the "undeniable" ramifications of the man's philosophy.

When Mr. Author-Man's family gathered around the dinner table, what did they discuss? Did he bounce his baby boy on his knee and feed him his mashed peas and carrots after a hearty round of contemplating the

---

1   And yes I used parentheses inside of parentheses. Why not send me a hundred messages about it? Quick, maybe I misspelled Fhatgn, too, better go check, got to focus on the important stuff, you know? What feeling eclipses the pleasure of superiority in knowing another made a mistake?

selfishness and futility of reproducing? Did the cosmic insignificance of all known human achievements, virtues and morals mean anything to this charlatan when he planned his little family vacations and doctors' visits for junior and told his wife he "loved" her?

Was little junior still a special snowflake in an endless scorching universe?

What stories and refrains and inspiring quotes did Mr. Author-Man regale his spawn with before bedtime? Perhaps this little quotable:

"The human race will disappear. Other races will appear and disappear in turn. The sky will become icy and void, pierced by the feeble light of half-dead stars. Which will also disappear. Everything will disappear. And what human beings do is just as free of sense as the free motion of elementary particles. Good, evil, morality, feelings? Pure 'Victorian fictions'. Only egotism exists." – If You Can't Guess Who Said This, Please Kill Yourself

Mr. Author-Man probably liked all the ker-azy monsters in Lovecraft's stories. He probably got into deep arguments online about the proper classification of Yog-Sothoth. He didn't yet know it, but he was just a dabbler, Lovecraft as just another form of entertainment, appearing on his shelves alongside Harry Potter, Mad Men and The Sopranos.

Mr. Author-Man was a living disgrace to the glorious man and his glorious philosophy.

He was perfect.

Mr. Author-Man was more than happy to sell Malcolm a copy of his book, just out from Innsmouth-Dagon Rock'em Sock'em Publications.

Thrills! Chills! Horror and Suspense!

The Great Azathoth will soon rise! The minions across the world scream for his arrival! Time is running out!

Only two intrepid PhD students at Miskatonic University have any hope of stopping this Lord Beyond Light. But to do so, they must awaken and partner with mankind's ultimate rival, Cthulhu!

Mixing action, intrigue and contemporary sexual and gender politics with classic Mythos adventure, and featuring a cast of Lovecraftian all-stars, this story has got it all! So what are you waiting for: heed the call, pick up your silver key, and open the door to cosmic adventure in The Unsung Mysteries at the Center of the Earth!

Author-Man was elated when Malcolm showed up later at his hotel room. Why, they were staying at the same hotel, on the same floor, Malcolm just noticed that's where Mr. Author-Man was staying. What a coincidence!

Would he sign the book?

Why sure!

The Mythos was all hokum, of course. Yog Sothery, as the great man himself had dismissed it.

But if you were going to find an audience to take your wrath out on, you could do worse than dressing it up in the appropriate accoutrements to punish a charlatan who supposedly had already come to grips with the futility of existence and the amoral nature of the universe.

The purging would begin.

What would Mr. Author-Man say when he woke up?

What could he say when he found the bodies; dead, gibberish signs and words carved into them, the lamps in the bedroom assembled into an arbitrary triangle?

What could he say when he found the bodies; eyelids shewn off, missing fingers, four puncture wounds forming a circle around their belly buttons?

All capricious, signifying nothing.

He'd felt bad about it, actually. Maybe he should just kill the pretentious authors themselves next time: Author-Man's wife and child were just along for the ride, innocent victims. But killing the family proved the point, right? Life and death are meaningless, right, so what does it matter? Eh, he would save the family and just kill the authors in the future, logical consistency and point-making be damned.

What grievance could Mr. Author-Man really have? Would he cry and wail despite "knowing" that he and his beloveds were no more important than the various pests and rodents humankind snuffed out without a second moment's thought?

It's not as cute to talk about the uncaring universe when it comes home. The uncaring universe appears a lot different when it comes home.

Oh Abel, Oh Absalom

VERNON CAMACHO IS a thirty-six year old Puerto Rican man who grew up in the Woodside Houses housing project in (no surprise here) Woodside, Queens. Someone who didn't know any better wouldn't think that being a Puerto Rican in Woodside was such a big deal. Shit, walk down Roosevelt Avenue in Woodside and you'll see all types of Latin American establishments, from Colombian to Ecuadorian to Brazilian. But those restaurants on Roosevelt Avenue are *South American*, with vastly different attitudes and cultures than Puerto Rico. Most of the South American expats in the neighborhood are the working poor, emphasis on both *working and poor*, and mainly just keep to themselves.

But Vernon, being a Puerto Rican, always felt some kinship to the stronger Puerto Rican culture across the East River, in East Harlem. That's not how he'd phrase it, exactly. That's how his parents had always phrased it. He'd like to disagree, but he really couldn't. He never liked Woodside, and as a kid he'd leave it as often as he could, instead finding comfort in the streets of East Harlem, festooned as they were with the colorful iconography praising a culture he knew nothing about and that meant nothing to him. More than once, he'd mistaken the Puerto Rican flag for an advertisement for Pepsi.

Partly based on his resentment of Woodside, and partly because he just enjoyed being a wiseass, he used to always insist that, in reality, he didn't live in Woodside. See, Woodside technically began east of 51st street, and his family lived in the western house of the project, on 49th street. So technically, he lived in Astoria. That didn't mean much for his purposes — shit, Astoria, with its Greek and Middle Eastern eateries and burgeoning yuppie population, had far less street credibility than Woodside. But even though his parents no doubt found his hair-splitting neighborhood distinctions obnoxious, they beamed at what it presaged: an attention to detail, Vernon's critical mind. A mind, they felt, that could enable young Vernon to accomplish more than they'd ever accomplished.

Plus, Vernon was light-skinned. That Catalonian blood rose up and hid all that dark, like thick cream on a Greek frappe. That was a joke that Vernon's father, Hector, always wanted to tell him – he'd like it, his father thought, because he always tells people he lives in Astoria. But Vernon's father was bad with words – both English and Spanish – so he didn't talk much to Vernon. Still, he always went out of his way to buy his son frappes, lighting up inside thinking about young Vernon, he of fair skin and that stubborn spirit and sharp mind, like the lawyers on television. Young Vernon would accomplish anything, if only he wanted to, if only he set his mind to it.

>< >< ><

Vernon Camacho, 36, waited in line with his plastic food plate, just like all the other inmates, to get his mac-and-cheese. Vernon was in prison, with two more months until his release, assuming he was released early for good behavior.

Vernon was serving a three-to-six-year conditional sentence for armed robbery.

>< >< ><

Vernon's father had died about four months earlier, from a heart attack. A massive heart attack, the doctors had said, as if that made any difference. Vernon's mother, Angelina, had since gone down to Puerto Rico. With her husband dead and her only child in prison, there wasn't much reason for her to stick around New York, especially not now, not in November, when the dying trees only made the gray skies that much harder to avoid.

As his release date got closer and closer, Vernon thought more and more of El Barrio, that bastard neighborhood of East Harlem. There was a mural on East 117th Street and Third Avenue that had all this Puerto Rican shit: tropical setting, quotes from people he didn't recognize, et cetera. The thing he always liked about that mural was the chicken with the guitar. It looked funny, how dedicated that cartoon chicken was to playing his cartoon guitar, all the serious-looking Puerto Rican scholars and celebrities in the mural completely ignoring the fact that, right next to them, a bright yellow cartoon chicken was shredding on the guitar. As he got older and his parents got more and more worried about him, he'd tell them how he liked seeing that chicken, and they'd loosen up a bit and think, oh, he's not a gangster, he's not a thug, what kind of thug would find a yellow cartoon chicken endearing?

East Harlem should be in jail, not me, Vernon thought. Yeah, it made no sense. But at his sentencing he wanted to tell the judge the truth: look, I'm here for the wrong reason. I wanted people to like me. I've got psychological problems. I'm depressed. It's East Harlem's fault. Where are they? They. The people of East Harlem. They never visited him: shit, most of them are gone, somehow gentrified-out by the Mexicans, of all people.

>< >< ><

He went the whole day without saying a word to anyone.

The friction of his rampaging thoughts was enough to make him tired and burnt-out, even though he did basically nothing all day, except some light reading and surreptitious "lights-out" jerking off. He wanted to get caught and punished for jerking off, so all his righteous indignation could be transferred to the worthy cause of advocating for the human right to self-pleasure. Then people would pay attention to him and congratulate him for his advocacy, tell him they had no idea he was so passionate and articulate. He was like a little wind-up toy, stuck in the corner, looking for a way to turn himself around.

He was bored, and was content with being boring for others. Let them experience a bit of this.

>< >< ><

The next day, he spoke to someone, a guard, a correctional officer maybe, he couldn't remember, but that person told him he'd been approved for early release. He'd be out in twenty-eight days. Oh, shit. He became instantly nostalgic for all those boring days in jail. There was something cozy about how boring those days had been, something safely soporific, like a dull headache and a warm blanket. He'd never been raped in jail, never really been fucked with, just stayed by himself in his minimum-security prison with his fellow first-timers and minor drug dealers and nobodies.

Who would he live with once he was released? What would he do?

He'd have to call his mother. Fuck.

He looked around his little cell, which he had to himself. There was a toilet in the right corner, a bare bed to his left, a shelf with an alarm clock and some books. He didn't know how big the cell was, the square footage or anything like that. He wasn't good at that shit. Everyone assumed Puerto Ricans knew handy-shit — how to fix cars or build stuff — but he never knew any of that. If someone told him that method X was the right way to build Y, and method X had been used, Vernon would eyeball it or make a face suggesting he was familiar with the method proposed and found it satisfactory.

>< >< ><

Vernon resolved to talk to someone today. Not communicate with someone, which he did daily with his wispy head nods, but actually *talk* to someone. He had some acquaintances he could hang out with, all Hispanic, darker-skinned Puerto Ricans and objectively dark-skinned Dominicans.

There were three of his pals at the table, eating chicken fingers and mac-and-cheese. There was Manny, stout little dark-skinned Manny from Mexico (Mexico, was it?); Hector, a bald, skinny, relatively lighter-skinned Puerto Rican with heavy creases around his mouth, as if he were a three-dimensional model made out of paper; and Frank, a skinny Puerto Rican of no real distinction. Both Hector and Frank looked like those too-skinny hustlers you always find on an uptown 6 train, talking too loudly about pussy or a hustle or 'dis nigga said dat' or something of the sort. Manny looked like the beefy dishwasher you catch out of the corner of your eye at some undistinguished local restaurant, that 5 foot 2 good-natured Mexican guy who points you in the direction of the bathroom who you then instantly forget about. When Vernon was out of jail, he'd never be able to I.D. Manny out of a line-up; the only thing he'd remember about Manny was how he felt bad about not being able to remember anything about him.

"'Sup Vernon," greeted Hector.

"Not much. Getting out of here soon, if you didn't hear. About a month."

"Word? Good to hear, man. Don't be getting yourself back up in here anytime soon. Rebuild your life out there."

"Yeah," he nodded. Anytime anyone says they are leaving, every other inmate turns into Oprah. Providing well-meaning but clichéd advice is the only temporary salvation anybody seems to seek in here. It's the easiest box to check off on the list of good deeds.

"No seriously man, I mean it. Look at me, man, I'm in here for fucking some dumb bullshit, black tar, stupid shit, I never even did it. I was fucking just ferrying it for some nigga cross-town. Not even fuckin' cross-town nigga, it was fucking, I took a bus from Park Avenue out to Second Avenue, shit fell out of my fucking pocket. Fucking stupid kid shit, man. Point is, I guess, is no matter what, don't do no stupid shit anymore, no matter how little you think it is."

Crackhead Frank nodded solemnly. Manny was inscrutable as always, like a thought never passed through his squat, beefy head.

"Word, I'm gonna be on the up-and-up, for real. I'll see you on the outside." Other inmates loved hearing that: see you on the outside, like they were all going to make it out.

"Knock on wood," Hector added, indeed, knocking on the wood table. That's another thing all these inmates seemed to share, some stupid belief in fate or mysticism or something. That way, they could all believe their incarceration was inevitably leading to some kind of redemption, like this was all some great big plan and not the insignificant bullshit of a bunch of impoverished nobodies. They were ledgers on a crime report, a check-mark on the C.O.'s daily log, a bit of annoying doggerel scrubbed out and forgotten about.

Nothing creates meaning like punishment. No priest or preacher in the world lived the concept of redemption like these sad fucks. All of them. Even the big bad tough guys, the hardcore guys, the guys who pre-tended not to give a shit. Redemption became more than a narrative with these people, it became something almost physical; you could see it if you looked, the way their heads were always nodding anytime someone spoke the Good Word (or something presented with the gravitas of the Good Word). They would even nod their heads before any of the Good Word was spoken: just participating in a public act associated with redemption and transcendence was enough to set them off, everyone vying to agree and extol the hardest, to be the most sincere, to be the most dedicated. Unno-ticed competitions would ensue, where one inmate would demonstrate his sincere desire to change his ways by nodding like a happy parrot and yelling "Amen" whenever the speaker's pitch got dramatic, only to be one-upped by someone who'd complement his "Amen" with a hand-clap, until a little passive-aggressive war of escalated woops and jeers and holy ghost conversions took place, two people not just being redeemed, but being the fucking best at redemption.

It was stupid, Vernon knew. But still, be polite ... .

"Word, knock on that wood for me."

"Will do man, for you, will do," Hector added, "for you man, for you."

Vernon mentally rolled his eyes at Hector's melodrama and walked to the cafeteria door to head back to his cell.

What should he do upon his release? Maybe get a tattoo. But why?
Having a tattoo was like adding value that couldn't be taken away. You
could be penniless and on-the-street, a complete piece of shit, but you still
have that tattoo. When you were dead, and some stranger looked at your
dead carcass — your dead nobody carcass, now even more of a nobody, literally a nobody — well, they will see that tattoo. That's something added.
Value added.

Or maybe a cowboy hat? Anytime Vernon had seen some guy with a
cowboy hat, he thought, man, that guy probably isn't ever bored. A guy
with a cowboy hat looks like someone going somewhere. A cowboy hat
provides context. Even if you're bored doing nothing, sitting in a lonesome
bar, well, with a cowboy hat, you're a mysterious drifter, a brooding badass. Well, maybe, but a Puerto Rican with a—

Something wrong sliced into his left ear and cascaded off the left side
of his face. His ear burned, inflamed, but it was a cold heat, like the life had
been drawn out of it.

He turned around hard on his right, and saw a thin black man he didn't
recognize. Well, he did recognize him, sort of. He recognized this guy as
that guy he could never get a bead on. The man was so dark he was like the
Alien creature, so dark you couldn't see his eyes, which he kept at half-lid,
no visible whites. This man was thin but tough, wiry, average height, maybe 5'7", 5'8", close-cropped hair, close-cropped everything. If this guy was
out in the streets of East Harlem, he would be the hanger-on outside some
head shop or barber shop, chewing gum, eyeing everyone but not really
focusing, all tight, all coiled. And now he was uncoiling, holding some kind
of something, something hard and seemingly metal.

It was a plate tray of some kind; but while all the plate trays Vernon
ever saw had been plastic, this one was gleaming and silver.

They squared off at each other, maybe a foot or two away. Vernon hoped
mystery-man would move first. Vernon didn't really know how to throw a
punch and knew he could only get away with that in close quarters.

He needn't worry. Abdul — the man's name was Abdul, Vernon suddenly remembered — roared forward, both hands swinging the tray like a pro-wrestler with a fold-out chair. Vernon barreled forward to meet him, shoulders first, jamming Abdul's fingers against the tray and lessening its impact. There was a dramatic toppling sound as the tray fell out of sight, which got everyone's attention. The anarchic sound of the chaos elicited a commensurate roar from the on-looking prisoners.

Vernon found his arm extended — he didn't even realize he threw a punch — and it connected. Technically. It connected in the sense that his arm extended until it ran a dead-stop into something, but there was no force there. No connection there, no depth. His arm and fist were like a middle-school teacher's chalkboard pointer.

Vernon suddenly got very nervous.

Now Vernon had his arms wrapped around Abdul, as if to shake him. Abdul kidney-punched him hard, fast, and repeatedly. Four or five punches landed before Vernon figured out where the pain came from.

Vernon bellowed, more out of frustration than anything, and with a quick fit of inspiration leveraged his greater weight to pile-drive Abdul into the nearest table. The mass of watching men moved around them like an amoeba around an acquired pellet.

Vernon had his arms wrapped tight around his skinnier aggressor, his forehead under Abdul's chin, nuzzling hard, jutting hard, hoping to strike Abdul's Adam's apple or jaw. When he could, he'd loosen his grip and hammer blows with his left hand, or throw little ineffectual punches to Abdul's midsection. Mainly, Vernon was just trying to smother him. Fantastically, he pictured there being nothing visible but Abdul's flailing arms tapping him on the back. Like a little boy seeing if his playmate had had "enough," Vernon arched his back to get a better look at his opponent. Somewhere, somehow, he planned on raining down a torrent of calculated knee strikes, but that never happened.

His sense of sight must have been elsewhere because Abdul's spindly claw lodged itself somewhere wet, somewhere unwelcome, and Vernon's eye flooded with the sharp sting of blood and sweat. A crushing palm jammed up his jaw and caused his tongue to mesh through his teeth.

And then he was on his back and the prison guards, playing hockey referee, decided this was enough and jerked them away from each other, hard. They both sprang back like they were on bungee cords.

"You fucking punk bitch!" Vernon yelled, more indignant than angry. Why the fuck did this asshole attack him? Abdul wasn't responding in any way to being dragged off; he just contorted and sagged wherever he was being dragged. Abdul kept his mouth shut and his demeanor unknowable, face stolid, like nothing had changed, head down, just back to the grind.

"Fucking bitch, fucking scratching little bitch. What fucking faggot scratches a nigga?" If any of his old friends had been around, they would have known Vernon was pissed (and not just by his tone): he rarely said 'nigga.'

>< >< ><

Back in his cell, Vernon nursed his wounds dramatically. Shit stung. Fucking low blow.

The guards had seen from the outset that he'd hadn't started it. They'd placed him in his cell brusquely and without respect, and gave him some curt order to stay put. That was C.O. speak for *we know you didn't do anything wrong, but just shut the fuck up, anyway.*

"Camacho, mail. First your own suite, now full-service mail delivery." That was Tony, the big jovial black prison guard. He always said flip shit like that. It seemed that if a black guy became too fat, he had to become nice. And jovial fat black Tony was nice. The fat creases around his eyes and those weird skin rolls made him look like a dog of some kind, some obese black Shar Pei. When Tony was walking behind you, that shit felt like Indiana Jones running from that boulder.

Tony slid the mail through the bars. It was a typical, plain letter, no return address, addressed to Mr. Vernon Camacho.

"Getting some TLC on your big day. Maybe it's a fan of your prize fight."

Vernon eyed the letter and liked thinking about himself as a prize fighter, with a bruised left eye, peering down at a mysterious fan letter, a letter urging him to never give up. Eh, whatever. But he enjoyed neither mysteries nor surprises, and prison wasn't the place to cultivate an interest in either.

Vernon slid open the letter. Inside was a single page of white, standard computer paper, with four simple, declarative sentences:

You are a rapist. Your son was the product of rape. Your son is dead. We killed him.

Vernon parsed the phrases in his head, again-and-again, to see if the meaning remained the same. Somehow, the dull headache and stinging eye pain still predominated over these mysterious new feelings. But slowly, his headache went from predictable to erratic and then his insides emitted sparks, a veritable electrical storm in his chest. Again, he read the letter. Then again and again.

"Yo, Tony. Tony! Tony! Tone-eeee!'

He lost himself for a moment, somewhere.

"What the fuck is it, man."

"Who sent this?" Vernon pushed the letter out toward him.

"Shit, how am I supposed to know. You know as much as I do," Tony responded, dumbstruck. Tony's brow furrowed and he looked exasperated and somewhat repulsed, as if Vernon had just offered him a blow job. This was an abrupt, unexpected, and unwelcome frivolity, and best dismissed immediately. "What the fuck is this shit, man? A rapist? This shit probably sent to the wrong dude." Tony's heart beat faster with thoughts of Vernon bringing a lawsuit for negligent infliction of emotional distress. Tony had to suppress the urge to crumple up the letter and throw it in the trash. But he flipped the envelope and checked again and, indeed, it was addressed to Vernon Camacho.

"Do you even have a son?"

"Yes. Yes."

"Fuck man, you never mentioned a son ...." and then Tony stopped himself, because why should Vernon tell him these things?, and there was an incipient tension in the air, and now it was best to shut up and do something. He gave the letter back to Vernon. "You wait here," Tony said without thinking, only days later realizing how self-evident that piece of advice was, "I'm going to go, get, talk, to someone." As Tony hustled out of sight, Vernon sat back down on his bench, staring.

Days later, the following facts were confirmed: Vernon's five-year old son, Cruz Luong, had been stabbed twice in the back of the head less than a block from P.S. 20, his elementary school, which was located in the neighborhood of Flushing, Queens. The murder had occurred only two days ago. There were no witnesses, no suspects. The only evidence was the two holes in the back of young Cruz Luong's head: mechanical, emotionless holes, as if they were created by the human equivalent of a paper hole puncher.

As most of the men in prison generally had not left childhood without some sort of scarring — be it mental or physical — an attack on a child, let alone the murder of a child, was a crime for which there was no pardon. The language of equivocation and the insistence on context that prisoners internalized to make sense of the trajectories of their lives was absent where a child was concerned. Where children were concerned, prisoners were the starkest of Manicheans.

Everyone learned about what happened, and everyone was consoling. The guys who had actively disliked Vernon now gave him sympathetic nods; people he was only casually acquainted with consoled him openly; and his actual friends swore to him a blood oath of fidelity that would rival the *familismo*.

"No one deserves that, man, no one," everyone said — at this moment, it was Tony saying it — and Vernon just nodded without affectation.

So sympathetic were his fellow inmates that none expressed any jealousy when Vernon's sentence was expedited and commuted to parole. His son's death and the decision to release him occurred within two days of each other. No one batted an eye.

Between being present with Vernon when he learned the news, and being keenly aware of Vernon's impending release date, Tony, whenever he was on mail duty, took it upon himself to rhapsodize at length with Vernon, his captive audience. Mailmen out on the street delay their route for a quickie or other mischief; Tony delayed his to play-act psychiatrist.

"And I ain't ever even see you cry, man. I have two kids, man, two boys, and I can't even imagine what you are going through. I feel you man, I feel you. I just want you to know, if you bottling all that shit up, man, it's ok, it's ok, you got to let that shit out sometime."

And Vernon just nodded, without affect. There was no point in talking about it. He felt gray and dull, a rainy immutable sky in human form. No one mentioned the reference to rape in the letter, and that was the only line of questioning, Vernon realized, that would wake him from this stupor. It'd leave him stuttering and dissembling, but he'd be awake, at least.

A couple of days before his release, he was given time to take care of some of the prosaic details of his release, i.e. make a few phone calls. Vernon moved with all the vigor of a man whose spine was parallel to the earth.

"Mom?" he asked when he heard the ringing end and the receiver click.

"Vernon." He heard the edge in her voice already. Well, it wasn't fair to call it an edge in her voice; it was just her natural timbre. A yappy dog about to go off.

"Mom. It's me, Vernon."

"Yes I know Vernon, I jus' said your name. I have a name too, you know, you don't nee' to call me 'Mom,' nobody else calls me that."

No one else called her 'Mom' because Vernon was her only child, obviously, but he knew better than to deploy reason.

"Well Mom, I'm out in two days. And I need somewhere to stay - "

"Well you're not coming down here, you can stay in New York."

He breathed deeply and closed his eyes. This was the cresting tide of an inevitable headache. It felt appropriate to have his nostrils burning with whatever pungent dust or debris was coming off this worn phone. Piece of shit phone looked like it'd been ransacked off the streets of New York, some Coney Island nostalgia piece.

"Where am I supposed to go, then."

"I said - dee apartment. Whee still got dee apartment, in Queens."

"Mom, I told you before. You are going to lose that apartment. It has to be your primary residence. It's NYCHA rules, they look into that."

"VER-NON" – the way she said it, you'd think he was a spoiled college boy begging his mommy for a bigger allowance – "don't talk on the phone about this shit, stoopid. It's under control. Just shut up, the Machatos next door got the key, go speak to them. It's good you're out, you watch the apartment.

"You probably don't got much time there, so I won't keep you on dee phone no longer. I see you. I'm glad you can stay in dee apartment. Call me once you get in and sit-choo-ated."

What had he expected? That she'd invite him down to Puerto Rico? Maybe. But what would that have done? In some hazy, indistinct rendering of his imagined future, his mother invited him down to Puerto Rico to begin anew, where he never brought up Cruz. And, since she didn't know anything about Cruz, she never brought Cruz up, either.

And in this reverie he'd continue on with his life, and there was no pain or doubt, and in time the brief tenure of Cruz's life required concentrated thought to remember, it being so distant and remote, to the point where he'd sometimes doubt whether Cruz ever even existed. For there was an unwritten rule that the life of a child must be avenged, but he'd like to check the exceptions to that rule. He intuited that enforcement of that societal norm was contingent upon some kind of bond with the child. How many men did he know who didn't give two shits about their child, who ducked child support and were somehow so nonchalant about the whole thing: offering at most presents, never presence. You bring up the ease which with these dudes abandon their kid, and they get mad at you, run through the whole gamut of excuses with you, tales of crazy 'baby mammas' to just boilerplate dismissals, just a 'c'mon son,' as if you should just know not to bring the issue up. Yet, if anyone ever hurt their kid, well, "nah nigga, now shit's on, nigga, that's my fam, nigga": all of a sudden these deadbeat dads become fuckin' fathers of the year, eager Cliff Huxtables.

He was at least being consistent, he figured.

>< >< ><

When Vernon was seventeen and believed in something like love, he and this girl promised they'd be faithful to each other. She was going to college upstate at Albany, a good school, and they made all the plans and commitments they should have; bus-this, Amtrak-that, and all was well and good, and then soon enough it was her day to move. He helped her pack up any last things — made sure the blue bulldog he won for her on Coney Island was next to her in the backseat — and they hugged really tight and she made that half-smile scrunchy face that showed off her high cheek bones. Then she and her family drove off and she was gone, and all those finely-wrought emotions were for nothing. Those promises they made to each other were the product of some liminal haze, and, with her gone, he had unknowingly but decisively entered a new period. A period where she wasn't around and wasn't going to be around, some chapter of his life that ended and was stowed away. That had been that.

That's what he felt when he was out of jail. All he did was walk out — escorted, of course — and, presto, all that prison bullshit was behind him. He was given a card that had a detective's name on it, presumably the same detective investigating his son's murder. Then he got in Mr. Machato's black beat-up Ford and off they went, back downstate to Queens. Mr. Machato didn't even say much — you'd think he was just picking Vernon up from a 7-11. Good old saintly Mr. Machato, with his wizened, stoic face, his crusty wife, and their two fully-grown, dependent children who were rarely ever mentioned.

They rode in stony silence. Mr. Machato didn't ask about prison life

because he didn't care. Inmates seemed too wiry and frenetic and ram-
bunctious, plotting, scheming, hustling; quiet Mr. Machato seemed like he
was from another planet, like he'd be shocked to learn people like those
prisoners even existed.

He barely even talked when they stopped at the roadside diner. Basically, he spoke just enough to tell the waitress his order, to let Vernon know
that he thought his father had been a good man and that he'd been sorry to
hear of his passing, and to explain how Vernon's mother was able to keep
her apartment:

"She sends us the check each month, written out in her name, and
we drop it off with the Super. That's it. They don't even know she's not
around. Your mom came back to New York to re-certify her income for the
apartment last month, so she may not be back for a while. I got no idea if
your apartment needs repairs, but be careful about that, I guess."

And with that Mr. Machato shrugged. Vernon knew it'd be unbecoming
to probe the arrangement set up between Mr. Machato and his mother, but
he damn well wanted to make sure that his mother was compensating Mr.
Machato for basically allowing her to keep two residences. But Vernon
said nothing, just nodded.

The ride from the prison to "home" was another liminal state, a feeling
of unreality, that mercilessly ended when Vernon glimpsed the Triborough
Bridge. He could have thought about the symbolism — driving through
the deprivation endemic to the South Bronx, across a bridge providing two
options, west to East Harlem, his old haunt, or east back to Queens — but
instead he defenestrated his pretensions, shut his eyes, tucked his neck
in disgrace and just wished to be doing something else, anywhere else.
He kept his eyes closed until the moment Mr. Machato pushed him gently,
apparently figuring he must be asleep. They had arrived and were parked
about a block away from the Woodside Houses.

Mr. Machato had a letter in his hand.

"We're home, Vernon. Welcome back." Vernon nodded and they both
left the car. Mr. Machato popped the trunk, Vernon got his stuff, and they

walked the block in silence.

At the front door, Mr. Machato again reminded Vernon that he'd already given him the keys, and then handed him the letter he'd been carrying. "This was left under my door yesterday, it's addressed to you. A friend, perhaps?" Even Mr. Machato, unhip as he was, blanched at the naïveté inherent in his question, and took that faux pas as an opportunity to expedite his departure. He forced Vernon to take $300, wished him well, reminded Vernon to knock if he needed anything to get adjusted, idled himself by checking his mail (it was a Sunday), and disappeared into the complex.

Vernon was tumbling the letter in his hand the whole time he pantomimed the unreality of being back in his childhood home. He imagined what it'd be like if he were being captured on camera for an unsuspecting audience. All they'd see was him, back in this apartment, checking to see if the lights worked, checking the apartment for dust, carrying a letter, carrying out the same list of listless activities as anyone else. They'd have no idea what this letter was capable of, how just looking at it induced some strong psychological reactions, made his stomach bottom-out, made him feel like he was walking on slanted ground through a perpendicular maze of askew, vicious angles.

Yes, here he was, the same two-bedroom apartment — the "2 BR," as he knew it from all those income forms — that he'd lived in all his life. And now he went into his bedroom and turned on the light, which flared hot for a brief second until it burnt out with an audible pop.

He unfurled the letter, and the strain of the dark made the back of his eyes ache and feel pregnant, as if this letter was actively evil and able to harm him just by being read.

We Will Be Contacting You Soon. We Want To Speak To You. You Want To Speak To Us.

He unpacked and slept without eating, without shaving, without shitting, without doing anything. He felt it immoral to find sleep in circum-

stances like this, but when he did, he thought of Kim-ly's big full lips, which
were most prominent whenever she looked confused. Which was often.

>< >< ><

On the subway the next day, he thought of his dead child mainly because
thoughts of his dead child weren't coming to him instinctively. That is to
say he proactively conjured up images of what his child might have been
like because he felt bad that, without his own guilt-stricken prodding, all
the little bouncing babies and school-aged children on the train would
have passed him by without causing him grief.

He just didn't care, really, and how on Earth could that be true?

He should go to the police, call that number he'd been given. Shouldn't
the police be contacting me? He could show them the letters, maybe get
some police protection ... but no, he wouldn't do that, he couldn't do that,
he had to see this through, perhaps out of the same impulse that introduced
ersatz images of a chipper light-skinned half-Vietnamese school-aged boy
as the screensaver of his subconscious.

He'd walked through El Barrio for less than thirty minutes until he
decided to go home to Queens. While on the 6 train from 59th street to 96th
Street, he thought the same jokes he had always thought. At 96th street:
please, all white people, please get off the train. Then, at 96th street, a
whole lot of professional and posh looking types disembarked. Then, up at
103rd street — no, seriously rich white people, if you are still on this train,
get the fuck off this train. As if privy to his imagination, almost everyone
in the subway car had emptied out at 96th street, leaving just some single
mommas with kids in tow and a smattering of the physically or economically disabled.

He got off at East 110th Street, ducked some young dark-skinned kid
asking/insisting "Yo, lemme get a swipe for the subway," ignored some
angry black man giving everyone a mean-mug, and ambled somberly
behind the hobbled, elderly Puerto Ricans who traversed these East Har-

lem subway steps since time immemorial. He walked east on East 110th street toward Third Avenue and, even though there were some atypical condos or bakeries here and there, it was just all the same bullshit. He didn't even make it to Third Avenue, as the combination of bummy-looking loiterers outside the public library and the truth-in-advertising banner of the Hellgate Post Office was enough to get him to hightail it back downtown and then across the East River to Queens.

He spoke to no one and was fine with it. If only it'd always been like that.

>< >< ><

"Hello good sir, do you know your way around this area?"

Vernon squinted his eyes and creased his forehead. He was back in Woodside and had been walking, head down, oblivious, when this stranger brought him back to Earth:

"Did you hear me, good sir? You do speak English, correct? It would be a sad state of affairs, if I, a Dutchman, could speak English, but you, Mr. Mexican-in-America, could not."

Vernon's forehead was still terse, eyes of squints, as if in rictus.

"Fuck you say, son? Bitch do I look five-three and brown? Who the fuck you be, saying shit like that to people, son. Nigga better get the fuck outta here before I beat your ass, son."

"Mijn hemel, there you go. Ghetto talk. That Ghee-toh talk goes straight to your head, ja?" He spoke English crisply, just the trace of an accent around the hard consonants and the strange lilt of certain words, like "ya."

Vernon kept squinting at this man. Vernon didn't know shit about this guy or what he was talking about. The man was well over six feet tall, muscular, bald and dome-headed, broad-shouldered in brown pleats and a tight brown T-shirt that looked basic but which Vernon knew was of some material or of some brand that made it expensive and chic. Vernon wasn't used to being intimidated by white people — by this he didn't just mean of European descent, like this guy was — but *white people*, you know, that ineffable middle-class whiteness that bleached out the aggression and volatility of generations past. This man was imposing, no doubt, but he was composed, too, and Vernon couldn't picture him lashing out unexpectedly, as if this man was contained behind some invisible frame.

"Nigga you fucking retarded, get the fuck outta here. You know where you are, nigga, you right by the projects." Vernon pointed one under-handed finger in the direction of the western house of the Woodside projects, only a block away. "Stupid fuck."

"I know where I am. And I'm not a nigga or a nigg-er. I'm white, obvious. Like you, you are white, too, ja?

"And is it wrong to call you good sir, Vernon? Are you not a good sir, Vernon?" He had no accent when he said Vernon, and that was unsettling.

The man said nothing for a few moments.

"So, I'm Dutch, from the Netherlands. What do you think of that?"

Vernon shook his head, like, *can you believe this guy?* But he didn't know how to extricate himself. "I don't think anything of it. You have something to say to me, then say it."

"Trying to keep composed are you? If you impress me with some knowledge of the Netherlands, I won't beat the ever-living shit out of you right now."

Vernon glared at him, which was the wrong move. The man sidled up closer to Vernon, so Vernon could literally feel the shadow casting over him from the man's height, get a close-up of the granular muscular detail of the man's forearm, get up-close-and-personal with that shaved thick dinosaur dome-of-a-head.

"Amsterdam, party town. Hookers and drugs. Maybe you should go back home to Amsterdam, cool off a little." He was playing the game and avoiding eye contact. His body language communicated his weakness.

"Not Amsterdam. Utrecht. More to the Netherlands than just Holland. Uh oh, looks like you are failing the test. It's not fun feeling weak, is it?

"I'm here to give you a message. I don't know why you've been selected, so to speak, but you have been. We know you won't do eh-nee-thing stupid. This just involves you, your child, and us. No reason to bring other people in it. If you do, we will kill them. Everyone, anyone.

"We are going to meet you tomorrow, southeast corner ... are you listening? ... we are going to meet joo, tomorrow, noon, southeast corner of 63rd Drive and Queens Boulevard, in Rego Park. M or R train, you know where, ja?

"No police, no friends, no any of that. We know you won't, we know you. We are not dumb, obviously, and, while it not as obvious, you are not dumb, either. If you want justice, you can get it. Tomorrow, ja?"

Vernon could see how muscular this man was; he half-expected the man to show off the ripples of muscles in his abs, proud of them like a family seal.

"But first, of my own interest, I must ask: Is it true? Are you a rapist? I mean, I know it is true, it must be. But I just want to make sure, to hear it from you."

>< >< ><

It never felt like rape. Whether some asshole could look at it after the fact and tell him technically this or technically that happened, and the occurrence or non-occurrence of this or that made something technically rape ... that was beside the point. It didn't feel like rape.

She had said "no," that was true. They had been alone in her apartment for the first time, unpacking her groceries, and he cupped the back of her neck with his hands and kissed her. She said nothing because his face smothered hers. When his face was off of hers but still close by, she looked askance and, if his hands hadn't been clamped around her neck, she would have been shaking her head.

He'd pressed forward. He thought cupping her neck was romantic and dramatic, and when that wasn't enough to woo her, he decided he'd take her on the kitchen table. That display of bombast would be enough to impress her. Then she whispered "no" when his weight was down on her, and "please, Vernon, please, no," in her stereotypical sexy fuck-me Vietnamese accent.

She hadn't struggled, or maybe she had, but not struggled by pushing him off her, but maybe by holding onto his shoulders and restraining him. No, not restraining him, more like enervating him, so he took her weakly, like the way she was weak, saying 'no,' and 'please.' Even her resistance was submissive, and when he entered her, there'd been a look of consternation on her face that didn't parse with the pleasant image of her humble face with those big fat beautiful dick-sucking lips. She always looked so sphinx-like and confused, as if she didn't know that being a pretty Asian woman with big lips gave her exploitable advantages.

But that inscrutability was broken through and she was in pain. But she took his thrusts — held him to lessen their impact, but she took them — while he whispered in her ear, "please, please, I need this," and she whispered back "please," too, and their words had different origins but that was lost somewhere and the words came out the same. But he wasn't dumb and he knew they meant different things except he was inside her and that's what mattered, and he pictured her pussy as warm and all-encompassing like those big lips, and only he was smart enough to somehow know that and take the initiative.

>< >< ><

The Dutchman's nose hair looked like crushed ant legs, Vernon thought, inexplicably, as the man darted forward and socked him hard in the jaw. The force of that punch knocked Vernon out of himself; he was on another plane of existence, a whirling top. He'd never been hit that hard, and he could never hit someone that hard, and all his tough-guy bravado bullshit spun right out of him. Still dazed, a solid punch to his gut brought him back down, down, down to earth, and this wasn't just a fight, it was something horrendous, it was getting hit by a car or struck by a terrible explosive or something. This, too, was unreality.

Vernon pulled his head up, gasping, and looked into that dense, implacable face, painted onto that round dome-skull. Strong, imposing men had bare heads, Vernon knew. He wanted to genuflect before that bare head, beg it not to hurt him anymore. Then, as if sensing that Vernon was prostrating before it, that bare head lunged forward and smashed into Vernon's nose, which was once something of structure but now emptied out like a stomped-upon balloon.

Through some miracle, Vernon landed flat on his back.

"Don't you pass out, now. Queens Boulevard and 63rd Drive, tomorrow, noon. Be there, you piece of shit. You stupid ghetto piece of stupid raping shit. Be there.

"We won't kill you or hurt you, I promise. We won't. Don't show up, and we will, we'll kill you and everyone you know."

Vernon's breathing was wet and congested and the back of his throat tasted salty and metallic. He didn't know how long he was out, but when he got to his feet, there were young boys on bikes staring at him from across the street, and a Middle Eastern bodega owner straining on his tiptoes to see what was going on, as if Vernon was on a ledge or something. Vernon got up, half-dazed, and spit up. He heard an excited, almost-goading "oh shit" from somewhere behind him, and heard someone nonsensically say "son got bodied for some Pop Tarts" and he heard laughing, but he didn't care and lurched forward, stumbling until he was back in his dim apartment.

He pulled out ancient pepperoni Hot Pockets from the freezer and threw them in the microwave. He ate them and felt somehow unworthy of them. He left the cheese-caked encasement on the round table and made his way to the bathroom, where he recognized himself as something swollen and puffy but still himself. He may have brushed his teeth or dotted his face with water, but soon enough he was out of his clothes and collapsed on the bed.

>< >< ><

Vernon had befriended Kim-ly, so to speak, because she was pretty and there was something voluptuous about her. It was obvious she was pretty, but he couldn't put his finger on what it was that attracted him so strongly to her. What first attracted him were those lips. Her lips looked like a duck bill when closed, they were so big and rich, and her eyes were almond-shaped and her skin was pretty and clean and glowing. He wouldn't and couldn't describe it in these terms, but all her features spoke of a virile fecundity that made him turn his head and hunger, like imbibing the wafting scent of freshly-baking bread.

And, to think, all this came about from this clueless Asian woman tending to fruit in some shitty little corner stand a block-or-so from his project.

When he first spoke to her, he situated himself and spoke as if it didn't matter how she responded: either way, he seemed to be suggesting, he was going to be a part of her life. He stood there, broad-shouldered, cocky, accentuating his New Yawk toughness, really emphasizing the heavy d in 'water,' and — this was so corny even he felt it was too much — ended their conversation by buying a single peach and biting into it luxuriantly like it was pure ambrosia.

He'd see her all the time — she always seemed to be working — and he'd help her out sometimes, bringing groceries back to her apartment, which was a two-bedroom apartment shared by four women. She'd nod and be effusively thankful, not saying or revealing much, just listening and saying she'd been in New York for three months and still wanted to visit the Statute of Liberty, and he'd sometimes laugh and she'd smile unknowingly, as if they were having a real conversation contingent upon what each person was saying to the other. All he knew was her name, that she was from Vietnam, that she had a husband-or-someone back home, and that she was probably here illegally, as anytime he recommended she go here-or-there to collect a benefit or get an I.D. she just coyly shook her head.

Once, he thought his lust for her had turned into love. Loving her would make no sense, since they had nothing in common other than that which everyone has in common, but love was supposed to be crazy, right? He'd noticed that the white T-shirt he was wearing was stained across the stomach with congealed strawberry jam, and he thought it looked like blood, and imagined, what if I were dying? This opened him up emotionally, and he looked up at her and she smiled unknowingly and she seemed to fill up that open space.

He came inside her and yelled his release loudly, to show his appreciation and make her feel better. She said nothing, just pivoted off the table and pulled her panties back on up under her skirt. Vernon was all endorphins, and kept looking at her like a solicitous dog, waiting for her to break out in smiles, as if his enthusiasm was contagious. She never did, and then Vernon's enthusiasm curdled briefly into self-pity until it sparked into resentment, and he said "ok then, whud-ever," and left, wishing he had some friends on hand to tell about the hot Vietnamese girl he'd finally bagged.

And after that one time, he didn't hang out around that fruit stand much anymore, except maybe he'd peek in here and there. Over a long course of time, he'd noticed a trend: she was rarely there. He thought maybe she'd moved back to Vietnam or some shit, until one time the little Asian proprietor spotted him and, in that annoying Asian way, pointed a squat finger at him and said, "You! You! You, get out! You not allowed here." Vernon made an arrogant, obnoxious face of dismissal, a loud "pshh," like he was just too hood for this fruit stand. His stance and patois got more ghetto, he said something like "fine, faggot, I don't need your fag shit," and practically crip-walked out of there. He heard someone behind the counter mock-tauntingly, "ooh shit, there goes father of the year, scumbag," and Vernon's stomach lurched up, but he maintained his cavalier composure until he was back on the street.

Then a couple days after that incident, he stalked the fruit stand again and, running into a Hispanic employee, played the concerned citizen and asked about Kim-ly. The man nodded knowingly and pantomimed a swollen belly, and Vernon said "pregnant?" and the Hispanic smiled and nodded mischievously.

And the months passed and he continued working his intermittent construction jobs, all the while pretending to be getting away with something even though he knew she probably wasn't looking for him and that she knew where he was if she wanted to find him, anyway. This fantasy of escape continued for a long time until, like a little boy tired of waiting to be found in hide-and-seek, he outed himself. He went to the fruit stand and asked another Hispanic if she still worked there — it could have been the same man who first told him she was pregnant, for all he knew — and the man just said, casually, "tomorrow," like it was nothing at all. And he was there tomorrow, and so was she, next to a young tanned baby, being ooohed and ahhed over by an avuncular Asian man.

>< >< ><

Vernon woke up sometime around 10 a.m. He took a shit, showered, and made a quick breakfast of buttered toast and did some other chores. There was a weird interlude where he went about his day as if things were normal. He checked himself in the mirror and yeah, the area under his nose had a big rouge smudge like he cut himself shaving, but in a really, really bad way. And he peeked at the clock on the microwave and rushed out the door like he was still on one of those construction jobs, and his body implored "late!" and for a moment he forgot what he was running late for.

Then he was getting off the R train at 63rd Drive-Rego Park, wondering if this was the last time he'd pass through a turnstile.

Even though he made sure to get off on the southeast corner of the intersection — where he was pretty sure he was supposed to meet the Dutch guy — he spun around wildly once he got to the surface, afraid he'd somehow missed them. The last few days moved too rapidly for him to interrogate his thought process, but he either took the Dutch man at his word, or felt obliged to endure whatever punishment awaited him.

Even before he made out any faces, he knew: this was the group he was looking for. There were five men, all fairly tall, hovering around six foot, all in fairly good shape. Varying hues of white, from alabaster to olive to something approaching burnt sienna. He felt a tap on his shoulder that screamed "walk with us, buddy," and he kept apace with the pack like a wayward fish rejoining its shoal.

"Glad you made it, Mr. Camacho." He didn't need to turn around to know that was the Dutchman. Odd, though, that he sounded genuine.

The pack all walked half a block down 63rd Drive before Vernon had any idea who was the leader. But all the group's focus on one man — all the soft touches on the man's wrist, someone pointing out a traffic signal to him, all the little nods appetent for praise — tipped Vernon off that the oldest gentleman, the one in the hat with the 360-degree brim, was the leader. Vernon's hunch was confirmed when they arrived at their destination, a small outdoor cafe with a stubby, rectangular wood table set up for serving. The hatted man sat on the west side of the table, his back to the street. The others, the functionaries — a group that included the Dutchman — sat two or three along the northern and southern sides of the table, respectively. Vernon, the guest of honor, was granted the glory of sitting on the eastern side, his back to the restaurant. There were no other guests; in fact, there weren't any other tables set up outside.

Vernon had miscounted, actually. There were six of them in total (seven if he counted himself), and the one he'd missed was definitely the odd man out. Of average height, brown, unkempt hair, a little disheveled and scrubby looking, could stand to lose 5-10 pounds, with a flabby chicken neck and a face made smooth with the extra cushion of flab. He wasn't as engaged as the others, didn't dote over the hatted man like the others, didn't have the fierce battle-scarred determination of the others, and didn't do much to make his presence felt. He avoided eye contact.

"It's a nice day for this, at least," said the hatted man. He was in his late thirties or early forties, fit, maybe even dashing, if dressed the right way. Vernon half-expected to see the functionaries staring at him expectantly when he failed to immediately respond to the hatted-man's comment. He braced himself for one of the more goonish functionaries to slap him hard on the back and bark "say something!," or maybe even something as dunderheaded as "when the boss speaks, you answer!" But the goons at the table looked like normal guys, for the most part, and instead of cradling their guns in anticipation, they looked rigid and maybe even annoyed. The hatted-man, Vernon surmised, would never say "annoyed"; he'd say "peeved" or some fancy shit like that.

"So, I'll make this brief, Mr. Camacho. Let me just state from the outset that, as you can imagine, we don't do this, ever. By that," he chuckled a bit, "I mean we don't, ahh, usually talk, informally, with the type of people, like you, who we deal with."

"And what, exactly, type of people is you talking about?" Vernon spat out the question in his usual default hood insouciance, as if that flying Dutchman hadn't beaten the moxie out of him less than 24 hours ago.

The Dutchman leaned in, smirk hidden behind his arm.

"Well, rapists, Vernon. You know that by now. You aren't stupid, despite your ... unfortunate diction.

"There are degrees of rape, of course. The violent street rapist is, of course, the worst. The date rapist: still terrible, but not as terrible. We don't say 'better.' Still awful, just not as awful.

"Our question is zero-sum. Rapist, or not a rapist. You are a rapist, although your crime was not as awful as most we've dealt with. In fact, your crime, I can say with only slight hesitation, is the least awful rape we've dealt with. Which is one of the reasons I've decided to talk with you."

Vernon's taut mouth and stone-cold glare served as objections to this characterization.

"Don't, Vernon, don't," he breathed heavily, "don't, look, we know you're a rapist. We know it, you know it, look," and on the hard 'k' on 'look,' Vernon caught a hint of the fast-talking New York shyster he was talking to. "Look, I already said your crime was the least awful crime we've dealt with."

"I didn't commit any crime like that. I wasn't in jail for rape."

The hatted-man gave him a hard stare. "Don't get smart with me. You know what I meant."

As if to shut Vernon up, the hatted-man continued. "You had sex with her once, didn't you. Ever think about that? You had sex with her once, and you conceived. Never struck you as odd?

"Did you know that sexual intercourse from rape is almost three times more likely to result in conception than voluntary sexual cohabitation?" Breaking out statistics, the quickening pace of his speech, the use of that curiously prim term 'sexual cohabitation': Vernon felt that this was the beginning of a speech that'd been rehearsed before.

"Some ignorant people think rape is about 'power.' That's a fashionable idea. Popular on college campuses. Complete nonsense. That's like saying bank robberies are undertaken because it's an opportunity to use guns. No, bank robbery is obviously about getting otherwise unobtainable money. Likewise, rape is a way to spread the seed. Either 'trading up' — getting a woman of greater genetic worth, also known as getting a girl 'out of your league,' or, in more desperate cases, allowing a man otherwise shut out from the evolutionary sweepstakes to put in a bid." The hatted-man smiled. One of the minions at the table swayed and nodded his head nonchalantly, as if keeping rhythm with a familiar song.

"Let me ask you a question, Vernon. When you went off to jail ... you went off to jail for armed robbery, correct? During the time you found yourself in such desperate straits that you needed to commit armed robbery ... you know what I bet you did all day? I bet you jerked off a whole bunch. I bet you jerked off a whole bunch after you got that first letter we sent you, too.

"How do I know that? Because you were nervous and desperate. And desperate men are horny men. Did you know that a man is more likely to cheat on his wife *after* he loses his job? Makes no sense, right?

"Wrong! Because a desperate man is a man who recognizes his sinking social status. His subconscious is telling his body: it's do-or-die time. The seed needs to be spread before all hope is lost. That's why spousal rape, as it is now called, occurs so frequently after the man gets laid off from work.

"You think you're in control, Vernon. You're not, not at all. Think about it! Think about it! What are the odds that you got Kim-ly pregnant on the first and only time you had sex with her? Did your body know you were raping her?"

Their server brought them all coffee and water right when the hatted-man said "did your body know you were raping her." The server continued serving, nonplussed.

"Thank you, Jackson. And you ... you, Vernon. You are interesting to me, I'll grant you that.

"You haven't even asked me anything regarding your son. Your son, remember? Your son, the son we killed, Vernon. Remember that?"

He said these final words in the same timbre as his earlier exegesis on the roots of rape.

Vernon leaned in and rubbed his hands together. "About that." What could he say?

He'd been tormented by feelings of parental inadequacy, of shame, of not even having a family history of abandonment to pin the blame on. He'd had nightmares of meeting his son in his pre-teens and finding him to be some skinny pussy-boy Asian faggot, getting knocked around the schoolyard and taunted for having a tiny little yellow pimple-for-a-dick. He'd had other dreams, alternative scenarios of shame: meeting his son when his son was older and in school for medicine or something, his son talking modestly about math or science or something, real casually, like it was nothing, leaving Vernon wishing he could explain that he too was smart, in his way, but his stuttering, simple language betraying any of his claims to profundity.

"About that, son," Vernon started, cringing in hot embarrassment, "you really think nothing going to happen to you?"

"No, I don't care about that. I wanted you to ask why we did it."

"Listen, you faggot."

"Please Vernon, don't act like that. We thought you were different."

Vernon sensed someone shaking his head.

"I don't understand your thinking, Vernon. Are you trying to threaten us? We outnumber you. We're armed, you're not. We obviously know where you live, we knew how to get to you in prison. We could have killed you there, if we wanted to. We have ... partners whose powers you can't even conceive of." The hatted man turned to the chubbier out-of-place guy and pointed with his thumb. "He can vouch for that," and one of the other men hit the chubby guy on the back affectionately, almost to rouse him up, but the chubby guy still kept his gaze askance.

"Please don't disappoint me, Vernon. I wanted you to ask why we did it. Someone, fill in for Vernon. He's not being helpful. Someone, ask me why we did this."

The other men around the table laughed while Vernon continued rubbing his palms, like a tough guy about to get his hands dirty.

"Why'd you do it, you bastard!" one of his minions play-acted.

"How could you, you monster!" another chimed in.

"Because," and now the hatted man betrayed his zealousness with a smile, "because, we had to. If we'd let him live, we'd be allowing rape to win, right? How is it that scum like you somehow instinctively learned to target the religious, the believers in shame, those who won't abort? Most pregnancies from rape end in abortion, certainly, but somehow, instinctively, you guys are getting better and better at making sure your seed lives on.

"Well, not anymore."

"You murderer!" another yelled in mock-horror.

"Yes, yes, it was terrible, as murder is. And yes, we are very sorry for that, although, of course, if you hadn't committed a terrible act, then we'd never need to commit our terrible act.

"It really doesn't matter. You are not the first, and you will not be the last, so what of it? Your son's survival was, prime facie, a tacit acceptance of the very premise for which we stand against: the proliferation and success of the act of rape. In other words, ceding to the moral demand to let your son live would be acquiescing to, on a biological level, the most ruthless and insidious crime. Ruthless, for obvious reasons, yet insidious, because by its very terms it takes moral hostage over the wicked fruit of its labor. The goal of rape is to spread the seed, and allowing the seed to flourish — for whatever supposed moral reason — surrenders to rape its only sought-after goal. Although, I should add, we are experimenting with new tactics," he said, with an implied nod-and-wink.

A couple moments of silence, and then the Dutchman piped up. "Wow. This guy is a rock, isn't he?"

"Vernon, don't you have anything to say? There are biological reasons why you would be so, shall we say, disinterested in your rape-product, but this ... don't you believe deeply in 'respect,'" – and here the hatted-man employed exaggerated hand gestures to puff himself up when he said 'respect' – "or such similar ghetto bullshit. Aren't you going to say something?"

Vernon nodded solemnly, but that was fake too, like his hand cleansing ritual. "I heard what you had to say, I heard it. I may not be smart as you," he said aggressively, "but I heard what you had to say. You best believe, I'll be checking in with you, for sure. You won't be getting away with this."

"Oh okay, there we go. The threats. That's better."

"I don't get this," Vernon continued, rotating the business card between his fingers, "what makes you think I won't just go to the police with this. I know the detective on the case. You don't think the police want to catch a child killer?"

"Feel free to. See what happens," the hatted-man said, matter-of-factly.

"What's your name, son."

"I won't tell you my name, daughter. Or I can tell you one of my many names, if you like. I'm not your son, by the way," and here the hatted-man again betrayed his exuberance with a smile, tipping Vernon off to the many easy jokes at his disposal, "and it's too late for this now. You had your chance to ask questions. You blew it. We'll be in touch."

And with that the hatted-man stood up, followed by his companions.

Vernon hadn't touched his coffee. "C'mon, you too," one of them said to him. Two of them were too close for comfort, and the one on his left tapped Vernon's elbow, as if to say, "rise!" Vernon got up warily.

The guy who touched him on the elbow pulled a gleaming silver pistol halfway out of his coat. "Ok. So you walk that way," the man pointed back to Queens Boulevard, "and you go home. I'm going to walk you back to the station, okay. You get on the subway, and you go home."

He stuck the gun against Vernon's solar plexus. Vernon walked forward, the man two solid steps behind him. Vernon didn't look back, and none of the men at the table said anything to mark his departure: like his experience with prison, all that had just transpired was just some discrete chunk of time that now felt like nothing at all, an unreality, cordoned off and compartmentalized into nothingness.

"What's your name, man," Vernon asked, still looking forward.

"Can't hear you. Not interested, either." Vernon didn't know what he was doing or what he was planning. He could see the foot traffic approaching on Queens Boulevard, and thought of spy movies, scenes of throwing somebody in his captor's way and running off. Then he'd look back and see his captor yell "fuck!" and his captor would try to maneuver through the crowd and get a clear shot, but he couldn't because there were too many people, and again his captor would yell "Fuck!" and ... scene ... fade to black.

But Vernon did nothing of the sort and just walked back to Queens Boulevard, his captor at his back.

"I don't get you. Not that it matters, but we thought you'd be a little more ... informative, in your way. I mean, it was disappointing how ... he loves a good debate on ethics. We all do. I think he thought you were something you weren't. Maybe someone more ... engaged. Your situation was ... unique, to say the least. Not like anything we've seen, tell you the truth. Don't you give a shit about this?"

"I do, man. I do. I do more than you think. Tell me, how can I get in touch with you again, if I wanted ... to talk."

Before Vernon could turn around fully, the man interrupted and made some gesture toward the subway. "We'll get in touch with you. We aren't far. We never are." Vernon detected a smile on the man's face, sensed it somehow, and instead of running or turning or overpowering him or doing something, he went down into the subway, through the turnstile, and got on the R train to head back to Woodside.

>< >< ><

Before he knew it he was back in his home. Well, not his home, but his mother's apartment. Where he used to call home. Back to Hot Pockets and dingy light and hot air redolent of musk, mold and age. It had all been a dream, in a sense, just a nightmare. He'd plunged unexpectantly into this netherworld, populated by bizarre characters of inexplicable beliefs and moralities.

What was this? What was he to do? Was this is it? His son dead; the mother of his child, left to grieve alone. Even that expression, mother of his child, was cumbersome. A wife was something, but the awkward phrase 'mother of my child' was klutzy, as if having to use that title was part of the punishment for having a bastard.

Look what apathy had gotten him. Here he was, so safe in his not caring. Like he didn't care if Kim-ly didn't love him and never loved him and never even understood him. Like he didn't care that he lived in his mother's project apartment, or that he hadn't had a real job for god-knows-how-long.

>< >< ><

The first and only time he'd ever mugged someone he'd been arrested, for godsakes, and that too was probably because he was too lazy to care.

Not lazy, but fatigued somehow. He always felt like he could collapse upon himself. Too lazy to live. When the cops busted him — minutes after he'd committed the robbery — he didn't really protest or run or anything. They just swooped in and got him, got stupid, lazy Vernon, the water-cooler joke who mugged two white kids right across the street from a fucking parked police car.

He had nothing of worth in him, fine, but his son didn't deserve that. Even if his son was going to be too weak, or too smart, or not like him, or something else ... even if he was a listless piece of shit who snickered at all the dunderheaded gangsta tough guy bullshit but wanted those same tough guys to accept him so badly. He couldn't escape anymore from the need to care.

>< >< ><

Emboldened, feeing a strange rush he'd never felt before, Vernon made his way to his bedroom and looked under his mattress. It couldn't still be here, nah ... he felt around for his gun, a little .22 he'd stashed about six years ago. He'd never actually used it before, and he never ran any drugs or anything illegal out of this apartment, so he'd never worried about getting busted ... but somehow it was gone. What the fuck? His mother knew about the gun, but would she really be proactive enough to get rid of it? Didn't seem like her.

He had a spark of inspiration and bounded over to Mr. Machato's apartment.

>< >< ><

"Hey Mr. Machato," he said excitedly, as Mr. Machato slowly opened the door. Vernon could see Mrs. Machato, decrepit and practically immobile but all smiles, sitting on the couch. She was ensconced with linens and doilies, just as he always remembered.

"Hello ... Vernon," she said very slowly, lifting an arm, not really to wave but to do her version of waving, which consisted of showing Vernon her palm.

"Hello, Missus Machato. Nice to see you again."

"Nice to see you too, Vernon," she said, and brought her attention back to the television.

Mr. Machato looked at him expectantly.

"Sorry to bother you. Before my mother left for Puerto Rico, did she give you anything? Like, any valuables, or a box, or anything like that?"

Mr. Machato froze for a moment, like he was processing something that did not compute. Then he nodded gravely, put up one finger, and ambled out of view. Several minutes later, he returned with a small cardboard box.

"Great. And, thanks for everything. And thank you too, Missus Machato."

At hearing herself referenced, Mrs. Machato turned again and did her signature gesture. "No … problem, Vernon. We love … you. Say hello … to your mother, for us." And with that, her hand went back to where it was.

He explored the box. He frowned in confusion when he saw the top layer consisted of innocuous T-shirts … until he felt the hard steel underneath them. Goddamn Mom, you selfish piece of shit. There was a whole mess in this box, but here was his .22. He checked the clip and, holy shit, it was still loaded, just like it was all those years ago. Only mom would repay the Machatos' kindness by gifting them an illegal, loaded .22 for storage.

He could feel the steel jutting like a foreign protuberance inside his puffy jacket. He raced down to the elevator and tapped his foot the whole time, as if Kim-ly was going to be outside waiting for his embrace.

It was a clear day, mid-afternoon, around 3 p.m. He didn't have a phone so he couldn't be sure of the time, which brought his mood down. Nowadays, if you didn't have a smartphone, you were poor. What'd it make you if you didn't have any phone at all?

>< >< ><

It wasn't hard getting into the Audubon Houses and he knew where to find Ms. Gloria Hernandez.

"Vernon," she said to him, a bit warily, a bit happily, when she saw him approach her apartment in the hallway.

"Ms. Hernandez," he nodded gently toward her. "Can I come in for a second?"

She sighed, the door half-ajar, and threw up her hands in a 'what does it matter' expression, but then turned back to him and smiled, sort of, an expression to show him her sour mood wasn't his fault. "Come in, Vernon. Why not? Vernon, back out on the streets, back from the past, why not come in? These times they can't get any stranger."

He couldn't read her general mood or what she was getting at. He stepped inside the apartment which looked neat and fastidious, but he didn't have any recollection of what it'd looked like in the past. He'd last been here, what, ten years ago, on some errand of his mother's?

"I'm glad you recognized me, that's a good sign," he said sheepishly and sat down.

"Can I get you anything? Coffee, tea?" she offered.

"Tea? Look at that? No no no, that's too fancy for me, you know," he said with a smile. "Some water would be great."

She brought him some water as he looked around the apartment. The place was orderly and clean and redolent of Palmolive. She was a boon to her building.

She asked about his mother and he told her he hadn't seen her and she was down in Puerto Rico. She asked whether he was staying in the Woodside Houses and looked mildly triumphant when he confirmed it, and mentioned the trick she told his mother about sending the rent checks to a neighbor to hold onto a NYCHA apartment while you lived elsewhere. They talked briefly about his stint in prison, how he was at heart a good guy and had always been a good kid, just had to keep his head above water and his nose clean, so to speak, an expression that bespoke of drugs even though he had always been sober. He didn't let his confusion show. He asked her about her children, and she snickered and corrected him, she only had one child, a young son, and he was good, and she mentioned he was away but didn't give more detail. She made an utterance that sounded like she was going to say "sister" but left the enunciation inchoate. She then looked at him like she fumbled something.

"Gloria " — she insisted he call her Gloria — "I - I'll be honest. I need your help, if you can provide it. I'll just say it. I had a son. He was a five, about five. He was murdered recently."

She cursed her condolences in English and Spanish. He knew people spoke their native tongue when they felt impassioned or unguarded.

"He was killed by this group that I don't understand. They were obsessed with ... with abortion and rape and had all these crazy theories about it. They killed him because – they believed – he was a child of rape. I know this sounds crazy, and to anyone else I'd say this sounds crazy, I know, but you ... I know. I know about you, and your ... history. Not saying that in a bad way. I just know. Know things."

They both knew what he was talking about. She was hard to read, but everything about her — her heavy clothing, her stout, thick body, her delayed body language — gave off a sense of weariness.

"You know, everyone knows, apparently, right?" She laughed spitefully. "So much for Ms. Hernandez and her ... operation. Everyone knows everything, apparently. And I'm always the last."

He put up his hand as if to ward her off the trail. "It's not like that, Ms. Hernandez. I don't care what you do, and I don't really know ... what you do. I just know it involves ... involved pregnant women and abortions and, you know, compensation, stuff like that. But I don't care. What you do is what you do. It's your business.

"But, I imagine that ... maybe I'm stupid, you know, but I imagine that's a small field. People got to know people. And maybe what I'm describing to you, my situation, sounds like something you may know about? Or maybe the same people? I'm just looking for a trail."

"We all do what we can do," she said. "Do you know what I did? I'll tell you. I got pregnant and had abortions on purpose, for money, and referred many other people I know to the same people, for the same reason, so you know. That's all. I never did anything more. I was just a supplier." She spoke gracefully but her pace picked up as she spoke, as if she enjoyed getting this off her chest. "But that's all over for me. Has been for a bit. You know, my social worker started snooping around in my affairs, in ... that group's affairs. His work colleague was found dead, and he disappeared, hasn't been heard from again."

Vernon nodded, said okay, not sure where this was going. "I just need a name, or somewhere to go. I don't care what you did."

"I know, Vernon, I know. You are a good man. I ask myself, what did I get myself into? These people were going to have abortions anyway. Why not something positive come out of it? And then, we'd get pregnant on purpose, and I'd think, it's our bodies, we can do what we want, we are the ones taking the risk. The money is – was – good. There's no harm in it. I didn't ask questions. But now everyone knows and I think my time is up."

"Please, Ms. Hernandez. For me. For my son. For my mom." Like his mom knew or gave a shit.

"Vernon," she waved him off. "You are not understanding me. I'm not blowing you off. I know. It's the same people, I'm sure of it. They do a lot. But Vernon. What I'm trying to say is there is nothing you can do. They are powerful and smart. I don't know why they do what they do or how they do what they do, but I know they are powerful and smart, and there's nothing you can do. You can't stop them."

"I don't want to do anything. You want to know my plan? I'm going to take my gun and kill as many of them as possible. That's it. That's all I can do. I have nothing other than that. They killed my son. No police. No nothing. Nothing but going and killing as many of them as I can. If they kill me, that's fine. I just want to kill as many of them as I can. I have nothing left and no other plans. I need to do something, and I'm realistic. That's all I can do and I've decided."

She bobbed her head slightly, and then gradually more so, impressed in a way with the simple clarity of his objective. "You know, Vernon, I'm a dead woman. I know that. Eventually, they will come for me. I don't know why they haven't; maybe because they know I can't do anything because

I still send people their way from time-to-time, because I don't ask questions, but I'm not dumb. This is one of those things, I guess, that not even
they can guess at. How would they know that your mother and I met randomly at a bingo game so many years ago? How could they know you've
heard what I've done? Funny, how these things work.

"Just know that I never did or knew anything about any murders.
That's not what I did, ever."

"I know, Ms. Gloria, I know."

She assured him several more times that the stuff with the abortions,
that's all she ever knew about. She wasn't surprised, to be honest, to learn
about this dimension to their operations but she'd never had any knowledge or role in that whatsoever.

She had some addresses for him. Some family planning clinics they
worked with, but she'd never seen any of the real players there. There was
a small warehouse she visited once, in Corona, Queens, several years ago,
where she'd been to a small gathering, saw things she didn't really understand but got the sensation it was some kind of power base of operations.

She'd never been back there, had no idea if it was still there, but she
gave him the address and wished him the best of luck. She kissed him on
the forehead, told him she admired his bravery, that he was a smart man,
going in with his eyes open, and that his son — if he could understand —
would be proud.

>< >< ><

Why he chose to spend his misspent youth — and misspent adulthood – in
East Harlem rather than Corona, Queens, was never clear to him. Corona, like East Harlem, was an overwhelmingly Hispanic neighborhood and
steeped in the culture. Maybe it'd been because of the cultural cache of
East Harlem. Everyone knew East Harlem was rough. The corner of East
125th and Lexington could look like the Apocalypse: lines of bums depos-
iting their pilfered recyclables; every disabled old-timer in the neighbor-

hood sitting on an upturned garbage can or leaning on a cane; out-of-it toothless women in wheelchairs waving little Puerto Rican flags; angry young men plotting and scheming and hustling, voicing their plans without shame or fear of repercussion. Corona may have its rough parts, but after disembarking the 7 train and walking north on 111st Street toward Northern Boulevard, he didn't see much of anything, except some old-timers and maybe some young families heading to Flushing Corona Park to take their pictures by the Unisphere.

And when he made it to Northern Boulevard and saw that, yes, it was still Northern Boulevard all the way out here — with its car franchises and blaring traffic — he had to fight the urge to turn around, as if this was some bullshit errand at a crowded Duane Reade.

He walked up the 112 block of Northern Boulevard, doing his best to guesstimate the right address. He tried his luck at the only lot that wasn't a car park or dealership.

It was a squat industrial unit – a factory, maybe, although he was conditioned to believe there were no factories in the boroughs anymore. All that shit had been torn down and turned into condos. Shit, he hadn't met anyone who worked at a factory, maybe not in his whole life.

There was a man standing outside wearing a tight black shirt, a double-breasted jacket over it, and blue jeans. He was white, about 6 foot, good shape. The fact that he was a white guy doing security out in Corona gave Vernon pause. The brief reverie, of forgone factories and old timers and tourists and the hood politics of Corona and East Harlem ... the jarring presence of that white guy ....

"Hey," Vernon shouted, no longer thinking. His brain was no longer acting in sequence, his lungs and heart on overdrive, marinating in adrenaline.

"Yes sir, how can I help you?" the man asked, flatly.

This was crazy, the part of his brain concerned with survival told him, through the electric jolt of nerves, frisson and nausea. You can still go home, forget all this.

"What kind of building is this?"

"It's a factory, sir."

"Yeah, a factory? What kind of factory?"

"Do you have business here, sir?"

"Yeah, man. I'm an interested customer. I heard about this place and I'm interested."

"Yeah? You need 1,000 aluminum cans? Do you normally solicit from businesses you don't know about?"

Vernon had no idea why he felt that this man should be more deferential.

"I'm here to see some people who work out of here. One of them is a tall, bald guy, from The Netherlands. He's from a place called 'You-trekt.' That sound familiar to you?"

Maybe the man's face hardened. If it did, it was by a matter of degree unknown to the human eye, but detectable to Vernon by some other, unknown sense.

"Yeah, and what do you want to see this man for?"

"That's my business. Is he here? I want to see him."

"Yeah? That so? You know man, you're pretty lucky, if 'lucky' is the right word."

"Yeah? Now what makes me so lucky?"

"Well, you're here, somehow. You don't seem too bright, though, if you don't mind my saying. I'm surprised it's gone this long with you, really. Really, I am."

"Is that so? Okay." Vernon turned around and mugged like he'd brought a crew that was lying in wait for his signal to strike. As he fidgeted and shifted around, he tried to lean in and get a look of what lay behind this guy and the entrance. He couldn't get a good look at anything, just the outline of a corner.

"So can you bring him up here?"

"Nah, he'll call you, I'm sure."

"I don't even have a phone."

The man guffawed. "Oh really, no phone?"

"Nope."

"Look at you, the man with no phone. Real mover-and-shaker here."

"Yep."

And they talked over each other, temporizing, Vernon insisting he be let in, or be allowed to speak to the Dutchman, his answers becoming more-and-more bowdlerized, not even monosyllabic, just grunts and huffs and sounds, as if they had a hypnotic, entrancing power to lull him into doing what he came here to do. This man wasn't moving, wasn't relenting, convinced of the power of his position.

"So you really not gonna move?"

"Nope. And I'm not going to tell you again, either."

"You not? Show me, what're you gonna do to stop me?"

And at this the man laughed, and looked around quickly like he, too, had a crew he was impressing, even though it was just the two of them. Like, 'can you believe this guy,' two men, weaned on movies, acting as if they were in one.

"Well, since you asked," the man said in a low voice, and moved his hand closer to his double-breasted suit jacket, and the man delayed again, looking around.

Vernon took out the .22, backed up, extended his arm, and must have caught the man off-guard because he saw only the attitude drained from his face, his skin drawn, and Vernon fired directly into the man's neck, one shot.

The goon's throat split and he fell back, his head smashing the ground, hard. Vernon heard low gurgling but didn't look further. He waited thirty interminable seconds. The sounds of the street were the same as before. The man wasn't moving.

He planned on frisking the body and checking his neck for a pulse, but the sight and touch of the gore derailed it, brought the experience into another realm.

Vernon put his back to the entrance, gun low but at the ready, and slowly, as stealthily as he could muster, made his way into the building.

The ceiling was high and the lights were low. He didn't know where to go, where to move, the dimensions of the building or how far back the building went. He couldn't hazard a guess. He walked carefully, in a crouch, about ten yards, keeping close to the walls and the shadows. There were no clanging machines, no gouts of smoke, no industrial manufacturing, not that he was really expecting that. There was a row of three, long wooden tables that reminded him of a school cafeteria. Shapes on the tables, papers perhaps, hard to see in the unrevealing light.

A door opened behind him. He ran in a loop, around a bend for cover.

He saw a white man, tall, light hair, in a dark sweater. The color and bulk of the sweater, along with the dim lights, left much a mystery. Vernon made sure there was no one else with him, and he ran up behind him and drew the gun to his head.

"Don't move or I'll kill you, okay?" He butted the front of the gun as gently as he could against the back of the man's head. The gun hit him harder than Vernon had anticipated.

The man's neck craned backward, flinched in a surprise, but didn't say anything, just put up his hands.

"The Dutchman, you know him?"

"Which one?"

"Tall, bald, knows how to fight, from You-Trecht."

The man's hands high above his head (*make him lower his hands, doesn't look good,* Vernon thought quickly to himself), lowered and pointed a single finger. Pointing back behind Vernon, to the door he came from.

Vernon turned, taking his attention off the man, which he knew was moronic, but he had to. There were three men there, two in the doorway, the other right behind them.

"Fuck." Vernon pulled the trigger without looking. He felt the spray back on his hands and clothes but didn't care, just ran forward, taking a moment to spin back around and fire another shot, where he saw the fallen man flailing and heard him screaming, lost control of himself and twirled to the floor, caught himself and kept running straight.

He barreled through the door at the end of the hallway and tumbled into a man in a dark suit. From the velocity and impact, the man hadn't been opening the door in any hurry, and the sudden collision splayed him across to the other side of the tight, narrow room. Vernon turned around, found that the silver knob had a lock, and engaged the lock. Click. No windows to this room. Good. Small. Almost like a classroom, something like a chalkboard but digital, a small learning nook, maybe.

He ran to the man in the dark suit and shook him, put the gun to his chest, looking to grill him, now on a full blown rampage. The man grabbed Vernon's wrists and pushed, doing his best to get himself level while throwing Vernon off balance. It didn't work. Vernon fired four shots directly into the man's gut. It was like slow-motion: firing at point blank range, firing while capturing the man's grimaced, stilted reaction; firing at the man splayed back against the outer wall, limbs akimbo; firing as the man slid down it. He shot him again, this time in the head, because he knew head shots killed and maybe shots to the gut didn't.

Vernon turned around, heart heaving, and faced the door.

There was another person here, in the corner. A man (*all men here*, he felt safe in concluding), but this man he recognized. The sloppy, chubby one from the lunch meeting. The one who looked like he didn't belong. He was sitting in the corner, again looking like he didn't belong, like he wanted to be anywhere else. He didn't look as disheveled, but still, more like a backend employee. Not someone client-ready. He wore a suit that fit oddly, too tight at the neck, too tight at the waist, a plain white button down, no tie.

"You should just kill me, then yourself. I'm telling you. Not as a threat. Kill as many of them as you can, but kill yourself after. You can't get out of here alive. It's better to be dead. Not for them, they're all true believers. I'm ... someone who made the wrong decision.

"But kill yourself. Kill as many of them as you can, let them kill you. They'll kill you quickly, just die in the gunfire. Don't escape, because then they'll send something after you. You've probably heard and seen enough to believe anything, but you won't believe the influence they have, the people and … things that are beyond people that they work with. Their clientele, if you will."

Vernon stood there, panting. Again, pregnant silence, momentary calm, maybe he was safe here, had time to think. Unlikely. He sensed a bulk behind the door.

"They know you're here. I'm sure they heard the gunshots. How many bullets do you have left in that?"

"I - enough."

"You don't need to intimidate me. I'm not trying to stop you. Kill me, if you want, but that may be a waste of a bullet. If they kill you, I'll do my best to take your gun and keep killing them."

Vernon nodded. He wasn't ready to believe he'd found a partner, needed to keep his guard up.

"Are they, are you a prisoner here?"

"Something like that, I suppose. I have some uses for them, I guess. I sold my services to protect someone. It's just the way it is. If I die, they won't go after her, no reason to. I'm already gone, vanished."

Vernon signaled toward the dead man against the wall. "Was he, he a bad guy? I mean —" he was panting and beginning to cramp up, which wasn't good, despite all the survival instincts he should be feeling, his shins were shaking and aching, his innards cramping, keep it together. "He wasn't like, a janitor or something. He knew what was going on here?"

"Yes, he knew what was going on here. Everyone here, honestly, knows what is being done. Not a lot of people here today. All over the City."

There was a loud rapping against the door and the presence of many bodies outside it.

"We know you are in there, Vernon," he heard through the muffling effects of the thick door.

"Back the fuck off, or I'll kill both of the guys in here. You know I'll do it."

In sotto voce: "There some exit here I don't know about?"

The man in the corner shook his head. "No. This is a classroom of sorts, unfortunately. Only exit is the one you came in from. Trapped. Do you have a second gun?"

"No," he said, and the man in the corner didn't question him, could tell he was telling the truth. He should have frisked that guard outside but had gotten spooked. Stupid. Not that it mattered, really.

"That Dutch guy ever here? The one from the lunch in Rego Park?"

"More than one Dutch guy there, but I think I know which one you're talking about. The bald one."

"Yeah."

"Yeah, I think so. It's your lucky day. He's rarely here, but I talked to him earlier today, actually. He was here."

"What is this place, anyway?"

"It's a lot of things. They do a lot, run some legitimate operations, I guess, all in support of that one underlying ... agenda, I guess."

He paused a beat, then continued in a sotto voce monotone. 'There's no God, at least not in the way we conceive of it. Or at least, there can't be the relationship with God we always sort of take for granted. It's not possible. I know that sounds strange to say, especially now, but it's true. Trust me. I've conversed, of sorts, with living things beyond our knowledge and intelligence. Perhaps they are gods, of sorts, in the sense a man seems a god to a lower animal. But not extraterrestrial. Just, different.

"But it's not possible for them to exist and for us to exist in the relationship with God that we learned about our whole life. Perhaps that's what motivates them, this group. They are obsessed with evolutionary psychology. Very mechanistic, very logical, very confident. Perhaps, knowing what they know, that makes sense. They know more of the workings of the world than perhaps almost everyone else.

"I don't know if that makes you feel better or not. I just thought, maybe you should know that. Maybe that takes some of the pressure off. Makes you feel better, I don't know. Less guilty. I don't know. Even knowing that, knowing what's true, you still can't shake the old feelings."

Vernon didn't respond and kept his gun drawn at the door.

"His name is Finn, by the way, if that's what you care about, killing him. I understand. His name is Finn."

"Finn!" the man in the corner yelled, now facing the door. "Finn, you out there! This guy is here to see you."

"I'm out here," he heard someone yell back, someone that sounded like the Dutchman. "I can't wait."

"So, he's out there," the man said to him, again in his resigned register. "Kill him if you can. But, there are a lot of Finns out there, so to speak."

"Ok. What's your name, by the way?"

"What does it matter? ... Alex. My name is Alex."

"Vernon."

"Glad to meet you, Vernon. I admire what you're doing."

"Thanks."

And more moments passed as he stared at the door. For how long he didn't know, both him and Alex sitting breathlessly, not talking, until a shot rang out from the hallway through the door. And then another, and another.

Vernon fired two shots at the door, now five separate holes. Shots aimed at the lock and then a solid kick against the door, which staggered weakly, and another solid kick which warped the door drastically, only a couple more kicks and it would fold completely like prey being overtaken by a dominant animal.

He fired more and more bullets and heard a grunt and saw the shadow of a body fall to the ground, and fired again at just the right time, after the door was kicked in, and got someone in the shoulder.

He fired and fired and never had to hear the click of an empty gun. He felt at his head and there was no left ear there anymore, knowing he put his fingers into a disfigurement of gore, couldn't really see anymore and his relationship with the physical world had altered. He was sliding down, fired, took out another body, felt at his stomach and touched a texture reserved for his insides, and that brought him back to reality, his impending death, and funny he could still feel the burning in his shins.

The world was an explosion of red hues, everything was a red hue, dripping exuberant yet dull brick-red paint, drenched, heavy drainage, emptying out, hot, heat, red, alarm bells ringing, knowing this was an end, to brace himself, filling his mind only with images he knew represented his son and of the conviction that his life could have gone in many different directions, but he pulled it together at the end to die fulfilled.

"It's Not Feelings of Anxiety; It's One, Constant Feeling: Anxiety"

"SO, THIS IS the little guy. This is the reason you only had one drink."

"Yup, here he is. Craig" — Miles pointed to his burbling baby son, gently bouncing on his wife Miranda's knees — "meet Henry."

"I like how formal you are with him already."

"All business, even at an early age."

Henry said his pleasantries to Miranda and crouched to address Craig, the first entry into the Klahnsman-family clan.

"Hey little man, how are you?"

Craig Klahnsman's eyes widened and a bubble of a smile appeared on his face. It was enough that somebody new was in front of him, someone with a friendly, funny voice. At this age, every new encounter tickled his pleasure center.

Henry waved his hand floppily. Craig did his best blubbery, uncoordinated pantomime.

"Look at those motor skills!" Henry said.

"I know. His future is already laid out for him. He'll be a surgeon."

"Motor skills don't run in your genes. Are you sure he's yours?"

Henry heightened the delivery with a supple turn and smirk while Miranda kicked out at him in jest.

"Ummm, I can certainly flail my arms and be just as uncoordinated as he is. Haven't you seen me ever, I don't know, try and fix anything?" Miles offered.

"Actually, no, I haven't," said Henry.

"That's right. There's a reason for that. I'll know for sure if he's mine if that's how he tries to shoot a hoop in fifteen years, or throw a baseball."

Henry laughed about how in fifteen years Craig would be about sixteen or seventeen, and that's when he'd first try shooting a hoop or throwing a baseball? Their comic riffing had lost nothing in the two years since Miles and Miranda-plus (the term Miles had adopted for Miranda while she carried their child) had left Chicago to return to Southern California.

Henry spent a couple more minutes playing the usual baby-games, mimicking Craig's movements and repeating words and giving him little high-fives.

"He does have your eyes, Miles, I'll give you that," Henry granted him. "You always did have cool eyes. Fortunately, he's pretty cute overall, so he must have Miranda's looks."

Miles delivered in his unbreaking, monotone delivery: "Unfortunately, the doctor said he also has my heart. It's pitch black."

"Don't listen to that goofball," Miranda told Craig, her charmingly chubby giddy mass of baby. She lovingly clutched Craig's chest. Craig giggled and cooed and enjoyed the touch and sensation of his protective fat being swaddled. "Don't listen to that goofball," she repeated again, in that inevitable sing-songy cadence people adopt whenever they speak to babies.

"He shits like me, too. Explosively. That's also how we know he's mine," Miles added.

"Well it's great you have him now. You can finally use all those extra diapers you stockpile."

"Stockpile? Do you know how much I shit? All those diapers were put to good use long before Craig was even born."

This riffing came effortlessly, yet, ironically, was simultaneously exhausting. Knowing this, Miles offered to go back out with Henry and leave his wife in peace. "I mean, I always thought, practically speaking, having a kid would lead me to drink more, not less, anyway. So it makes sense why we should go out for another," he stated in his matter-of-fact comic monotone. He received the exhaled snorts of laughter he sought, got Miranda's "ho ho ho" — which was both criticism and tacit approval — and went back out with Henry. She always wanted to keep up with their back-

and-forth but Miles suspected she found it tiring over time.

"I'll only be gone like another hour or so. Be home before bedtime."

"I know baby," Miranda said softly, and kissed him tenderly on the lips.

They decided on a bar to try, on Miles' recommendation ("I assume no responsibility if you don't like this bar," Miles had said. He hated feeling responsible for recommending something someone didn't like.) Henry assured him it was fine and so they went.

They sat at the counter in the brightly-lit bar.

"So, man, a kid. Look at you, got a house, with a garage and everything? And a real live kid. You are, as you always said, a 'Real Person' now."

A Real Person. Having a child, a family, a mortgage. Being a Real Person. Being literally responsible for the health, well-being and development of an autonomous being that inherited your genes and served as your proxy representative to future generations — that's ... Real Person Shit.

"I know, I know. Bartender, I'll need twelve more drinks," he joked to the guy behind the counter, who he could tell was half-listening in on their conversation.

"Sounds like you have a young kid? Who knows, you might need it," the bartender joined in, lips almost invisible behind his mountain man hirsuteness. Like this kid knew anything about that. A line like that may have meant more coming from the archetypical hoary, grizzled bartender who has seen it all. This bartender was a kid. Miles noted this all impassively — it didn't really bother him too much, except for the knowledge that this kid could make his jokes and go home to his studio apartment, sleep until noon and get high at night with his young, hot artiste friends.

"So, how is everything going, for real though?" Henry pressed him.

"Good, pretty good, I guess."

There was an unusual silence.

"So, what is it, you mention Real Person stuff and then it gets all serious? That's when 'Shit Gets Real.'"

Henry snorted his approval of the punctured silence.

"I guess things are fine, job is still shitty and lame, but at least it's shitty and lame back in California. Glad they finally transferred me. It's cool to own a house. Sucks having to drive though. You know, the usual. Or, as we say in California, 'the yoojzh.' If you moved out here, you'd pick up all the slang.

"How do you like your time out here? Sure beats freezing your balls off in Chicago, eh?"

Henry was just visiting on a work trip.

"So," Henry didn't take the bait to switch topics from Real Person Shit, "I take it you no longer believe that there is 'no value in creating human life.'" He said this last part in a bit of a stentorian, didactic tone. It was a playful dig at Miles' longly-held, freely-espoused views back in college, but it was a bit unfair, too, as Miles had always expressed it matter-of-factly and respectably. He was never some rabid proselytizer, but when the conversation of a higher power or the joys of life-giving or just general plans for the future had come up — usually in so mundane a question as to whether he ever planned on having kids, and if not, why not? — he had always stuck to his guns and explained his position if asked. Most of his friends had agreed but never articulated it and were content just plodding onward, while others just respectfully disagreed out of allegiance to a deeply held faith in a higher-purpose or disagreed but had no articulate reason for doing so.

"I never sounded like that."

"Well, you know what I meant. I always remembered that rather pungent turn of phrase. It's a good line. 'No Value in Creating Human Life.'"

"Hmm, well ... of course there is no objective or inherent value in creating human life. I still believe that, I suppose. Except for having Craig, of course. That's the universe's only one exception to that general rule."

At this Henry scoffed and padded his drink against the coaster for emphasis. "Aww man, you sold out. What would 'Miles of Years Past' say to that?"

To that Miles shrugged in an 'ain't I a stinker' way. "Cognitive dissonance, man. How would any of us be able to survive without cognitive dissonance? Craig is a cool kid, though. He's great. I love him. He's a keeper. Even if he has to live with the shame of not having as cool of a name as his father."

That was a polite feint, of course: Miles had argued in the past that procreating because you 'love' a child is solipsistic and selfish.

"I don't know. Why does anyone do anything?" Miles intended that to be the end of it. He had a slight headache.

"Touché." And they continued their conversation and their beers, both of them having to drink light, Miles for his family, Henry because he needed to finalize a presentation for a conference later in the week.

"So, does having a kid make you no longer wish you could fuck other women?" This was a call-back to when they worked in the same office back in Chicago and would talk harmlessly about their desirable female colleagues.

"No, unfortunately not."

"Ahh, figured," Henry responded knowingly.

A pause. "It has made me not want to fuck other kids though."

That joke was a winner, as it got Henry to spit-take his beer back into his cup.

Nailed it.

>< >< ><

Miles ended up being a little more intoxicated than he wanted to be. He wasn't drunk, but his head sat swimmingly and he felt the rising cresting of pressure in his forehead as he tucked Craig into bed.

The mess of shit in Craig's diaper was a sharp knife through the booze induced fog, and blew away any creeping sentimentalism Miles may have been feeling about fatherhood. Jesus. Craig looked up at him with awe and reverence — and whatever emotions he indicated by his spitting and giddy screeching — while Daddy fumbled around with the diaper. Miles had done this countless times already, but he always had some stop-and-start problems with wrapping the diaper properly.

Craig said nothing. Miles' only critic was himself.

>< >< ><

It'd been two hours since he did anything that could remotely qualify as work. That must be a record. Not one internal note input into the Bullhorn software, not a candidate contacted, not even an email answered. Not that there were many emails to answer — six unmarked emails by his count — and maybe he could assuage himself by responding to those six inconsequential emails and feel like he was getting something done. He was supposed to be hustling, being proactive, and bringing in clients and candidates so he'd have MORE emails to respond to. That was the nature of this work. Not having work wasn't a good thing.

He was not cut out for sales. It just wasn't in his blood. He was a reactor — he'd done well in college and even his early entry-level jobs because the teachers and bosses gave him work and, being fairly responsible and detail-oriented, he completed the work fairly well. But sales was a proactive sport. You couldn't just operate like he wanted to: come to work, watch the clock and wait to go home. No, you needed a certain kind of competitiveness, a passion, a need to close deals and feel validated. He needed to be validated, of course, but by loved ones, not corporate bosses.

There was just something ... what was wrong with him? This was a good job, he'd done well in the past, he deserved this posting, he was sent out to expand the Southern California office for a reason. That's what his wife said and other people said, too, but of course, they didn't know.

He just assumed the paterfamilias instinct would have taken over. Miles had so many people riding on him now — a family — but still he kept this distance, of being above the fray, as if he were too good and special to debase himself hustling HR representatives for menial work orders to fill. He'd gotten some early scores on the board through dint of luck — met some "walking invoices," as his boss back in Chicago had called them, highly qualified candidates that just reached out to him, just happened to be perfect for the jobs they had on the job board. Even though everyone knows the essential ingredient in the recruiting game is luck, he got a good reputation for being nothing but the conduit between qualified candidates and their jobs.

Then the luck started running out, the job board slowed down, his boss' patience was wearing a little thin with his lack of hustle, but then, boom! Pregnancy, a transfer request to head out to the fledgling California office. His boss, he suspected, had been sorry to get rid of him on a personal level but not-so-sorry otherwise. And now here he was, in his little office with only two job orders to work on — a lowly secretarial fill and a part-time library assistant fill — job orders that every other agency in California had in their databases. He had those jobs, had a sea of untapped and untouched HR representatives.

Representatives that, at this pace, would remain untapped. What was wrong with him? He just ... couldn't do it. He wanted nothing more than to do it. He wanted orders to fill, candidates to interview and place, backslaps and high-fives. He wanted it, and he could imagine it, but yet here he was, not doing it. Did he feel above it? Was he afraid of failing? Was the fantasy of success enough, did the fantasy conjure up the same chemical cocktail as the actual accomplishment? These were all interesting questions, but the reality of the situation was the Reality: he ate lunch, checked and re-checked his email and the effluvia of the Internet with the dedication of someone trying to decipher a pattern.

His printer had been non-functional for the last three days. They had an assistant who was supposed to help with those technical issues. He resolved to fix it himself to make himself feel good, only to punish himself later for spending his time on something someone else was responsible for, that had no relation to his bottom line. He knew this, yet still, he did it, sliding open the printer and examining it (he may as well have been looking inside the human brain), looking serious as if the illusion of competence needed stoic resolve to sustain.

But of course, he couldn't fix it — it kept saying there was a fucking typeface load error; isn't typeface what gets printed OUT, not something inside the printer? — and doing something successfully was an optimistic pipe dream to the ever-frustrating reality of knowingly spending his time on a distraction and managing to fuck that up, too. Better call the college dropout with the generic tribal tattoos to fix the problem.

>< >< ><

He sat around the dinner table with Miranda and his son. His family unit. Craig was eating iron-fortified grain soup sweetened with honey, which seemed a bit intense for a baby, but what did he know: this was a new day and age. They'd found the recipe on a Young Parents blog in the comments section: he was amazed, here was a recipe left by an absolute stranger, upvoted and approved of by other absolute strangers, and here they were feeding it to their child. Maybe the blog poster was an absolute sadist? But Craig seemed to like it, edging his pudgy little face closer and closer to sip out the slurry. "New textures and tastes," indeed.

There was an agreed-upon moratorium on asking about work. He didn't ask her about her reduced work schedule, and she didn't ask him about his job. She was curious and, maybe she didn't want to admit it, a bit nervous, as any time she asked about his work he got sullen and a little evasive, as if he needed a night of respite to regrow his protective armor. No one likes talking about their jobs, but there was a pained desperation in his eyes when she used to ask about how it was going, almost like an internal straining of his heart.

So she focused on other things.

She was talking about some show on Netflix she'd gotten into as he sat, mesmerized by the enthusiasm of little Craig. Whatever world of discovery and adventure little Craig inhabited, Miles wanted to be a part of it. Craig sipped again and smiled wildly, a sense of unfettered joy that'd be meretricious on anyone old enough to be self-conscious. Even Miranda's chatter about the nuances of the show, its themes and plots and intrigues, complemented the atmosphere. Miles wished time would stop and his world could subsist solely of Miranda and Craig, solely of their love and affections, where the only thing that mattered was the cultivation of childhood glee and entertaining his fluency for popular culture.

"Juice!" Craig yelled, as he grabbed his sippy cup. He often extended his arm when he did that and pointed at the closet, where Miranda kept the extra juice boxes when they weren't in the fridge. Clever kid, that Craig. Craig's pointing at the closet, coupled with his yelled "Juice" sounding like "Jews!" was ripe for a future Anne Frank joke, assuming the proper sardonic audience.

This was not that audience.

Little Craig bounded up off his chair and headed closer to Miles, sashaying his hips as he ran like a take-no-prisoners Diva, a fair part of the juice he was drinking already missing his mouth. Funny, Miles thought, why Craig was walking like that? His legs seemed off their joints, pumping awkwardly like the emaciated sticks of a runty gazelle. In another circumstance, it would be funny to watch.

Craig tripped, and hard. His soft forehead landed squarely — smack-dab — on his juice cup and his knee overarched onto the ground at a weird angle.

Crying filled the room. Not the usual I'm-hungry-but-I-know-what-hunger-is-so-I-know-this-will-be-taken-care-of type of crying, but rather the dreaded I-don't-know-what-happened-and-I-don't know-how-to-calibrate-my-response sort of crying. The crying of smashed glass and midnight screams.

"Honey!" Miranda yelled, as she swooped up Craig. "You take charge of him for one second!"

Wait, what? Since when was he taking charge, and when was that responsibility given over to him? How was the fall his fault?

"I-" he started. "I'm sorry, I, he just fell," Miles stammered.

"You ok, Little Guy? You took a fall there, huh? Eager Beaver took a fall, huh?" Miranda consoled him.

Miles looked at Craig, distraught and crying, and even at that virgin age maybe Craig could detect some of Daddy's guilt. Somewhere in Daddy's look of empathy and humaneness there was understanding, of what it feels like to be overwhelmed and distraught and crying, and maybe Craig knew that Daddy understood him. Maybe, for it is difficult to detect the tonal and attitudinal shifts in a baby's fits, but his crying shifted from pain and fear to the desire to be loved, to be enveloped by that sad but understanding creature that was his father.

Craig produced a muffled, inward hacking cough, like there was an old man somewhere in his throat, handkerchief-up, struggling to breathe. It could have been funny, in another circumstance. Craig, 18 months-old, going on 108 years-old.

Craig's body shook a little bit, a shaking that started down from the bottom and made its way up, like a too-small elevator shaft dealing with an ascending cargo carriage. And — ding — final stop, top floor, doors open and the tired workers spilled out the contents — chunky, dewy vomit, thick, squat and squamous like a runny brick. The rice particles looked like half-maggots, but that was fine, expected. What's worse was the unexplained: the intense, burgundy-like tubules threaded through the vomit like asbestos fiber.

"Oh, god, honey!"

After he was done, Craig vacantly mulled and chewed his mouth, like how a dog smacks its lips after being sick. Craig stared up at his father, silent and droopy-eyed.

"I'll get a towel," Miles declared.

"Baby, what did you eat?" his wife asked, gently patting him and rubbing the poor baby.

No one said a word. Miles quietly cleaned up the little puddle, which was still practically steaming. It looked like too-thick oatmeal with raspberry-flavored syrup.

"He seems better, but I want to take him to the emergency room." She said it patiently, without any sense of panic in her voice.

"I agree. I'm sure he is fine, babies get sick sometimes, but I think that's best. Let's go."

"I'm sure he's fine, I can just do it. I know you have a big day tomorrow. I'm sure it's nothing." They spoke formally, almost diplomatically, in measured tones. Of course, babies get sick — diarrhea, fever, stomach aches — nothing to get too worked over. Running to the emergency room for one upset stomach is probably overkill; why, I bet if her grandfather were still alive, he'd say something supportive and endearing in that old-timey way, about how when her father was sick he'd give him nothing but ginger ale and a little whisky. Something like that.

"I want to come, too. It's important."

She nodded, not pushing her original position. She knew fuzzy details about his meeting the next day: he'd been fretting about it for a week or so. "It's about 8:30 now. Hopefully, it will be nothing, we can be in and out in a couple of hours." The closest hospital with a pediatric care facility was about forty-five minutes away.

>< >< ><

He drove and she stayed in the backseat, comforting Craig.

Emergency rooms were surreal, in their way, in how you never imagined them to be as bad and poorly-run as they actually were. But still, how on earth was this reality, this polyglot incubator for disease, a Towel of Babel cast of several languages, all the germy hosts crammed together in one overflowing hall, transmitting their various ailments to one another in close quarters? Several people stood in the hallway because there weren't enough seats. Half of these people were probably uninsured, he fumed, and he silenced himself, not letting his fear degenerate into cruelty. Everyone here had their problems, no need to make things worse.

After well over an hour, they met with a young, enthusiastic doctor. He checked little Craig out, gave him an allergy test, checked his stomach and throat, the whole nine yards. The conclusion: a clean bill of health. Babies, you know? Just watch what he eats, monitor him, check for fever, and come back if anything develops.

They got home around midnight. They stayed up together, relieved, and coaxed little Craig to sleep. It was 1:30 a.m. by the time they'd gotten ready for bed. Fatigue and a powerful headache sunk Miles into bed like a heavy blanket.

He squeezed Miranda's hand, and she squeezed back. The chaos of being a parent was beyond platitudinous, a given, the basis of the hackiest small talk. Under that small talk, he always wondered, there must have been despair. Not wondered. Knew. The responsibility to take care of a life, a life you've created with a partner you've dedicated your life to. He was a drowning man, and he'd fit himself a brand new iron dumbbell.

He'd joked about that with other new parents and they all laughed and empathetically agreed.

Tell me about it.

But no, really.

It can be tough.

No, really, I mean it.

How do you deal with it?

Back to platitudes.

>< >< ><

The meeting the next day wasn't an explosive disaster, but then again, nothing is usually explosive. This was more like a slow gas leak, a building collapsing into itself, death by a million oversights. He didn't get enough sleep and looked sloppy. There were dust balls on his suit jacket he hadn't noticed; his work shirt was more creased and visibly sweat-stained around the collar than appropriate; usually Miranda double-checked him before he went into work for important meetings, but he insisted she should sleep in, he could handle it.

He showed up a little late, by about ten minutes. He skipped breakfast entirely and felt weak. The usual easy-going jesting of his supervisor, Mark, was nowhere to be found; not surprising, since Mark's supervisor was also in attendance. Mark's supervisor told Miles his name but Miles didn't do a good enough job of remembering it, and he referred to him as a pronoun, signaling to everyone he forgot. Unprofessional. Mark looked disappointed, like he'd been personally let down. Mark transitioned from Mark to Mr. Cunningham.

>< >< ><

The curious thing about having a partner-for-life is you end up not talking about upsetting things. You have to maintain an equilibrium. That's the curious thing. Love is supposed to be passionate, intense, boundary-less. But of course, no one acts like that.

So when he asked how her day was going, she said it had gone well, that Craig had been healthy and happy all day, but said nothing about how she was feeling, personally. What disappointed her, saddened her, and excited her? Likewise, when she inquired about how his meeting went, he told her it went "not great" and "fine," but he "didn't want to talk about it." That's a curious turn of phrase, isn't it? Why do we never want to talk about the most important things with the person we've selected to presumably share everything with? No, instead he'd share his insecurities and frustrations at work with Henry, who'd, in turn, relate with his occupational frustrations, but of course it wasn't the same or helpful.

Because, the reality is, we go through our experiences essentially alone.

Miranda mentioned how she was excited to get back to work full-time, in that undetermined future when Craig was sufficiently older. The grass is always greener, he supposed.

If he was serving in the stay-at-home role and not earning money, he'd be eager to get back to traditionally paid work, too. That sentiment usually dissipated, though, at the precise moment he actually started working for another.

The co-pay for the hospital was $150. He was thankful it had been so low, and that his employer provided his family reasonably comprehensive medical insurance.

He was feeling deflated from work, from his commute home, from this persistent ambient headache that stayed with him. But he was happy to see Miranda, be in her company, and even happier to be around Craig. There was something about those quizzical, curious eyes, that belly-aching laugh and frantic pace of his that could convince one that life was nothing but a series of new experiences and opportunities. To be that young.

Even in his late teens, Miles still remembered being excited about sensuality, the joy and pleasure of sex, the unwritten future, all those possibilities. Now that was gifted to this little guy, his son. *When would that excitement end for him?* Miles wondered. Maybe around sixteen, when Miles remembered it had begun to unravel for him. That indelible quote from his then-girlfriend's surly stepfather, trotted out whenever he'd come back from a long day at work and the young lovers had made the mistake of being too young and loving.

"One day, it'll be your turn to eat that shit sandwich. You just wait," was her stepfather's repeated refrain.

Little Craig carried a plastic guitar toy and ran, hunched over, flapping as he walked like he had flippers for feet. He dropped the toy in his Thomas the Tank Engine bin and ran straight back to Mommy, right into her tummy like he was a fastball and she was the catcher. He was hunched-over the whole time.

"Look at little Quasimodo over there."

She made an exaggerated, playful movement, as if he was a sentient ton of bricks. "Ooh, big boy, built up speed there!"

Craig curled into her midsection, then stood up on her inner thigh, looking over her shoulder to Daddy.

Miles rubbed his son's head, massaging his temples with his thumb.

He was unabashedly petting his son like a puppy, but Craig seemed to like it. Miles grew up with pet dogs, and that was his longest-standing experience with touch as a sign of love. He even sometimes found himself rubbing Miranda, kneading her inner thigh, cuddling her, a hand on her tummy.

Craig was still hunched over, Miles noted. Craig made a propeller-like noise and drooled.

>< >< ><

The next day at work was a little icy and he kept his head down. No one talked to him — the jury's still out on whether that was good or not.

It was when he was cleaning the dishes after Miranda's dinner the next night that he noticed it again, equivocally. Craig was running around at a funny angle.

He pointed this out to Miranda, who was reading an old *Travel and Leisure* magazine on the couch.

She lifted him up and put him up to her belly.

"Baby's never too young to learn about good posture," and she put her hands to her sides and sat up straight like a wooden British solider.

She put him back down on the ground in front of her. "Now you try," and she again assumed the position.

He giggled.

Miles moved quietly behind Craig and put a comforting hand on his lower back. He delicately attempted to lift up his shoulders to get him standing straight.

Craig burst out crying, a high pitched yipping, as if someone stepped on his toes. He doddered back a few steps, still at that angle.

"Oh honey, I'm sorry." Miles lifted Craig up and kissed his head until he stopped crying. Craig was a good boy, in that he rarely was overtaken with those never-ending stereotypical crying jags. He slept easy and was a good sport.

Miles — oh so delicately — tried to straighten out his son's back again. He resisted, squiggling out of his grasp.

He pointed out the posture to Miranda. "Baby's just being silly, I'll straighten him out," but it went no further and soon she took him up to bed.

He checked some work emails while she was putting him to sleep, ruing about how that presentation had gone. *Who are you fooling?* he thought. *You stayed up late on purpose. You were eager for an excuse to not get enough sleep. You love having a reason to fail.*

The work emails were just background on his computer, skimmed over in between .gifs of sexually compliant young women, adoring eyes, bouncing flesh. He wasn't even getting hard, but appreciated the calming, narcotizing effects of the pornography.

He had to shake out all the dandruff when he took off his work shirt to go to bed. He'd been scratching at his head all day and all night.

Eventually they both found themselves in bed, after Craig had drifted off to sleep.

In between snuggling and sensitivities, he asked her whether she ever got Craig to straighten up. She deflected a bit — she hating talking about anything remotely substantive before bed, but admitted he'd been a stubborn silly little boy, you know how he gets.

No, I don't.

>< >< ><

This was an easy assignment and he was fucking it up. He was just as smart as everybody else, and there was no reason for what should be a basic assignment to throw him off course so much. He just overthought it. He was instructed to use some discretion, collate the analyses of sales reports and identify the recurrent trends. A relatively simple summary job. But he hadn't been provided some of the documents and findings cited in the reports. His internet was slow. He started the assignment by adding too much detail, but had to keep the tone and level of detail consistent throughout. Some sections had too much, some too little. He had excuses — he always had excuses, and some were legitimate. He didn't control the internet; he didn't control what his boss could or couldn't provide him. Of course, the credibility of excuses never mattered in the Winner Culture, did it? Just the Results, right?

He responded with lightning speed to any email the boss sent out, to sustain the fiction that he was a competent employee, while continuing to underperform on the analysis itself.

He scratched the back of his head for long enough for a head in a near-by cubicle to turn. "Shit," he said as he blew off the hair debris and scabs that covered the documents. He looked down at his crotch area, which ran amok with strands of hairs and ugly dandruff.

He petered out at work and came home late, so when he complained about failing at work, his wife could point to his staying late as proof that he was a good employee and he could internally satisfy his contrarian impulse by knowing the truth — that he hadn't even been working late at all, just dawdling in his car.

Craig was walking in a crouched position again, something that he'd been doing all day, according to Miranda, although he'd been sleepy and slept most of the day. She'd touched and inspected him all over but didn't see any bruises or injuries. They dangled a cookie over his head, just out of reach, to see if he'd straighten himself up. He cooed and reached for it, eager and happy as ever, but his back refused to straighten out proper-ly. Miranda tried again to physically encourage it. Craig screamed like an alarm with malfunctioning batteries, a scream sharp enough to stop them in their tracks.

They should take him to a doctor tomorrow. Doctors, doctors, doctors. Kids get sick, but poor baby.

He held Miranda at night and kissed the back of her neck. Frenzied butterflies occupied his gut. He kissed the back of her neck again and held her tightly from behind, in the spoon position she liked. He pressed him-self against her until his stomach was flat against her back, as if he could connect his body to another he'd stop feeling that anxious buzzing.

"I'm scared, to be honest, baby."

She didn't respond. He held her tight again for emphasis, and she meekly squeezed his hand, a sop to his anxieties.

"I'm sorry, I just am. I want him to be ok."

"I know. We will find out tomorrow. I'll take him first thing to Dr. Glick-man. I need you to be strong though, you know. If he's not well, I need you there with me."

"I know," he said in a sullen whisper. He declared his love for her over and over again over the years, his utter devotion and he meant it, and she meant it in kind. He told her a million different ways that he was weak, ineffectual. "You're too good for me," he'd always say to her, his cry for help and understanding that she'd misinterpret as loving modesty. "You're the good one!" she'd say, because he cleaned the dishes or hugged her tenderly or let her indulge whatever hobbies she wanted, as if it required any competence as a provider or husband to be a decent human being.

But when it came to the big things, he'd fail; he'd always fail.

Since she'd been on Wellbutrin for the past year, she'd become less anxious, more determined, less victim to mood swings. There was no anti-depression or anti-anxiety medicines left for him to try: his frequent prescriber card was thoroughly stamped. He was retrogressing in medical advancements, so desperate he was trying Prozac. He assured her he'd stay strong and swallowed up his emotions, as if it were a switch to be turned on and off, like anyone could reveal themselves in a moment of weakness, resolve to do better, and instantly be back on the right track.

He waited until she fell asleep, and masturbated joylessly into the sheets, imagining a sexually voracious, younger Miranda reverse-cow-girling her former coworker who always made eyes at her. He emptied himself into the sheets and was too depleted to detach the stickiness from his inner thigh or change his damp boxers.

>< >< ><

The assignment was barely passable but he sent it in anyway, doing nothing else but distracting himself with listicles and clickbait, dreading the reply from his supervisor.

Craig wouldn't straighten out, but the doctor was at a loss as to what could be wrong with him. En route to the orthopedic surgeon referral, Craig threw up all over himself in the baby seat. The baby seat was a horror show, a miasma of porridge-like fluids.

The surgeon was at a loss, too. In the X-Rays everything looked fine, the surgeon assured them. Craig was only a year and a half old, his musculature was still adjusting, don't worry too much, he'd seen this before. Be glad it's not something serious.

>< >< ><

Late at night, a couple days later. His boss had had a serious talk with him earlier: his performance needed to improve, significantly. They would talk about a regiment, structure to his day. More input, more calls, more results: simply a numbers game. Ok, he agreed. What else could he do?

He surfed the Internet late at night while Miranda put Craig to bed. Miles surfed the webcam sites and made small talk with the regular coterie of models he spoke to. He tipped them to hear their affections and see them smile; he asked them to be bouncy and happy, and they did it. He didn't even request nudity or care to see it. He just wanted their affection, these pretty ladies who listened to him, or pretended to listen to him, who provided what he wanted when he asked for it and seemed perpetually grateful for what he provided in return. He never did hard drugs but imagined the reason people did them was because the sensation was superior to the real world; it was the same with this. This was calming, aesthetic and anesthetic, rewarding and gratifying and pleasurable.

>< >< ><

He called his mother the next day. She moved down to Florida with her boyfriend and talked about what she'd been up to, arts festivals she'd been to, restaurants they had gone to. She asked about "little Craig" and he told her about his posture and recent-flare up, and she told him to expect that, little kids get sick, just keep an eye on him, and she regaled him with a colorful anecdote about a stomach problem he'd had as a little boy and how it went away.

He called his father, who expressed more concern and told him to keep him updated about how Craig was doing. If he didn't call his father, he'd never hear from him; his mother at least called on her own accord to have someone to tell her stories to. His father was overworked, as always, could never find good help to assist him with his business. He, too, mentioned how nervous he'd been as a new father, but not to worry, things work out in the end, which was a curious thing to say in a world of colon cancer, schizophrenia and disabling freak accidents. Miles' father hadn't even been a good father, really, treated his son like a burden rather than a blessing, so what good was his advice?

He called Henry.

"Hey man, good to hear from you," Henry started. Miles' flinty telephone timbre and his unfocused demeanor clued Henry in to his psychological state.

"Hey man, how is everything going? How is ... how is the depression doing?" Henry probed.

"The depression is doing great. I mean, as in separate from me. I'm doing terribly, but the depression itself, man, it's going great. Never been stronger!" There was Miles, always with the joking, and the conversation proceeded apace, verbal feints and deflections and other coping mechanisms. The conversation was substantive but of no great lasting effect, because that's how things were when you were a yawning chasm.

>< >< ><

Miles was at a bar after work, by himself. He was supposed to meet a friend, but the friend cancelled after Miles had arrived. Miles wasn't going home yet. He had chalked out a couple of hours for socialization. Miranda had always talked about the need to wrest away some "fun time" for yourself after work, to keep a healthy separation between work and life. He was going to indulge that, with a friend or not.

He never drank alone; that was the tell-tale sign of a problem. He didn't really drink at all, really. He had to fight his urge to invest everything with a meaning that wasn't there; after having a child, everything seemed pregnant with importance. But he could have one drink. No reason to be alarmist.

He limited himself to only two drinks, two tasty stouts. He was nestled in the corner, gave the fetching bartender two bucks per drink as a tip and enjoyed her bubbly response even if it was no doubt honed and calibrated.

It was approximately 7:30 p.m. He texted Miranda that he loved her, perhaps out of guilt of making harmless eyes at the bartender. He just liked her looks of approbation; whether they were genuine or not, he was hard-wired to feel good from them.

A feminine hand appeared out of view and tilted his empty beer glass. The woman next to him lifted up the glass, to her eye, like it was an over-sized magnifying glass. She turned to look at him, viewing him through the bottom of the empty glass.

"Looks like this is empty! We can't have that. What were you drinking? Let's get another. Barkeep!" She put the glass up and spoke through it like it was a megaphone.

"Someone's had enough," he said, which was a stupid thing to say.

"Nope, only had one. You're alone, I'm alone, let's be alone together. Whatcha drinking?"

He turned and looked at her. She was beautiful in an alluring, unprac-ticed way, dimples and skin-tone that was vaguely ethnic. If someone put a gun to his head, he'd guess half-Filipino. She looked to be in her ear-ly or mid-twenties. She was a couple inches shorter than him, thin and well-proportioned, cropped short hair and a sizable bust obvious under her brightly-colored T-shirt.

"Hah, as enticing as that sounds" — wrong word — "I'm just killing time. I got to go back, my wife is making dinner."

"Oh, it's not like that, you. I'm just being a friendly goofball. Don't you want to make friends with a friendly goofball?" She lowered her chin and looked up at him, batting her eyes in such an overemphasized way that it had to be self-aware.

"Well, you will have to pack in all the friendship-making in about, thirty minutes or an hour or so."

She ordered two stouts — the same stout he'd been imbibing — and paid in cash. "Don't worry, tell the wifey you'll be home soon. I got an hour to kill and a friend to make."

They talked about her — she graduated a couple years ago from the University of Chicago, which opened up a whole rich mine of conversation; she was new to California and loved the weather, which allowed her to wear T-shirts all the time (at which point she pointed at herself excitedly and jiggled); he had been sort of right about her ethnicity: she was half-Swiss, a quarter-Filipino and a quarter-Chilean; she was currently working as an executive assistant for a fashion company but was really big into improv and comedy and was hoping to break into that.

He told her about himself, and, as they were becoming friends, he revealed a fair deal about himself: his marriage, his young'un, work gripes and new parenthood fears. When he told her he was a new father, she talked about how "real" that was — "whoa, what an adult" — and he said, "I know, don't remind me" and they laughed because that's the popular banality.

She asked him to guess what she thought about when she thought of having children? "Tell me," he said, and she made the shrieky noise and stabbing motions from *Psycho*.

"So, if your child is sick, why aren't you home with him?"

"Hmmm," he said, pushing his emptied third beer away from him. He waved the comely bartender away. No more drinks.

He explained that, well, everyone said it was just a temporary thing, young children got sick. He made it evident that her comment killed the good-natured flow of the conversation.

"I don't know about that. Vomiting is always a bad sign."

He had a lot to say in response to that, but he felt groggy and there was no point. This was stupid, he didn't need to convince some flake.

"Miles, what are you going to do about your job, too? Aren't you nervous about getting fired? Sounds like it's a possibility. Sounds like a terrible time for you guys to lose health insurance."

Miles turned to her, intentionally amplifying his deserved look of bewilderment.

"I'll figure it out," he said harshly. "It was great meeting you, best of luck on your … comedy thing." He started getting up.

"You probably shouldn't drive home. Maybe call your wife, tell her to pick you up. From the bar. Responsibility isn't for everyone."

"Excuse me!" For him to publicly stand-up to anyone — especially an attractive lady — was an anomaly. He always felt like everyone assumed he'd be in the wrong, especially if fighting with a woman. "I don't know where you get off on telling me this—"

"I was just saying. You don't seem like someone who likes being married or having a child or responsibility. I meant that as a compliment. But sounds like you are stuck with it. So it goes."

Before he responded, she continued:

"You seem really unhappy, honestly. I can understand why. You said you never planned on having a child, a family. And now you're stuck with it."

This was stupid, this conversation was over. "Thanks for the drink," is all he said. "But you don't know anything about me or my situation."

"I know you want to kill yourself. You should. That's the only solution you have. You aren't cut out for this. You made a huge mistake and you should off yourself before you become a huge burden to your family."

He turned, to whom he wasn't sure. Maybe the comely bartender. For an instant he really, truly believed he might take the empty beer glass by the handle and smash it against her skull. He perspicaciously could imagine the bulk of the glass, her wide-eyed expression as the glass hit her head, even the angle of the shattered glass and her face-plant descent to the floor. He didn't do it, of course, instead looked around for someone, as if someone could confirm she really just said something so fucking hurtful and outrageous.

He turned around and she was gone. There was no empty barstool, even. It was occupied by the same middle-aged man in the light blue button-down, the same man who'd been having drinks with his two coworkers when Miles had first entered the bar. There was no empty beer stein in front of him.

He signaled to the pretty bartender. The male bartender came instead, and he asked to get her attention. He did so. The lag time, the normal inconveniences and frustrations of the bar experience felt atypical given the strangeness of this sensation. Unexplainable visitations, mental breakdowns, and still, having to deal with the usual quotidian hassles.

He made eyes at her and she came over.

"Change your mind? Want another?"

"No, ugh, can I pay out? Receipt."

"I'd love to take your money twice, but you already paid for your drinks."

"I want to pay for the third. Did you see the girl sitting next to me before?"

Her expression was hard to read, perhaps a hint of confusion, impatience, rounded out with a bit of embarrassment whenever a man, by himself, asks about a disappeared girl.

"No, sorry. All I know is your drinks are paid out. Two Young's Double Chocolates. Trust me, if they weren't paid out, you'd know. Enjoy your night."

"Okay." The moderately busy bar wasn't the time and place for an argument.

As he assembled himself, he asked the man next to him, did you see that girl who was sitting here before? The man had no idea, they'd been sitting there for several hours. Ok.

He texted his wife, an abstractly apologetic sort of text, and told her he was on his way home.

>< >< ><

She greeted him, and he greeted both her and their son lovingly and gratefully. He made expressions of being overjoyed with their companionship and love. He complimented her cooking effusively, to the point that even she, ever receptive to culinary praise, thought it a bit much.

Traces of Craig's unusual stances were apparent whenever Miles focused on it, when he tried to look. For the most part, he didn't, and let his wife lead. She didn't mention it to him, so he didn't bring it up. *I'm sure it's fine. The surgeon said it was fine, if it persists we will take him to another specialist in a week or so, it's fine.*

After putting Craig to bed, he had some alone time with his wife on the couch. They watched television together, his left arm limply around her midsection, until she adjusted to cover herself with the afghan. They watched an interesting but depressing documentary on a boom town in the Midwest.

Afterward, he was checking his emails and she was at the counter, doing something that involved the sink.

A soaring guitar melody came out of the laptop speakers, and then stopped dramatically. He smirked lasciviously at her and acted as if he was a lounge singer, the laptop his piano, Miranda the object of his seduction.

"There was a beauty living on the edge of town, she always put the top up and the hammer down, and she taught me everything I'll ever know about the mystery and the muscle of love," he sang in his best warbling Meat Loaf impression.

"Aww baby."

He continued singing, matching the operatic intensity of the song's build-up, continued his impassioned singing to the part of the song where the instruments dropped out and it was just him and Meat Loaf, belting over the staccato, pounding drum line:

"I'll probably never know where she disappeared

But I can see her rising up out of the back seat now

Just like an angel rising up from a tomb."

He continued his quavering singing. "Oh baby, you're so good," she said, somewhat sullenly. He sung the refrain dramatically: "Objects in the Rearview Mirror May Appear Closer Than They Are....."

"Oh baby," she said softly. She had mixed feelings about his singing. He had a nice voice and definite passion. His commitment at times was meant as a lark, but the emotion behind it was too sad for her sometimes. He seemed too crestfallen, too empathetic to the words, too overtaken by the power of art, almost disappointed when the experience was over and he was no longer singing and he was back to reality.

They held each other at night. He kissed the back of her head and told her he loved her. He didn't hear a response. He kissed the back of her head and meant to say something but it came out almost as a sneeze, a wet blubbering gasping. She felt the spit-up on the back of her head, used a hand to streak it out. "Baby!" she yelled, startled.

"I'm sorry," he covered his mouth. He was crying, it seemed.

"I said I loved you, silly. Didn't you hear me?" She held his hand.

"I'm sorry, I don't know what's wrong with me," he looked down, the hot tears coming from seemingly nowhere.

"Oh honey, it's ok, it's ok. Here let me get you a tissue." And she reached over and retrieved a tissue, nestling it on his face as she turned toward him.

"It's ok, I just, I just feel so overburdened, so overburdened, I can't deal with it."

"Ok," she said, and turned over back to her side. The doting was gone, the coaxing was gone. She took his comment as a shot against her parenting and contributions. Saying he "can't deal with it" was just the sort of exaggeration he'd say to get her sympathies. They were like tilt-a-whirls, each vying to see which could be the most off-balance.

"Baby," he pleaded. He wanted her to coax him, caress him, supplicate him, take care of him. Her babying voice was usually grating but now he wanted that security more than anything.

"Go to sleep, you will feel better in the morning, ok?"

He kept his hand on her back and rubbed it slightly, until her lack of response led him to roll over on his side. He cried softly into his pillow, perhaps out of exhaustion, desperation, confusion, or the thought of facing another day and all the portending fear. He sobbed with enough passion to rouse her to comfort him, to kiss and apologize, but she wasn't sure if that was the pragmatic thing to do. A marriage, a life together, is an organization as much as it is an emotional union, and things had to run smoothly. She couldn't placate him every time he got upset.

He couldn't express everything he felt — that he couldn't explain what happened at the bar, that perhaps he was having a nervous breakdown, that he was rudderless and adrift, had no right to think he could bring life into this world, totally unequipped for the task, a task he didn't ask for or want.

There were worse people in the world than him. He was good, he tried, he was here, he consoled himself.

He slept.

>< >< ><

His phone rang at work, just before a scheduled meeting.

"Hello?"

"Hello," came the response, a male voice, deeper than his, familiar yet aloof. He couldn't place it. He looked at the phone display but it was blank. "You should honestly kill yourself. It'll make everyone in your family happier. It's been a long time coming, you know?"

He focused himself, narrowed all his senses into themselves. Living in the moment. He took note of his breathing, the blood rushing in his ears

and head, the sweaty slick grip of the phone in his hand, the slight discomfort of his inner thigh in the way he sat. He focused on all of this, to know
this was real, to know this was reality, to catalog as many experiences as he
could to make sure they all could not be part of one trans-sensory delusion.

"Who is this?"

The phone went dead.

He needed to take a medical leave, he decided. Of course, it seemed
suspicious, right in the midst of his lackluster work performance. Miles
felt ashamed, hated to let down his boss, hated to let anyone down, for
them to think he was conniving or scheming or incompetent, even when
he was. Maybe his obvious issues at work would bolster his claim that he
needed some time off. Things were getting to him, you know? Issues at
home, maybe.

He'd talk it over with Miranda that night, see how it might actually
work, the nuts-and-bolts of it. He felt rejuvenated already, the prospect of
escape, time-off, waking up later and rekindling his love, his bonds with his
family, just the three of them, the days of possibility unfolding before then.

All you need is love.

After another unproductive day at work — he was acting as if he'd
already been given the time off — he called Henry. Henry was his best
friend, he figured. Of course, Miranda was his "best friend," his life partner,
but Henry was his true best friend. At some point when two people decide
to form a family unit, some topics of conversation get sidelined to preserve
the union. Usually, topics of conversation that would serve to puncture
illusions.

He had told her, ad nauseam, all throughout their years together, that
he was depressed and felt worthless. Of course he wasn't worthless, she'd
told him, he was the sweetest, most loving guy. Sometimes she'd invert it,
tell him that the depression he suffered from was what made him who he
was, what made him such a good father, such an understanding, compas-
sionate figure, such a loyal friend, always there to help people. And he did
help people: he always kept in contact with friends, pitched in more than

he needed to, followed up. Such a good person. It was when he wasn't involved, when activity wasn't overtaking him, when he could reflect upon himself; that was when he began to despair.

He'd told her a million times, but it only seemed to strengthen her love for him. It wasn't a joke. It wasn't a stage in his life that he'd get over, he told everyone who would listen; but at some point, he decided he'd grown up and couldn't burden everyone with his problems.

Oh remember this, remember that: a phase, a thing everyone goes through.

Everyone goes through.

Everyone goes through.

Everyone goes through.

Of course people struggle inwardly. But you move on, you persevere through.

He called Henry and talked and talked, wanting Henry to tell him what to do. Henry refused, it wasn't his place. Henry suggested not taking time off: didn't want to compromise the job and make a bad impression, and Miles' heart sank. He wanted to be told he could flee, seek refuge, and convince himself it was actually the right thing to do. He didn't want to stay and suffer and be outed as a failure.

"Do you ever — do you ever think that sometimes some people just shouldn't exist? I feel like, I feel like I'm not right for this world. I shouldn't exist. I'm defective. The world is, like, telling me I'm defective.

"I should fade out. Some people are just defective, and they get strained out of the gene pool. There's been an error here, and it's like, sometimes I feel like the world is weighted against me. Straining me out. I'm defective and I need to be erased There's this lyric I think of sometimes: 'addiction and depression are just swimming in my cum.' That's me. I'm just defective like that."

That was too much. There wasn't any humor there to leaven the sadness. He overshot his mark. Kvetching worked when it was just dribs and drabs, just a susurrus, a pinhole release of accumulated despair.

Henry remained silent for too long. He admitted he was out of his depth here, and that Miles needed to talk to Miranda about this, or a health professional, seriously.

Miles didn't want to hear it, laughed it off as knowingly self-aggrandizing and self-important. Of course he was just being stupid.

He just had to get out of the office. He could work from home, sure. He emailed the relevant parties and didn't wait for a response.

>< >< ><

Was Miranda not home? There was no indication she was here, odd. He called out for her and there was no response. He checked his phone to see if there were any messages from her, but no, there weren't.

He heard gurgling upstairs. The house wasn't very big, just one short flight up and around the corner to Craig's room, but he shouldn't be able to hear him unless he was listening to the baby monitor. When Craig was asleep, the door was closed. Craig was never left alone, also. Why would Craig be here if Miranda wasn't?

Again the gurgling. When he heard it, it was combustible, the wet gurgling of a stalled pipe, a backwash, a flooded engine. Too loud.

He sat down on the couch, eyes fixed on the short staircase and the figure that made its way down it.

His phone rang and he knew it was Miranda before he even looked at it.

Craig slowly seeped down the staircase, on all fours, his spine an elevated domed point. He leaned gauntly on his side, in obvious distress. The distortions of his musculature were such that his head dragged forward and his front limbs had trouble even making constant contact with the ground; his back, arched up as it was, made him resemble a pinioned marionette.

"Craig?" Miles mouthed, nothing coming out. "Craig," he repeated, this time sotto voiced, and gasped to himself at recognizing his own voice, for it was his voice and this was real and actually happening.

"Craig, baby, baby? My baby?"

He answered the vibrating phone and brought it to his ear and said nothing, mouth agape.

Craig, with his unknowing face, looked up at his father. His unknowing face of pestilent, congealed sores, his mouth suppurating cruelly, his eyes voiding of life. His spit-up added an almost laminating bright sheen to the crusting, curdled ooze around his mouth. He crawled on his side like a wounded animal. He reached out and tumbled and something about the severity of the fall reignited the traditional fear centers that Miles recognized, the panic of a fallen child.

Miles ran and hovered over Craig, not sure how to grab him, not sure how to scoop him up and drive him to his bosom, to protect him.

He listened to his wife's hysterical yelling through the phone.

"He's mutating, he's mutating, Dear God, I didn't know what to do, I panicked. I ran. I'm sorry.

"I'm dying. I ran, I didn't know what to do. I'm dying. My, my privates ... my private area, it's dissolving. It ... hurts so badly. It's ... dissolving. Please, what is going on, help us! Help us! The back of my head, where you kissed me last night, it hurts so much, it's like, it's like someone hammered the back of my head. I'm ... I'm in agony. I'm dying ... . "

He was not meant for this world, and this is what his indecision, his vacillation, his fear to take the plunge had resulted in. He was toxic. He'd known it all his life. It was time to be done with it, to do what the world had been telling him to do for as long as he'd been cognizant enough to recognize it.

He didn't hate himself, honestly. He was a good person.

He just didn't fit. He just didn't fit within the contours of the world. He was defective. He'd known it his whole life, every fiber and feeling within his being had told him so, but he'd let the cult of positive thinking delude him otherwise, pretend that the traditional flow of life was something he could take part in.

He took out the sharpest knife in the drawer and tore out his throat, baptized, rectified, stretching out in contrition for his failures, praying to whomever placed him in this world to take pity on him, for existence had not been his fault.

Made in the USA
Columbia, SC
15 October 2017